IN A DISTANT GALAXY,
THE PEACEFUL PLANET LORIEN
WAS DECIMATED BY
THE BRUTAL MOGADORIANS.

The last survivors of Lorien—the Garde—were sent to Earth as children. Scattered across the continents, they developed their Legacies and readied themselves to defend their adopted home world.

The Garde thwarted the Mogadorian invasion of Earth.

In the process, the Garde changed the very nature of Earth. Legacies, the extraordinary powers from the planet Lorien, began to manifest in human beings.

These new Legacies frighten some humans, while others look for ways to manipulate the new Garde to their benefit.

And while the Legacies are meant to protect Earth, not every Garde will use their powers for good.

I AM PITTACUS LORE.
RECORDER OF THE FATES,
CHRONICLER OF THE LEGACIES.

I TELL THE TALES OF THOSE
WHO WOULD SHAPE WORLDS.

RETURN TO ZERO

BOOK THREE OF THE ◇ LORIEN LEGACIES REBORN ◇

PITTACUS LORE

HARPER
An Imprint of HarperCollinsPublishers

Library of Congress Control Number: 2019000130
ISBN 978-0-06-249380-4
ISBN 978-0-06-291315-9 (intl. ed.)

19 20 21 22 23   PC/LSCH   10 9 8 7 6 5 4 3 2 1

First Edition

CHAPTER ONE

DANIELA MORALES
EARTH GARDE COMMAND—WASHINGTON, DC

DANIELA GAZED UP AT THE HOLOGRAM OF THE globe as it did a slow rotation above the polished mahogany conference table. The lights in the briefing room's domed ceiling automatically dimmed whenever the operations map was active, so she stood there bathed in the projection's vivid blue glow. She traced her fingers across the back of one of the twenty vinyl chairs that surrounded the table. She'd been sitting right there, months ago, when she was assigned to Melanie Jackson's "good works and public relations" team. Daniela still remembered the positive vibes in the air that day, how everyone was smiling, even her. Earth Garde was going to let her help rebuild New York City. Her home.

Now, the room was empty. There was no briefing

scheduled today and the mood around headquarters was decidedly uncheerful.

Daniela shook her head and reminded herself that, despite recent craziness, life was pretty good. She cracked a disbelieving smile, the way she did whenever she considered how far she'd gotten from Harlem. Not like physically far, at least not at the moment. NYC was three hours away on the train, faster if Earth Garde assigned her a helicopter. And they often did. How baller was that? She should put in a request to go visit her mom once she wasn't confined to headquarters anymore. It had been too long and her mom was probably worried. Especially if she'd been watching the news.

Thinking about her mom, it was hard to believe the gulf between this life and her old one. Where had she been two years ago? Hooking up with boys in Harlem River Park? Getting fired from her job for being rude to customers? She certainly hadn't been hanging around any high-tech military briefing rooms in state-of-the-art buildings just down the block from the Pentagon.

The invasion changed everything, of course. She developed Legacies. She may or may not have robbed a bank. She met John Smith. She helped save humanity.

And now? She'd been all over the world. Seen some crap straight out of those dorky sci-fi movies her stepdad—rest his soul—used to watch all the time. She'd made friends that weren't even *human*. She'd helped rebuild what the Mogadorians had broken.

Daniela liked to think she was making a difference. Even if sometimes all she did was sit on a beach and babysit Melanie. She frowned at the holographic globe. All the places she could go, all the good she could be doing. Instead, she was stuck at headquarters. Grounded. At least until the fallout from Switzerland blew over.

It had seemed like a cake assignment at the time. Hang out at the mansion of the billionaire tech guru Wade Sydal, who, of course, was a family friend of the well-connected Melanie. Ride around on his new spaceship that he'd reverse-engineered from Mogadorian tech. Eat lobster.

Daniela still hadn't wrapped her head around how it all went to hell. Apparently, Sydal was involved with some shady people who helped him acquire black-market alien technology. Without telling them what he was up to, Sydal brought Daniela and her Earth Garde teammates Melanie and Caleb to Switzerland so that they could watch his back. The British lady selling him Mogadorian ooze had some mercenaries and Garde of her own—Nigel and Taylor—although they were actually double agents. Before the deal could even be completed, freaking Number Five and that maniac Einar showed up to do, like, a citizen's arrest on all the adults. It all popped off. They fought, even more Garde showed up and they fought some more.

"Bananas," Daniela muttered.

Sydal had been killed in the process of bailing on his Earth Garde escort like a scared little bitch. There were a ton of soft-focus tributes to him on TV. The official story was that Einar killed him, even though she was pretty sure one of the Brit's mercenaries took out Sydal with a rocket. But no one around headquarters was interested in Daniela's version of the events, especially not with video of Einar's unhinged speech playing on cable news 24/7.

Daniela surprised herself with how often she thought about Einar's screed. He'd definitely come off like the type of dude who sent mail bombs from his basement, but some of what he said actually made sense, especially in light of the whole Sydal-being-corrupt-as-hell thing. Daniela didn't know anything about cabals and conspiracies. No one filled her in on that stuff while she was acting as a glorified side-kick to the pretty face fronting Earth Garde. But it sure sounded like Einar and his people had some legitimate beef with how the Human Garde were being treated. He'd convinced some to run away with him, including Caleb, who Daniela didn't think had ever broken a rule in his life, much less disobeyed the UN.

Ultimately, Number Nine had let Einar and his followers escape. After one ugly battle, none of them had wanted to fight each other again. At the time, Daniela never considered rolling with Einar. Her gut told her to stick with Nine and his people. He wouldn't steer her wrong.

But Nine was back at the Academy with his students and Daniela was stuck here at Earth Garde headquarters with a bunch of adults who gave her the hairy eyeball and wouldn't let her leave.

Daniela breathed out a sigh through her nose. When

would things get less complicated?

When would they let her out of here?

The globe rotated so Europe was facing Daniela. With the press of a button, she called up the operations overlay. A dot pulsed over Switzerland. Daniela poked her finger into the hologram and a text pop-up appeared:

CLEANUP OPERATION UNDER WAY. UNKNOWN
EXTRATERRESTRIAL SUBSTANCE BELIEVED AT LARGE.

On the hologram, Daniela could check on the progress of all of Earth Garde's operations. Sometimes the details were vague due to the limits of her security clearance, but she could still get a pretty good idea about what Earth Garde was working on. Right now, there were hardly any glowing dots on the map. There were only a few dozen trained Human Garde to begin with and operations had been scaled way back since Switzerland. Garde like Daniela could rebuild all the world's exploded landmarks and Melanie could smile all pretty for the cameras, but all it took was one unhinged Icelandic kid rambling about taking over the planet to shake the public's confidence in their fledgling organization.

"Didn't hear them complaining when I was busting my ass laying down stonework for them," Daniela muttered, thinking about all the foundations she'd supplemented using her stone-vision. She tapped a few buttons on a tablet computer mounted on the conference table. "Let's see who still wants our help . . ."

The glowing dots on the projection increased tenfold. Here were the open requests from countries for Earth Garde assistance. Waving her fingers through the map, Daniela accessed a few of them at random. Sickness in Kenya, an oil field under threat in Egypt, drug cartels in Mexico—all potential jobs for Earth Garde. More requests than they had personnel to handle.

"Oh, Puerto Rico's got a bridge near collapse?" Daniela asked the empty room. "I could help with that, if I wasn't cooped up in here answering the same dumb questions over and over."

Officials had been interrogating her about Switzerland on pretty much the daily over the last two weeks. There were different faces from different governments and intelligence agencies, some of them were nice and some of them were gruff and one of them even tried to ply her with cookies like she was five years old, but their questions were all the same.

"What happened in Engelberg?"

"Do you know where the rogue Garde might be hiding?"

"Do you think the Loric known as Number Nine had anything to do with the attack?"

"Did Caleb Crane tell you he planned to defect?"

With a frustrated swipe of her hand, Daniela gave the transparent globe a spin. The hologram blurred, blue lines flickering.

Daniela always answered their questions honestly. Or tried to, at least. She really didn't know much. The only time she bent the truth a little was when they asked about

6

Caleb. Of course she'd noticed how strange he'd been acting. She knew that Caleb and his clique from the Academy were tangled up in some weirdness. She'd been assigned to help extract them from that crazy religious cult a couple of months back, hadn't she? She remembered how, on the way to Switzerland, it had seemed like Caleb was trying to warn her that something bonkers might go down.

But Daniela played dumb about that. She wasn't a snitch. She liked Caleb. She'd survived alongside him, Nigel and Ran back at Patience Creek. Just because they'd chosen different sides back in Switzerland didn't mean they were bad guys or defectors or terrorists or whatever else the so-so-serious diplomats and generals implied when they peppered her with questions.

Daniela wondered, not for the first time, what Melanie might be telling the interrogators. Back in Engelberg, she'd been too shell-shocked to say anything when Nine had let Caleb and the others leave. But, on the flight back, Daniela had seen a dark look on Melanie's face. "I can't believe he let them escape" was all she'd said to Daniela.

They'd been kept separate since returning—Daniela was stuck in the barracks, but she was pretty sure Melanie got to go back to her dad's estate in Maryland. Or maybe Melanie was just avoiding her. She probably didn't appreciate how Daniela had literally slapped some sense into her in the middle of battle. Daniela smirked at the memory.

"Girl's over there crying instead of using her super-strength," Daniela mumbled with an incredulous shake of her head. "And I'm *not* going to give her a smack?"

"You're not supposed to be in here," a voice answered.

Daniela spun around just as a man in a very expensive suit entered the room. His brown hair was slicked back, his face bright and wrinkle-free, even though he was probably in his forties. He had a European accent that she couldn't quite place. She'd seen him around before, in the halls of Earth Garde HQ. He was a diplomat or something. The guy carried a tablet computer, glancing down at it every few seconds, like he was too busy for this conversation.

"I'm sorry—who are you?" Daniela asked with a cocked eyebrow, unable to keep the surliness out of her voice. Dudes who thought they were hot shit always brought it out of her. "Since when can't I be in here?"

The man crossed the room and turned off the operations map. The blue glow faded, the normal lights coming on.

"We were actually just coming to talk to you about that," the man said, a bit of impatience in his voice. "Had to search all over the complex for you, Ms. Morales."

The "we" he was talking about became clear as a trio of Peacekeepers entered the room. Daniela squinted at the soldiers. They were stone-faced, dressed in body armor and carrying those shock-collar Inhibitor cannons that Sydal Corp produced.

A lump rose in Daniela's throat. The vibe here was all wrong.

Why would these guys be dressed for combat inside headquarters?

8

"Am I supposed to know you, man?" Daniela asked the guy in the suit. She casually circled around the table.

He smiled. "My name is Greger Karlsson. Usually, I work with your friend Nine at the Academy, but I've been asked to supervise the installation of Earth Garde's new safety protocols."

"Safety protocols? What's that got to do with me?"

Greger glanced down at his tablet, double-checking some bit of data. "Now, according to your psychological profile, there's a high likelihood of you interpreting what I'm about to tell you in a negative way. Let's try to maintain a cool head and approach this matter with maturity, yes?"

"I mean, you're already pissing me off with that tone and we just met like thirty seconds ago, so no promises."

Daniela thought one of the soldiers almost cracked a smile at that. Greger continued on like he hadn't heard her.

"The UN has determined that, in light of recent events, measures must be taken to ensure Garde do not become a threat to the public. Going forward, it will be mandatory for all Garde to have an Inhibitor chip implanted."

Daniela's eyes narrowed. She'd heard Ran say something about Inhibitor chips back in Switzerland. The government had apparently put them into her and Kopano without asking permission. She got the feeling Greger here wasn't asking either.

"You want to stick one of those things in my brain," Daniela said. "And I'm supposed to be *mature* about that?"

"It's a very simple procedure. We have a healer on hand.

Once it's done, you won't even know it's there."

"I haven't done anything wrong," Daniela said, her voice rising. "All I've done is help people."

"Your model service is all noted in your file," Greger said with a smile. "If that behavior continues, you'll have nothing to worry about."

Daniela glanced at the Peacekeepers. "This is some stop-and-frisk shit, man."

"I don't know what that means."

"Yeah. Of course not." She edged farther around the conference table, making sure it was directly between her and the soldiers. "So, what? You put this chip in me and give me a shock whenever I'm late to a meeting?"

Greger actually chuckled. "It's not meant as a punishment, Ms. Morales. It's a worst-case scenario. A last resort. The Inhibitor will only be used if your conduct becomes dangerous."

"And who decides that? You?"

"No, actually, you'll be assigned a trained Peacekeeper as a handler who will monitor your behavior and assist you in the field. We got the idea from the Loric themselves, actually. Back on their home planet, we understand that their Garde also had minders. They called them Cêpan."

Daniela took a deep breath. She was out of questions, except for the big one. *Here we go. Moment of truth.*

"What if I say no?"

"I'm afraid it isn't optional. The agreement you signed with Earth Garde in conjunction with the Garde Accord gives us unlimited discretion to implement safety measures necessary to protect the human race."

"Who's protecting me from you?" Daniela asked sharply. "I'm part of the human race, too."

"That, Ms. Morales, is a matter of some contention."

Daniela's hands shook. This creep just told her she wasn't human.

"Don't you need my mom's permission before you like cut my head open?"

"Again, as per your agreement with Earth Garde, the organization has guardianship over you now, not your mother." Greger smiled patiently. "Any other questions?"

Daniela shrugged her shoulders, loosening them up. One of the soldiers behind Greger twitched, watching her closely. She was officially out of ways to stall what was about to happen.

"Guess you've got it all figured out," she said coldly. "One more thing, though. What did you say about my psychological profile? About how I'd process some totalitarian-ass news like this?"

Greger glanced down at his tablet. "I said—"

Daniela didn't let him finish. With a burst of telekinesis, she flung the conference table at the Peacekeepers. Only one of them managed to get his weapon up in time, the electrified collar fired from his cannon deflecting harmlessly off the table. Daniela's eyes sparked silver as she unleashed a current of stone-energy, cementing the table to the conference room wall, thereby trapping the Peacekeepers behind it. She stepped over the broken hologram projector, glaring at Greger.

"Honestly," he said, shrinking back. "This is futile."

"My ass," Daniela replied. She snatched the tablet away from him and, in one smooth motion, backhanded the man across the face with it. He fell with an undignified shriek, clutching a broken nose.

Daniela made for the door, already reminding herself of the HQ's layout. There would be more guards throughout the building, but Daniela thought she could avoid most of them if she snuck down the service stairwell. The easiest way out from there would be through the cafeteria. She knew some of the workers down there liked to smoke on the back loading dock. They wouldn't give her any trouble. But she needed to be quick.

She stepped out of the conference room, turned down the hall and was immediately struck by a massive weight in the middle of her chest.

Daniela actually heard her ribs crack. She managed only a whistling scream and hit the ground, bouncing off the tiles from the force of the blow.

Melanie stood over her, fist cocked back, ready to punch Daniela again. The photogenic face of Earth Garde looked grim, her blond hair tied back in an all-business ponytail.

Of course. She *would* be a sellout.

"Stay down, Daniela," Melanie said. She tried to sound hard, but Daniela saw through that—she knew how easily the girl scared. "I'll hit you again if you make me."

Daniela couldn't have stood up if she wanted to. She couldn't even focus enough to encase Melanie's stupid head in a block of stone. She couldn't breathe.

"Wow, you really messed her up," said an Asian girl as she sidled up next to Melanie. She looked like she'd just stepped off a runway, her black hair in a bun, her slim frame clad in a metallic sleeveless dress.

Melanie looked down at her fist. "He told me to hit her if she came out unescorted."

The unfamiliar girl crouched next to Daniela and laid a hand gently on her breastbone. She felt the familiar sensation of a healing Legacy, the probing tendrils of restorative energy—but not enough. This girl wasn't actually helping her; she was just assessing the damage. Daniela still couldn't get in even a whisper of breath. She arched her back painfully, trying to find an angle that would relieve the pressure.

"You punctured her lung," the healer said, clucking her tongue. "My goodness, you Earth Garde people are all so barbaric."

"Just heal her, would you, Jiao?" Melanie said, looking away from Daniela's pleading eyes.

"Not until she's sedated," Jiao replied. She stroked Daniela's cheek with the back of her hand. "Nothing personal, darling. We'll all be on the same side soon enough."

Just then, Greger stumbled out of the conference room. He held a handkerchief to his bloody nose. Daniela would've taken more pride in that if she wasn't slowly suffocating.

"Well done, girls," he said nasally as he produced a

syringe from inside his jacket pocket. "Well done."

Daniela closed her eyes. There was no way she was getting out of this.

Her last thought, as she felt the pinprick in the side of her neck and the darkness closed in, was that she should've gone with Caleb and the others.

Two weeks ago she'd been in Switzerland.

Two weeks ago she could've escaped.

CHAPTER TWO

TAYLOR COOK
THE HUMAN GARDE ACADEMY—POINT REYES, CALIFORNIA
TWO WEEKS EARLIER

"HEY, TAYLOR, RIGHT? YOU ALL GOOD?"

Taylor blinked and turned away from her window. From across the spacecraft's aisle, that Earth Garde girl who'd shown up with Caleb was giving her a concerned look. Taylor thought her name was Daniela.

"What?" Taylor asked tiredly. The corners of her eyes stung, her cheeks were still hot with windburn.

"I asked if you're okay," Daniela said. "You were grinding your teeth."

Taylor touched her mouth. "Was I?" Was she? Jesus. She made a conscious effort to unclench her jaw. "Been a long few . . ." Days? Weeks? "I'm tired as hell," Taylor concluded. "And too pissed off to sleep."

"That was some crazy shit," Daniela said, laughing

incredulously. "Most bananas situation I've been in since the invasion."

"Yeah," Taylor replied. "Sure was bananas."

Professor Nine came down the aisle from the cockpit, looking grim. He nodded at Taylor before addressing Daniela.

"Earth Garde's already up my ass," he said. "They've got transportation for you and Melanie waiting at the Academy. They want you back in Washington . . ."

Taylor tuned them out, returning to her window as Lexa's spacecraft descended. When the Academy came into view, Taylor could see Maiken Megalos doing hyperspeed laps around the track. Maiken stopped her run, staring up at the ship as it swooped in overhead. Then, she darted towards the student union. Maiken was well known as a busybody. She'd want to be the one to break the news that Professor Nine and some of his wayward charges had returned to campus. She'd tell everyone.

Which meant Taylor didn't have long to catch Miki, if the guy was even still on campus. It turned out the tweeb was actually hiding a Legacy that let him transform into wind and was also spying for the Foundation. He'd helped sneak Taylor off campus once she'd convinced the Foundation she was on their side. She badly wanted to bust him.

She could at least do that. One small victory after so much failure.

The engines on Lexa's spacecraft weren't even cool, the exit ramp barely in the dirt, when Taylor made a wordless beeline off the ship and headed for the student union. Most of the others were too tired to notice. Nine had a small group of Peacekeepers to deal with, and Daniela and a still-sniffling Melanie were with him, probably arranging their return to Earth Garde. Nigel had his mother, Bea, to worry about—the black tendrils curling under her skin looked a lot like what Taylor had seen on the Blackstone soldiers back in Siberia. The woman wasn't well, but Taylor wasn't in the mood to offer her healing. And then there was that spy lady, Agent Walker, the one responsible for "handling" Kopano and Ran for that shady Watchtower group operating within Earth Garde. Walker was focused on looking after Rabiya, the Foundation teleporter that was allegedly now on their side, their new recruit looking around the Academy with shining eyes like she was stoked to be here.

That left no one to follow Taylor.

Well, no one except for Kopano.

"I know that walk," Kopano said, his longer legs matching her stride for stride. "We are about to do something badass."

Taylor glanced over at him, too drained for jokes. Frankly, she didn't understand how he could be so upbeat after getting kidnapped, having a chip installed in his head and then fighting a massive battle against a genuine Loric. But Kopano was going to Kopano.

"Got to get Miki," Taylor said, her voice scratchy.

"Yeah, we talked about him on the flight back," Kopano replied.

"I know."

"And we decided not to do anything rash."

Taylor picked up speed. "Who decided? Not me."

All the voices in the student union abruptly fell silent when Taylor shoved the double doors open with her telekinesis. There was Maiken, front and center, probably having just finished telling everyone about how she'd seen Lexa's ship land. The girl edged away from Taylor with a nervous look.

Taylor couldn't blame them for staring. Her face was windburned, her hair greasy and matted. She wore a heavy-duty black snowsuit, totally inappropriate for California, looking like she'd just gotten back from climbing the Himalayas or, more accurately, like she'd fallen off a mountain. The suit was ripped in patches and smeared with mud and blood, mostly not her own.

Taylor scanned the room. Maiken, Nicolas Lambert, Omar Azoulay, Simon Clement, a girl with aquamarine hair whose name Taylor didn't know, about forty others.

Where was he?

Simon, the French boy with the Legacy of knowledge transference, finally broke the silence. "*Mon Dieu.* Taylor, what happened to you?"

She said nothing. Her eyes bounced from table to table.

"Holy shit, Kopano," Nicolas exclaimed. "They let you out of prison?"

Kopano had followed Taylor inside, slightly out of breath from trying to keep pace with her. He wore a dress shirt and slacks, not a winter getup like Taylor, but his clothes were similarly ripped and bloody. Unlike Taylor, he immediately processed the fact that they were making a scene.

"Hi, guys," he said sheepishly. "I'm back. And, um, I wasn't in prison. It's a long story."

"I think I speak for everyone when I say we'd love to hear your story," Maiken said to Kopano, still side-eyeing Taylor.

There.

At the back. A table of tweebs.

"Well—," Kopano started to say.

"You," Taylor said, and she pointed right at Miki.

That took everyone by surprise, except maybe him. The tweebs sitting with Miki all turned to look at him, but soon they were yelling and shooting to their feet as Taylor telekinetically swiped their table out of the way. Taylor strode into their midst, ignoring questions and complaints, until she loomed over Miki. He didn't even stand up.

"I'm not going to fight you," Miki told her. Everyone around them exchanged looks—like, what would Taylor want to fight Miki for?

"Good," Taylor said. "If you're thinking of running, don't bother. All we did on the ride home was think about ways to stop you."

Miki squinted at her, then cracked an uncertain smile. "I think you're bluffing. But I'm not going to run either."

"It wouldn't be running, really," Kopano said, relief in his voice. "Breezing. That's a more accurate term."

"Breezing," Miki said. "I like it. I won't do that either."

"Who cares what we call it?" Taylor snapped. "You'll come peacefully then?"

"Sure," Miki replied. "Where are we going?"

"Professor Nine wants to see you."

Behind them, Nicolas let out an exaggerated *ooohh* that failed to lighten the moment. Taylor grabbed the smaller boy by his upper arm and marched him right out of the student union without another word.

Kopano rubbed his hands together.

"So," he said. "What's for lunch?"

Outside, Miki wiggled his arm in Taylor's grip.

"You don't have to drag me all the way there," he said as Taylor pulled him across the lawn, towards the administration building. When she didn't respond, he added, "You're hurting me."

Taylor glanced down at Miki. His eyes were wet and earnest. She hadn't even realized how tightly she'd been squeezing his narrow bicep. Her mind was singularly focused on putting one foot in front of the other. She was operating on no sleep. It was hard to calculate on account of the time zones, but she was pretty sure she was fighting Mogadorians in Siberia just a couple of days ago. From Siberia to Switzerland. Always in danger. From Switzerland back here. She'd traveled halfway around the world, catching fitful naps on private jets or Loric spacecraft.

What had all that stress accomplished? She had three less friends, for starters. Her big infiltration plan had taken one Foundation member into custody—*one*—and she was Nigel's mother, at that. Not to mention, it almost seemed like the woman wanted to be captured.

And now, she had Miki. No more moles burrowed into the Academy. So that was something. A small victory.

But what good were those?

The more Taylor saw of the world outside of South Dakota, the less it made sense. Everything was a mess, and the corrupt people at the top just kept getting away with their shady plans, driving good people like her —like Isabela and Caleb and Ran—further and further towards the edge. How far would she have to go to win against an organization like the Foundation that completely lacked morals and boundaries? What would "winning" even look like?

"Ow," Miki said. "Taylor. Come on."

Taylor realized that she'd been digging her nails into his skin. She let him go.

"Sorry," Taylor mumbled.

"It's okay," Miki said, rubbing his arm. "So what happened? Did you get them?"

Taylor glared at Miki again. She knew that he could escape if he wanted. She *had* been bluffing before about having a plan to stop him from using his Legacy. The best they'd been able to brainstorm was arming themselves with some high-powered vacuums. If Miki wanted to fly out of here, she couldn't stop him.

But he looked relieved to be caught.

"We got . . ." Taylor rubbed a hand over her face. "We got

one of them. A leader, I think. But I'm not sure it matters."

"Oh," Miki said, crestfallen. "I was hoping you would tell me it was all over."

"Sorry, but remind me why you care, exactly?" Taylor replied. "Don't you work for those jerks?"

"Not willingly," Miki said. "I could've told them about your plans. Your secret meetings with Professor Nine and the others. But I didn't."

"Or maybe this is all just a cover to get you in tighter with us so you can do maximum damage."

Miki chuckled. "Seriously? That's way paranoid, Taylor."

"You'd be paranoid too if you'd seen half the crap I have."

"I can't blame you for not trusting me," Miki said. "I wouldn't trust me either. So if it makes you feel better, I'll let you guys lock me up in the cells underneath administration. I won't try to escape, even though we both know I could. I'll sit down there until you're ready to trust me."

As they closed in on the shiny glass façade of the administration building, Taylor slowed down a little bit.

"How do you know there are cells under there?" Taylor asked.

"I'm the wind. I've explored every inch of this place. Did you not know?"

Taylor shook her head. "No."

"I assume that's where Professor Nine is going to put me. They've already got Dr. Linda there and this mercenary bastard Alejandro." Miki smiled. "I think Isabela kicked the shit out of him. That was cool of her. He was my Foundation contact. He really needed to catch a beating."

Just like on the night that he'd spirited her away from the Academy, Taylor was surprised by Miki's candor. In spite of herself, she was starting to like him.

"Why do you do it?" she asked. "Work for them, I mean."

Miki exhaled through his nose. "Have you ever heard of the Nome Nine?"

"Is that like a tiny version of Professor Nine?"

He snorted. "Not *gnome* with a *g*. *Nome* with an *n*. It's where I'm from in Alaska."

"I've never been," Taylor said.

"Yeah. Not many people have. It's protected land for indigenous people. A few years ago, one of the big gas companies found a rich oil vein in the ocean just outside the boundary of our waters. My parents were actually convinced that they fudged the report and that the oil was on our land, but the government didn't listen or didn't care. They let the company go ahead with building one of those big offshore rigs, even though they always spill and even though my people relied on those waters for . . . well, for everything."

Taylor nodded. "Okay? So did a spill happen?"

"Thing never got the chance to spill because my parents and some of their friends blew it up. The press called them the Nome Nine."

"Oh," Taylor replied. "That's intense."

"They got arrested like a week before the Mogadorian warships showed up, so the story didn't really make the news. I was in foster care when I developed my Legacies.

And that's where the Foundation found me." Miki swiped his hand through the air at the memory, flattening the grass up ahead with a burst of telekinesis. "This lawyer showed up and said he could get my parents out of prison, even though they were basically terrorists. Not only that, he said that he could prevent the gas company from coming back and rebuilding their rig."

Taylor already knew how the story would end. "And all you had to do was work for them."

"Bingo," Miki said. "I didn't know what the Foundation was then. There was barely even an Earth Garde or an Academy. I didn't care whose side I was on. I just wanted to help my parents and save our home."

Taylor plucked at a hole in her bulky snowsuit. She felt a little guilty for handling Miki so roughly.

"I probably would've done the same thing," she admitted.

"Thing is, I've been thinking a lot about what my parents would have done in my position. Or what they would think if I told them about the deal I made." Miki looked down at his sneakers. "I think they'd be pissed at me. So ashamed they'd probably insist on going back to prison. They're that hard-core. I'm finally ready to do what my mom and dad would've encouraged me to do from the start. And that's blow the whole thing up. Screw the Foundation. I'm done being their puppet."

Miki's story was a lot to take in. Taylor had been around a lot of liars recently, but he seemed sincere.

Moments later, they stood in front of the administration building. Professor Nine waited for them there, flexing the fingers on his cybernetic hand. He looked, as ever, like he wanted to punch something. He'd been wearing that sour expression ever since Switzerland and their run-in with his old friend Number Five. Taylor felt Miki shrink back from Nine's look.

"All right, you," Nine said, waving his hand at Miki. "Let's see it."

"See what?"

"You know what." Nine snapped his fingers. "I heard you've been holding out on us, wendigo."

"Oh, that."

With an uncertain glance in Taylor's direction, Miki transformed himself. One moment he was standing next to Taylor, the next he was gone—except not entirely. If she squinted, Taylor could still make out Miki's particles as they swirled through the air. He looked like a small cloud of dust. A breeze now, Miki floated through the air around Nine's head, before reappearing on the other side of Taylor.

"Cute," Nine said, smoothing down his hair. "We could help you with that. Train you. Figure out what you're capable of."

"I know," Miki said. "I'd like that."

Nine clamped his robotic hand on Miki's shoulder. "Let's go inside." He looked at Taylor. "Earth Garde wants to talk to you. They want to talk to all of us. I told them they can wait. You should get some rest."

"Not yet," she said. "There's some *other* people I need to talk to."

Nine squinted at her. "What? Who?"

Taylor nodded back at the student union. "My people."

"Your people . . ." Nine raised an eyebrow at that. "I don't know what you've got in mind. Maybe we should talk it out first. Or, at least, I could go with you . . ."

"No offense," Taylor replied, "but I think this is something we Human Garde have to hash out among ourselves."

Nine's lips compressed. That was the face the big lunk made when he was trying to figure out the angles. The self-appointed professor was more of a straight-ahead-hit-something type, but he was really trying to be more circumspect. To see the big picture.

"You aren't going to incite a mass rebellion, are you?" Nine asked. "I can only handle, like, one of those a month."

"They already know something is up," Taylor said. "We can't keep them in the dark forever."

Nine thought this over. "I trust you," he said finally. "Do what you've gotta do."

Taylor went back to the student union. This time, she didn't blast open the doors. Instead, she slipped in unnoticed via the side entrance. Everyone was focused on Kopano, who sat at a central table with a massive burrito bowl in front of him. They were all talking at once, so Taylor watched and listened.

"They told us you were taken away for your own

protection," Lisbette said to Kopano. "Was that not true?"

Taylor found herself taking stock of Lisbette. She was from Bolivia. She could create and manipulate ice. She was way more into using her Legacy to erect glittery sculptures than, like, stabby icicles, but she still showed good control. She could be useful.

"Uh, I guess that's one way to put it," Kopano replied. He shoveled some rice and beans into his mouth, using the food as a method of deflection. "Sorry, guys, I'm *really* hungry . . ."

"Gosh, me too," Maiken said. "I'm always starving after I run." She reached out and snagged some tortilla chips off Kopano's plate, eating them at high velocity. "Seriously, though, Kopano, you have to tell us what's going on . . ."

Maiken was Greek. Nosy and talkative. Fast as hell.

"I'm not sure how much I *can* tell you," Kopano replied, swallowing. Taylor could see that a part of him was enjoying the attention. "It's sort of top secret."

"Is no one going to mention how Taylor just hauled Miki out of here like she's some kind of cop?" That came from Danny, a Canadian tweeb, whose lunch Taylor had ruined when she flung aside Miki's table.

"She looked pissed," said Greta Schmidt, a German Garde whose Legacy allowed her to see in all different spectrums of light.

"She *always* looks pissed," Danny replied.

"I don't know," Anika Jindal spoke up, setting down the plastic cutlery she was using on her lunch. "Taylor's always been really nice about healing me. If she's mad at Miki, she probably has a good reason."

Anika was new at the Academy, newer even than Taylor. She was from Delhi and her Legacy was magnetism. She didn't have good control yet and so was frequently pulling sharp metal objects towards herself. Taylor had fixed her up multiple times.

"Forget about Taylor and Miki," boomed Nicolas Lambert, the Belgian with superstrength, as he loomed over Kopano. "I want to know what these secret missions you guys keep going on are all about."

"The first time wasn't a secret mission," Kopano replied innocently. "We just got in trouble sneaking off campus."

"*Merde*, Nic, let the guy eat," said Simon. He was seated across from the Moroccan fire-breather Omar Azoulay, the two of them engaged in a game of chess. Omar was more focused on his next move than all the conversations around him.

"It doesn't bother you that they don't tell us anything?" Nic asked Simon.

"Not really," Simon replied.

"It bothers me," Maiken put in.

"Like, we go here too," Nic continued, glaring at Kopano, who kept on cheerfully eating. "We deserve to know what's going on."

"Checkmate, you French fool," Omar said.

"It's not even your turn," Simon replied distractedly. He reached across the table and grabbed Omar's bracelet. "Did you forget how to play? Let me recharge this."

"I wish I could tell you guys more," Kopano said. "I'm—"

"You *could* tell us more," Nic butted in. "You just don't want to. You guys are a clique. Trying to keep all the action to yourselves."

"How long have you been at the Academy, Nic?" The question came from the girl with the spiky turquoise-dyed hair who Taylor hadn't seen before.

"I've been here since the beginning, 'Nemo,'" Nic replied with air quotes. "What does that matter?"

"So you've been safe in here for almost two years. You don't know how crazy life's gotten out in the real world," Nemo replied. "Whatever Kopano and the others were doing, I'm sure they were helping people like us."

"They still shouldn't keep us in the dark. It's not fair," Nic countered with a surly frown. "Like I'm not good enough for their secret missions? Look at me. I can do more than swim for a long time, at least."

Nemo rolled her eyes. "Legacy-shaming. Real nice."

Someone cleared their throat next to Taylor. She turned her head to find that Nigel had sidled up beside her along the wall. His eyes were red-rimmed, his posture like a wilted flower. If anyone had a rougher last few weeks than Taylor, it was Nigel. She started to say something, to put a hand on his shoulder, but he jerked his chin in Kopano's direction.

"You going to let the big lad take all the heat?"

Taylor returned her gaze to Kopano, who had leaned back in his chair and was now blotting at his mouth with a napkin while Nic stood over him.

"My friends, truly, I wish I could tell you more about our many adventures," Kopano declared grandly, "but they are highly classified."

"Aw, that's horseshit," Nic complained. "Classified by who?"

"We should say something to Professor Nine or one of the other administrators," Maiken said. "This situation is really detracting from my ability to learn."

Taylor sighed. She pushed away from the wall. Looking beyond the crowded tables and arguing students, Taylor saw there were a few members of the kitchen staff hovering around the buffet, plus a Peacekeeper guarding the back exit. She couldn't tell if they were eavesdropping. Couldn't take any chances.

She turned to Nigel. "Can you put us in a sound bubble so no one outside can hear?"

"You and me?"

"No," Taylor said, shaking her head. She motioned to the Garde at the tables surrounding Kopano. "All of us."

"What're you going to do?"

"There's too many secrets," Taylor replied. "I'm sick of it."

With that, she strode forward, into the midst of her classmates. They fell gradually silent as they realized Taylor had been standing there for a good portion of their argument. Nic spun away from Kopano and sized her up.

"What'd you do with Miki?" he asked.

Taylor held up a finger. She waited until she sensed a

change in the air and could no longer hear the birds chirping outside the student union. Nigel had done as she asked.

"You want to know what's been going on?" Taylor looked straight at Nic, then past him, at all the faces turned in her direction.

"Uh, I mean, you could go take a shower first . . . ," Lisbette said quietly. "We'd wait."

Taylor ignored her, taking a deep breath. She could tell by the expectant looks that her classmates were all ears.

"We first found out about the Foundation when they kidnapped me . . . ," she began.

Taylor told them everything.

About the Foundation and Bea Barnaby.

About the mole at the Academy.

About Watchtower, the clandestine organization working within Earth Garde.

About Sydal Corp and the weapon designer's ties to both Earth Garde and the Foundation.

About all the factions interested in controlling them or profiting off them or simply eradicating them.

And then Taylor told them what might happen next.

It was nearly sunset when Taylor finally finished fielding what seemed like endless questions from her classmates. The size of the crowd kept growing, her classmates leaving to go get their roommates or friends, to let them know big stuff was happening. Classes got skipped. Every student came through eventually. She felt like she had to keep explaining the same things over and over, but she stayed patient. At one point, Professor Nine and Dr. Goode popped in to watch, but they respectfully stayed outside Nigel's sound bubble.

Her mouth was dry from talking. Still in her battle-shredded snowsuit, now unzipped to the waist, Taylor trudged back towards the dormitory feeling like she could sleep for a year. Luckily, Kopano was at her side and seemed happy to let her lean against his shoulder.

"That was very cool," he told her.

Taylor rubbed her jaw. "I'm freaking exhausted."

"You know, when the first generation of Human Garde got their Legacies, John Smith pulled us all into a vision and explained everything about the Mogadorians. For the longest time, I thought I dreamed it."

"Yeah," Taylor said tiredly, "you told me about that."

"You reminded me of him just now," Kopano said.

Taylor snorted. "Of John Smith? Really? Your idol?"

"You are my new idol."

Taylor squeezed his arm. "I'm glad that's who you were thinking of, because the whole time I was talking I kept thinking about Einar."

"Yuck. Why?"

"His whole speech about us sticking together. About liberating us. He's an insane, murderous asshole, but some of that stuff made sense. He wanted to get it all out in the open."

"I sense a 'but' coming," Kopano said. "I hope there's a 'but' coming."

As they neared the entrance to the dorms, Taylor's eyes started to feel heavy. Her bed. So close. She took a long pause, getting her thoughts together.

"*But*," she said at last, "he was wrong about one thing, especially. About us needing to be liberated. We don't need that. We already have a place where we can be free."

"We do?"

Taylor waved a hand in front of her, encompassing the grounds, the lights flickering on in the buildings, the Garde hanging around in small groups, probably discussing all the insane stuff she'd just told them.

"It's here," she said. "This is our place. And we're going to fight for it."

CHAPTER THREE

CALEB CRANE
ROME, ITALY

AS HE STOOD IN THE DOORWAY OF THE MASTER bedroom, which was roughly the size of the entire first floor of his house back in Nebraska, Caleb was struck by how every inch of the villa seemed to glitter. He'd read somewhere that all the gold ever mined in human history would fit into just three Olympic swimming pools. Caleb figured this place had to account for at least a bathtub's worth. The marble floor tiles were flecked with gold. Veins of gold ran through the massive bed's wooden posts. The bizarre painting on the wall—topless angels with flaming swords chasing after a grinning man in a sparkling race car—was housed in an ornate gold frame.

Caleb couldn't quite wrap his head around the style. The guy who lived here was superrich. Got it. Understood. But why did he feel the need to constantly remind himself of the fact? Something was definitely wrong with anyone who needed to be so flashy.

Then again, the villa's owner was a member of the Foundation, so bad taste was just the tip of the iceberg of his psychological problems.

The bedroom was empty, just like all the other rooms Caleb had checked so far. The top floor was clear. He was about to go in search of the others when something jabbed him in the small of the back.

"Stop looking at boobs," commanded a voice behind him. "We're trying to do an infiltration here."

Caleb spun around to find Isabela smirking at him. She held a nectarine in one hand and a knife in the other, the handle still pointed at Caleb.

"You shouldn't sneak up on me," Caleb said, blushing as he realized how it must have looked to Isabela: like he was ogling that skeevy painting. "One of my duplicates could've attacked you."

"Oh please, all your selves love me," she replied, brushing past him. "Anyway. The place is empty. We've checked everywhere."

"Just like the last one," Caleb said sourly.

Two weeks had gone by since Switzerland. Two weeks since Caleb turned his back on Earth Garde and teamed up with Einar (a psychopath), Five (also a psychopath) and Duanphen (surprisingly normal by comparison). After a couple of days resting up on Einar's cramped spaceship, they had tried to track down more of his former Foundation contacts. Even after the mess in Switzerland, they all agreed that bringing Foundation members to justice was the best use of their time. Well, Isabela thought they should be partying and enjoying the wealth they'd amassed, but the rest of them wanted to do something productive.

In Greece they found a conspirator's estate deserted. They'd tried another name with another mansion, this time in Croatia. No one home. And then, they'd come here, to the villa of a former Formula One driver turned angel investor, apparently a big spender on the Human Garde black market. But he was gone, too.

"Rome seems like it'll be more fun than Crete," Isabela said cheerily. "But the other mansion was much nicer. This place is kinda trashy, don't you think?"

"It hurts my eyes," Caleb said, always happy to be able to agree with Isabela about something. He cleared his throat. "Also, I wasn't looking at those boobs before. Just so you know."

Isabela considered the painting like she was at a museum, tapping her knife on her chin. "Why not? Don't you like them?"

Caleb opened his mouth but didn't manage a response.

Random articles of clothing were pooled on the bedroom floor or sloppily hung from half-open drawers. The door to the walk-in closet was ajar, empty hangers piled in one corner. From the look of things, the race car driver must have packed in a hurry. Maybe he sensed the avenging angels from his painting were finally catching up to him.

Isabela plucked a lavender silk shirt from the ground and tossed it into Caleb's face.

"Put that on and we can go clubbing," Isabela said.

Caleb disentangled himself from the shirt and made a face. "You need to take this more seriously."

"Oh, right, we're on a *mission*." Isabela dropped her voice to a whisper and wiggled her fingers at him. "Psh. I would've stayed at the Academy if I wanted lectures, Caleb."

"It doesn't bother you that none of Einar's leads on the Foundation have panned out? That we haven't accomplished anything? That we're basically fugitives without a plan?"

"We have a spaceship filled with money. What do we need a plan for?" She grazed her knife against the bed frame. "Think this is real gold?"

"Isabela. Come on."

"You should be happy we haven't found any Foundation people," Isabela said, her eyes darkening as she focused on Caleb. "Einar and Five would probably want to kill them, you and Ran would say no and I'd have to listen to all the arguing."

"We said we wouldn't kill anyone," Caleb replied. "We aren't murderers. We're trying to bring these people to justice."

Isabela scoffed. "You're sweet."

"You mean that as an insult."

"Obviously." Isabela waved her knife through the air as she spoke. "Who do you think will help with this 'justice,' hmm? Earth Garde wants to arrest us. Every government thinks we are *terroristas*. The Foundation buys its way out of any trouble. If you want justice, killing them is really the best we can do."

"You don't really believe that," Caleb said quietly.

She popped the last slice of fruit into her mouth and tossed away the pit. "Look, I'm with you. Killing is a big waste of effort. We have a saying—*se correr o bicho pega; se ficar o bicho come*. If you run, the beast catches you; if you stay, the beast eats you. Get it?"

"Damned if you do, damned if you don't."

"Exactly! So if there is nothing we can do without screwing ourselves, our best option is to go screw."

"I'm not sure that means what you think it does."

"Forget all this fighting. We can do *anything*." She jumped up on the bed. "We have money; we have powers; we can— Ah!"

Isabela lost her balance as the bed shifted weirdly beneath her feet. She would've fallen off, but Caleb hopped forward and she braced herself on his shoulder.

"A waterbed," Isabela declared, stomping down on the rippling mattress. "How ridiculous. Now we know that this man is evil."

Isabela pushed off Caleb's shoulder and navigated the bed's waves until she stood on the pillows directly beneath the painting. She flipped her knife into an overhand grip.

"He must have had this made special, yes? What do you think he asked for? Sistine Chapel but for a horny loser?"

Caleb cracked a smile and tried to think up a joke. He wasn't the best when it came to riffing, especially not with Isabela. Before he could formulate something witty, Isabela slashed her knife through the canvas. Caleb cringed.

"I mean, someone did spend time painting that . . . ," he said weakly.

"Yes, and they got paid and then probably spent a week washing their eyeballs." Isabela flopped into a sitting position, the motion 'accidentally' plunging her knife into the waterbed. She left it there, a steady trickle of water bubbling up around the handle. "Oops."

"So, we're vandals now," Caleb said. "That's what we left Earth Garde for."

She stood up and gently slapped his cheek, her fingers still sticky from the nectarine. "I don't know why *you* left," Isabela said. "Me? I was tired of being told what to do. You might not want to admit it, but I think you like this too." She gave the leaking bed an emphatic kick. "You're tired of orders. But you have that little thing inside—a conscience or whatever—it keeps telling you that you need to do something *important*. The sooner you stop listening to that, the happier you'll be."

Once again, Caleb's mind filled with half-formed sentences, none of which would do as responses to Isabela. His mouth hung open and he made a conscious effort to snap it shut so that he wouldn't look like a total idiot. Isabela didn't notice. She had already started across the room, towards the attached bathroom.

"Did you check in here?" she asked over her shoulder as she nudged open the door.

"No, not yet. I—"

Isabela's shriek cut him off. Caleb jolted forward, pushing into the bathroom right behind her. He half expected to find some Foundation assassin lurking in the shower or a bomb affixed to the shimmering bidet. But there was no threat at all.

There was only a Jacuzzi.

Isabela clutched his arm. "Are you seeing this? I think it has a whirlpool." She brushed her fingers through her hair. "Do you know how greasy I feel cooped up on that spaceship?"

She didn't look greasy to Caleb. As usual, her skin was perfect, her hair flawless. But then, that was all thanks to Isabela's shape-shifting Legacy. Caleb had seen Isabela's true form, the burn scars that she'd gotten in an accident before the invasion. He squinted at her, trying to see through her façade. Could she really be so cynical about their situation? Would he really be happier if he ignored the tug of his conscience and went full-on YOLO like Isabela recommended? Was he even capable of that? Did people still say YOLO? Even thinking that acronym gave him anxiety.

Isabela unzipped the Jacuzzi's cover and shoved it aside. She turned on the jets, steam immediately rising. The gold inlaid wall-to-wall mirrors over the sink began to fog up. She reached around to her hip and unzipped her skirt, shimmying out of it in the same fluid motion as she began peeling off her shirt.

Caleb gulped.

She glanced over her shoulder at Caleb like she'd totally forgotten him, although that was obviously just another one of her games.

"Coming in?" she asked, one arm draped demurely across her chest.

"No, uh, I—"

"Then shut the door," she said with a wave. "You're letting in the cold."

His cheeks hot, Caleb backed out of the room. As he closed the door behind him, he swore he could hear Isabela laughing over the bubbling tub.

"Seriously, dude? That's your decision?"

A duplicate stood next to Caleb. When had he gotten loose?

"Remember when she made out with us on the beach?" the duplicate asked. "That was dope."

"I remember," Caleb said. "Shut up."

Caleb absorbed the duplicate and went in search of Ran and the rest who, hopefully, were all fully clothed. He found most of them gathered downstairs in the villa's expansive living room—or maybe the rich guy who lived here called it something fancy like a "parlor" or a "salon." Whatever. There was a big-screen TV mounted on one wall, an endless leather sectional and a bar. That made it a living room, no matter how many nude sculptures stood watch around the edges.

Duanphen nodded at Caleb as he walked into the room. She sat at the bar, her long legs crossed, idly scratching her fingers across the dark stubble growing in on her once clean-shaven scalp. In the time Caleb had been traveling with her, Duanphen hadn't said much. She was difficult to read, seemingly content to go with the flow. Like Isabela, she seemed happy just to be out of her past life and in the world uncontrolled. Even seated, there was a readiness about her, like she could snap into action at a moment's notice.

"Find anything?" she asked Caleb.

He shook his head. "You guys?"

Duanphen dragged her finger across the bar, making a squiggle in the dust. "This man has been gone for weeks. Even the maid stopped coming."

"Another dead end," Caleb said with a sigh. "What should we—?"

"Morons! Liars!"

Caleb and Duanphen both turned at the shout. Across the room, Einar paced back and forth behind the couch. He pushed a hand through his hair and left a tuft sticking up. The Icelandic boy had seemed so fastidious when Caleb first saw him in his collection of expensive dress shirts and slacks, but since Switzerland he had stopped taking so much pride in his appearance. Back in Greece, when they rested at the abandoned mansion, Caleb had walked in on Einar ironing one of his shirts. Lost in thought, he'd let the iron linger too long and left a brown scorch mark on the sleeve. Then, he'd thrown the appliance at the wall. Caleb had left the room before Einar noticed him watching.

"I thought we agreed to not let him watch TV," Caleb said.

"You try to stop him," Duanphen said lazily.

The big screen was tuned to the BBC. There was Einar, speaking directly into the camera, his unblinking gaze either passionate or unhinged, depending on your interpretation. Caleb had seen this clip before. He'd been there when it was filmed. The video was captured on Isabela's cell phone right before the battle broke out. They had never discussed uploading it to YouTube; Einar had gone ahead and done that without asking permission, snagging Isabela's cell phone while the rest of them slept. He'd expected his speech to be a call to revolution for the Garde suffering under repressive regimes—Foundation or otherwise—around the world.

"This is how we do it. By banding together. By not abiding by any law they pass to control us. We will not be their pawns. They will not be our masters," the Einar on-screen ranted.

Caleb wished they could delete the clip off the internet, but that wouldn't do any good now. It was out there. Picked up by every news service in the world. At first, Einar had been practically giddy that his message was getting boosted by the mainstream media.

Now, though, Einar realized his error. They all did.

He looked like a crazy person.

Which, Caleb supposed, was pretty accurate.

The clip froze on a still of Einar where a bit of spit flecked off his lips. That image stayed in the top corner of the screen as the broadcast cut back to the studio, where a prim newscaster sat behind a desk.

"The Garde terrorist known as Einar would go on to describe humanity as 'leeches' before he and his minions, one of which is believed to be an actual Loric alien, murdered the inventor and philanthropist Wade Sydal. Earth Garde assured the BBC that steps are being taken to bring these perpetrators to justice and to prevent further incidents. Two weeks have gone by and the rogue Garde remain at large . . ."

"Terrorist!" Einar shouted, drowning out the rest of the broadcast. "They didn't even mention the substance of my argument. They didn't listen at all."

"I am not a minion," Number Five grumbled.

The Loric sat on the couch, arms folded, curled in on himself, draped in the same baggy sweat suit he always wore, grass stains faded on the knees from the brawl in Switzerland. Caleb couldn't swear to it, but he thought Five looked thinner since then. Honestly, he tried not to look in the Loric's direction too often. Five was sensitive about the inky splotches that disfigured him, had a shorter temper than Einar and had nearly killed Caleb two weeks ago. He wasn't eager to provoke the Garde.

An accused terrorist and a psychotic Garde. That's who he had ditched Earth Garde for. In the heat of the moment, after that bloody battle, it had seemed to make so much sense . . .

Caleb caught himself fingering the vial of black ooze that he had pocketed back in Switzerland, hidden now in his coat pocket. Sydal had been buying a whole suitcase of the goo from Bea Barnaby—Nigel's mom, a member of the Foundation; he still couldn't get his brain around that one. The substance had driven Five into a rage, which Caleb supposed wasn't surprising, as it appeared to be the same gunk that had disfigured him and still writhed beneath his skin. Caleb hadn't told the others that he'd swiped a vial. He wasn't even sure why he'd done it in the first place. Only Isabela knew and she kept quiet about it.

"Also, we weren't the ones who blew up Sydal," Einar continued. "Not that I'm sorry it happened. But these journalists are getting everything wrong." Einar noticed that Caleb was in the room and glowered. "If only our plan hadn't been derailed . . ."

Caleb stared at him, saying nothing. It was Caleb who had broken Einar's psychological grip on Wade Sydal and the others, preventing him from taking them prisoner. Einar was still obviously bitter about that, and about the beating that Caleb had put on him. Also, the fact that Caleb could use his duplicates to work around Einar's emotional manipulation Legacy surely didn't sit well with him. Einar was used to being in control.

"Caleb," a soft voice said. "Can you come here?"

With a sigh of relief, Caleb turned to look at Ran. Here, at least, was someone he could depend on to not do anything crazy. If Ran hadn't stepped forward to join Einar's crew back in Switzerland, Caleb didn't think he would've found the courage to do the same. Caleb knew that, for Ran, this alliance was a matter of convenience. She wanted out of Earth Garde and Einar had transportation and the skills to evade their pursuers.

Caleb understood Ran's position. She'd been treated horribly—tagged with an Inhibitor chip and forced into a spy program with the mission to bring down Einar. Caleb thought it was odd that Earth Garde hadn't bothered trying to take down Einar until he started killing members of the Foundation. Didn't they know about Einar when he was going around kidnapping healers for the Foundation? Had the Foundation simply covered their tracks or had Earth Garde turned a blind eye? Judging by the symbiotic relationship between Earth Garde, Sydal Corp and the Foundation, Caleb thought it was a little of both.

Every day since Switzerland, Caleb dreaded that Ran would decide she was better off on her own. He swallowed as he followed her out of the living room and back down the hallway she had emerged from, hoping that they weren't about to have that conversation. She glanced in his direction and must have read the worry in his expression because she reached out to touch his shoulder.

"What's wrong?" she asked.

"Nothing, I—" Caleb checked behind him to make sure they were out of earshot. "Just wondering what we're doing here."

"In Italy?"

"With these people."

"Ah."

"Do you think we made a mistake?" Caleb asked. "Two weeks and we haven't made any progress. Heck, I'm not even sure what progress would look like . . ."

"They are a means to an end," Ran replied. "I will never trust Einar after what he did to Nigel. But he is right about one thing: We have a better chance surviving together than apart."

Caleb nodded and fell silent. He reflected on the speech Einar had given, the one they were now using clips of on TV to label him a terrorist. The funny thing was, Caleb actually agreed with what Einar had said about the Garde needing to find their own way, about them not being able to trust the people in power. It had actually inspired Caleb to take Einar's side.

Not that he would ever tell Einar that. It was the right message coming from the absolutely worst messenger.

Ran led Caleb through the dining room and out onto a wide terrace that overlooked a cobblestone backstreet. The villa was only a few blocks from the tourist-filled Piazza di Spagna, but here it was quiet. Nestled across the street were a small café and a pasta shop, neither of them crowded. The midafternoon sun was shining and Caleb took a deep breath of the brisk air. A bell tolled in the distance.

"It's nice out here," he said. "Too bad the rest of the place sucks."

"At the café," Ran said quietly. "Do you see that woman?

Careful, do not make it obvious we have noticed her."

Caleb edged closer to the terrace's railing, peeking down at the café's outdoor seating. Of course he saw the woman—she was the only one there. She was middle-aged, dark-haired, dressed in pants and a heavy knit sweater. Totally ordinary.

"What about her?" Caleb asked.

"She has not ordered anything," Ran said. "Before her, there was a man sitting there. He also did not order anything. He left and she came minutes later. Sat in the exact same spot."

"Hmm," Caleb grunted.

He took a closer look at the woman and, as he did, her eyes flitted in his direction. Caleb edged back so she couldn't see him.

"Definitely weird," Caleb said. "But I've felt paranoid nonstop since leaving Earth Garde. So maybe let's not jump to any conclusions about some lady."

"If the Foundation knew enough to evacuate the people we've been looking for because of Einar, would it not stand to reason that they would post sentries here to trap him? To trap us?"

"We didn't have any problems in Greece," Caleb said thoughtfully. He took another look at the woman. She held her hands out in front of her, staring at them, like she was checking her nails.

"I have a bad feeling," Ran said. "I know Isabela wanted to stay here. We could all use some time off that ship. But this is not right."

"What's going on?" Einar appeared on the terrace, Five and Duanphen behind him. Caleb could tell he was still angry about the news report and suppressing a scowl.

"I think we are being watched," Ran said.

Einar came to stand next to Caleb so he could get a look at the woman. When Einar appeared, she looked straight at him, blatantly staring now, not even bothering to hide it.

"She could be anyone," Caleb said cautiously, suddenly more worried for the woman's safety than their own. "Or nobody."

Five put a hand on Einar's shoulder. "Step back. She might recognize you."

"Just some woman," Einar said, looking at Ran. "Is that all?"

Ran hesitated. "There was a man before. Same spot. It seemed like surveillance."

"I see," Einar replied. He clapped his hands, a disturbing vigor in his eyes. "Shall we go say hello?"

He left the veranda without waiting to see if the others would follow. Ran and Caleb exchanged a look, then went after him.

"Let's not overreact," Caleb said.

"Haven't you been complaining that all our Foundation leads are garbage?" Einar asked. "Well, that is a lead down there."

Caleb could already tell Einar wouldn't be talked out of approaching that woman. But at least he could make sure no one got hurt and that they didn't get in any deeper trouble.

"Uh, Five . . . ," Caleb began, clearing his throat to keep his voice from cracking. "No offense, but you're pretty conspicuous. Maybe you should get up in the air. There are a lot of narrow streets around here. If there's an ambush coming, you'll be able to spot it and scoop us up."

Five stared at Caleb with his single, unblinking eye. "Einar?" he asked, after a moment.

"Yes, yes," Einar replied. "That sounds like a good plan. Our ship is still hovering up there. We'll need you to bring us back to it if a hasty exit becomes necessary."

"What about me?" Duanphen asked. It took Caleb a moment to realize that she was talking to him and not Einar.

"Get Isabela," Caleb said. "She's in the bath."

"Of course she is," Ran murmured.

"Watch our backs from the terrace," Caleb continued to Duanphen. "Tell her to get ready to shape-shift into a diversion. The pope or something."

Duanphen nodded and jogged towards the stairs. Five went with her, heading for the roof, a more discreet place for him to leap into the air than the veranda.

Seconds later they were on the street, Einar leading the way, Ran and Caleb on his heels.

"We aren't going to hurt anyone," Caleb said, trying to match Einar's determined gait.

"That depends on her, doesn't it?" he replied.

The woman at the café had gotten up while they made their way downstairs. She was already halfway down the street, heading for the crowded plaza beyond. She walked backwards, eyes on them, lips curled in a smile. Baiting them.

"Enough," Ran said. "This is a trap. We'd be stupid to follow."

Ran's warning didn't stop Einar. He stalked down the narrow lane with his fists clenched at his sides.

"Where are you going?" Einar called to the woman. "Why don't you stay and have a chat?"

"Oh, I know how you like to talk, talk, talk," the woman replied. She stopped walking and stood in the mouth of the alley. "Reckon I wouldn't get a word in edgewise with you, Einar."

Her English was perfect. In fact, she sounded to Caleb like she had a Southern accent.

"If you know me," Einar said through his teeth as he continued towards her, "then you know that I'll make you talk. But I don't want to waste my time chasing around some flunky. Tell us who sent you and where we can find them and I might let you leave breathing."

"You ain't nearly so scary as on TV." The woman sniffed the air. "You stink, though. I can smell your rot from here."

A bent old man turned the corner and nearly bumped into the woman. She reached out and squeezed his hand in apology. And then, much to Caleb's surprise, all hell broke loose.

The woman started screaming. *"Dove sono? Dove sono?"* Her eyes cast about wildly. *"Un diavolo mi ha posseduto!"*

"What the hell?" Caleb said.

Einar stopped advancing as the woman fell to her knees,

people from the plaza beginning to trickle into the street to see what the commotion was about.

"We should go," Ran said. "She's drawing too much attention."

Meanwhile, the old man continued down the street towards them like nothing happened, completely oblivious to the commotion. In fact, he seemed more interested in the three Garde than he did the panicking woman behind him. It was the old man's smile—an odd twist of his chapped lips—that set off an alarm for Caleb.

"What's with him?" Caleb said, pointing out the approaching octogenarian.

Ran and Einar, both distracted by the woman, turned their attention to the old man only when he was almost on top of them. He reached out a gnarled hand towards Einar's face.

"Judgment has come for you, abomination," the old man pronounced, his accent somehow just like the woman's had been before she started shrieking in Italian.

Einar shrank back, pushing Ran and Caleb away as he did so. Then, with a telekinetic force that made the hair on Caleb's arms stand up, Einar sent the old man flying into the nearest wall.

"Jesus!" Caleb shouted. "What did you do?"

"Go," Einar said. "Get back."

The old man slumped against the café's front, his narrow rib cage rising and falling, breath whistling through his nose. And yet, he still wore that demented smile and kept staring at the Garde.

Ran rounded on Einar, eyes wide. "Why did you do that? You could have killed him."

"We need to leave immediately," Einar insisted.

He was right. The quiet street outside the villa was now a full-blown scene. The woman who first lured them down here was still shaking and holding herself while a group of people tried to make sense of what she was saying. Nearby, a handful of customers from inside the café checked on the old man. An apron-wearing Italian scrutinized the Garde.

"*Lo hai attaccato?*" he asked them.

As Caleb watched, the old man groped for the apron wearer's leg and, as he touched him, the younger man's face changed. He wasn't angrily making accusations in Italian anymore. He was smiling at them and speaking English.

"Just a bit of fun, pal," he pronounced, smiling at Einar. "Next time, you won't see me coming."

"Come on!" Einar yelled at Ran and Caleb. He turned and sprinted back towards the villa.

As he and Ran chased after Einar, a thought occurred to Caleb that made him even more uneasy about this bizarre encounter. Back in Switzerland, Einar had been shot in the throat by Bea Barnaby and nearly bled to death.

And yet, this was the most frightened that Caleb had ever seen him.

CHAPTER FOUR

TAYLOR COOK
THE HUMAN GARDE ACADEMY—POINT REYES, CALIFORNIA

KOPANO SET HIS BOOK DOWN IN THE GRASS AND yawned theatrically. "This Holden Caulfield is a real whiner, huh?"

Taylor stirred. She'd been so lost in thought that she had forgotten to blink and now her eyes stung from staring into the cloudless blue sky. She'd also lost track of the fact that Kopano was there, even though her head was propped up on his thigh. The two of them were sprawled in the grass outside the student union. A passerby who didn't know any better would've thought they looked pretty chill: an ordinary couple enjoying the bright sun on a cool day.

Taylor would've scoffed at that. As if she could ever chill. The only reason she was lying around out here was because Kopano insisted. She would've much rather been pacing beneath the training center, watching the security monitors and waiting.

For what? Well, she wasn't quite sure yet. The next bad thing.

She peered up at Kopano. "I don't know Holden. What's his Legacy? Is he new?"

Kopano laughed and picked up his book, shaking it at her. "He's fictional. Aren't you reading this? It was assigned for literature class."

"Lit class was canceled," she replied. "Professor Kellogg was too scared to keep working here, just like half the faculty."

"We're still supposed to do the reading."

Taylor rolled her eyes. "There's more important stuff going on than homework, Kopano. Besides, I read that back at my old school. I think you've got to be an angst-filled teenage boy to get anything out of it."

Kopano looked down at the book. "Maybe that's why I'm not into it. I'm not angry enough. I just want to yell at this Holden—*Cheer up, my dude!*—and then slap him on the butt like all your American jocks do."

"I mean, you *should* be angry, though," Taylor said. "Earth Garde forced you into a secret spy program and put a chip in your head against your will." She chuckled bitterly. "Those Watchtower people don't care about your grades. They just want you to do their dirty work. Why bother keeping up with the reading?"

"I'm here until Agent Walker decides we should report

back," Kopano replied, lowering his voice like he was letting Taylor in on a secret. "And I don't think she plans to do that. Now that people like Professor Nine and Malcolm know about Watchtower, it'll get shut down. So what else am I going to do while I wait? I like the class. I don't want to be behind once everything is sorted out and things go back to normal."

"Go back to normal," Taylor repeated and looked away.

She shaded her eyes with her hand, mostly so that Kopano couldn't see the scorn on her face. He was so naïve. He still thought things would just go back to how it was when the two of them first arrived at the Academy. He really thought that any day now he'd resume taking classes the way he had before.

Kopano refused to wrap his head around the fact that he was basically a fugitive. Or, at the very least, a deserter. So far, Agent Walker had been able to shield him. She kept filing phony reports with Watchtower that said she and Kopano were investigating leads in their hunt for Einar, while they were actually hiding out at the Academy and doing nothing of the sort. After the PR nightmare of Switzerland, Taylor got the sense that Earth Garde had bigger things to worry about than Kopano's whereabouts, but eventually they would circle back to him and Walker. Nothing would ever go back to normal.

"Why do you look mad all of a sudden?" Kopano asked her.

Taylor sat up. "Honestly? Your constant positivity is driving me a little insane."

Kopano didn't appear to take this personally. "Do you remember the solemn vow I made you when we first got here?"

"You promised to keep my Academy experience as boring and normal as possible," Taylor said. Then, she gently flicked Kopano's forehead. "You really botched that, didn't you?"

Kopano's smile faltered. "Yes, but . . ."

"It's okay," Taylor said, guilty now for making Kopano feel bad. She rubbed his shoulder. "I release you from your promise. I don't want boring anymore. I haven't wanted that since the night Einar kidnapped me."

"Obviously boring is out of the question," Kopano replied, puffing out his chest. "But maybe it wouldn't hurt to relax sometimes, eh? Enjoy a sunny day in the company of a handsome young admirer."

Taylor made an exaggerated look around. "Where would I find one of those?"

Kopano gave her a flat look. "You don't take me seriously, but I am full of wisdom. You must learn to breathe, Taylor. To enjoy the smaller things. If you become too focused on all the work we must do, you'll crack under the pressure. The kids here believe in you. They need you to lead them. And to lead them, you need to keep yourself sane."

Jesus. Taylor sucked in a breath. Kopano was right, but it

was still weird as hell to hear.

When had she become a leader?

Kopano must have been able to read the uncertainty in her eyes. "I know better than anyone that you didn't come here to be in charge," he said, then chuckled. "You didn't want to come here at all."

"From the day we met, you've been going on about being heroes and our responsibility to use our Legacies for good," Taylor countered. "You must have brainwashed me."

Kopano winked at her. "Maybe enhanced charisma is another one of my Legacies."

"Maybe it's supermodesty."

"Yes, that too, most definitely," Kopano replied without missing a beat. "Anyway, as I was saying, you might not have wanted to be a leader, but you are one now. And when you are a leader, it matters how the others see you acting. Everyone here has seen the news, the videos of Einar, the loudmouths who think we should all be locked up. It makes them nervous. Scared, even. But if they see you out here, being chill, letting yourself relax in my absurdly muscular arms—"

Taylor snorted.

"—they'll think, hey, things are not so terrifying. They'll think—oh, right, life is dope here at the Academy and I am doing a good thing and this is a place worth fighting for."

"They'll think all that just from seeing us together, huh?"

"It would be more effective if we made out a little,

yes . . . ," Kopano said thoughtfully.

Taylor chuckled and looked around. Further out in the grass, a couple tweebs tossed a Frisbee back and forth without actually touching it. Past them, Lisbette Flores and Nic Lambert recorded the measurements of a tree for a biology class project. Nic said something—probably gross—and Lisbette slapped him hard on the arm with her clipboard.

"You're right," Taylor told Kopano. She took a deep breath of the fresh air. "It's okay for us to relax a little."

And then, as if on cue, because nothing could even stay nice for like five seconds, Taylor spotted Nigel. The scrawny Brit's shoulders had been hunched more than normal since they'd come back from Switzerland a couple of weeks ago. If Kopano thought that Taylor needed to chill out, she could hardly imagine what he thought about Nigel, who was perpetually scowling, skipping classes and barely taking care of himself.

"Uh-oh," Kopano said as he too spotted Nigel.

Taylor got to her feet and Kopano followed suit. Both of them knew immediately that Nigel wasn't here to hang out.

"Saw a bunch of Peacekeepers massing at the entrance," Nigel said without any greeting. "Greger Karlsson is with them. They're coming in. Something's going down."

"Maybe they are coming to tell us what a good job we're doing," Kopano suggested half-heartedly.

"Go find Rabiya," Taylor said immediately. "Get her to create some Loralite so we can teleport out of here if things go bad. And then you two stay out of sight. You aren't supposed to be here and we don't want to give Greger any more excuses to cause problems."

"On it," Kopano said, and jogged off towards the dorms to look for Rabiya.

"Get everyone together," Taylor told Nigel. "Like we talked about."

When Greger Karlsson and his Peacekeepers arrived at the administration building, Professor Nine was waiting for them with two dozen Garde at his back. Two dozen students who Taylor had picked because they could handle themselves. Two dozen who listened to her. And more watching from the dorms in case they were needed. She'd told them that they might need to show their strength. She'd planned for this and her classmates had mobilized quickly.

"You aren't welcome here, Greger," Nine said, by way of opening the discussion. "Not after the shit you pulled with Ran and Kopano."

"Ironic," Greger replied. "Because you are the one who is not welcome."

Taylor stood a few steps behind Nine, her face stony. For the last two weeks—as they replayed that video of Einar on the news over and over, as the world lamented what a tragic loss of life Wade Sydal was, as talking heads shouted over how Garde should be disciplined—Taylor had prepared for this. Really, she started preparing the day she got back from Switzerland.

Greger extended an envelope bearing the official seal of the UN. He flinched when Nine snatched the paper out of his hand.

"That is from the UN," Greger said, taking a quick step back. "You have been terminated as headmaster of this training facility."

"Bullshit."

The tiny hairs on the back of Taylor's neck stood up. She had the sudden feeling that she was being watched. Greger and his Peacekeepers were all warily keeping their eyes on Nine, though. She must have just been feeling the tension in the air. Not surprising, considering they were a bunch of teenagers taking a stand against a massive multi-government organization.

"Don't be dense, Nine," Greger was saying. "After everything that's happened, did you honestly expect them to keep you on? You've let this place get out of control. The public has no faith in you."

Nine opened the envelope but didn't so much as glance at the letter. He tore it up while staring right at Greger, then let the wind carry away the pieces. That made Taylor smirk.

"You want me out," Nine snarled, "you're going to need an army."

"That can be arranged," Greger replied.

The Peacekeepers backing Greger didn't seem eager to make this a physical confrontation, though. The Garde at Nine's back—Taylor, Nigel, Nicolas, Maiken, the rest—they didn't so much as blink. She had told them to remain stoic and silent, to not invite trouble, but also to make it clear they weren't playing. This wasn't field day. This wasn't capture the flag.

Greger glanced at one of the Peacekeepers, and Taylor realized that was Colonel Ray Archibald, the commander of the Academy's entire detachment of so-called protectors. She hadn't recognized him in his body armor.

"Well, Colonel? The Loric known as Number Nine is now on Academy grounds illegally." Greger made this pronouncement like Nine wasn't standing a few feet away with a feral grin on his face. "How should we proceed?"

Archibald's nostrils flared while Greger spoke. He took a long look at Nine and the rest of the Garde. Then, he replied to Greger, his voice neutral and flat.

"You asked for an escort onto campus to deliver your message," Archibald said. "That is all the activity my people are cleared for at this time, Mr. Karlsson. Anything else will need to be run up the chain of command. If there's no pressing safety concern here, we'll be heading back to base."

Archibald wasn't stupid. He could see how the odds were stacked against his Peacekeepers. But Taylor thought she detected something else in his tone. He didn't like Greger. He didn't approve of firing Nine.

Taylor spotted a flash of anger in Greger's eyes when Archibald failed to play his role, but he covered quickly. He straightened his tie and turned his attention to the students lined up behind Nine.

"I would like to remind everyone here that they are

serving at the pleasure of Earth Garde," Greger said. "Your actions are regulated under the Garde Accord. Any attempt to obstruct this change in the Academy's leadership will be seen as a serious violation of your contract. There will be consequences and . . ."

Greger's voice got smaller and smaller until it was muted entirely, even though his mouth still moved. It took Taylor a moment to realize that Nigel had muted him.

"What's that, Greger?" Nine asked with a laugh. "I can't hear you."

The Earth Garde liaison stomped his foot and made a cutting motion with his hand, but his voice wasn't restored. Some of the Garde snickered.

Archibald sighed and shook his head. "Peacekeepers!" he yelled. "On me."

The colonel turned sharply on his heel and led his soldiers back towards their camp. Greger scurried after them, getting into Archibald's ear as soon as he was out of Nigel's range.

When they'd gone, there was a collective breath exhaled by the Garde. Some of them started laughing, mocking the way Greger had stomped his feet. Nine turned to look at his students, pushing loose strands of hair out of his face.

"I appreciate the support, guys," he said.

"We got your back, Professor," Nic said.

"Hopefully, we got our message across," Nine continued. "With any luck, Earth Garde will pull their heads out of their asses, fire Karlsson and we can get back to training."

Dr. Goode, who had been standing quietly beside Nine throughout the confrontation, stroked his chin. "I'm not so certain it will be that easy."

"No," Nigel agreed. "That bellend will go put on his big-boy britches and then they'll be back."

"If it comes to that," Taylor said, "we'll be ready."

CHAPTER FIVE

"WELL, HELLO, DARLING," BEA SAID. "HOW WAS school today?"

Nigel rolled his eyes. She had asked him the same thing yesterday. And the day before.

"Get some new material, Mum," he replied as he dragged a chair into his mother's cell, the legs screeching across the floor in a way that he hoped was extra insolent.

"Isn't that what a mother is supposed to ask when her child comes home?" Bea asked, her head tilted. She held up a wrinkled women's magazine, which Nigel had given her last week after she requested something to read. "I've read this feature about being a stay-at-home mother thrice over but I suppose I still don't have a handle on the material."

"Telling, innit? That you've started to think of this place like home?"

"Hmm. You do too, don't you?" Bea smiled. "I'm merely pleased that we're together."

Nigel frowned. At first, it had been a delight to see his mother locked in this subbasement cell, the powerful woman's lavish lifestyle reduced to a stiff cot, a stainless-steel sink and a toilet. However, Bea didn't seem at all fazed by her environment. She sat on her bed with legs crossed and back straight, imperious even in track pants and a hoodie taken from the lost and found, like this prison was her domain and she'd deigned to allow Nigel to visit.

Two weeks. The woman had been down here two weeks and didn't seem at all rattled.

"Right, we can do the happy-family bit," Nigel said, sitting down opposite his mom. "School was fine, I suppose. Learned a lot."

That wasn't exactly true. Nigel's class in conversational Chinese, which he was failing, had been canceled entirely, much to his relief. Meanwhile, his hour of social studies had been overseen by Dr. Susan Chen, the dean of academics, who was substituting for the fuzzy little historian who usually lectured. While her teaching was as sharp as ever, Nigel could tell by the amount of iced coffee she gulped down and the frayed quality of her braid that Dr. Chen was exhausted. She was teaching all nine periods now, in addition to her usual advising duties.

Half the faculty had resigned or taken sudden leaves of absence in the last two weeks. More since yesterday, when Greger made his move on Nine's job. Nigel didn't have a head count of the kitchen crew and maintenance staff, but they'd thinned out considerably too.

A lot of gaps in the adult population around here, all since the news of Wade Sydal's death went public and the video of Einar ranting at the scene like a little Icelandic Hitler had gone viral. People who had worked at the Academy since it opened suddenly weren't so eager to show up anymore.

The whole thing irked Nigel to no end. The students here always had amazing powers, which, at the bare minimum, made them capable of at least maiming any normal human. That wasn't new. The only thing that'd changed was the wall-to-wall news coverage of how dangerous Garde could be if left unchecked.

Thanks, Einar.

So yeah. School wasn't exactly fine. But Nigel wasn't about to tell Bea all that.

"I talked to Jessa today," Nigel said, changing the subject.

Bea's eyes lit up at the mention of her daughter. "How is she?" she asked. Her expression tightened a half second later. "What did you tell her?"

Nigel let himself enjoy Bea's discomfort for a moment. His sister, Jessa, didn't know anything about Bea's ties to the Foundation and it was clear Bea preferred to keep it that way. Nigel supposed it was important to Bea that at least one of her children thought of her as a good mother.

"Well, for starters, I told her that we're alive," Nigel said flatly.

In the process of kidnapping Nigel and fleeing to Switzerland, Bea had conspired to kill Nigel's Earth Garde escort and then burned down their family estate. Jessa was completely in the dark about that plan and had spent the last month believing that her family was dead. Nigel had delayed contacting her until Lexa could provide a secure outside line—it was a certainty that Earth Garde was eavesdropping on all outgoing communications from the Academy. Nigel went back and forth on how much to tell Jessa. At first, he'd wanted to spill his guts, unmask their parents once and for all. But he ultimately decided that would just be cruel. Jessa had a happy, normal life. She deserved to stay that way.

"I told her that some anti-Garde terrorists tried to kill us back in London," Nigel continued. "I told her you're with me in Earth Garde's protective custody. So, not entirely a lie."

"But what about the money?" Bea asked. "Did she get it?"

"That's all you care about, isn't it?" Nigel replied.

The money in question was the hefty sum Wade Sydal had paid Bea for a supply of Mogadorian ooze. Sydal ended up exploding in his knockoff spacecraft moments later, thanks to a rocket fired by one of Bea's mercenaries. As businesswomen went, Nigel figured Bea had to be one of the most cold-blooded alive.

"I care about ensuring that our family survives the world to come," Bea responded. "That we do more than survive.

That we have the means to flourish."

"You were in MogPro, you dunce," Nigel said, referencing the secret organization of Mog-supporting humans that the Foundation had grown from. "You thought our family and the rest of humanity would *flourish* under Setrákus Ra?"

"Given the information we had at the time, we believed we were backing the winning side," Bea replied with a flip of her hand. "Unfortunately, all the variables weren't known to us. No one anticipated the Loric weaponizing our own children, for instance. The Foundation has a much stronger grasp of the current situation. Better informed. Better able to profit."

Nigel pointedly looked around Bea's cell. "Mum, I don't think you've got a grasp of your own situation, much less what's going on in the world."

"This?" Bea smiled, plucking at one of her sweatshirt's frayed strings. "This is only temporary. I'm happy to remain in your custody for now. With Einar on his little rampage, my position with the Foundation was quite shaky. I thought they might kill me themselves, if only to limit their own exposure. It's what I would've done, after all. That's why I needed to cut that deal with Sydal, to put something away for you children."

"And then you offed him," Nigel said.

"Well, for all his big ideas, the man was a simpleton. He was never actually part of the Foundation. He simply enjoyed the resources we could provide him. He cozied up to us and Earth Garde, playing both sides. It was only a matter of time until someone cut him off. Permanently, as it were."

"I still don't understand why."

"Are they saying that I killed him?" Bea asked with an amused tilt of her head. "On the news, I mean. Are they blaming Bea Barnaby? The Blackstone mercenaries? Are they talking about the Foundation? Is that the story? No?"

Nigel glared at her. She knew. Of course she knew that her name hadn't come up in connection with Sydal. Even though Einar's speech was everywhere, the parts where he ranted about the conspiracy had been fluffed off as the ravings of a teenager off his meds.

"Here's what I imagine is happening," Bea continued, her eyes twinkling, like she'd been waiting to spring this trap. "The Garde are being blamed for what happened in Switzerland. People are afraid. The public is coming to realize how a random selection of superpowered teenagers can be a danger to society. They are realizing that a silly private school overseen by an impotent body like the UN is simply not enough to protect the world we know. As a result, the preciously idealistic vision of those who first founded Earth Garde is crumbling. How close am I?"

"Not even," Nigel lied. "Your face is all over the news. And they didn't choose a nice picture either. Got a bit of the double chin, yeah? The Queen herself came on the telly to call you a disgrace to England. Even the other Tories think you're scum."

Bea chuckled. "My dear, the Foundation was only a secret organization because that was more profitable in a post-invasion world where everyone wanted to believe the Loric and their Legacies would lead us towards utopia. A united Earth where we all link arms and stand together against alien invaders isn't a place where old-fashioned free-market capitalists like your dearly departed father and I could thrive in the open. We recognized that. We understood that there was always going to be a blissful period of time where all the world's countries pretended to get along. After all, we defeated an alien menace together, didn't we? But that time is ending. Tell me, Nigel, when Earth Garde and the Academy come apart, who will the leaders of the free world call in to fix things? Perhaps a well-funded organization with a worldwide infrastructure already in place and a proven track record of controlling dangerous Garde? And what if that same organization, through a series of stock buyouts and a tragically untimely death, now owned a controlling stake in the world's biggest manufacturer of anti-Garde technology, hmm?"

Nigel stared at her, willing himself to believe that it was all the lies of a desperate woman trying to get into his head. "You're talking out your ass."

"I give it two more weeks before I'm free," Bea said. "Be a dear and, once you've finished your homework, go over to the faculty building and pick me out a nice office. I think the California air will agree with—"

Bea doubled over suddenly, overcome by a coughing fit. Her stern posture fell away just as her magazine slipped onto the floor. Nigel stood up, cringing at the sounds she made.

He had to stop himself from going to her side. For all the hate he felt, she was still his mother. It wasn't easy to see her ill.

After a minute, Bea caught her breath. She dragged the back of her hand across her mouth. Nigel handed her a tissue and she blotted at her nose and the corners of her eyes.

He could see the black veins now. The dark slivers moving beneath Bea's skin like worms. Back in Switzerland, Number Five had shattered a vial of that viscous ooze across Bea's face, rubbed it into her cuts. The stuff was still inside of her, making her sick.

"We can heal you," Nigel said, standing over Bea now, making an effort to keep his voice steady. "All you have to do is provide us with a list of names. Everyone who's in the Foundation. Tell us every way that they've weaseled their way into Earth Garde and we'll fix you up before that poison kills you."

Bea looked up at her son and Nigel was surprised by what he saw in her eyes. She approved of his negotiation technique.

"An interesting offer," Bea said. "But I shall hold out for a better deal."

"It's the only deal you'll be getting."

"I'm afraid my answer is still no, dear," Bea said. "Maybe if I actually believed that you'd let me die, I'd be more open to bargaining. But you and the Cook girl couldn't even let that horrible shit Einar expire, after everything he put you through back in Iceland. After he murdered your father."

"He'll pay for his crimes," Nigel said. "And so will you."

"Maybe. But in the meantime, I hardly believe you'll let your own mother perish."

"We don't know what that stuff could be doing to you," Nigel countered, trying a new tack.

"The Foundation ran experiments," Bea said. "I know how much time I've got. I'm not worried. You shouldn't be either. Like I said, two weeks. Maximum. And then one of my healers will come in here and fix me up, if your friend Taylor hasn't caved already."

Nigel let a breath hiss through his nostrils. She wouldn't give anything up. Not today. Maybe not ever. His mother would apparently rather let that Mogadorian sludge eat away at her insides than betray some of her rich friends.

"Right, then," Nigel said, making an effort to keep his voice breezy. "We'll see how you're feeling tomorrow. Ta-ta for now."

His mother said her own insufferably pleasant good-bye, but Nigel couldn't hear her over the sound of him dragging the chair out of her cell. He sealed the bulletproof glass door behind him without taking a look back at Bea. He couldn't bear to see her smug expression.

Nigel made it partway down the row of cells before he let loose a roar and flung the chair away from him. It bounced harmlessly off one of the cell doors and Nigel heard a gasp. He turned his head and saw, in a narrow room identical to his mother's, Dr. Linda Matheson. The Academy's resident psychologist, guidance counselor and mole for the Foundation. Hair frazzled and eyes bloodshot, she stood pressed against the very back of her cell, clearly startled by his violent outburst. Linda relaxed a bit when she realized that it was Nigel out there having a tantrum and not some assassin come to kill her.

"Nigel . . . ," Linda began, having some difficulty capturing the soothing yet judgmental tone she once had such mastery of during their weekly sessions. "Is everything okay?"

"Cram it, Linda," Nigel replied, and continued on.

He passed the cell where Miki slept facing the wall, snoring gently. The Academy's secret little jail was built to withstand a Garde's telekinetic abilities, but they weren't designed to be airtight. Earth Garde obviously didn't want anyone to suffocate. Therefore, Nigel figured, Miki could slip out whenever he wanted, but he hadn't tried anything yet and Taylor didn't think that he would. Like that Rabiya girl they'd brought back from Switzerland, Miki wanted to be good.

Alejandro Regerio, on the other hand, seemed eager to escape. The Foundation's pretty-boy thug-for-hire stood right up against the glass as Nigel walked by his cell. The guy's face was still cut up from the beating Isabela gave him when she was posing as Dr. Linda. Nigel would have loved to have seen that. After Isabela escaped the Academy, she tipped Professor Nine to Alejandro's location—locked in the trunk of Dr. Linda's car. Nine took him into custody but had hesitated to report his existence to Earth Garde because doing so would create questions about why Isabela was off campus yet again.

"You can't keep me here," Alejandro barked at Nigel, slapping his hand against the glass. "Let me out, you scrawny punk."

"Mate, nobody gives a shit about you," Nigel replied, using his Legacy to throw his voice so that the sound came from behind Alejandro. He cracked a smile when the man flinched and spun around, only to find there was no one there. Everything else might suck, but at least he could still dunk on this loser.

Nigel ignored Alejandro's profanity-laden shouts. He punched in the key code he'd gotten from Malcolm and shoved through the heavy security door, the only exit from the Academy's small prison. Or detention area. Apparently, that's what Earth Garde had called it when they insisted on installing it. Of course Nine and Malcolm had been aware of the cells, but in over a year of operating the Academy they had never seen the need to use them.

Funny that now most of the occupants were human.

Still, Earth Garde had wanted them here, Nigel thought. If Nigel had been in a more optimistic mood, he would've seen that as the organization feeling it was better to be safe than sorry. But, in the mood he was in now, it seemed to Nigel like another example of humanity being scared of Garde. He wondered, not for the first time, what Ran would think of these cells. His best friend had lost so much trust for the

Academy and Earth Garde that she'd gone and joined forces with the guy who nearly murdered Nigel, who successfully killed his dad and who had everyone in the world talking about what a danger Garde were to humanity. And, insanely, he didn't even blame Ran for ditching him. He couldn't bring himself to be mad at her. He just missed her.

All Ran had wanted to do was opt out of fighting. All Nigel wanted to do was help people. And it seemed that all Earth Garde wanted to do, with the exception of the good people at the Academy, was stick them in cages.

Maybe his mother was right. Maybe a war with humanity was inevitable. Maybe he was kidding himself to think otherwise.

Damn it. She was in his head again.

Beyond the detention area was a chilly passageway with corrugated steel walls and harsh lighting. Nigel moved through it at a swift clip—subterranean hallways took him back to Patience Creek and the terror he had faced there. He preferred to get to open space as quickly as possible.

The prison was hidden beneath the administration building. Nigel made a series of turns through the dismal maintenance tunnels, picturing himself walking aboveground, in the sun. He was taking a mole's route from admin to the training center.

He pushed through another series of security doors until he found himself in the open chamber beneath Nine's beloved obstacle course. The room always smelled like grease, the gears and wiring of Nine's many sadistic traps visible in the ceiling. Not long ago, Nigel had relished sneaking down there with the rest of the Fugitive Six, making their plans to bring down the Foundation. There was the table where they'd bounced around ideas over tea supplied by Malcolm. There was the bulletin board upon which they had tacked up all their leads and information.

It had almost seemed like a game.

The room felt bigger now without all the others gathered here. Or maybe not bigger, exactly. Emptier.

Since Switzerland, Lexa had set up a row of monitors and laptops on the table that the three of them—Lexa, Nine and Malcolm—took shifts keeping tabs on. There was no one else on the faculty they could trust with the task and, although Nigel had volunteered to help, the adults (and, well, Nine) didn't seem eager to burden their students with that responsibility. The screens were tuned to a spiderweb of cameras around the Academy. The views included the subterranean prison that Nigel had just come from, but that wasn't the biggest concern. Most of the cameras were focused on the Academy's perimeter, specifically the Peacekeeper encampment and the routes patrolled by Colonel Ray Archibald's soldiers. Nine and the others hadn't come out and said it, but they were definitely expecting the Peacekeepers to, at some point, take a sterner hand with the running of the Academy. So far, the soldiers hadn't changed their routine at all. They weren't aiming their guns inward. But there were a lot of them. And more getting bused in every day.

They were amassing an army out there. Just like Greger

promised. Taylor had the student body primed to resist whatever came next, but Nigel wasn't sure how long they could hold out. That's why he needed to get information on the Foundation from his mother—armed with that, maybe they could expose the truth and make the public see that Garde weren't the real enemy.

Ugh. Now he was starting to think like Einar.

Malcolm stood watch over the monitors. He flicked a glance in Nigel's direction, but didn't otherwise acknowledge him. Malcolm held his phone out in front of him, a bewildered look on his face.

"This isn't the time for selfies, Doc . . ."

Nigel began to trail off almost as soon as the joke started, his voice an awkward whisper by the end of his sentence. Something didn't feel right.

"Are you alone, Dr. Goode?" a voice asked.

Nigel clamped his jaw shut as he realized Malcolm was on a video call.

"Yes, Greger, I'm alone," Malcolm lied, purposely not looking in Nigel's direction.

"Where are you, exactly?" Greger asked. "That doesn't look like your office."

"I'm doing some maintenance under the training center," Malcolm replied. Nigel appreciated how easily the old scientist lied. Here was a man once interrogated by Mogadorians; he wasn't going to give anything away to some slick pencil pusher like Greger.

"Good. You're keeping busy," Greger said. "It's quite

important we maintain a sense of normalcy around the Academy during these fraught times."

"Excuse me, Greger," Malcolm jumped in, an edge to his voice. "But how exactly did you get this number?"

Even though he couldn't see Greger, Nigel could hear the sleazy smile in his voice. He completely ignored Malcolm's question. "I've always found you to be a pragmatic and intelligent man, Dr. Goode. That's why I've nominated you to take over operations at the Academy."

Malcolm's eyebrows shot up. "Excuse me?"

"You and I both know that Number Nine is out of control," Greger continued. "He never should have been given such a powerful position there but, after the invasion, we all felt such a great debt to the Loric. While we certainly appreciate what his kind have done for us, considering his recent performance, it's simply not practical to keep him on any longer."

"I disagree with that assessment," Malcolm replied coldly.

"We both know how this ends," Greger said with a sigh. "Wouldn't you rather be in charge there, Dr. Goode, rather than let Earth Garde appoint a total outsider? It would be a smooth transition. Not to mention, your support in these matters will go a long way to ensuring all our Garde remain happy and healthy."

"I don't respond kindly to threats, Greger."

"I wouldn't threaten you, Malcolm. I *like* you. I am merely trying to impress upon you the gravity of the situation."

"I see," Malcolm replied. "Consider me unimpressed,

Greger. Kindly take your job and shove it."

Malcolm disconnected. As soon as he did, he let out a jagged sigh and groped behind him for a chair. Nigel came forward, shaking his head.

"Well played, Doc," Nigel said, finally stepping forward. "Put that wanker in his place."

Malcolm nodded, his gaze distant as he stared down at his blank phone. He flopped backwards into the chair, looking like he'd been punched in the stomach.

"Dr. Goode?" Nigel asked. "What's the matter?"

Malcolm held up his phone. The ID from the disconnected call was still displayed there.

Sam.

"That son of a bitch," Malcolm said quietly. "He just called me from my son's phone."

Nigel swallowed. "Oh."

"Yes," Malcolm said as he tossed the phone onto the table in front of him. "His implication seems to be that Earth Garde has taken him prisoner."

Sam Goode. From what Nigel knew, the guy had been working for Watchtower, the same secretive offshoot of Earth Garde that swept up Ran and Kopano. Sam and Number Six had been working with the group willingly, though. Sam had played by the rules and now it sounded like Greger was using him as leverage. So maybe it wasn't just the Academy's students that were in trouble with Earth Garde.

"I'm sure your boy's fine, Doc," Nigel said, attempting to sound reassuring and sincere, always a difficult task for him.

"I've seen him in action a time or two. He's got the stuff."

"Yes, Nigel, thank you . . . ," Malcolm replied distantly. "I just . . . I thought our years of being on the run and finding each other locked in cells were behind us. I—"

Something on one of the monitors distracted Malcolm. He leaned forward, squinting at an infrared feed from a camera pointed out at the ocean.

"Do you see that?" he asked Nigel. "That heat signature?"

Nigel leaned in over Malcolm's shoulder. He did notice something odd in the air over the ocean. There was something out there letting out sporadic bursts of heat, although nothing visible to the naked eye.

"What is that?" Nigel asked. "A thunderstorm?"

"No," Malcolm replied, reaching for his walkie-talkie. "That's traveling way too fast to be a storm. That—that is something *else*. And it's headed this way."

CHAPTER SIX

KOPANO POLISHED OFF THE LAST GREASY BITE OF his second meat loaf sandwich, licked the tips of his fingers and then leaned back in his chair with a satisfied belch. "So good."

Across the table, Simon picked at a salad. "That was horrific to watch."

"I feel great," Kopano declared, rubbing the sides of his belly.

"How do you have a girlfriend?" Simon replied, shaking his head.

The kitchen only served meat loaf like once a month and while a lot of the Academy kids turned their noses up at greasy slices of ground beef, Kopano loved the stuff. It reminded him of the kafta he used to buy from a stall outside his family's apartment complex in Lagos. The cooks didn't usually reheat the previous night's leftovers for lunch, but they'd been short-staffed since yesterday and Kopano guessed they had to improvise. Whoever came up with the frankly brilliant idea to sandwich some meat loaf between toasted rye bread with melty slices of bright orange cheese deserved a Nobel Prize. America was wonderful.

Kopano's meat loaf–induced euphoria dimmed slightly when he spotted Karen Walker entering the lunchroom. The agent had stuck mostly to the administration building since the two of them arrived. Kopano knew that she was helping Malcolm and Lexa with the Academy's security systems and that she'd been reporting in a steady stream of excuses to Watchtower while figuring out her next move. *Their* next move, technically. She was supposed to be Kopano's handler, although Walker seemed pretty comfortable abdicating that responsibility so that Kopano could return to his normal life here. However, based on the grim look on her face and the beeline she made towards his table, he could tell something had changed.

"I need a word with Kopano," Walker said to Simon. The French boy grabbed his tray and cleared out, letting her take his seat.

"What's up, Karen?" Kopano asked with a smile. "You should eat a sandwich. You look thin."

Walker ignored his suggestion. "I've been officially called back to Washington," she said. "The chaos after Switzerland had the Earth Garde brass scrambling, but it seems like someone finally looked into my reports. They know your Inhibitor is down and that I lost Ran. I'm supposed to report for debriefing. I'll definitely be fired. Maybe detained. You're supposed to come with me. You'll most likely be assigned to a new handler and have another Inhibitor installed."

"I see," Kopano replied, his smile faltering.

He'd been taking a lot of flak from Taylor lately about his positive attitude. She thought that he should be angrier about what had happened to him. She wasn't wrong, but it's not like Kopano was happy to have been kidnapped and conscripted. He was pissed. To show that anger, though—to let it change him—that would be letting the bad guys win.

"I think I'll stay here," Kopano said after a pause. He looked Walker in the eyes and flattened his lips to let her know that he was serious.

"I figured you'd say that," Walker replied. "I couldn't force you to turn yourself in, even if I wanted to. But you should know that they'll come for you, eventually. Could mean trouble for the Academy."

"Maybe," Kopano said. "But I believe in Earth Garde. I believe that these conspiracies will get sorted out and that we'll go back to helping people, like we're meant to."

"I hope you're right." Walker's tone was one Kopano heard often from Taylor and Nigel—weary skepticism, like he was a fool to be so optimistic. Still, he pressed on.

"You should stay here, too," Kopano suggested. "The instructors keep quitting. You could teach a class in spy craft. That would be sweet."

Walker pinched the bridge of her nose. "I have a lot to answer for—"

"Like me," said a voice behind Kopano.

Rabiya stood at Kopano's shoulder, dressed in a purple tracksuit and a Lycra hijab. Walker visibly winced at the sight of her, perhaps remembering how she'd been complicit in smuggling the teleporter out of the UAE, a territory not governed by Earth Garde.

"Will they be coming for me too?" Rabiya asked. She'd obviously been eavesdropping.

"Surprisingly, you didn't even come up," Walker said. "I don't think your father reported your . . . your emancipation."

"This is good news," Kopano said, opening his arms. "See? We can all stay at the Academy. Eventually, Earth Garde will understand that we aren't dangerous. This will all blow over."

Walker frowned. She clearly didn't agree, but she said nothing. Rabiya laid a hand on Kopano's shoulder.

"Come on," she said. "We've got fitness."

"I thought you Academy kids were supposed to be in better shape," Rabiya teased over her shoulder. "What's wrong with you?"

Doubled over with his hands on his knees, Kopano sucked in a deep breath and held up his index finger indicating that he needed a minute. Kopano's sandwich addiction had him doubled over on the track, only a half mile in to what was supposed to be a four-mile run, feeling like his stomach was invading his lungs. He could use his Legacy to make his body lighter, but he'd already been scolded for that before— it wasn't actually exercise if he cheated.

Rabiya circled back to stand beside him. Her tracksuit made a rhythmic swishing sound as she jogged in place. She'd barely even broken a sweat.

"You look unwell," she observed.

"I ate too much," Kopano replied, straightening up with a groan and rubbing his sides.

"I know. I saw you at lunch. What did you call it? Fuel for your ever-growing muscles?"

"I don't remember saying that," Kopano said, stifling a belch.

Rabiya waved her hand at their surroundings. There wasn't anyone else on the track and they were in the section that cut through the woods. "At least, there is no one to see if you need to poop your pants."

"I'm not—!" Kopano protested. "Disgusting."

Rabiya kicked a foot back into her hand, stretching her hamstring. "So, are we running or what?"

Kopano's stomach bubbled at the thought. "Maybe we could just walk awhile."

"Good with me," Rabiya replied. "I don't think anyone cares if we hit our fitness goals today."

"No," Kopano agreed. "Doesn't seem like it."

The Australian personal trainer—a former distance runner and Olympic medalist that typically oversaw their conditioning—had left campus with some of the other faculty after Greger announced Professor Nine's firing. Nine himself was busy with his own classes, mainly working with tweebs to unlock their primary Legacies, so he'd told the kids in Kopano's fitness block to see to their own workouts.

Just Rabiya and Kopano had showed up at the track. The two of them were the only ones taking classes seriously and they weren't even really students.

In the aftermath of Switzerland, Professor Nine had barely blinked when Kopano introduced him to Rabiya. Kopano had explained the deal they cut with her against Agent Walker's wishes and Nine had basically waved it through. After losing two students and an Earth Garde operative, taking in Rabiya wasn't such a big deal. Nine never added Rabiya to the official Academy roster, but got her enrolled in classes. To the other students, she was simply a new arrival.

With both Ran and Isabela on the run, Nine had installed Rabiya in Taylor's pod. "Your girlfriend is the perfect American, like the nice girls on the sitcoms," Rabiya had told him during one of their other runs, a statement that made Kopano blush mostly because he and Taylor hadn't had the formal discussion about their status. However, Kopano also knew that Taylor still harbored some residual ill will from Rabiya's role in ambushing them when she was a pawn of the Foundation, and that it was only Kopano vouching for her that kept Rabiya from getting stuck down in the cells with Miki and Mrs. Barnaby. Taylor was busy organizing the students into a rebel army anyway. She didn't have time for new friends.

So Kopano had taken it upon himself to show Rabiya the ropes. He liked her. She had a dry sense of humor that surprised him. And, unlike Nigel and Taylor, she wasn't constantly talking about how they'd all soon be subjugated by a murderous cabal.

"It's good news that your father hasn't reported you missing, right?" Kopano said, thinking back to their conversation with Walker. "You get to stay here."

"Yes. Good news," Rabiya said. She tried to make her words sound bright, but there was a note of hurt in her voice. "I'm starting to think the sheikh might be happy I'm gone."

Kopano scratched his chin. "You know, when my dad found out I had Legacies, he immediately started scheming how he could turn a profit off me. Kept me a secret from Earth Garde for months until we got in trouble with some bad men . . ."

"At least you were valued," Rabiya said with a shake of her head. "Men like my father have a reputation for being overprotective of their daughters. He used to baby me so much, at least until I started moving objects with my mind. After that, he could barely look at me. I think it bothered him that he was no longer the most powerful person in our house. When my brother became sick and the Foundation approached us, I think he saw it as an opportunity to get all this Garde madness out from under his roof."

"What was it like working for them?" Kopano asked.

"They treated us like movie stars as long as we did what they asked," Rabiya replied. "I saw more of the world in a few months with them than I had in my entire life. At first, it was fun. All I did was move people from place to place. And I was helping to save my brother's life . . ."

"Bad deeds for good reasons," Kopano said. "My dad used to say that."

"It wasn't until we started kidnapping the healers that I saw how the Foundation really thought of us," Rabiya continued. "As assets. Property. When Einar left me behind and no one from the Foundation came to save me, that's when I learned how little I was valued." Rabiya sighed. "When you and your friends showed up and rescued me, I saw how much you cared about each other. Einar always bad-mouthed the Academy as the UN trying to control us. Maybe that's true in some ways. But at least here you stand up for one another."

Kopano's stomach grumbled when he puffed out his chest, but he did it anyway. "The intentions of this place are good," he said, then paused, thinking about Nine's dismissal. "At least, they used to be."

"A ripe fruit will always draw the attention of worms," Rabiya said. "*My* dad used to say that. I think he was talking about keeping me away from boys, but it still applies. Anyway. I like it here. Even if it's not all like I imagined."

"It's not?"

"For one, I didn't picture so much jogging," Rabiya said with a half smile. "I don't know. I get that it's called an academy, but I didn't think it would feel so much like regular school. I expected brilliant young Garde using their incredible powers to create world-changing inventions and wonders. Instead, you all play a dumb game where you try to shove each other around with telekinesis."

"Thrust, they call it," Kopano said with a chuckle. "You know, on my first day here, this guy Lofton broke his wrist playing that. Now he's graduated to Earth Garde."

"Sounds like one of our best and brightest."

Kopano lowered his voice, even though there was no one else around. "It isn't all like I imagined either. I thought we would be zipping around the world helping people and fighting bad guys. Like superheroes." He paused. "Well, I guess it's sort of been like that, actually. But everything is more complicated. Nastier. When you realize that the bad guys aren't cartoon characters and are actually people, it can get kind of intense."

"I know what you mean," Rabiya replied. Her sneakers crunched on the track as they rounded a bend that brought them in view of the fence at the Academy's western border. "Like I said, it felt like a game with the Foundation. Until I was hung up in a meat locker with those sickos threatening to burn me alive."

Kopano breathed out through his nose. "I'm sorry that happened to you."

"Everyone here has been through something, in one way or another," Rabiya said, after a moment. She reached over and gave Kopano's hand a squeeze. "The only way we truly overcome those bad experiences is by refusing to let them change us."

"Yes!" Kopano agreed happily. "This is what I've been trying to tell Taylor and Nigel, but . . ."

It took him a moment to realize that Rabiya hadn't let go of his hand. He raised his eyebrows in confusion, peering down at the smaller girl. Her gaze pointed straight ahead, at the point where the tree line broke open upon the Pacific Ocean, a peaceful expression on her face, like she didn't even realize she was holding Kopano's hand.

"Rabiya, hey—," Kopano said, worming his hand free.

"Sorry, sorry," she replied quickly, yanking her hand back so she could pull at her hijab, perhaps wishing she could cover her face and hide the rising color there. "I was just thinking about how nice you are to be my friend here when I don't know anyone and—I didn't mean anything by it."

"It's cool," Kopano replied lamely. He thought that he should say something more to ease the sudden awkwardness, but that's when he noticed a strange shimmer on the horizon over the ocean. He stopped in his tracks.

"Come on, let's keep going," Rabiya said over her shoulder. "I promise I won't make things weird again."

But weirdness, it seemed, was already coming their way. Kopano pointed out towards the ocean.

"Do you see that?"

Kopano shaded his eyes, trying to get a good look at the patch of sky where the sunlight bent unnaturally. There was a ripple in the air, sort of like heat lines from pavement during the summer. And it was getting closer.

"What is—?" Rabiya let out a cry of surprise as a crackle of reddish energy splintered off from the ripple and then another. It was like a small, fast-moving lightning storm.

Kopano blinked and, suddenly, the ripple was gone. In its place was a Mogadorian skimmer. The bug-like ship was dented and covered in scorch marks. Clearly, its cloaking system had just failed. The ship barely cleared the trees and then started descending towards the track, coming in fast for an emergency landing.

"Is that Einar and the others?" Rabiya asked.

Kopano squinted. He'd gotten a good look at Einar's ship back in Switzerland. It was beaten up, just like this one, but in different places. This skimmer looked like a slightly different model.

"No," Kopano breathed. "No. This is someone else."

"Someone else?" Rabiya raised her voice, alarmed. "Mogadorians?"

The knot in Kopano's stomach returned. Mogadorians. Of course. Who else would be flying one of those ships? Taylor said she'd encountered some of them during her hellish visit to Siberia . . .

"Get back to campus," Kopano said. "Warn the others!"

"What about you?"

Kopano tightened his molecules, making his skin harder than diamond. "These things cannot hurt me."

Rabiya didn't protest. A funnel of blue light erupted from

her palm, a jagged growth of Loralite appearing on the track at her feet. She touched it and, in a flash, was gone, transported to one of the stones she'd installed back on campus.

Kopano could wait for Rabiya to come back with help. Play it safe. That was the smart thing to do.

But come on. Mogadorians. The real bad guys. Adventure. Action.

This was why he'd come here.

He bounded forward, feet thudding against the track's packed dirt with his increased mass.

The skimmer wobbled as it descended, flares of crimson energy arcing loose from where a chrome panel had ripped off under the left wing. The ship's nose bobbed upwards as the pilot tried to pull back and slow down, but the skimmer still hit the track at high velocity, divots of dirt and rocks kicked up in its wake, armor shrieking in protest as it peeled off the ship's underside.

At least, Kopano thought, he wouldn't have to run laps for a while.

As the vessel skidded to a stop, Kopano was right there to meet it. Debris bounced off his hardened skin as he charged. He couldn't see through the skimmer's gleaming front windows, but he knew how these ships were laid out. He knew the cockpit was right in the front.

Kopano loosened his molecules just as he reached the ship and passed straight into it, through armor, through alien circuits and overheated engine parts and straight into the cockpit. He grinned at the surprise on the Mogadorian pilot's face. It must have been a strange sight, his ghostlike form emerging from her controls. She even let out a startled scream.

"Boo," Kopano said.

He went solid just long enough to grab the pilot by the shoulders—she wore some kind of obsidian armor that was icy to the touch—and then turned them both transparent. He registered, quickly, that there wasn't a regiment of Mogs waiting in the space behind her. In fact, the skimmer seemed empty. Odd.

Still holding the Mog pilot, Kopano kept up his momentum. He phased them straight through the back of her pilot's chair, which she hadn't even finished unbuckling from, and then out the ship's side wall.

The Mogadorian screamed again, this time in anger. "Get off me, fool!"

"As you wish."

When they hit the track, Kopano turned them both solid and flung the Mogadorian to the ground. She landed hard on her shoulder and Kopano thought he heard a bone break.

"Hello," Kopano said, standing over the Mog. "I am the welcoming committee. Stay down and I won't hurt you anymore."

Even as he said these lines—pretty badass, he thought, if only there were more people around to hear, that would've been cool—Kopano was trying not to blatantly stare at this Mogadorian girl. He'd never seen one of the aliens in person before.

Her skin was pale gray, almost the color of stone. The sides of her head were shaved, a coil of ink-black hair that probably reached to her waist when loose piled atop her skull. A jagged tattoo started at her collar, reached up her neck and curled around her ear. She wore patchy black body armor that was dented in so many places it couldn't be very effective, including a hole in the breastplate where the previous wearer must have been shot or stabbed right in the heart. The Mog was also young. Probably Kopano's age, assuming the Mogs aged the same way as humans. Sixteen or seventeen, tops. That was strange, too. He'd never seen a young Mogadorian before. Only the vicious, belligerent bald things that exploded into ash all over the news.

The Mog rolled away from him and hopped to her feet. She was as tall as him and extremely skinny, her armor too loose at the joints. The Mog did something to the arm that she'd landed on, wrenching the shoulder like she was popping it back into place. She grimaced and flexed her fingers.

"Ow," she said dryly.

"I told you to stay down," Kopano replied, this warning a little shakier than his last. She was a pretty intimidating sight.

In response, the Mog detached what looked like a small club from her belt. She gave it a shake and the handle extended in both directions. One end opened up like a flower, terminating in a spiked mace head made of pure obsidian. She flipped the weapon from hand to hand.

"I'm not here to fight you," the Mog said, but then seemed

to reconsider. "Unless this is part of it?"

"You're not . . . ?" Kopano cocked his head. "Wait. Part of what?"

"The training," she replied. Then, she grinned, her sharp canines glinting. "Of course. An initiation. Such was the way on my planet too."

And then she came at him, swinging the mace for Kopano's chest. He hardened his molecules and let the blow connect with his sternum, smiling confidently.

Pang. The mace-head bounced off Kopano with a noise like a cymbal. He skin wasn't broken, but it *hurt.* An icy sensation spread through his torso, causing Kopano to stumble back.

"Ow," Kopano grunted. "What is that thing made of?"

In response, she swung again and this time Kopano went intangible. The mace passed through him and this—somehow—was even more painful than the last strike. He felt the freezing cold spread throughout his body. The feeling shocked him and it was all he could do not to turn solid with the mace still inside him. He leaped back, panting and holding his chest.

"Okay," he said. "Give me that."

With his telekinesis, Kopano yanked the mace away from the Mog. She let out a cry of surprise as the handle ripped loose from her fingers. The weapon spun towards Kopano, under his control.

And then it stopped. Held in midair.

He stared at the Mogadorian. Her hand was extended, her

gaze focused on the mace. She was pulling it back to her.

"You're . . . you're telekinetic," Kopano whispered. He didn't know why he was whispering.

"Do you always talk so much during battle?" the Mog asked.

They struggled over the mace, the weapon bobbing in the air between them. She was strong. Maybe as strong as Kopano, he thought. Maybe stronger.

"Okay, I think that's enough, you two."

The voice came from over Kopano's shoulder, back in the direction of the skimmer. The Mogadorian girl wasn't alone after all.

A ramp jerkily extended from the skimmer's belly, not reaching all the way to the ground as the wrecked spacecraft continued to belch smoke. The speaker hopped down from there and approached. He wasn't Mogadorian. He looked human, with shaggy blond hair and a patchy beard to match. There was a cut on his eyebrow that he only noticed when a trickle of blood dribbled into his eye. He waved a hand over the wound, healing it.

"Rough landing," the guy said.

"I warned you all the skimmers were damaged," the Mog said sullenly.

"It's fine. No harm done."

He looked human, but he wasn't. Kopano knew exactly who the Mog's passenger was, would've recognized him anywhere. He heard the slap of metal on skin as the Mog's mace flew back into her hand, Kopano too star-struck to care about maintaining his end of the telekinetic tug-of-war.

"Hey, I'm—"

"John Smith," Kopano blurted. "You're *the* John Smith."

"Yeah," John replied, sheepishly rubbing the back of his neck. "Would you mind bringing us to Professor Nine?"

CHAPTER SEVEN

TAYLOR COOK
ADMINISTRATION BUILDING
THE HUMAN GARDE ACADEMY—POINT REYES, CALIFORNIA

"UNTIL THE ONGOING ISSUE WITH THE ACADEMY'S leadership is resolved—that's me he's talking about, I'm the issue—it would be prudent for all Academy support staff to remain off campus. Salaries will be paid in full during this work stoppage."

Nine glanced up from the email displayed on his laptop, shaking his head. Taylor, seated in the chair across from his desk, chewed the inside of her cheek.

"When did Greger send that?" she asked.

"This morning," Nine replied, shutting the laptop with more force than necessary. "This is bullshit. I fought an intergalactic warlord and now I'm getting owned by an empty suit with an iPhone."

"How much staff have we lost?"

"I don't know," Nine snapped, standing up and going to the window. "Dr. Chen and Malcolm are trying to keep people working. Figured the request to stay would be better coming from a—from a human," he said bitterly.

"At least the Peacekeepers haven't come to drag you away yet," Taylor offered.

"Yeah. Not yet, at least. Not until Karlsson clears all the normies from campus." He tapped his metal fingers on the glass. "I wonder how many Peacekeepers I can take."

"How many *we* can take," Taylor corrected. "Let the staff go if they want to go. We don't need them. You original Garde got by just fine training yourselves."

Nine turned back to look at her. She was expecting to see the usual brow-furrowed anger curdling Nine's face, the macho bluster she was so used to. Unexpectedly, though, there was a deep sadness in his eyes.

"This is going to make me sound like a grandpa," Nine said. "But I really wanted a better life for you guys than what we went through."

"You're trying—"

The walkie-talkie on Nine's hip crackled to life. "Nine? Come in."

That was Malcolm. Three little words, but Taylor didn't like the tension there.

"I read you," Nine replied into the device. "What's up?"

"A Mogadorian skimmer just crashed out by the track."

Nine's eyebrows shot up. "You're kidding."

Taylor stepped closer. "Could it be Isabela and the others?

Maybe they came back?"

"We've got a visual," Dr. Goode said. "Kopano appears to be engaged in a battle with a Mog warrior."

Nine's mechanical hand tightened around his walkie-talkie, the plastic creaking. "It's just one shit storm after the next."

Taylor was already heading for the office door. "We have to get out there."

"Elevator's too slow," Nine said, waving Taylor back to him as he popped the window. "This way."

Nine hooked her around the waist and, with his antigravity, booked it down the side of the building. After teleporting across the world and transforming into wind, Taylor didn't even blink.

On the ground, Maiken skidded to a stop in front of them, tufts of grass kicked up in her wake. Rabiya clung to the speedster in the piggyback position, stumbling loose when Maiken came to a stop.

Maiken's words came out fast and breathless. "There you guys are! Rabiya! Kopano! The track! Mogadorians!"

"Damn, slow down, we already know," Nine said. "Rabiya? Get us there."

"Yes, sir," she replied as she funneled energy into the ground, a chunk of Loralite rising up.

Maiken's eyes were wide as she looked at Taylor. "Are we being invaded again?"

Taylor thought back to her experience in Siberia. Howling Mogadorians lurching out of the darkness with their energy weapons, gunning down soldiers next to her as she sprinted through the snow, other people's blood warm on her face. She shuddered, but tried not to let Maiken see.

"If they're invading, they chose the wrong place," Taylor said coldly.

"Ready," Rabiya announced.

They all linked hands—Maiken somewhat reluctantly—as Rabiya touched the newly formed Loralite stalagmite. There was a flash of blue, a disorienting spinning sensation and then they were on the track. Twenty yards ahead of them, acrid black smoke curled up from a wrecked skimmer.

There was a Mogadorian girl standing right in front of Taylor. She must have been inspecting the Loralite stone because she leaped back with a startled cry when the four of them materialized around it. The Mog was tall, lean and angry-looking. She carried a weapon that looked like a souped-up version of one of those medieval head-whackers.

Reacting fast, Taylor made to shove the Mog with her telekinesis. But then, she noticed Kopano. He was just standing there over the Mog's shoulder, a stupid grin on his face. There was a guy with him, blond and with a scruffy beard, immediately familiar.

"Oh, there he is," the blond guy said to Kopano, nodding at Nine. "Perfect timing."

"Guys!" Kopano hollered, raising his arms in triumph. "Check it out! It's freaking John Smith!"

For a minute there, when John and Nine were bro-hugging

each other and laughing, Taylor actually thought that things were looking up.

"Damn, John, it's good to see you," Nine declared. He eyed the Mogadorian girl. "I get the feeling this is going to be one hell of a story."

"Yeah," John replied. "Long story short, I need your help. Can we go somewhere away from the burning ship?"

He needed their help.

John Smith needed their help.

Maybe if she was more like Kopano—a total fangirl—that simple statement would've thrilled her.

But it just pissed Taylor off.

They left the skimmer behind and teleported back to campus. Taylor caught John looking at her in that same strange, wistful way that he had when she met him briefly in South Dakota.

"I remember you," John said, when Taylor caught him staring. "You're a healer."

"Taylor Cook," she said, reminding him of her name.

"That's right," John said. "How's it been going?"

Taylor snorted, no idea how to answer that question. She opted for honesty. "Pretty shitty, actually. There's a global conspiracy under way to enslave our people."

John scratched his cheek, looking away. "Yeah. We should talk about that."

"After we get to your thing," Taylor said dryly. "Which I'm sure is very important."

Kopano caught up with them, slinging an arm around Taylor's shoulder. "Taylor told me all about how you saved her from Harvesters," he said, smiling brightly at John. "It sounded very badass. I wish I'd been there to see the looks on their faces."

"It wasn't that big of a deal," John said. "I just happened to be passing by."

"Yeah, it wasn't that big of a deal," Taylor agreed, shrugging off Kopano's arm as she picked up speed. "I've been in much worse trouble since. We all have. But I guess you weren't 'passing by' those times."

Kopano gave her an incredulous look. John swallowed, not replying. He didn't say much of anything the rest of the way to the administration building.

They all packed into Nine's office on the top floor. Lexa, Malcolm and Nigel came up from the subbasement to join them. The adults hugged John and greeted him warmly, like a long-lost relative had come back home. Agent Walker joined them as well, although she got a brisk handshake instead of a hug.

Nine settled in behind his desk. John, Malcolm and Lexa sat down in the chairs in front of him. Kopano flopped down on the leather couch to the side, right next to the Mog girl, like he'd completely forgotten that they'd been brawling ten minutes ago. Walker stood over Kopano's shoulder. The Mog, to her credit, looked as anxious about this whole situation as Taylor felt. Maiken and Rabiya both lingered by the door to Nine's office, not sure if they should stay or go, neither wanting to miss anything. Nigel leaned against the wall, his arms crossed, not making any acerbic remarks for once. Taylor, meanwhile, stood behind Nine. A security feed on Nine's computer showed a team of Peacekeepers coming over the fence to investigate the smoldering skimmer and set up a perimeter.

"Just gave Greger another reason to bust in here," Taylor muttered.

Nine gave her a look. "He's already got all the reasons he needs. Chill."

"My original plan was to land their entire ship here," John said sheepishly, overhearing. "But then I decided stealth was a smarter approach considering everything going on with the Earth Garde."

"What do you mean 'entire ship'?" Nine asked.

Before John could respond, the Mog let loose a low, ominous growl. Everyone turned in her direction. It took Taylor a moment to realize that the noise wasn't a threat; it was her stomach rumbling.

"I—I apologize," the Mog said. She shifted uncomfortably, her armor scratching the upholstery. "Would it be possible to get some food?"

Nine stared at the emaciated warrior for a moment. "Maiken? Could you see what's left over from lunch?"

"Sure," Maiken replied, and dashed off.

Taylor knew how Maiken worked. At hyperspeed, it might only take her a minute or two to grab a snack and then she'd spend an equal amount of time spreading gossip. The way she talked, soon everyone would know that John Smith was here with a strange Mogadorian girl.

That might actually improve morale, Taylor thought. Nothing bad could happen to them if John Smith himself were around. At least, that's what many of the students would believe.

"We should probably start with your new friend," Nine said. "I'm trying real hard to be cordial and shit, but you know I've got a standing policy to smack down any Mog I see."

"Your ward already tried that," the Mog said with a side-eye directed at Kopano. "It did not go well for him."

"Ward," Nigel repeated, chuckling. "Do all Mogs talk like aristocrats? No wonder Mum liked them so much."

Kopano frowned at the Mog. "Um, I think I was winning."

"You were not," she stated.

"Shut up, all of you," Nine said, looking at John. "Why did you bring one of them here, dude? What's going on?"

"She can speak for herself," John replied.

The Mog hopped to her feet. Everyone's eyes tracked her, ready for trouble—well, except for John, who seemed mostly amused. She bowed deeply at the waist.

"I am Vontezza Aoh-Atet, trueborn daughter of the deceased General Aoh-Atet, co—"

"Commander of the Mogadorian warship *Osiris*," Taylor finished, not even realizing she was speaking aloud until everyone in the room was staring at her.

Vontezza cocked her head. "You know me, human?"

"Yeah, I'm a big fan of your podcast," Taylor said. "Actually, I was on a Mog warship—or what was left of it, anyway—in Siberia. Your ship was hiding behind the moon, sending out a broadcast on loop." She looked in John's direction. "Asking for him."

John nodded. "Yeah. I heard it, too. Eventually."

Vontezza's gaze lingered on Taylor, sizing her up. Taylor stared back. After a moment of that, Vontezza seemed satisfied and turned back to Nine, resuming her overly formal speech.

"Number Nine of the formidable Loric Garde. Your mercy is legendary."

Nine snickered. "It is?"

"I told her she didn't have to do this part," John said. "She insisted."

Vontezza ignored their sidebar. "I humbly request sanctuary at your Academy so that I may train the gifts granted to me by your people and use them for the betterment of humanity, thus beginning down the path of reparations for centuries of Mogadorian aggression."

"Jesus," Nine said. "What?"

"This is absolutely mental," Nigel muttered, pinching the bridge of his nose.

"Gifts?" Malcolm asked. "Do you mean . . . ?"

"She's got Legacies, Doc," Kopano said. "Telekinesis, anyway."

"That isn't possible," Rabiya said.

"She wouldn't be the first, actually," Walker said.

Nine waved a hand at Vontezza. "Okay, okay, sit down. You're weirding me out with all this courtly stuff."

"As you wish," Vontezza replied, settling on the edge of the couch next to Kopano.

Malcolm turned around in his chair so that he could peer at Vontezza. "This is fascinating. When did you receive your Legacies?"

Vontezza met Malcolm's eyes, her posture rigid like she was under some kind of military inspection. "I developed my telekinesis at the same time as the humans."

"Wait. During the invasion?" Kopano asked. "You were one of the first?"

"Yes."

"Lorien picked you," Kopano said, awe in his voice. "Even though you were on one of the enemy warships."

"Surprised we didn't see you on the ground trying to kill us," Nigel said.

"This is actually the first time I have been off that warship in years," Vontezza said. Her feet moved and it looked to Taylor like she was squeezing her toes inside her boots. "My father was a general, in command of a regiment preparing to attack Earth. My mother was a priestess and a scholar—"

Nine laughed. "The Mogs had scholars?"

"Yes," Vontezza replied, unoffended by the sarcasm. "She taught the Great Book, the writings of Setrákus Ra. When I showed her my Legacies she became skeptical of her faith in our Beloved Leader. You see, he wrote that Legacies would be impossible for our people without his experimentation. It was our justification for invading Lorien and then Earth. We truly believed that these other races were hoarding the Loric energy for their own selfish ends and that we could never progress as a people unless we controlled it ourselves . . ."

As Vontezza went on, Taylor couldn't help but think about how similar the goals of the Foundation sounded to the Mogadorians. Well, the group had grown out of the Mog-Pro contingent. It made sense they'd share a screwed-up worldview.

"And then I was pulled into John Smith's telepathic vision," Vontezza continued. "Where the history of Setrákus Ra was revealed. How he was Loric and betrayed his people, then manipulated the Mogadorians into war . . ."

"I was in that vision!" Kopano said, slapping his leg. "It was sweet."

"Glad you liked it," John said wryly.

Kopano eyed Vontezza. "I didn't see you there, though . . ."

"I didn't see you either, large one," she replied simply. "Many of the human young were too busy mewling or panicking to notice my presence."

"Tough-as-nails Mog in a room full of humans," Nigel said. "You didn't freak out at all, huh?"

"I assumed it was some kind of trap and attempted a tactical retreat," Vontezza replied. "But the back door of the chamber would not open."

"Oh, so you were hiding in the back," Kopano said.

"Tactical retreat," Vontezza snapped.

"Okay, okay. What happened next?" Taylor asked.

"Soon after that, Setrákus Ra was badly injured in battle. There was a rumor that he was dead. Because of my telekinesis, my mother believed that I was the rightful heir to power. She convinced my father and they led a mutiny against our warship's captain. The crew was divided virtually in half. There was a battle . . ." Vontezza brushed at a smudge on the shoulder plate of her armor. "My mother was killed in the fighting, but her side—*my side*—ended up winning."

Taylor wasn't sure what the protocol was when a Mogadorian told you their mother had died. Kopano was the first one to speak up.

"I'm sorry about your mom," he said.

Nine made a face. "You know how many people lost families because of the Mogs? They wiped out an entire planet and would've done the same here."

Lexa nodded in agreement. John kept his expression neutral, not weighing in.

"*She* didn't wipe out any planets, though," Rabiya said from the doorway. "You can't blame her for the actions of her people."

"We can't always choose where we come from," Nigel muttered.

"You've got some smart students," John said to Nine.

"Give me a break," Nine replied, crossing his arms.

"So why did you end up hiding behind the moon for like two years?" Kopano asked.

There was a tiredness in Vontezza's dark eyes that Taylor could see growing, but she answered Kopano dutifully.

"After the mutiny, I found myself suddenly in control of the warship. I still did not fully understand what was happening to me, much less what all this meant to Mogadorian society. I chose to pull back to a defensive position until I could decide what to do." She paused. "When my shipmates learned that Setrákus Ra was still alive, there was a second mutiny by those who wished to reenter the fight. By the time I regained control of the ship, the invasion was over and Setrákus Ra was dead."

Taylor noticed the way Nine's fingers dug at his cybernetic arm while Vontezza spoke. Setrákus Ra might have been dead, but the damage he caused wasn't forgotten.

"Damn," Kopano said. "How many mutinies can one ship have?"

"Seven," Vontezza replied with a straight face. "There were seven in total in my time as captain of the *Osiris*."

The condition of her armor made more sense now. It sounded like she'd been fighting nonstop. Taylor found herself staring at the puncture in Vontezza's breastplate, where it looked like a sword had been plunged.

Just then, Maiken zipped back into the room carrying a tray of food. A blueberry muffin, some chicken, pretzels, an apple. She extended the tray to Vontezza, careful not to get too close.

"Sorry, uh, I don't really know what you people eat," Maiken said.

Vontezza took the tray. "Thank you. This is perfect."

"How did you survive all those battles?" Kopano asked,

wanting to squeeze in more questions before Vontezza started to eat.

"My Legacy," she replied, touching the hole in her armor. "I would have died if not for that."

"So you've developed a primary Legacy?" Dr. Goode asked. "What is it? Can you control it?"

Vontezza grimaced. "I don't need to control it. It works on its own."

Without warning, Vontezza picked up a fork from her tray and jammed it into the soft flesh of her forearm. Taylor gasped. Kopano flinched backwards. Maiken looked like she might faint.

The Mogadorian removed the fork and held up her arm, showing off three punctures dark with fresh blood. As they watched, the wounds sealed up on their own. Vontezza picked up a napkin and wiped the blood away. It was as if it'd never happened.

"You could have chosen a less dramatic way of showing them," John told her.

She cocked her head in response. "I learned I possessed this Legacy when my own father drove his blade into my chest while I slept. That was the sixth mutiny. According to my crew, I was dead for five hours before my flesh grew back." She looked at John. "Is that less dramatic?"

Nine laughed incredulously. "A Mog who can't be killed. That's perfect."

"Why did you stay up there so long?" Taylor asked. Her gaze slid to John Smith. "And why come here now?"

"I have been reaching out to the Garde since shortly after the invasion," Vontezza answered. "But most of my time was spent trying to keep my crew alive and stop them from killing each other. You would be surprised how time flies when you're trapped aboard a spacecraft with a population who know nothing except war." She sighed. "At this point, we are nearly out of fuel and rations. We no longer have the capacity to run both our shields and life support. Much of our equipment is damaged. The *Osiris* must land now or what's left of my crew is doomed." Her stomach growled again and Vontezza glanced longingly at the tray of food on her lap. "Forgive me, but I would very much like to stop talking now."

"I can take it from here," John said. Vontezza nodded gratefully and immediately began to devour a cold leg of chicken.

Nine leaned forward, looking closely at John. "Why do I get the feeling I'm not going to like what you say next?"

John shrugged. "I heard Vontezza broadcast when I was scavenging the wreck of a warship in China. We made a deal."

"You made a deal," Nine repeated.

"Her warship will safely land and the remainder of her crew will turn themselves over to the authorities and be sent to Alaska with the others. Except Vontezza will stay here. So that she can be trained."

"You want us to take in a Mog," Nine said flatly, then laughed. "Do you have any idea what's been going on here? Technically, this isn't even my office anymore. I've been

fired. And, no offense to you, kid—" Nine gestured at Vontezza, who was too busy eating to notice. "But I don't care
about some Mog right now, whether she's got Legacies or
not."

"I'm not letting her be sent to Alaska," John stated. "We
should've never let Adam go there and—"

"Is that what this is?" Nine asked. "You feel bad about
Adam and you're trying to make up for it with this rando?
He *chose* to be imprisoned."

"John told me of this Adamus and he sounds honorable,"
Vontezza said, swallowing a large bite. "What's left of my
crew have agreed to join him in this northern prison and
work on reeducating the less forward-thinking of our people. Bringing them to the light is not easy.

"You made that clear with all the mutinies," Nigel said
dryly.

"If Mogs are ever to find a home on this planet and coex-
ist with humanity, then we must show them we are capable
of good," Vontezza continued. "I wish to set an example by
attending your Academy and, perhaps one day, joining Earth
Garde. I want to repay Earth for the violence done by my
people."

Nigel snorted. "Guess you don't get any news up in space.
We aren't exactly Earth's favorite people right now."

"Um, they like us more than Mogadorians, at least," Maiken said, making a face.

"You said you made a deal," Taylor said to John, her eyes

narrowed. "What do you get out of this?"

"I need the force field technology built into Vontezza's warship."

Malcolm pursed his lips. "For what, John?"

"For what I'm building," he replied.

John reached under his shirt, producing a pendant with the azure glow of Loralite. Nine made a noise of recognition, yanked open a drawer on his desk and revealed his own identical pendant. Taylor found herself clutching the necklace that Kopano made her for Christmas that also contained a chunk of Loralite, wondering at the significance of these items.

"I call it New Lorien," John said. "It's a place where our people can be safe. Especially once I have enough of the force field generators. Vontezza's will be the third one I've acquired."

"You're going to seal it off," Nine said, a note of disbelief in his voice. "Like Setrákus Ra's base in West Virginia."

"Yeah," John replied. "That's the plan."

Taylor was grateful that Kopano raised his hand and interjected. "I'm lost. What's New Lorien?"

"It's a friggin' cave," Nine said dismissively. "A cave in the Indian Himalayas where one of our dead friends used to hide out. Now John spends all his time there practicing the sitar or some bullshit."

"It's more than a cave," John snapped, glaring at Nine. He took a breath and calmly turned to Kopano. "It's more than a cave. It's a sanctuary that the Loric would use on their previous visits to Earth. We've been building it up. Myself, Marina and Ella—"

"That's Number Seven and, um, the other one," Kopano said as an aside to the others who either already knew that or were more interested in what John had to say.

"There's a small village nearby that are very welcoming of our kind," John continued. "I've been in talks with the Indian government. Last week, they agreed to grant us status as an autonomous territory."

"They *what*?" Lexa exclaimed.

Walker mimed plugging her ears. "I should *not* be hearing this."

"You're one of us, Karen," Nine said. "Whether you like it or not."

"They gave you a country," Malcolm said to John, his eyes wide. "Is that what you're telling us?"

"Autonomous territory," John corrected him, sheepishly rubbing the back of his neck. "But yeah."

"Wow, cool! When can I come visit?" Kopano said.

"Anytime you want," John replied. "All Garde will be welcome once we've got the place secure. I'm hoping that we'll be able to do classes and training there." He looked to Nine. "Sort of like what you've set up here."

"But without the UN looking over your shoulder," Nine said, his voice even.

"Right."

"Do they know about this?" Malcolm asked. "The UN, I mean. Earth Garde."

"This was one of those situations when I thought it'd be better to beg forgiveness than ask permission," John replied. "I'm trying to keep the place on the low until it's safe."

Nine clapped his hands. "Well, sounds great, John. Thanks for dropping by to let us know you're opening a competing Academy."

John sighed. "It's not always a competition, Nine. I'm trying to plan ahead. Don't you think it'd be good for us to have a place where we can train if things go wrong? I know you don't have the tightest grip on this place right now—"

"Hey!" Taylor stepped forward before Nine could respond, standing beside her professor. "Who are you to show up here like this? Where the hell have you been? I know, I know—everyone worships the almighty Number Four. My boyfriend's probably thought about getting your face tattooed on his butt."

"Boyfriend," Kopano repeated with a grin. "Wait. What?"

"You're supposed to be hot shit," Taylor continued, gaining steam. "But from what I've heard so far, you've been hiding out in some mountain while the rest of us are out here suffering. Did you know there's a group of rich assholes calling themselves the Foundation who are trying to enslave us? Do you even care?"

"Please, Taylor, this isn't productive," Dr. Goode said in an attempt to calm her down.

"Nah, Dr. Goode, all due respect, but Taylor's right," Nigel added, pushing off from the wall so he could look at John. "You remember me, mate? You benched me during the invasion for my own protection. Cut the cord after that, didn't ya?" Nigel motioned to Dr. Goode. "The old man here ain't telling you for some reason, but his kid's been snatched by Earth Garde. Locked up somewhere. I remember you two being pretty buddy-buddy. Haven't checked in on that relationship, have ya?"

John turned to Malcolm. "Is this true?"

"I believe so," Malcolm said. He held up his hands. "We only just found out, John. You know as well as I do that Sam and Six can take care of themselves."

"Oh, don't let him off the hook, Dr. Goode," Taylor said.

John turned around to look at Walker. "Do you know where they might be holding them?"

She shook her head. "When Watchtower recruited Kopano and Ran, I met them at a secret facility in Nova Scotia. That place was being shut down. I heard talk about a new, upgraded detention center, but it was on a need-to-know basis and if I didn't need to know then, they certainly wouldn't tell me now that I'm AWOL."

Taylor snapped her fingers to get John's attention. "You know what she means by 'recruiting'? Earth Garde put Inhibitor chips in Kopano and Ran. Forced them to go on a mission they didn't really want to do. So now we're thinking maybe this Earth Garde thing we're working towards isn't so noble after all. The one place we have that any of us feels even close to safe is here, this Academy, and if you haven't noticed the general vibe since you waltzed in, I'll tell you—we're hanging on by a thread. And you're in here talking about India and force fields and helping Mogadorians. Let me channel my friend Isabela when I say, *Bitch, please.*"

Kopano's eyes widened and Rabiya smirked. Vontezza continued to eat, basically oblivious. Malcolm and Lexa discreetly looked into space, while Maiken hopped from foot to foot like she couldn't wait to share the details of Taylor telling off the hero of the invasion. John just stared at her, digesting everything.

Nine cleared his throat, breaking the silence. "I cosign all of that."

John looked down at his hands, folded there in his lap, gathering his thoughts. He actually appeared chastened when he finally met Taylor's eyes.

"I know I've missed a lot. I've made mistakes. After the invasion, I was just so tired of fighting. I couldn't face the possibility that someone else I cared about could be hurt. But, of course, people *are* getting hurt, and me sitting out isn't helping . . ." He shook his head. "I won't make excuses. I'm here now and I hear what you're saying. I thought that I could take my time with New Lorien. I didn't think we'd need a safe haven—not yet, at least. Hopefully not ever. But it's looking like we do. We gave up too much when we signed

RETURN TO ZERO

onto that Garde Accord. I thought we'd be able to trust the UN but—"

"We can only trust each other," Taylor said, cringing inwardly as she realized that she was echoing Einar.

"I agree," John said. "That's why I came here. I need your help."

120

CHAPTER EIGHT

"ARE YOU EVER GOING TO EXPLAIN WHAT THE HELL that was back there?" Caleb snapped, making no effort to conceal his impatience.

"We watched from the window," Duanphen said. "I don't understand what I saw."

"I was on the ground and I don't understand it," Caleb told her.

"Ugh, I can't believe we're back on this butt-smelling ship already," Isabela added unhelpfully.

Ran agreed with all these statements, but she always found it more useful to keep quiet and observe rather than join the confused chorus. She stood in the doorway to the skimmer's cockpit, shoulder against the cool metal frame, arms crossed. They were all crammed in there. Five flew the ship, keeping them cloaked and at high speed as they fled Italy. The rest of them gathered around Einar, who knelt on the floor, a half-dozen tablet computers spread out before him.

"I'll show you," Einar muttered, paging through a tablet's files with frustrated, manic flicks of his fingers. "I know it's in one of these."

The tablets all once belonged to members of the Foundation. Ran didn't want to know exactly how Einar acquired them, although she could guess. They contained the identities of other Foundation members, their contacts and lackeys, location data and bid histories on the Garde they had purchased at auction. But not one tablet contained *all* the information. There was no skeleton key that would unlock the entire shadowy network. The Foundation was purposely kept compartmentalized—no member had access to more than a sliver of all the organization's secrets. As they traveled across Europe, they learned that the tablets were quickly becoming obsolete. The Foundation knew some of its members had been compromised and were adjusting.

"You could just tell us," Caleb said. "Use your words. You usually love that."

"Better to see for yourselves what we're up against," Einar replied without looking up.

"You keep saying that."

"Yes," Einar agreed. "Because you keep making me repeat myself."

"Here they go again," Isabela said with a roll of her eyes

that Ran found just as predictable as Einar and Caleb bickering. "Let me know when we're landing somewhere good. I'll be in my closet questioning my life decisions."

Isabela brushed by Ran on her way out of the cockpit, departing for the storage room she'd turned into a bedroom. Caleb kept his sleeping bag against a bulkhead near the exit ramp. Five slept in the cockpit. Einar, who didn't sleep nearly enough, stayed in the ship's armory, which lacked weapons but now had plenty of stolen money, artwork and jewelry. Duanphen and Ran shared the cramped passenger area, which was really just two hard benches along opposite walls. They were practically on top of each other all the time and Isabela was right about the smell. The entire ship reeked of armpits, stale breath and chicken nuggets. These skimmers were built for ferrying Mogadorians from their warships to ground combat. They weren't homes. They weren't even dorm rooms.

Ran wasn't going to sulk about it like Isabela, but she'd definitely been looking forward to some time off the ship. It was the claustrophobia that made them so quick to snap at each other.

"You almost killed an old man," Caleb said to Einar.

"But I didn't," Einar replied. "Believe me. I could've hit him harder."

"Oh, so it was all under control?"

"Yes."

"Why don't I believe you?"

"I don't care what you believe, Caleb," Einar said through

his teeth. He tossed a tablet aside with a force that suggested otherwise, picking up another in the same angry motion. "Stop badgering me for five seconds so I can find what I'm looking for."

Duanphen looked between the two boys, as if not entirely sure what they were fighting about or whether she should intervene. When she glanced in Ran's direction, Ran offered a subtle shake of her head. *Don't bother. Let it play out.*

This tug-of-war for control between Einar and Caleb had been going on since this mismatched group first flung themselves together. In Ran's estimation, both guys were going through some serious existential crises. Caleb had abandoned what Isabela referred to as his "Boy Scout lifestyle" and was now constantly trying to justify that decision by checking Einar and keeping them on mission—even if that mission was often as elusive as the Foundation. Meanwhile, Einar's abundance of confidence had dwindled since his big speech in Switzerland failed to turn him into an icon for the Human Garde. Instead, he'd been branded a terrorist. No one had rallied to his cause except those aboard this skimmer and, even for them, teaming with Einar was something of a matter of necessity. Einar had nearly been killed. He had no plan. He was spiraling. Making a fuss about what happened in Italy was his way of exerting some control, even if it was totally misplaced.

So Ran let the two of them argue. If it was ever really necessary, she would obviously side with Caleb. It wasn't so long ago that Einar had used his telekinesis to break her ribs and then nearly killed her best friend. But, for now, their quarrels were no more serious than Isabela's constant complaints about her living conditions. They were a pressure release.

"Aha!" Einar shouted, holding up a tablet in both hands. "I told you it was here!"

"Finally," Caleb muttered. He came to stand alongside Einar, to look down at the tablet. Duanphen and Ran joined the huddle and soon the skimmer's autopilot kicked on and Five came back too.

With all their attention, Einar seemed a bit restored to his old, authoritative self.

"This tablet comes from a Blackstone mercenary I took out back in Iceland," Einar explained. "Unbeknownst to the Foundation, they sometimes record their combat engagements. This is from after the invasion, when the Foundation was just starting up . . ."

"Play it, please," Ran said simply, having had enough of the exposition. Einar's lips quirked into a brief frown, but he did as she asked.

The screen came alive with grainy, green-tinted video. A group of mercenaries in gunmetal body armor appeared—the Blackstone outfit that Ran was all too familiar with—crammed into what looked like a suburban living room with wood-paneled walls, shag carpet and flower-print furniture. There were five mercenaries in total, all of them wearing gloves and helmets with visors, and all of them devoted to wrestling one skinny, wriggling teenager.

"My son is possessed!" a resonant baritone voice shouted from off-screen. *"There's a devil in my son!"*

"Would someone please shut up the preacher?" one of the mercenaries snarled.

Ran focused on the boy at the center of the scrum. He wore pajama pants and a tank top, splotches of acne visible on his narrow shoulders. Probably about fifteen years old. He had wild, wavy brown hair that had been tied back in a ponytail until the mercenaries started grappling with him.

How was this one boy holding back a group of combat-trained adults? Telekinesis. Not the precision control that Ran had practiced in her time at the Academy, but the raw, desperate force of a new Garde fighting for their life. Grown men were thrown backwards by sudden bursts of force or else slammed up against the ceiling. Random objects from around the room spun through the frame—ceramic angels, mostly, but also a large metallic crucifix that hit the face guard of one mercenary with enough force to crack it open.

"It isn't the devil, Daddy!" the boy shouted. *"It's a gift! I could see into your heart when I touched you! I saw your sins—"*

"Lies!" the off-screen father bellowed back.

While the two argued, the mercenaries were trying to tug the scrawny boy into a straitjacket. Apparently, this was before the invention of Inhibitors.

Fed up with the screaming and the tchotchkes breaking across his shoulders, the mercenary with the shattered face mask lunged forward and delivered a right hook to the kid's jaw. The punch dropped him to his knees and immediately some Blackstone guys wrenched his arms back.

"*Careful with him, Crenshaw,*" one of the other men reprimanded the puncher. "*They want him in one piece.*"

"*Someone had to do it,*" said Crenshaw. "*Done playing nice with these hicks.*"

"*You're compromised, clear the area immediately,*" replied the first. "*Remember, no skin-to-skin contact—*"

A sudden burst of telekinesis flung aside the mercenaries pinning the boy's arms, allowing him to pop to his feet and thrust his hand through Crenshaw's broken visor. The boy's mouth was bloody, which made his crooked smile all the more off-putting.

And then, suddenly, the boy's body went limp, collapsing to the floor like a puppet with cut strings.

One of the mercenaries started screaming, "*Subdue Crenshaw! Subdue—!*"

But they were too slow. The mercenary Crenshaw now wore the boy's odd smile. He pulled a sidearm swiftly from his hip and opened fire on his colleagues.

The video cut off when the soldier doing the recording pitched over backwards from getting shot in the chest.

Caleb broke the silence in the cockpit. "What did . . . ? What did that kid just do?"

"The Foundation described his Legacy as tactile consciousness transfer," Einar replied, replaying the scene on the tablet, this time on mute.

"He's a possessor," Five said. "A body jumper."

"Yes," confirmed Einar. "His name is Lucas Sanders and with a touch he can transfer his consciousness into another body. Once in a new body, he can transfer into another and another, all with a touch."

Ran thought back to the woman watching the villa in Italy, how she'd traded seats with a man when she'd shown up, which was why Ran noticed her in the first place.

"I thought it was a team of agents running surveillance," she said aloud. "But it was just him. Taking control of locals."

"Most likely," Einar said. "We're lucky you spotted him when you did. If he had gotten close enough to us to initiate contact . . ." Ran noticed how Einar's gaze flicked in Five's direction, likely imagining the damage that could've been done if this Lucas guy took control of the Loric. "While in a host body, Lucas doesn't have his telekinesis. However, he is able to access the host's memories. Look through them. That's how the Foundation wanted to use him. For petty reasons, like finding out if your wife was cheating on you. Or for financial gain, like by stealing trade secrets right out of an inventor's mind. But Lucas proved too unstable to be useful. At least that's what I heard."

"What happens to the people he possesses?" Caleb asked.

"They report being aware of their actions although incapable of stopping themselves. They describe it as dreamlike."

"You know a lot about this guy," Caleb said.

"Lucas was one of the first Foundation recruits, along with me," Einar said, speaking frankly. "We were mostly kept separate, except for some training exercises, but I saw enough to know he was completely out of his mind."

Caleb shot Ran a look to point out the irony of Einar call-ing someone else crazy. Ran didn't find it ironic, though. She found it worrying.

"I never heard of him when I was with the Foundation," Duanphen said.

"No, you came along later," Einar replied. "By then, Lucas was dead. Or, at least, he was supposed to be."

"What do you mean?" Five asked.

"Lucas was insane. He *is* insane," Einar corrected himself. "His father was a Christian fundamentalist who believed that Legacies were a plague sent by the devil. Lucas also believed that, with the added delusion that he was an arch-angel, heaven-sent to stop those with Legacies. Or, really, anyone he didn't like. There were rumors about things he did on Foundation missions—killings beyond those sanc-tioned by our handlers. Attacks on other Garde. All in the name of judgment."

"Hold on," Caleb interjected. "Why does all that religious stuff sound so familiar?"

"Lucas's father is—well, *was*, Reverend James Robert Sanders. Reverend Jimbo. The leader of the Harvesters."

"You killed that man," Ran said.

"Yes," Einar agreed. "And I would do it again."

Caleb pinched the bridge of his nose. "Jesus Christ."

"That's exactly how Lucas thinks of himself," Einar said.

"A Garde who hates his own kind," Ran murmured. "A valuable weapon in the hands of a group like the Foundation."

Five grunted his agreement.

"The Foundation spends most of their time exploiting Garde for profit," continued Einar. "But they also aren't shy about eliminating those of us who they feel are a danger to humanity. I'd heard that Lucas was quote-unquote *retired*. Too many escape attempts, too difficult to control. I thought they killed him. I should've known they would never dispose of an asset that valuable. He must have been imprisoned somewhere until they had a reason to let him loose."

"You're a pretty good reason," Caleb said.

"Yes, it seems the best way to control Lucas is to let him do what he loves," Einar said, pursing his lips. "Hunt Garde and judge them."

"But how did he find us?" Duanphen asked.

Caleb glanced down at the tablets still scattered on the floor at Einar's feet. "Could they be tracking those?"

Einar shook his head. "No. Here is where the Foundation's paranoia plays to our advantage. For their own security, their computers cannot be traced."

"If they had a tracker on us, we'd be getting attacked twenty-four/seven," Five said.

"They know which of their people we've identified," Caleb replied. "If they're smart enough to evacuate them from their mansions, it stands to reason they could also be staking out those locations."

"Perhaps if it was Blackstone waiting for us, I would agree," Ran said. "But it was only this boy. How would he know to be in Italy? It must be more than a lucky guess."

"So, they *are* tracking us," Caleb said, screwing up his face. "But not in a way that's consistent."

"Makes no sense," Five grumbled.

Ran turned to look at Einar. "More importantly, if we encounter this boy again, how do we stop him?"

"Well, obviously, don't let him touch you," Einar replied. "If the body he possesses is rendered unconscious, Lucas is flung back to his own. It's why I hit that old man so hard—"

"This is sick," Caleb said, looking at Einar. "It's even worse than what you do. We can't beat up on his hosts just because they had the bad luck for this guy to touch them."

"Does his Legacy have a range?" Duanphen asked. "Does he need to maintain a certain distance from his actual body?"

"No," Einar replied. "In all likelihood, Lucas's body is under guard in a Foundation facility somewhere. At least, if we knock out one of his hosts, we could send him back there. Buy us some time."

"What we should be doing is searching for his location," Five said. "Cut the head off the monster." Caleb shot Five a look and the Loric held up his hands. "Metaphorically."

"It is not a bad idea," Ran said. "If this Lucas chooses to threaten us, we should respond in kind."

"And if we can find this facility, we might dig up some dirt on the Foundation that actually sticks," Caleb said, coming around to the idea.

Einar smiled. He looked energized. At last, they had a mission that wasn't just stumbling towards dead ends. He bent down to gather up the tablets. "I have an idea where to start looking. Just give me time to do some research."

"Here, let me help," Duanphen said. She picked up some of the tablets and followed Einar out of the cockpit.

Caleb blew out his cheeks. "Well, I guess I should go tell Isabela everything she missed. Tell her to avoid letting strange men touch her."

Ran raised an eyebrow.

"I mean, I won't use those words exactly . . ."

Caleb exited the cockpit. Ran couldn't help but smile a little as she watched him attempting to straighten his blond hair as he left. The boy was like a moth to the flame when it came to Isabela.

With a grunt, Five returned to the pilot's seat. They were alone. Ran lingered a moment, unsure of how to approach speaking to the intimidating Loric. There was something on her mind, a thought that had been nagging at her for months now, one that had only grown more persistent with the discovery of this Lucas character. She had a question and Five was the only one around capable of answering it.

She padded forward and sat down in the copilot seat. Five's one eye rolled in her direction, but he didn't say anything.

"May I ask you a question?"

Five fully turned in her direction, a look of surprise on his face. His brow furrowed and unclenched. His mouth opened and closed. Ran gazed steadily at him, her own expression impassive. She knew Five was damaged; that social interactions weren't always easy for him. She gave him time to respond.

"A question," he repeated finally. "Sure."

"The Loric entity traveled to Earth from your dying planet, yes?"

Five looked at her strangely. "That's what you want to talk about? Ancient history?"

"It's a starting point. To be honest, I have many questions," Ran replied. "I've had them for some time, actually, but never ordered my thoughts enough to ask them. I've had a lot of time with my thoughts on this ship."

"Okay," Five grunted. He was obviously still confused by Ran's approach—she didn't even fully understand why she'd chosen this moment or even this Loric to speak with—but he decided to play along. "Yeah. The Loric entity fled here during the annihilation of Lorien. A piece of it was actually already here because some of the Elders anticipated what Setrákus Ra was up to but . . . yeah. Why do you want to know about that crap?"

"Those who don't study history are doomed to repeat it," Ran replied.

"Uh-huh. Heard that one before."

Ran relaxed in her seat a bit, growing more comfortable that Five wouldn't suddenly shut down the conversation or otherwise flip out.

"This entity is a being of pure energy. Your people didn't fully understand it. Mine certainly don't. But we all agree that it's capable of bestowing Legacies."

Five turned to look out the windscreen at the dark clouds coasting by. "Pretty much sums it up," he replied with a yawn.

"And you believe this entity is intelligent?"

Five pursed his lips. "What do you mean?"

"That it isn't a phenomenon like an earthquake or a tornado. It's aware. It knows what it's doing."

Five drummed his fingers on the steering wheel, thinking that over. "I don't remember much of Lorien. I was young when my parents blasted me across the damn universe. But I know my people worshipped the entity like a god. Not the way you humans have gods who hang out in the clouds and judge people when they die. More like Mother Nature. A nurturing force of general goodness or some shit."

"So not something that thinks or communicates like us," Ran said. "Something that just *is*."

"I didn't say it doesn't communicate." Five's look darkened and Ran worried that he might not say anything more. He picked at one of the dark splotches on the back of his hand, where the Mogadorian ooze had eaten into him. "Some of the other Garde—my Garde, the numbered ones— they spoke to the entity. One of them was even carrying an extra bit of its power around for a while. They . . . they don't like me very much. They never told me what it said to them or what they saw."

"I see."

Five cleared his throat. "Setrákus Ra claimed that the Loric energy wasn't anything more than a resource that could be harnessed and used. That ooze you saw back in Switzerland—that's created by corrupting the Loric energy. Setrákus Ra thought that if he could master that process, he could give Legacies and take them away. Eliminate the randomness of it all."

Five held out his arm so Ran could see where the dark, scab-like blots covered him. She couldn't swear to it, but she thought Five's condition had worsened since they fought back in Switzerland and he had transformed his entire body into the flowing, viscous ooze. The stuff was eating away at him.

"Nice, right?" Five asked, referring to his skin. "That's the result of all Setrákus Ra's hard work."

"I am sorry that happened to you," Ran said.

Five merely grunted in response and tugged his sweatshirt sleeves down to his knuckles. Ran was quiet for a moment, trying to figure out how to best phrase her next thought.

"I know that he was an atrocious, evil man," Ran said tentatively. "But I can understand Setrákus Ra's desire to control Legacies."

Five's lips curled back. "You can," he said flatly.

"If the entity is an intelligent life-form, why would it bestow a Legacy onto a boy with such hatred in his heart?"

Five frowned. "I wasn't always like this."

"No, no," Ran said quickly. "Not you. The boy in the video."

"Oh. Him."

"Why would he get Legacies?" Ran asked again. "And that power. To take control of another person. To make them a prisoner in their own body. What good can that possibly do the world? For that matter . . ." Ran glanced surreptitiously over her shoulder. "What is the benefit to a Garde like Einar? Manipulating people—"

"He soothes me," Five interrupted, although not with any malice. "I know what you guys think of him. I know he's hurt you. Hurt your annoying British friend especially. But I . . . I've never been able to control my emotions. It's even worse sometimes after what happened to me . . . what happened during the invasion. I feel pain and rage and . . . I just lose it. When it gets like that, Einar can help me feel normal again. He helps me forget what a toilet my life has been."

Five spoke quietly, with little inflection. It was the most Ran had ever heard him say at once. She had hoped to drag a few answers about the nature of their Legacies from their Loric associate. She'd never expected to have him open up about himself. Not with his brutal reputation. She thought about putting a hand on his arm, but decided against it. Better to maintain a companionable distance. She looked out at the sky, matching the direction of Five's gaze.

"I did not know," she said. "Maybe there is a use and I'm just not seeing it . . ."

"You talking about that Lucas kid? Or yourself?"

Ran smiled inwardly. "Is it that obvious?"

"I paid attention back in Switzerland," Five said. "You said you didn't want to be anyone's weapon."

"I . . ." Ran looked down at her hands.

She thought about how the ceiling of her apartment collapsed when the Mogadorians opened fire on Tokyo. She could hear her little brothers crying. Panicked, she shoved debris away with her newly discovered telekinesis—she didn't even know what she was doing, how hard she was pushing. She freed herself. But her brothers stopped crying after that.

"I have hurt people with these Legacies," she said quietly. "People I didn't mean to hurt. I did bring my friend back to life but it was . . . it was luck. And I could've just as easily killed him. I don't understand why the entity would give me these powers. I don't understand what purpose I'm supposed to serve."

Five breathed out slowly through his nose. "I used to love to fly. Then Setrákus Ra told me that back on Lorien, flying was almost as common as telekinesis. It's a nothing power, he said. He told me that my strongest Legacy, the one that matters, is this . . ." A flash of silver as Five briefly transformed his skin into the same metal as the steering column. "My skin. What is it good for except absorbing damage and dishing out pain?"

"You have thought about this too," Ran said.

"Yeah, I had a lot of time to think after the invasion. I was on an island, pretty sure I was going to die any day. A girl who hates my guts was watching me, worried I might do something evil." He snorted. "Even she lost interest eventually and moved on. It was just me until Einar showed up, told me about these Foundation people and how they wanted to enslave the Garde. Like you said before about history . . . it was the cycle starting over again."

"So you believe we have these Legacies to fight the Foundation?" Ran asked. "That is our purpose."

"No, not exactly," Five said. "I think what we are—what Garde are—is a self-defense mechanism. The entity cares about the Loric and Lorien or humanity and Earth only so far as it gets to continue existing. It needs a place to live. We're given Legacies to defend it. We aren't here to improve life or save society or any of that happy horseshit. We're here to make sure some ancient ball of energy gets to go on burning. That's it."

"That is . . ." Ran paused. "That is bleak."

Five showed his teeth, an approximation of a smile. "You know who ruled on Lorien? A council of Elders—the oldest and most powerful of the Garde. It was a peaceful place before the end. Almost a utopia, to hear the other refugees tell it. But Setrákus Ra told me what came before there was a Council of the Elders."

Ran wasn't sure she wanted to know what Five would say next. She was getting more answers than she'd bargained for.

"Setrákus Ra was a liar," she said quietly.

"Sure was," Five agreed. "And maybe this was a lie. But to hear him tell it, there were plenty of Loric without Legacies who wanted to control the Garde, or who didn't like a bunch of random jerks having superpowers. There was a war."

"What happened?" Ran asked, even though she could guess the answer.

"The Garde took control of the planet and all the normal Loric that stood against them were wiped out," Five answered simply. "Like you said, history repeats itself."

CHAPTER NINE

AS HE PULLED ON HIS THREADBARE CONVERSE IN their pod's common area, Nigel could somehow hear Kopano snoring through the closed door to his room. He didn't understand how the big lad could sleep so soundly all the time. Nigel was jealous. He hadn't gotten a good night's rest in weeks. He was always half expecting to wake up and find Bea standing over him, sipping a cup of tea and holding an Inhibitor attached to Nigel's neck.

Ran suffered from insomnia, didn't she? Used to run around campus at night until she tired herself out, winning the battle with her body. That wasn't Nigel's style, though. Sometimes, he went up to the vacant room that he and Caleb once used for band practice and plucked at a guitar until his fingers hurt. That didn't help him sleep, though.

Thinking about the friends who bailed on him to hang with a murderer always failed to ease his mind. Surprise, surprise.

Shoes on, Nigel slipped out of his dorm room. It was nearly dawn, anyway. The Academy was beginning to come to life. He heard showers running and sleepy grumbling as he made for the stairwell. The first classes of the day began in an hour. Nigel was pretty sure he was scheduled for Physics of Legacies then. That was a special class designed by Dr. Goode where they studied the scientific laws that their Legacies were breaking, in an attempt to better understand their powers. He'd been tossed in that class so he could learn more about sound waves. It was kind of interesting, as far as lots of squiggly lines and gibberish formulas went.

He'd skipped the last few classes. No one had said anything. There was no reprimand coming his way. Even Dr. Goode and the other remaining instructors knew to give him space.

Maybe he'd pop in that morning. The lecture might help him catch a few winks. A boy could hope.

Outside, the morning air was damp and cold. The sky was just beginning to lighten, casting the campus in a dreamlike gray haze. Nigel cut across the wet grass of the lawn towards the student union. The other day, his evil mother had commented that he was "skinnier than usual," and when Nigel looked in the mirror that morning he did notice his cheekbones jutting more than normal. Better try to eat something.

Nigel found a small group of other early risers inside, all

of them bleary-eyed and slump-shouldered like him. The students were huddled up near the food line, engaged in a discussion. Something wasn't right.

Every morning since they'd staffed this place up, the student union had smelled like coffee and bacon. But not today.

The kitchen was empty.

"What's all this, then?" Nigel asked as he joined the other students.

"There's no food," Omar Azoulay told him.

"I'm starving," groaned Danny, the fourteen-year-old Canadian tweeb, his brown hair long and floppy like some boy-band reject. "What're we supposed to do?"

Nigel sighed. The rest of the kitchen staff must have called it quits. He couldn't blame them for not sticking around. There were plenty of food service jobs out there that didn't require a security clearance. Starving the students of resources seemed to be Greger's plan to get Nine to accept his termination. The Earth Garde liaison must not have realized how stubborn Nine was—or how much the student body supported him.

"Get a grip," Nigel told the whiney tweeb as he hopped over the counter and entered the kitchen. "Just because the help's taken a powder doesn't mean the pantry's empty."

Nigel rifled through the cabinets, quickly finding where the staff stored the packaged muffins and single-serving cereal boxes. He tugged these bins out and floated them towards the buffet line with his telekinesis.

"Help me put these out," he told the others, who were just

standing there watching him.

"They said we'd be taken care of if we came here," Danny said. He looked almost dazed. "Now we're just . . . we're on our own?"

The word "wanker" was on the tip of Nigel's tongue, but he managed to hold back. The kid wasn't just upset about the lack of a healthy breakfast. He was scared. Many of these Garde hadn't done more than watch the invasion play out on TV. Since then, they'd been sheltered by Earth Garde. They'd never faced down what Nigel and his friends had.

"Bloody hell. You're a sorry bunch," Nigel said, crossing his arms. "You're supposed to be Garde. Most fearsome beings on the planet. Would-be protectors of the free world. And here I find you huddled about like some wet babies, afraid to make breakfast? I'm embarrassed to be amongst ya."

"Okay, Nigel, we get it," Lisbette said. "What should we do?"

"Someone go check the fridges and get the juices out. Put 'em in the nice vase-looking things."

"Carafes," Lisbette said. "They're called carafes."

"I don't *carafe* what they're called," Nigel replied. He waved to the empty space on the buffet where the drinks were supposed to be. "You make ice, don't you? Fill that up and then go get the drinks."

Lisbette made a face at him but did as she was told. Omar raised his hand.

"My family owned a restaurant," Omar said. "I can scramble eggs."

Nigel held out his hands like a blessing had been bestowed on them from on high. "So what are you waiting for? Get to it. You can even use that fire-breathing of yours to roast the sausages. I'll get Nine to give you extra credit for practicing."

"Gross," Lisbette protested. "I don't want his fire-spit on my food."

"Someone put out plates and silverware. And someone else get coffee brewing, or the professors will probably lose their minds . . ." As Nigel divvied out tasks for the others, the irony wasn't lost on him. He'd grown up tended to by a team of obedient servants. He couldn't actually scramble any eggs or even work a coffee machine himself. His abilities maxed out at slapping the bread slices together for a peanut butter and jelly sandwich. At least the aristocrat in him knew how to order around the help.

Soon, the student union was humming with activity. It almost seemed normal. As more students trickled in, some of them were too tired to even notice that it was Omar behind the kitchen counter instead of the usual attendants.

"One tiny battle at a time," Nigel muttered.

Across the room, Nigel took note of Dr. Susan Chen entering. The dean of academics looked like she'd gotten dressed in a hurry. She forewent her usual thermos of coffee, instead heading directly to the bulletin board where announcements were posted. Nigel met her there.

"Oi, Susan, you and the other grand masters know that the kitchen staff's all gone on vacation?"

Dr. Chen gave him a tired look. "Mr. Karlsson of Earth

Garde sent out notice last night that no human personnel were to report to work until the Academy's so-called leadership issues are resolved. The kitchen and maintenance staff don't live on campus, like the faculty, so I doubt the Peacekeepers would let them back through even if they did choose to violate Greger's decree."

"That's his strategy, then," Nigel said with a snort. "Deprive us of pancakes."

On the bulletin board, Dr. Chen tacked up a notice about canceled classes. Nigel did a quick once-over of the list. It seemed like almost half the Academy's staff were taking indefinite leaves of absence.

"We held a meeting before dawn. Not all the staff want to see Nine replaced by some bureaucrat. And there are some of us, like me, who believe that our first responsibility is to you Garde. What we're doing here is important."

"Right on, Dr. Chen," Nigel said, patting the woman's arm. "Just make sure that if shit goes all topsy-turvy, you keep you and your fellow teachers out of harm's way."

Dr. Chen looked up at Nigel with slightly widened eyes. She was trying to keep a cool head, but Nigel could tell that she was as rattled as anyone. It was no accident that Greger had used the word "evacuate" in his memo to the teachers. You evacuated war zones, not schools.

"I should hope it won't come to that," she replied. "Myself and some of the other instructors sent letters to the UN, protesting Nine's removal. With resistance from the student body as well, I expect them to reconsider. I know the incident in Switzerland is heavy on everyone's mind, but given enough time, I hope Earth Garde will see reason. Also, Ray Archibald is a good man. He knows his mission is to protect you Garde, not enforce the whims of some bureaucrat."

It sounded a bit like Dr. Chen was trying to talk herself into the possibility of cooler heads prevailing. Nigel scratched his pockmarked jawline, trying to keep his mother's voice and her dark promises about the Academy's future out of his head.

"Let's hope everyone at Earth Garde has your good sense, Dr. Chen," he said.

"Check it out! They're talking about us!"

Someone had turned on the student union's big screen to a broadcast of one of the morning news shows, already in full swing on America's East Coast. Nigel bristled when he saw Melanie Jackson on-screen. The last time he'd seen the Earth Garde figurehead was in Switzerland, all teary-eyed and snot-nosed, crying over that dead technocrat Sydal who'd been trying to buy black-market Mogadorian ooze from Nigel's mother. Nigel remembered how, on the flight back from Switzerland, Melanie wouldn't hear a single negative word about Sydal. She was in a state of shock, basically, so Nigel had cut her some slack. Still, he couldn't forget how her eyes had swept the passenger compartment, looking at her fellow Garde like they were monstrous.

Melanie looked much better on TV than she had a few weeks ago. Her blond hair pulled back in a neat ponytail, her face made-up for the cameras, the girl basically glowing. She wore a pastel sweater and a prominent gold cross.

"Excuse me, Dr. Chen," Nigel said, nodding to the screen. "But I get the feeling this is about to be some truly shite TV."

Nigel moved closer to the screen, Dr. Chen following after him. Everyone else in the student union had already stopped what they were doing to peer up at the screen.

"I'm grateful for the chance to sit down with you today, George, to hopefully put some of those fears to rest," Melanie was saying, in response to a question from the patiently smiling host. "I was there in Switzerland, as you know. I've seen firsthand what it looks like when a person like me, with my abilities, goes rogue. People are right to be worried. But we at Earth Garde are taking steps to make sure that never happens again."

"What kind of steps?" the host inquired.

"Before his—" Melanie's bottom lip quivered and she made a show of composing herself. "Before his untimely death, Wade Sydal was working on a device capable of disrupting a Garde's Legacies. We actually believe this is why he was targeted for assassination. The chip is about the size of a fingernail—amazing, right?—and can safely and remotely prevent a Garde from using their Legacies."

"By frying their brain," Nigel muttered.

"I've actually already had my Inhibitor installed," Melanie continued, tossing back her hair and tilting her head towards the host. "Do you see my scar?"

The host leaned forward. "I don't see anything."

She smiled. "Of course you don't. The surgery is quick and Earth Garde has great healers ready to aid in the recovery. I was out for about an hour and now I'm completely safe."

"They're . . . they're going to make us get brain surgery?" Lisbette asked, looking around the room with wide eyes.

"This is Orwellian," Dr. Chen said.

"You mentioned that these chips can be controlled remotely," the host said. "Who is going to do that? Earth Garde, I assume. But who specifically?"

"Great question," Melanie replied. "We're actually borrowing a concept from the Loric for that. On their planet, they had people called Cêpans. These were people without Legacies who were trained to handle Garde. They acted as teachers, bodyguards and friends. Starting at the Academy level, each Garde will be assigned a Cêpan who will directly oversee their training and monitor their behavior for dangerous patterns."

"I'll make some dangerous patterns on their faces if that lot tries to chip me," Nigel said.

Dr. Chen shook her head. "What she's saying undermines everything we've built here. We're trying to give you an approximation of a normal school experience, at least. Not this—this *nannying*."

"And this process is in motion already?" the host inquired.

"It is," Melanie replied. "Everyone in Earth Garde has already received their Inhibitor and been matched with a Cêpan. It's rolling out to the Academy as soon as some logistics are worked out."

"What happens to Garde who don't go along with this? Like the at-large terrorist Einar Magnusson?"

"Well, people like Einar and his cohorts are in clear violation of the Garde Accord," Melanie said coldly. "They'll be hunted down, chipped and detained until it's determined they aren't a danger to themselves or others."

The host seemed to consider this for a moment. His tone shifted unexpectedly. "All due respect, Ms. Jackson—and I'm as frightened at the possibility of a dangerous rogue Garde as anyone—but this strikes me as a bit of a dangerous overcorrection. What you're talking about is performing an invasive surgery on teenagers before they've even done anything wrong."

Nigel clapped his hands. "Hell yes! This bloke gets it!"

Melanie's smile never faltered. "Can I tell you something that a lot of people don't know, George? It's going to sound slightly crazy because, well, we live in a pretty crazy world now. When I received my Legacies—and any of the other first-generation Garde will back me up on this—I also had a vision of like Loric history. A warning, basically. And you know what? Setrákus Ra, the sick monster who invaded our planet and killed how many? Two million people? He was a Loric. He had Legacies. He was insane, obviously, and not like the Loric who rescued us and signed on to the Garde Accord that makes Earth Garde possible—but still. Imagine if the Loric had the good sense to stick a simple microchip in Setrákus Ra back when he was just *slightly* crazy. Imagine how many people would still be alive. Heck, I might not even have Legacies because there would've never been an invasion, if those people had just shown a little foresight."

"Bollocks," Nigel said, running a hand across his Mohawk. "She actually went there."

"That's—that's a great deal to take in," the host replied, on his back foot now. "And we need to take a break. But we'll be back with—"

A loud tone blared, drowning out the TV and its commercials. It took Nigel a moment to realize that the Academy's emergency PA system had been activated. The school-wide messaging system was controlled from the Peacekeeper camp and was meant to notify students of incoming threats. Outside of fire-drill-style tests every six months, the system had never been used in all of Nigel's time at the Academy.

"Attention, students of the Human Garde Academy." That was Greger's voice, coldly authoritative, booming over the speakers. "The following students are required to report immediately to the Peacekeeper encampment for mandatory processing. Daniel Abernathy, Omar Azoulay, Nigel Barnaby . . ."

Everyone in the student union stood still as Greger rattled off ten names in alphabetical order. Nigel glanced out the front windows, where he could see lights blinking on in the dorms, any classmates who were still sleeping were now awake thanks to the announcement. He imagined he could hear Professor Nine dropping off the ceiling—Nigel always imagined that Nine slept upside down because of his antigravity Legacy—pulling on some clothes and cursing up a storm. The knobs at Earth Garde were making their move.

There was silence in the student union as Greger finished his list of names and simply cut off his broadcast. Everyone jumped at screams from the TV, a commercial with kids clamoring for chicken nuggets putting a bunch of Garde on edge.

Omar caught Nigel's eye from the kitchen. He had a pan in one hand, an egg-covered spatula in the other. He cocked his head uncertainly, as if to ask Nigel if they were really going. Nigel shook his head emphatically.

A chair squeaked across the floor and Nigel turned to see Danny nervously standing up from his table.

"Oi," Nigel said. "Where you going, mate?"

"I—" Danny pointed up at the ceiling, an awe in his voice like God himself had paged him. "He called my name. I'm supposed to . . ."

Nigel sauntered around to block the exit. *"Oh, Danny Boy,"* he sang. *"Your ass, your ass is showing . . ."*

Nobody laughed. Everyone stared at him. Nigel scratched awkwardly behind his ear. So maybe half-assed parodies of lame Irish ballads weren't going to get the job done.

"Right, then, listen up, Danny, and everyone else, whether you got called or not," Nigel began, using his Legacy to ratchet up his volume just a bit, giving himself some leaderly vibrato. "Some of us just got summoned to the principal's office, yeah? Usually, that means detention, but the way things are going it sounds like our so-called guardians got something a bit more drastic in mind. Like a lobotomy. Now,

I don't know about you lot, but I haven't done fuck all but be a good little Garde who listens to his teachers and busts his ass in training."

Dr. Chen, still standing just a few feet away, raised an eyebrow at that but didn't interrupt.

"I didn't sign up to let anyone stab around in my brain. Nobody in here did. I don't care if the Queen herself wobbles out here and tells me it's for the good of mankind. Earth Garde can't just go changing the rules on us."

A number of his classmates—Omar and Lisbette included—nodded their heads in agreement. But just as many stood by with glazed eyes and shrunken shoulders, looking like they wished they'd hid under the bed that morning.

Nigel waved to Dr. Chen. "Even the dean of academics here don't think this is on the level. Isn't that right, Susan?"

Dr. Chen stared at Nigel for just a moment before she turned to the other students, her hands on her hips, adopting a posture much like she did when at the front of the classroom.

"This entire . . . change in policy was not run by me or any of the other administrators. I would suggest you all hold off reporting until the staff has had an opportunity to discuss this matter."

Inwardly, Nigel breathed a sigh of relief that Dr. Chen had backed him up. Even skittish Danny eased back into his seat when someone with actual authority spoke. The vibe in the room changed. Though some were brighter than others, Nigel could see sparks of resolve in the eyes of his classmates.

"Right, then," Nigel concluded with a clap of his hands. "Spread the word. We stay here. We watch out for each other." His eyes zeroed in first on Danny and then on some of the others who still looked like they might break, emulating a growl that Nine would've appreciated. "Anyone who crosses over to Earth Garde is a bloody sellout."

CHAPTER TEN

"I'LL NEED A PRIVATE SUITE. THE BIGGEST YOU have." Isabela didn't bother to hide her Portuguese accent. After all, the soccer star she was pretending to be wouldn't speak perfect English. "And we are *not* to be disturbed."

"Of course, of course," said the hotel manager, an obsequious middle-aged man in a vivid white suit. "As it happens, our penthouse is available."

"Perfect," Isabela replied. "I'll take it."

Giggles echoed across the hotel lobby's beige and silver tiles. Isabela spotted a pair of girls in their twenties, half-hidden behind one of the decorative silk curtains draped from the ceiling. The two of them were tan, pretty and clad in fashionable dresses. For a moment, Isabela envied them.

The girls had their cell phones out and were sneakily trying to snap photos of her.

Of *him*, actually. Today, Isabela was a man. Bronzed, lean, a brilliant smile, dark hair gelled immaculately. She could re-create this appearance from memory; her youngest sister had worshipped the soccer star, posters of him and his abs all over her bedroom walls. Isabela had opted for the version without those horrible frosted tips.

She winked at the girls, shot them with a finger-gun that made one of them swoon, then leaned across the counter. She lowered her voice to speak to the hotel manager, who was busily typing on his keyboard.

"Bro, I thought this place was supposed to be private," she said, making the soccer star's voice icy.

The manager glanced up, saw the girls and quickly snapped his fingers in the direction of a thickly built bell-hop who lumbered across the lobby to chase them off.

"Sincerest apologies, sir," said the manager.

"*Tudo bem*," replied Isabela, flashing an endorsement-worthy smile. She glanced over her shoulder. "Where's my assistant? Yo, bring the bag here."

Even though he wore a pair of sunglasses and a baseball cap with the brim pulled low, Isabela spotted Caleb's nervous tics as he approached the counter and set down the leather satchel in front of the manager. At least with his character of put-upon assistant, he wouldn't give anything away. Not that anyone—even the manager, right there in front of him—paid

Caleb any mind. Why look at him when they could be ogling Isabela's soccer superstar. The only thing that could screw them over was if Caleb let a duplicate pop loose. She silently prayed the boy would keep control. Isabela couldn't stand another minute on Einar's dinky spaceship.

She shoved the bag towards the manager.

"It's cool if I pay in cash, right? I want to keep this visit on the low. You can take a nice tip for yourself, of course, and put the rest on credit at the casino. I might want to do some gambling."

The manager flicked open the bag, glanced over the neatly stacked bundles of euros inside and nodded once. "But, of course, sir. Cash is always welcome in Casablanca. Here is your room key."

"Appreciate it, boss," Isabela said, because she imagined the soccer player being the type who would call subordinates "boss" ironically. She swiveled away from the front desk and extended both of her arms. "Ladies? Shall we?"

Ran and Duanphen stood a few feet away, both of them somehow looking even more awkward than Caleb, both of them glaring daggers at Isabela. She made a kissy face to remind them of their roles—a pair of smoke-shows that wouldn't look out of place with a celebrity athlete. Isabela had lent them a couple of her tightest dresses from the collection she was amassing on this world tour of shoplifting, then heavily applied eye makeup and lip gloss until the two badass Garde looked almost like genuine groupies. Caleb couldn't even bring himself to look in their direction, which was how Isabela knew her makeover efforts hadn't gone to waste.

In response to Isabela, Ran half-heartedly batted her eye-lashes in a way that was less alluring and more like she'd lost a contact lens. It was better than Duanphen, at least, who simply stared blankly at Isabela's athletic hunk. At least they both had the good sense to tuck in under Isabela's arms, allowing her to lead them across the lobby to the elevator. Caleb followed after them, dragging the luggage.

Isabela sensed that the manager and his bellhop were still watching, so she couldn't resist. She let her hands stray casually downwards until they were resting on the girls' butts.

Ran turned her head and whispered. "I am going to hurt you."

"Nice! Dirty talk. That's goo— Yow!"

Isabela jumped and yanked her hand away as an electric shock traveled from Duanphen's backside directly into her fingers.

"Oh, you bitch," Isabela muttered.

Duanphen and Ran exchanged a look and then both of them laughed. Even though it was at her expense, Isabela didn't mind. There hadn't been much fun over the last couple of weeks, a fact that still baffled Isabela. They were free, in possession of a spaceship and, like, millions of dollars. They could go anywhere. In her case, she could be anyone.

"Jesus, you guys are going to get us made," Caleb grumbled as he jabbed the button for the elevator.

Ah. The buzzkill. Right on cue.

"Made," Isabela repeated. "Listen to you."

"It means caught."

"I know what it means, *idiota*," she replied. Isabela hadn't actually heard that expression before but had inferred from Caleb's sweaty armpits that he was still afraid they'd be found out.

The elevator doors whooshed open immediately and they all piled inside. As they ascended towards the penthouse—a floor accessible only via a swipe of Isabela's gold-plated key card—the girls scooted to one side of the elevator to get away from the soccer player's wandering hands. Isabela wiggled her eyebrows at Duanphen.

"I *will* shock you again," she said.

"I kind of liked it," Isabela replied with a leer.

Ran put a hand over her face. "Isabela. Wow."

"That wasn't exactly inconspicuous," Caleb complained.

Isabela rounded on him. She was taller than Caleb in this form, a fact she enjoyed.

"Oh, relax," Isabela said. She straightened his collar. "We're in. Everything is fine."

"You could've made yourself look like anyone," Caleb said. "You didn't have to choose someone famous."

Ran gestured at Isabela. "This man is famous?"

"He's one of the best soccer players in the world," Caleb replied. "He's also gross, so she got that part right."

"My sister used to flick it to him all the time," said Isabela with a shrug. "You don't get it. People bend over backwards for guys like him. They can pay with cash and bring their entourages around and no one bats an eye. No one even notices. It's called hiding in plain sight."

Before Caleb could formulate a response, they arrived at the penthouse level and Isabela swaggered out of the elevator. She made a little cooing sound at the sight of the room—probably a weird visual coming from the soccer player, but whatever. There was no audience now. She could stop being macho and enjoy.

A sunken common area equipped with chic leather furniture led to a trio of bedrooms; floor-to-ceiling windows across one wall offered a sweeping view of the Atlantic's white-capped waves. A table was set with an assortment of cookies and fresh fruit, a bottle of champagne on ice and fresh orchids. The whole tableau was only slightly sullied by Five looming over the food.

"These cookies are dry," he commented, munching away.

Of course, Einar and Five were already there. They had let themselves in via the penthouse's exclusive rooftop garden. They'd gotten lucky that the place's top floor was vacant and there was a discreet flight path in from over the ocean. Even with Isabela serving as a distraction, there was no way Five and his messed-up face could walk across the lobby with Einar, the world's most wanted terrorist. Hiding in plain sight only worked up to a point.

Isabela changed back into her true form—well, her unburned true form—and went to the table, narrowing her eyes at Five. The cookie tray was already half empty. She slapped a biscotti out of his hand.

"Stop eating them if you don't like them," she commanded.

Five rubbed the back of his hand, scowling at Isabela. "I'm hungry."

"Eat some fruit," she said, popping a strawberry into her mouth and then flipping one in Five's direction. He caught it with his telekinesis and let it rotate in the air as he examined it.

"Did anyone see you flying up here?" Caleb asked, parking the luggage next to the door.

"Of course not," Einar replied. "We aren't stupid."

Caleb studied Einar for a moment, clearly not convinced. Einar simply ignored him, already absorbed by the big-screen television on the far wall. That one was always watching the news. He loved to wallow in how much the world hated him.

Caleb turned to look at Five. The Loric nodded once.

"We were careful," Five said flatly. "You can relax."

"He can never relax," Isabela said. "He's not wired that way."

Ran tugged at the hem of the dress she'd borrowed from Isabela. "I would very much like to get changed."

"Same," said Duanphen.

"But you guys look so hot," moaned Isabela.

They ignored her, pulling some of their normal, boring clothes free from the luggage and then retreating to one of the bedrooms.

"You're sure this Blackstone guy will be here?" Caleb directed this question at the back of Einar's head.

"He isn't just any Blackstone guy," Einar replied coldly. "He's Derek King. CEO of the entire organization."

Einar flicked his wrist and floated a tablet in Caleb's direction, a picture of their target displayed on the screen. Derek King was a square-jawed man in his early fifties with a full head of graying hair that he kept swept back, and sharp emerald-green eyes. In the image, he clenched a fist around some dice, hunched over a craps table. He had a couple of scars on his cheek, shrapnel from some long-ago battle—the scars not bad enough to disfigure him, just enough to give his face some weathered character. He was pretty handsome for an older dude, Isabela supposed.

"Not bad," Isabela said, watching Caleb from the corner of her eyes. "I won't mind seducing him."

Caleb looked at her. She pretended not to notice. He swallowed hard and then muttered. "If he even shows up."

"It's a near certainty he'll be here," Einar said with an exasperated sigh as he turned away from the TV. "The picture you're looking at was taken in this very casino. The Blackstone Group has been charged with crimes in a dozen countries and is being sued by citizens in a dozen more. For all the wealth his private army has generated, there are only so many places where Mr. King is welcome. Morocco happens to be his favorite."

"You know him pretty well," Caleb replied. "He your best friend or something?"

"Yes, Caleb, he's my best friend," Einar replied sarcastically. "We did have dinner a few times, actually. He wanted to use my Legacies to 'convince' some governments to allow Blackstone to operate inside their borders. Bea always turned him down. Said it would be too much exposure. Anyway, you should be happy that I listened when he prattled on about hard eights and which hotels have the best complimentary massages, otherwise we'd have absolutely nothing to go on."

Caleb picked up an apricot from the snack tray, then sullenly tossed it back down. "And you think we can get this guy to talk? A former Green Beret who's been commanding mercenaries for a decade? A guy who's gotten paid millions to clean up the Foundation's messes?"

"He's not a Green Beret anymore," Einar replied. "He's a suit."

"He'll talk," Five said flatly.

"Without killing him?"

"Obviously, he can't talk if he's dead," Einar replied with a chuckle. He shot Isabela a meaningful look. "As long as Isabela can do her part."

She waved her hand in response. "Please. Horny old men are my specialty."

Caleb looked at her, started to say something, but let it go. All out of objections, he started to disconsolately pick at the tray of cookies.

"You believe that this Blackstone man will know how to find Lucas Sanders." Ran joined the conversation as she emerged from the other room, dressed in boring jeans and a T-shirt.

"If we assume that the Foundation is holding Lucas at a secure location, then it's likely Blackstone provides security there," Einar said. "King will know where his people are stationed. Isabela will lure him somewhere private, we'll take out his bodyguards and find out what we want to know. And then—" Einar looked pointedly at Caleb. "We'll let him go back to the casino floor and I'll amp up his anger and envy to the point where he makes a scene and gets himself arrested. That will cover our escape and, I assume, satisfy Caleb's humanitarian streak. A bad person gets thrown in a Moroccan jail and no one gets hurt."

"Except the bodyguards if they step to us," Five commented, chewing. "But we won't hurt them too bad."

"The hunted will become the hunter," Duanphen said, settling in on one of the couches.

"I still feel pretty hunted," Caleb said, gazing down at the cookies like they were some kind of battle plan. "What if King doesn't know where that body-snatching jerk is operating from?"

"Then we will pry some other information out of him," Einar said. "It will bring us closer to the Foundation."

Caleb shook his head. "You keep saying stuff like that, but we aren't getting anywhere."

Einar's eyes flashed. Isabela could tell he was trying to remain calm. It seemed easier to control others' emotions than his own. But Einar had promised not to use his Legacy against any of them and so far he'd stuck by that. Not that his tricks worked on Caleb, anyway. But still. Caleb was so annoying sometimes; she wouldn't have blamed Einar for giving it a shot.

"Why did you even come with us?" Einar asked. "To complain in my ear incessantly?"

"To stop you from making a bigger mess than you already have," Caleb replied sharply. "To stop you from killing people."

"I know we're all trying to get along and play for the same team now," Five said, "but, just so we're clear, if I decide to kill someone, you won't be able to stop me."

"We stopped you in Switzerland," Ran remarked from the couch, an eyebrow raised.

"Yeah, fine," Five said. "But you had help."

"I was going easy on you," Ran replied.

Five laughed, thought this over and then shrugged. "Fair enough."

Einar and Caleb were still glaring at each other, as usual. Isabela grabbed Caleb by the arm.

"Stop, okay?" She took a demonstrative deep breath of the room's filtered, lilac-scented air. "It doesn't smell like pits here. This is a step up. If this Blackstone guy doesn't show up tonight, I say . . . so what? We can wait. Chill for a while."

"There's a killer Harvester Garde chasing us," Caleb said. "We can't stay here forever."

"Italy is far away and I doubt that creep has a spaceship," Isabela replied. "We're fine, Caleb. Seriously."

"Oh, seriously?" He pulled his arm free. "You don't take anything seriously."

Isabela shrugged. This was true. She ambled across the room, taking in the view from the window. The Atlantic was pale blue here, choppy and beautiful. The horizon stretched on forever.

She could disappear over that horizon. It would be easy. Swipe a few stacks of the money Einar had just lying around on his spaceship. A hundred thousand or so would get her started. She could be anyone. She could go anywhere.

She didn't need to put up with this shit. That terrible little spaceship and the constant bickering. No one was actively hunting her or, if they were, they didn't stand much chance of ever finding her. She wasn't a revolutionary like Einar or some wannabe pacifist like Ran. These Foundation people were bad, obviously, and deserved whatever they got—but Isabela wasn't passionate about being the one to deliver justice. She could read the writing on the wall. They were screwed. There was always going to be corruption. There were always going to be people trying to kill and exploit them. Better to just opt out of the whole dumb conflict and live the sweet life that their Legacies provided.

So why hadn't she bailed? It'd been two weeks of this crap. She was beyond tired of it.

In the window's reflection, she saw Caleb's dumb, handsome face, screwed up as usual with some inner turmoil. She really, really loved tormenting Caleb. That was it. She wouldn't leave until she was thoroughly bored with that.

One of these days, though. Poof. *Desenrascanço.*

"We paid for two nights; we shouldn't stay longer than

that," Caleb was saying. "We still don't know how we're being tracked. Not to mention"—he gestured at Isabela—"all we need is for your alter ego to post something on Instagram that says he's in Spain or Italy or somewhere other than here, and then people will realize we're imposters."

Isabela closed her eyes, for a moment shutting out the allure of the ocean and escape. "What are the chances of that? You're so paranoid." She spun away from the window, gave Caleb a look and sauntered over to the luggage. "If it makes you feel better, I'll keep an eye on his Insta."

She pulled out the makeup bag that contained the pieces of her cell phone and tossed them onto a glass end table—the phone, its battery and the SIM card clattering around. She started to piece the device together when she realized that everyone was staring at her.

"What?" Isabela asked.

"Whose phone is that?" Caleb asked.

"Mine."

"Whose phone was it before that?"

"That *sacana* from California," Isabela replied. She couldn't remember his name, so she looked to Einar. "The one I was impersonating when you jumped me."

"Alejandro Regerio," Einar supplied the name as he massaged his temples. "You still have his phone?"

"Uh, *yes*, you knew that I had it," Isabela replied. "I recorded your whole stupid speech on here. You used it to upload to YouTube."

"Yes, but I thought you'd be smart enough to get rid of it

166

after that," Einar replied. "I can't micromanage everything."

"Why would I get rid of it?" Isabela asked. She popped the battery into the back of the phone. "This thing is prepaid. It's still got minutes."

"Isabela," Ran said calmly. "The Foundation is tracking us. We aren't sure how. Has it not occurred to you that they might be using the phone of one of their former employees?"

Isabela hesitated with her fingers poised to slip in the SIM card. She thought back to Italy, where that Lucas freak had first caught up with them.

"No," Isabela said. "No way. I keep it in pieces. I never put it together in Italy. They can't track it if it's taken apart."

"You don't know if that's true," Caleb said. "They could have a tracking device in there or something."

Five upended the dish of strawberries, which he had finished, and loudly slurped the juices. He didn't look nearly as agitated as the rest of them.

"Look, as someone who spent years trying to stay off the grid, if the Foundation were able to track that phone, they'd be all over us," Five said.

Isabela pointed at Five. "See? Listen to the crazy one."

"We shouldn't take any chances," Caleb said. He came forward with his hand extended. "Come on. Let's get rid of the thing."

She shrank back from Caleb. "Hold up. The Academy has the number for this phone."

"All the more reason to get rid of it," Einar said.

"What if they need to call us?" Isabela focused on Caleb.

"What if you want to drunk-dial Taylor?"

"I'm not . . . I don't . . ." Caleb shook his head. "You can just steal another one, Isabela."

"Am I the only one watching this?" Duanphen asked. She'd been staying out of this latest argument from her spot by the TV. She waved at the screen, where Al Jazeera was on, recapping some story from earlier in the day.

A story about Garde getting chips put in their heads. They all fell silent, listening to the latest report on the change in Earth Garde policy.

Einar was the first one to speak, although quietly. "This is my fault," he said, slouching back into the couch. "I thought I could force them to give us justice. Instead . . ."

"Instead, you made it worse for all of us," Caleb replied, though his heart didn't seem into the rebuke.

"My Cêpan was a piece-of-shit coward," Five grumbled. The dark splotches that broke up his skin writhed, a sure sign that he was angry. "This is what I was talking about," he said to Ran. "This is what they do when they're scared."

Ran said nothing. She looked lost in thought, fingering the spot on her temple where a chip had once been installed.

"They're going to do that to everyone at the Academy," Isabela said with an incredulous laugh. "It's insane."

The urge to run came over her again, but not the urge to disappear. It was a feeling that she shouldn't be halfway across the world in a lavish hotel suite. Her friends—Taylor, Nigel, Kopano, even her dumb-ass ex-boyfriend Lofton serving for Earth Garde somewhere—they were in danger. She wanted to do something.

Caleb took the cell phone out of her hands before she realized what he was doing. He popped the battery in and powered it on, then held the phone out to Isabela.

"Call them," he said. "Tell them that we're here to help."

CHAPTER ELEVEN

TAYLOR COOK
THE HUMAN GARDE ACADEMY—POINT REYES, CALIFORNIA

NINE WAS ON A TEAR.

"I wake up—because, *sorry*, I needed to sleep. I mean, I barely slept at all because of all the shit running through my head, but I did close my eyes, okay? I wake up to this dumbass Greger making announcements about my students, so I hustle up to my office to try to figure out what's going on. And there's John. Sitting behind my desk. Reading through our files."

Taylor stood in front of the Academy's toolshed, a place she had never ventured before. She gave the door a tug before realizing that the maintenance staff who hadn't shown up for work that morning had left behind a padlock. She glanced over her shoulder at Nine, who was glowering into the distance and ranting.

"He gives me a look like . . . *Why aren't you taking care of this?*" Nine continued. *"Why is this Greger guy all up in your shit?"*

Taylor sighed. "Do you have a key for this?"

"What?" Nine patted his pockets. "Damn. I don't know what I did with them."

Nine grabbed the padlock and with little effort snapped it off the shed's door. He crunched the useless hunk of metal in his cybernetic hand and then whipped it into the air, flinging the lock clear across campus. Taylor cringed.

"If that hits someone in the head, I'm going to have to heal them," she said.

Nine didn't hear her. "Guy shows up for a day and thinks he's in charge," he grumbled.

Taylor surveyed the inside of the toolshed, which basically looked like a larger version of what her dad had back at home. She started gathering what they would need—hammers and nails, a blowtorch, some loose boards that were lying around.

Meanwhile, outside, Nine dumped the contents of his wheelbarrow next to the shed. Thirty speakers in a pile, their wires tangled, some of them still featuring chunks of the drywall they'd been ripped from. Tearing down the Academy's PA system as quickly as possible had turned into something of a contest that morning. Taylor wasn't paying attention to the count, but she thought Maiken won. Now, Greger's announcements only reached campus from the distant speakers of the Peacekeeper encampment.

That hadn't stopped him. Greger's announcements continued, running down the list of students in alphabetical order, one batch every hour.

"He's not in charge," Taylor said as she loaded up the empty wheelbarrow. "He's just a really pushy guest."

"I know what people think of me," Nine said quietly. "I'm the meathead of the original Garde. I get it. But I'm also the one who stuck around. That tried to build something. And John . . ." The joints on Nine's metallic hand creaked. "Dude always made his own plans and did things his way, whether the rest of us were on board or not. He's the big hero, right? Except nobody knows about all the times he royally fucked up and almost got us all killed. It was like . . . every week."

Taylor patted Nine on the shoulder. "Will it make you feel better to smash some stuff?"

"Yes. Yes, it will."

So, they went to work.

Only one road led onto campus from the Peacekeeper encampment. That was where the students built their barricade.

They banged nails through boards and laid them in strips across the pavement. A chain of students ferried desks from the classrooms out onto the quad where they broke the furniture apart. They tangled the metal legs into brambles of steel, melting these sections together with either the blowtorch or Omar's fire-breath. Other students took the ceramic desktops and wedged them vertically into the grass near the road, creating a low wall. At some point, John Smith joined them, wordlessly assisting their construction efforts with his stone-vision.

"Won't stop the Peacekeepers from marching in through the woods, but at least they won't be able to drive a convoy right to our front door," Nine said to Taylor, wiping sweat off his forehead. The two of them stood near the student union, surveying the barricade-building from a slight rise. "Plus, everyone's a lot less spooked now that we've got them working."

"You should make a schedule," Taylor said, shaking out her hand that was tired from gripping a hammer. "Assign students the tasks that the support staff would normally handle. Get some people to cook dinner. Set up patrol shifts."

"Good idea," Nine replied.

"I know."

"We'll see if you still feel that way when you're fixing a clogged toilet," Nine said with a smile. "Hmm. What other students here annoy the shit out of—"

A noise from Nine's back pocket cut him off. Bouncy and familiar, Taylor quickly identified the ringtone as a song by that *other* Taylor. She gave Nine an incredulous look as he quickly yanked his phone out of his pocket.

"Say something," he snapped. "I dare you."

She held up her hands. "It's cool. I was a tween girl once too."

Nine scowled at her. His eyebrows shot up as he looked at the caller ID.

"Huh," he said, hitting the button for speakerphone. "Well, well, well," he said loudly. "About time my field agents reported in."

There was a long pause on the other line. Taylor's face broke into a relieved smile when Caleb's familiar, nervous voice responded.

"Um, are we really field agents?"

"I'm practicing for when I have to testify in front of the UN," Nine replied.

"We aren't agents of shit, *idiota*." Taylor's smile grew even wider as Isabela came on the line. "Did you let everyone's brains get drilled, Professor Man-Bun? Are we too late?"

"Isabela! Caleb!" Taylor spoke up before Nine could say anything through his clenched teeth, elbowing in closer to the phone. "Are you guys okay?"

"Ah, good, someone smart is there," Isabela said. Taylor could sense the genuine relief behind Isabela's usual barbs. "Hello, my most beautiful friend. What's new?"

Taylor chuckled. "Where to start . . ."

"Did you hook up with Kopano yet?"

"Isabela!" She glanced around to make sure Kopano wasn't nearby, but he was off hauling desks out of a classroom.

"What?"

"We're fine, Taylor," Caleb cut in. "All six of us are fine."

Six of them. So they'd stuck together. The Academy crew and Einar's psychos.

"Not that I don't want to hear about Taylor's love life,"

Nine said. "But where the hell are you?"

"Uh, probably better we don't say," Caleb replied. "In case someone is monitoring the call. But we saw the news, saw what's happening there and thought we should call, see if you need any help."

"Is the news wrong?" Isabela asked. "You don't sound brainwashed."

"So far it's all bark and no bite," Nine said.

"It's only students and some faculty left on campus," Taylor added. "There are basically no classes. You'd love it, Isabela."

"My dream!"

"We can come back," Caleb said firmly. "We *should* come back. Help you fight."

"Probably not the best idea," Nine said. "Hopefully, this all blows over. But if the shit hits the fan, I feel better knowing you guys are out there."

"To save you, you mean," Isabela said.

"I never need saving," Nine replied.

Someone in the background laughed.

"Also, John Smith just showed up out of nowhere," Taylor added. "Maybe to help, maybe to just get in the way. Don't mind Nine. He's feeling a little insecure."

Isabela made a cooing sound. "Is he as hot as on TV?"

"He needs to shave," Taylor replied.

"I'm glad you guys checked in," Nine said. "If we weren't stuck on campus, I'd go smash down some doors myself, but since I can't, you'll have to do it for me. We're pretty sure that

Earth Garde has already scooped up some people, like Six and Malcolm's son, Sam."

"The one who can talk to machines," Caleb said.

"Figures that a guy with his Legacy would disappear the day before they announce we're all getting chips in our heads," Taylor said.

"They might have been working for Earth Garde, but there's no way Six and Sam would go along with this mess. Greger all but told Malcolm that he's got them in custody somewhere. Probably wherever they're holding the Garde who won't cooperate," Nine continued. "Not that we here at the Human Garde Academy are telling you to break any laws or spring anyone from a secret government prison. But we're also not *not* telling you to do that."

"Uh, hold on a second," Caleb said, and then must have hit the mute button because all sound cut out from their end. Nine looked at Taylor, then muted their line as well.

"As someone not known for his impulse control, let me ask you," Nine said, "involving them is a good idea, right? We aren't going to make things worse letting that Einar nut-job and my old buddy Five do work for us?"

Taylor thought about the unique group of personalities on the other side of this phone call. "The fact that they haven't killed each other yet or made the news for blowing something up is an encouraging sign. Besides, we need *someone* out there doing what we can't."

Caleb came back on the line. "So, it turns out we might already be looking for this secret prison or, anyway, a place where the Foundation is holding dangerous Garde."

Taylor raised an eyebrow. "You are?"

"Well, we haven't made much progress so far—"

"Don't tell them that," someone—definitely Einar—snapped in the background.

"But if we get any leads or if we find Six and Sam, we will definitely try to rescue them," Caleb said. "I mean, obviously."

"Very reassuring," Nine said dryly.

"Hold on a second," Caleb said. "Ran wants to talk to you."

The connection jostled as it passed between hands and then the speaker function clicked off so that Ran's gentle voice came through much clearer.

"Hello, Taylor, Professor Nine," Ran said. "Is Nigel there with you?"

Nine fidgeted with the joint on one of his mechanical knuckles, then used his telekinesis to float the phone closer to Taylor. Clearly, he didn't want to field this one.

"Hey, Ran," Taylor said. "He's not with us right this second. Last time I saw him, he was headed under the training center to . . . to . . . ." To pointlessly interrogate his evil mother? Taylor didn't know how to phrase that, so she just trailed off. "Do you want me to get him for you?"

Ran hesitated. "No. That's okay. Please tell him that I called and I'm thinking about him."

"I'll do that," Taylor replied.

"That's all—" Ran started to say, but it sounded like

someone yanked the phone out of her hand. A gruff voice came on.

"You there, Nine?"

Nine's expression darkened. "What do you want, Five?"

"Just wanted to say that I'm looking forward to saving your Academy because you're such a loser and can't do it yourself. Later, bitch."

And the line went dead. Taylor snatched the phone away before Nine could punch it out of the air.

"Very mature," she said.

"That dude should've stayed soaking in an ooze puddle," Nine replied.

With the phone in hand, Taylor abruptly thought of calling her dad. She'd considered that often during the last couple of weeks. Taylor kept telling herself that she didn't call because she didn't want to worry him, but that couldn't really be true—her dad was obviously already worried. What would she tell him, though? He'd supported their crazy plan to infiltrate the Foundation, which involved destroying their family farm. That had gotten Taylor welcomed back into the secret organization, but it hadn't helped bring them down. In fact, the situation was worse than ever. How could she tell him that it was all for nothing? She dreaded that conversation, so she kept putting it off.

Taylor gave the phone back to Nine. "Do you think our families are safe?" she asked. "What's going to happen to them if we don't do what Earth Garde wants?"

Nine paused, breathing out through his nose. "Man. I always forget that you guys have families and shit."

"That's real nice, Nine."

"No, I mean, it almost made it easier for us OGs. We didn't have anyone to tie us down when we were on the run. Well . . . some of us didn't, anyway." Nine shook his head, getting out of his memories. "I doubt they'll do anything to your families. So far, they've been all about public relations, right? How would that look if they started threatening parents? No. Right now, they want to look like the sane, law-abiding ones."

"I hope you're right," Taylor replied.

As the two of them lapsed into silence, John left a group of students telekinetically piling up desks and walked up the path to join them. Taylor was glad to see him pitching in, even if it was clear John had ulterior motives for showing up at the Academy. She glanced at the sky, half expecting to see a Mogadorian warship looming above them.

"Kind of reminds you of the old days, doesn't it?" John said to Nine as he stopped in front of them. "Scrapping together whatever we could, making it work . . ."

"In the old days, we would just go on the run," Nine said.

John hesitated. "That's an option, you know. If this escalates any further, we could . . ."

"Run off to India with you?" Taylor asked, her eyebrows raised. "Are you kidding?"

"I know you'd be giving up a lot," John said cautiously.

"But if I can make New Lorien safe . . ."

"If we did that, we'd be back to zero," Nine replied. "No life. On the run, fugitives, looking over our shoulders. You remember what that was like?"

"Of course."

Nine gazed out at the students, many of them taking a break now, passing around jugs of water. "And you want that for all of them?" He didn't let John answer. "No. I know you don't."

"We want this Earth Garde thing to work," Taylor added. "But we have to show them that we aren't their property. We should have a say in how things are run, who our instructors are, whether or not we get Inhibitors."

John nodded. "Well, I'm going to visit the Peacekeeper encampment to let them know when and where the *Osiris* is landing," John said. "Maybe you'd like to come."

It took Taylor a beat to realize that John was talking to her and not Nine. "What? Me?"

John shrugged. "The Academy should have a representative, don't you think? Seems like you could speak for the other students here."

Taylor didn't know what to say. Luckily, Nine was there to fill the silence.

"So you're just going to walk over to the Peacekeepers and tell them that there's a Mogadorian warship planning to land up the coast tomorrow," Nine said flatly. "That's your plan."

As he spoke, Nine walked over so that he stood beside

John instead of across from him. This let the two of them avoid eye contact and instead gaze out across the campus. Taylor assumed this was some kind of passive-aggressive guy ritual.

"Earth Garde should be happy to see the last of the Mogadorians brought to justice," John said. "And I'm going to tell them that I negotiated their surrender with the help of some students from the Academy."

"But we didn't have shit to do with this," Nine replied.

"Didn't you?" John responded. He smiled at Taylor. "You heard Vontezza's broadcast while working for the Foundation and reported it to Nine. He got me involved because—well, because I can fly in space?"

"That's a lie, though," Taylor said.

"A harmless one," John replied. "Anyway, it could make for some good PR for the Academy, which it seems like you guys could really use at the moment." John hesitated for a moment, a tic that Taylor knew meant he was going to say something that Nine wouldn't like. "I could also bring a couple of your students with me tomorrow. Might make for a good learning experience."

Taylor snorted. So there it was. The ask. Nine had mentioned that John was up early that morning looking through the school's roster. He needed help.

Nine came to the same conclusion, his tone brusque. "You want to use some of my kids, stop dicking around and just ask, bro."

John grimaced. "The force field generator is a big piece of equipment. I could use a hand with it, especially with the Mogs and Earth Garde around. Kopano's ability to phase through matter would be helpful."

"Can't you just copy it?" Nine asked.

"Yeah, but I can't be everywhere at once," John said. "I've only got one set of hands."

Taylor almost said something. She didn't want Kopano off campus right now. But he would be so excited to go on a mission with John, she couldn't bring herself to speak up. And besides, she was still considering her own offer from John that would put her face-to-face with representatives from Earth Garde. What would she say? What would the students here *want* her to say?

"And also there's this guy Miki with strong telekinesis and wind transformation," John continued. "He'd make transporting the generator easier."

"Miki's in a timeout right now on account of being a scummy little spy," Nine replied. Then, he shrugged. "But if you need him, go ahead and take him. Just be aware, he might try to run off or otherwise screw you over."

"I'll keep that in mind," John said. "So, yeah, that's my favor."

"It'll be up to Kopano and Miki if they want to help you," Nine said. "But I don't have a problem with it."

John nodded. "Thanks. You said the head of the UN Peacekeepers here is Ray Archibald?"

"Yeah."

"What do you make of him?"

"Military guy. Kind of a dick. You know the type. A little bit like our old buddy Lawson."

"Good enough." John glanced at Taylor. "That's who we'll talk to."

"You'll probably find him out by your crash site, holding down a perimeter around the wreck. Malcolm went out there last night to let them know there aren't any Mogadorians invading. Didn't want to give them any excuse to rush onto campus. He told them it was you."

"Then they'll be expecting me."

"Yeah. Maybe you can get a chip drilled into your head while you're there."

"That's not going to happen."

"No," Nine agreed. "I guess Greger hasn't gotten to 'S' in the alphabet yet."

"Anything you want us tell him, Nine?" John asked.

Taylor's lips screwed up for a moment. Even though her mind was racing as she rehearsed possible conversations with the Earth Garde bosses, she hadn't missed John twice assuming that she was coming with him. She started to say something, but then snapped her mouth shut. Why act like she'd pass up this opportunity to shout at some powerful jerks? It was turning out to be her favorite pastime.

"Well, when you're over with Archibald, you could let him know that jamming Inhibitors into the brains of my students is a really terrible idea," Nine said with a look at Taylor.

"Definitely," she agreed.

"Also, please inform Greger Karlsson that I'm going to knock his teeth out."

"I thought sitting behind a desk would've stopped you from talking that way," John said with a smirk. Nine didn't seem amused.

"We'll tell them," Taylor inserted. "Maybe I'll filter your message a bit. But I'll tell them."

"And probably don't mention Vontezza," Nine added.

"Obviously," John said with a sigh. "Anything else?"

"Tell them you respect my authority and that I'm doing a good-ass job," Nine said.

"You got it," John said.

Nine gave Taylor's shoulder a squeeze. "Good luck. And if you're not back in an hour, I'll be leading the search party."

Taylor smiled at him, trying not to feel nervous. This was the kind of chance Kopano was talking about—an opportunity to lead, to make a difference. Or, at the very least, to see firsthand what the Academy was up against.

"So," Taylor said, turning to John. "Are we flying over or what?"

"No reason for anything so dramatic," John said with an easygoing smile that made Taylor want to strangle him. "We'll just walk right over and say hi."

Walk right over. Into the encampment of a bunch of

soldiers who wanted to install electrified microchips into her head. Stroll on by for a pop in. It suddenly sounded like a pretty shaky plan to Taylor.

But when John Smith started to walk away, she followed.

CHAPTER TWELVE

CALEB CRANE
LE ROYAL MANSOUR—CASABLANCA, MOROCCO

IT WAS CLOSING IN ON THREE IN THE MORNING and the casino floor of Le Royal Mansour was still as busy as it had been two hours earlier when Caleb first took up his post on the balcony. At first, he'd felt like he stuck out like a sore thumb. He wore slacks and a white dress shirt that fit him perfectly but chafed for reasons he couldn't articulate. He'd selected a chaise lounge close to the balcony's railing that afforded him an unobstructed view of the rows of table games below, but also had him reclining in a way that felt way too prone. Too exposed.

Leaning back on his elbows on the plush couch in stuffy clothes, Caleb felt like a model in a bad cologne ad. He sat up and tried to make his expression neutral.

He was a cool guy and he belonged. Yeah, totally.

Caleb kept expecting someone from the hotel's security staff to bounce him. But this wasn't like America, where you couldn't get near a casino until you were twenty-one. The gambling age in Morocco was eighteen and he got the impression that law was only loosely enforced. He was pretty sure those were a group of teenage boys smoking cigarettes and playing poker right below him. No one bothered him at all, unless he counted the waitress who brought him an unsolicited mug of tea.

"To calm your nerves so you can win big," the waitress had said as she set the steaming mug on the glass end table beside him.

Did he look nervous? Was he giving off that vibe? Oh man. Caleb chewed his thumbnail, then stopped because he knew that made him look suspicious. He took a sip of the tea too quickly and burned his tongue.

He was bad at this. Like, really bad.

Relax. Don't pop a dupe. No one's paying any attention to you.

He kept sitting up and leaning back and straightening again and then reclining, unable to decide what the proper position for a stakeout was. Or, rather, what was the proper position for a person *not* on a stakeout.

His gaze tracked across the green felt of the blackjack tables and the spinning black and red of the roulette wheel. There was a steady flow of gamblers to watch, a predictable cycle—a shiny-eyed guest elbowed their way to a spot at a table, watched their chips dwindle and then let a fresh victim take their place. The clouds of cigar smoke that wafted in the air gave Caleb the feeling that he was peeking in on a sweaty, feverish dream.

As he got used to the click of chips and splutter of decks shuffling, and once he realized that every scream from below wasn't because someone had identified him, Caleb was able to let his mind wander a bit. He hoped that his friends back at the Academy were okay. Caleb thought back on their short phone conversation earlier that day.

"You're supposed to know all the secrets," Caleb had said to Einar after muting their line. "Any idea where Earth Garde would be imprisoning uncooperative Garde?"

"No, I don't know where Earth Garde stores their delinquents," Einar replied. He stroked his chin. "But I have a feeling that Derek King might. There's a reason the Foundation always used him and his men to hunt down Garde. He's plugged in."

"If they've got a place strong enough to hold Six and Sam, they could be using that same place to hide that body-jumping turd," Five said.

Caleb shook his head. "But that would mean Earth Garde's working with the Foundation."

Einar smiled. "You're finally catching up." He waved at the phone. "Tell your friends we'll go looking for their prison. In fact, we'd *love* to help. If King cooperates, we could have some information for them as soon as tonight."

Derek King. The CEO of Blackstone Group. The guy who

gave the orders to mercenaries who had tried to kill Caleb and his friends on multiple occasions.

The guy standing right there, at the head of the craps table, a stupid grin on his handsome face. King wore a tan suit with a lavender dress shirt deeply unbuttoned, his chest bronzed and waxed. A blond woman with a huge mane of curly hair and an hourglass figure was tucked under his arm. She was clad in a low-cut and sparkling red-and-blue dress, looking like a human version of a firework. Derek put his fist in the woman's face, the dice clutched there. She puckered her lips and blew on them.

"Blech," Caleb said.

Caleb couldn't be sure, but he thought Isabela tried about six different looks before catching King's eye. She'd sauntered by the craps table as a dazzling Middle Eastern woman, retreated to an elevator when King didn't take an interest and came back as an icy-eyed blonde in a chic business suit. When that didn't take, Isabela had reappeared as a freckled redhead with a playful smile, then a striking woman clearly modeled after Lexa from the Academy, and eventually even a lithe young man. These were just the appearances she chose that Caleb managed to notice, the ones who glanced up in his direction and winked, or blew a kiss, or briefly flashed a stretch of leg.

Isabela. She couldn't take anything serious.

After hours of trying, it had been the voluptuous trailer-park beauty queen who had caught King's eye. Apparently,

King's tastes skewed towards the cliché. As Caleb watched, Isabela tossed her head back and laughed brightly at some remark King made. Caleb winced.

"I only see one bodyguard. What about you?"

It took some effort for Caleb not to leap to his feet and then more effort not to let loose a duplicate. Ran had sidled up beside him without his even noticing. She'd changed back into Isabela's slinky dress, although this time she'd added a pair of silver leggings.

"Jesus," he said. "You scared me."

"You were very focused."

Caleb cleared his throat. "Yeah, uh, I only see the one big guy, too . . ."

He nodded discreetly towards King's shadow, a rather large man who stood a respectful distance from the craps table but hadn't budged since King arrived. He wore a charcoal suit over his massive frame, dark red hair pulled back in a ponytail, a scar creating a canyon in his otherwise thick beard. He looked like a modern-day Viking.

"He's not wearing an earpiece," Ran observed. "If he was, I would think maybe there are more guards. But it's just the one."

"Einar was right," Caleb admitted begrudgingly. "King feels safe here. This was a good place to target him." He took his eyes off Isabela for a moment to look at Ran, searching for reassurance in her typically serene face. "We're doing the right thing, aren't we? I mean, a part of me still feels like we should be rushing straight back to the Academy."

As usual, Ran considered her words before speaking. "This man, King, he is our enemy. If we can hurt Blackstone, that will hurt the Foundation as well. Also, he could know something about Sam and Six."

Caleb nodded. They'd been over all this before, but he was still searching for a reason not to go along with Einar's idea to interrogate King, even though the plan was already in motion.

He turned his attention back to the craps table. King leaned forward and tossed the dice. They bounced off the back wall and a cheer went up from the gathered crowd. He must have rolled a high number. Or not? Caleb had no idea how craps worked. As Caleb watched, Isabela leaned up to whisper something in King's ear.

"This is gross," Caleb said.

Ran patted his back gently. "It's the mission."

Caleb sighed. "I know, I know. It's just like . . . this guy is evil. And Isabela is . . . I don't know. Forget it. I don't know why it's bothering me so much."

Ran flashed a small smile. "You don't?"

"Why are you looking at me like that?"

"No reason." Ran tilted her chin towards the gaming floor. "It's happening."

Caleb looked down in time to see the croupier passing King a tray filled with tight-packed chips. King handed that off to his large bodyguard, put his arm around Isabela and escorted her away from the craps table. They were on the move.

Caleb shot to his feet, then brushed some wrinkles out of his shirt to appear unhurried. Ran hooked a hand through his arm and the two of them made their way slowly along the balcony level, headed towards the elevator bank.

Down below, King briefly parted from his bodyguard, the brute stopping by a teller's window to turn the chips into a wad of cash. King spent this time letting his hands wander along Isabela's back. She said something and King laughed delightedly. Caleb wondered what it was.

"Does this man really only have one bodyguard?"

That was Duanphen, joining them from the other side of the overlook, where she'd also been keeping watch.

"It appears so," Ran said.

"Good. This will be easy."

"Don't say that," Caleb replied. "You'll jinx us."

They waited for Isabela, King and the bodyguard to board the elevator. Caleb slouched his shoulders.

"Do we look casual enough?"

Ran arched an eyebrow. "Yes, Caleb."

"Last car on the right," Duanphen reported.

They all looked up towards the gold-plated arrow above the elevators that ticked off the floors, watching the last car on the right tick upwards and upwards until, finally, it stopped. Fifteenth floor.

"Just one below our penthouse," Ran said.

"That'll make it easier," Duanphen replied.

Caleb groaned. "The 'e' word again. Haven't you ever been

on one of these missions before? They consistently go sideways."

"Actually, ours tended to go pretty well," Duanphen said. "Until you Academy people showed up in Switzerland."

Caleb punched the button, calling for another elevator. Once they were inside, his foot tapped compulsively, a fact he didn't realize until Ran gave him a gentle nudge.

"Sorry," Caleb said.

As the doors started to close, Duanphen cocked her head to the side. Caleb followed her gaze and caught a glimpse of a wavy-haired girl with a wooly unibrow passing by on the walkway.

"What is it?" He asked Duanphen.

"Nothing," she replied. "I thought I saw someone familiar."

The doors closed and the elevator hissed upwards. Seconds later, the three of them stepped into a typically posh hallway—gold trimming, recessed lighting and doors with ornamental knockers. There was a mirror on the ceiling that Caleb thought was unnecessarily dizzying.

Straight ahead, in front of the door nearest the elevator, King's bodyguard was just beginning to lower his thick frame into an absurdly fragile-looking wicker chair. The bodyguard appraised the three of them with bored, tired eyes, his butt hanging over the seat like he wasn't sure if he should finish sitting down.

Ran looped her arm through Caleb's again and they

stumbled off the elevator in unison, like a pair of messed-up kids coming back from a long night. Duanphen followed behind them, body straight, not bothering with any kind of ruse.

"This ain't your floor," the bodyguard said, deciding to stand up after all.

"No English," Ran replied as they staggered closer.

The bodyguard didn't buy it, not even for a second. His hand darted inside his coat, probably reaching for a weapon.

Too slow.

Ran and Caleb split apart and Duanphen lunged between them. She grabbed the bodyguard's throat and sent a jolt through him.

The bodyguard's knees wobbled and it looked for a moment like he might pass out straightaway. He was a large man, though. Big enough to withstand a shock. He rallied and managed to throw a desperate punch at Duanphen's face.

"Stop—stop, you—you prick—" the bodyguard said through gnashing teeth.

Caleb popped a duplicate to grab the bodyguard's arm. The duplicate danced and twitched as he too was shocked by Duanphen's touch, but held back the bodyguard until the large man collapsed from the volts. Duanphen kept ahold of him for a couple of seconds after he was down.

"Okay, okay," Caleb said. "He's out."

Duanphen stopped shocking the bodyguard but said nothing in response. She brushed off her hands and waited.

"Gotta get him out of sight," Caleb said as he loosed

another pair of duplicates to pick up the unconscious body-guard.

Meanwhile, Ran tried the door to King's hotel room. It was open. Just like they'd planned.

"Took you long enough. This creep was extremely handsy."

Isabela—not the blond lifeguard stereotype, but the real thing—stood over the prone body of Derek King. Caleb found himself smiling with a combination of relief and admiration as he entered the room. It appeared that King had attempted to undress but only managed to get as far as his belt and one shoe—the shoe that Isabela apparently brained him with. There was a decent cut on his forehead, blood trickling down into his eye. King kept dazedly trying to push himself up and, every time, Isabela stepped down on his back, pressing him to the floor.

"Hot," said one of Caleb's duplicates as he observed Isabela striking her glorious pose over the beaten CEO. Caleb cringed at the remark, but he didn't think Isabela heard it.

"Stay down, stupid," Isabela was saying to King.

"Who—who are you?" King mumbled.

"Quiet," Isabela reprimanded him, digging her heel into his back.

Meanwhile, the duplicates had managed to wrestle King's unconscious bodyguard into the room and dumped him on the floor. Once there, they began systematically tearing up bedsheets and using the scraps to bind the large man's wrists and ankles. They wouldn't be the most secure bonds for such a huge guy, but hopefully they'd be long gone by the time he woke up.

Duanphen stood in the doorway for a few seconds, watching and listening for any alarms raised from neighboring rooms. It was quiet. The whole encounter had lasted less than a minute. She closed the door to King's room and locked it behind her.

"Let's get him up," Ran said, coming to stand over King.

Caleb and Ran each grabbed an arm and yanked King to his feet. His eyes were glassy and blinking, still recovering from Isabela knocking him upside the head. Isabela reached out and pinched his cheek.

"Thanks for teaching me craps," she said. "Bye-bye."

Ran and Caleb dragged King towards his room's balcony. At first, he hobbled alongside them, too dazed to fight back. But, when Ran used her telekinesis to push open the balcony doors and the night air rushed in, something clicked on in the man's brain. He started to dig his heels into the carpet and his words became sharper.

"What are you doing?" he demanded. "Don't—don't—!"

It struck Caleb how it must seem to King like they were about to pitch him over the balcony's marble railing.

"We aren't going to hurt you," Caleb said, trying to sound coolly dispassionate.

"You already hurt me," King replied.

"We aren't going to hurt you *more*, then," Caleb said. He didn't want this guy getting too comfortable, though, so he added lamely, "Unless you make us."

Once they were out on the balcony, Ran grabbed a ceramic ashtray off a table and used her Legacy to charge it until it shone bright red. She held the glowing object out over the balcony's edge, waved it back and forth twice, then grunted as she absorbed the energy back into her body, not letting the ashtray detonate.

"What the hell are you doing?" King asked her.

Five floated down from above. His part of this mission had been to hover above the hotel and wait for Ran's signal. King shrank back when the one-eyed Loric grabbed him by the shirtfront.

"Hold—hold on—" King stammered.

"You hold on," Five grunted.

Five started to rise up again, this time with King in his grasp, but hesitated when he realized Caleb was still holding the older man's arm.

"You can let go now," Five said.

"I'm going with you," Caleb replied. "I know this guy's a scumbag, but I'm not leaving him alone with you two for even a few minutes."

Five's lips curled back and he started to snarl some threat, but Ran put a hand on his shoulder. That surprised Caleb.

"Take Caleb," she said to Five. "We'll clean up here and be there soon."

From inside the hotel room, Isabela shouted, "Oh my God, this dude has so many watches!" Clearly, the process of rummaging through King's luggage had begun.

Caleb watched Five, both of them still holding on to King,

who had gone completely silent since the Loric showed up. After a moment, Five shrugged.

"Whatever. Grab on," he said.

Caleb didn't hesitate to wrap his arms around Five's neck in a piggyback position, even though it felt ridiculous and awkward.

King was trying to be stoic now, but he let out a squeak when Five lifted off, still holding the older man by the front of his dress shirt. Caleb thought he could hear fabric ripping. King must have heard it too because he groped at Five's forearms to hold on.

It wasn't much of a flight, really. More like a big leap. Five landed them on the private rooftop garden attached to their penthouse. And there was Einar, seated at a small metal table with a half-eaten steak in front of him, surrounded on all sides by vined trellises and flowers drooping low in the moonlight. A candle flickered on the table, the fire shining in Einar's eyes.

"Hello, Derek," Einar said, a piece of bloody meat paused just in front of his lips. "Thanks for dropping in."

Caleb rolled his eyes. How long had Einar been sitting up here in that exact position with that lukewarm steak in front of him, all so he could deliver that line?

Five shoved King forward. The businessman stumbled— he was still only wearing one shoe. With his telekinesis, Five yanked a chair out from under the table opposite Einar and tilted it so King could fall into it.

"Einar, hold on, hold on—" There was a note of panic in King's voice as Five shoved the chair closer to the table. Caleb stood aside, watching, his hands clasped behind his back.

"Why are you so scared, Derek?" Einar asked with a teasing smile. "I only wanted to catch up."

"I know what you've been doing to Foundation people," King said. He glanced over his shoulder at Five and Caleb, his Adam's apple bobbing in fear. Caleb's stomach turned at being lumped in with these killers. "I'm not working with them anymore," King continued. "I'll tell you whatever you want to know."

Einar raised his eyebrows in surprise. When discussing this interrogation, they'd all expected to have to resort to more threats, or possibly let Einar manipulate King with his Legacy. Einar set down his cutlery and reconsidered King.

"What do you mean you're not working with them anymore?" Einar asked. "I never did a mission for the Foundation that didn't use Blackstone as support personnel."

"They canceled our contract," King said. "Don't need us anymore. They've got the UN boys now."

Caleb stepped forward. "What do you mean by that?"

King glanced over his shoulder. "After Switzerland, the Foundation got in good with Earth Garde. I think that was always their plan. They presented themselves as a nonprofit that's been rescuing abused Garde from non–Earth Garde countries."

"The UN bought that?"

"Sure. Those suckers lapped it up."

"There are good people at Earth Garde, though," Caleb murmured. "I mean, there have to be . . ."

Caleb realized belatedly that he'd already derailed their interrogation. Einar looked exasperated and even King was staring at him like he was the biggest schmuck on the planet.

"Yeah, there's some bleeding-heart types at the UN," King said. "But mostly those guys go to the same cocktail parties as the Foundation people." He glanced at Einar. "Who's the new kid, Einar? He seems a little wet behind the ears to be running with you."

"Don't worry about him," Einar said. "Worry about me."

"Oh, I am." King touched the knot on his forehead, winced and plucked a napkin off the table to dab at the blood. "You know how many good men I lost on those Foundation ops? Was getting so the money they paid didn't cover my costs to train new recruits. I'm glad they let me go when they did. Frankly, you people scare the shit out of me. I'll tell you whatever you want to know."

"How do we find Lucas Sanders?" Einar asked.

"Who?"

"The body-jumper," Einar elaborated. "Blackstone apprehended him months ago."

"That maniac?" King breathed out through his nose. "If I knew, I'd tell you."

Einar's eyes narrowed in suspicion, but Caleb jumped in

before he could ask another question.

"Do you know anything about a prison built to house Garde?"

King thought for a moment. "Actually, the Foundation did have a place in Mexico. Right in the middle of the Chihuahuan Desert. They bought it cheap off the Mexican government and were making some upgrades. Had some of my people assigned there to act as security, clear out the cartels, that kind of thing. Seemed like they were gearing up to hold a lot of you freaks—you people there."

"Why are you speaking in the past tense?" Einar asked.

"I lost the contract on that place a few weeks back, that's why," King replied with a note of bitterness. "Those UN white helmets took over."

"Peacekeepers," Caleb said.

"Yeah. Foundation said something about a subcontract from Earth Garde. Guess they're on the up-and-up now, can't be associating with mercenaries like me. History of every great business, right? Things are illegal until they aren't. Like prohibition, right?"

"Spare us the history lessons, King," Einar said.

"Sorry, sorry," King said with a nervous smile, remembering himself. "Look, if you're trying to track down Lucas Sanders or any of the other Garde that the Foundation have stashed—the ones they can't get to work in the field for them, anyway—" King glanced at Einar. "That's the first place I would check."

"How are they tracking us?" Caleb and Einar asked this question in unison, then both glared at each other. Five snorted, amused.

"They aren't tracking *you*," King answered. "They're tracking *us*. Foundation members whose identities you've compromised. Everyone got their futures read by that pre-cognitive girl they've got."

Einar snorted. "Salma? The one they dress up like a gypsy? She can only see what? Two hours into the future? We used to joke that she couldn't see past her own eyebrow, and that's who you people have doing security? Barnaby auctioning her off is one thing, but using her against us? Insulting."

Caleb remembered the girl Duanphen had caught a glimpse of in the lobby. He started to say something, but King talked over him.

"I guess she's been practicing since you went rogue," King said. "Her readings aren't totally accurate, but she gave us odds on you paying us a visit. Said we might want to change up our routines if we were above forty-two percent. Not sure how they came up with that number. If they're tracking you, that's how. They're staking out your most likely futures."

"What percentage were you?" Einar asked.

"Twenty-four," King said with a chuckle. "I always did like a long shot."

"Was she just here?" Caleb asked. "Salma?"

"No," King said. "My reading was weeks ago. Guess my odds changed."

Einar's steely gaze bored into King, his fingers drumming on the table. Meanwhile, King had relaxed back in his chair, like they were old friends having a chat. The man was being way more cooperative than they'd expected.

But then, if you wanted to hide something from Einar, wouldn't your best chance be to make him think he didn't need to use his Legacy?

"He's lying," Caleb said. "This is too easy."

Einar pursed his lips. "Damn it. I agree with Caleb."

King held up his hands. "What do you mea—?"

And just like that, King's body language changed. He stretched his arms across the table, bumping Einar's plate in his attempt to grab hold of Einar's hands. Einar recoiled and Five lunged forward to shove King back into his seat. The businessman, suddenly vibrating with panic, settled for grasping the sides of the table.

"You have to get out of here," he told Einar.

"What did you do to him?" Caleb asked.

"I'm making him care about me," Einar replied, straightening his cuffs and eyeing King. "I'm the center of his world now."

"You're my everything," King agreed. "But I lied to you before. The Foundation's psychic didn't put me at twenty-four percent. It was *ninety*-four. And it was hours ago. They know you're here, Einar."

Caleb's stomach tightened. He looked over at Five, the Loric scowling at King. "You should get the ship," Caleb said. "We might need to book."

"He's right," Einar said, standing up. "We shouldn't stay here."

"No," King said. "You really shouldn't. I lied about something else, too. I do know where Lucas Sanders is."

Einar leaned forward. "Where?"

"He's downstairs," King said. "Inside my bodyguard."

CHAPTER THIRTEEN

TAYLOR COOK

THE HUMAN GARDE ACADEMY—POINT REYES, CALIFORNIA

PEACEKEEPERS LINED THE PATHWAY LEADING FROM the Academy to their encampment, their weapons down, all of their eyes shining with varying degrees of awe, respect and fear. As she marched through their ranks, Taylor couldn't help but square her shoulders a little bit. It was empowering, to be looked at like that. Kopano would've loved it. Even though those stares weren't really directed at her, Taylor was at least adjacent.

"Mr. Smith!" A dark-haired Peacekeeper with a thick New York accent shoved through some of his fellow guards. Taylor braced herself, but he wasn't armed. He came right up to John and insisted on shaking his hand. "I was in the city during the invasion. You saved my life, man! I always wanted to thank you. I joined the frigging Peacekeepers *because* of you."

"You don't have to thank me," John said, patting the Peacekeeper's shoulder.

"I don't buy into this whole Inhibitor thing either," the Peacekeeper blurted. "That's probably why they're transferring me out—"

"Give him some room, LaRussa!" one of the other Peacekeepers shouted. With a regretful smile, LaRussa sank back into the crowd. The escort John and Taylor had picked up out at the crash site marched them onward, deeper into what Taylor now thought of as enemy territory.

"You get that a lot?" Taylor asked, under her breath.

"Yeah," John replied. "It never stops being awkward."

Taylor turned her attention to the encampment. She'd been here before, once during her group's ill-fated odyssey off campus and again during her supervised meeting with her dad. She remembered the squat metal buildings that served as bunkhouses and mess halls, the armory, the tall fences with their mounted security cameras and the incongruous picnic area and cabin set aside for family visitations.

What she didn't remember were the tents. The canvas enclosures filled every space between buildings, the population of Peacekeepers in the encampment swelling to fill them. Taylor couldn't be sure of the head count, but it seemed like there were at least five times as many soldiers stationed here than there had been during her last visit.

Well, Greger *had* promised them an army.

The Academy had cameras pointed at the Peacekeeper encampment. They would know if the soldiers made a move, but they weren't capable of seeing the interior of the camp. She didn't know there would be so many of them. When Taylor got back, she'd suggest to Nine that they sneak someone over the fence to plant some more eyes.

Assuming she made it back.

Taylor expected to be led to the building where the Peacekeepers conducted their official briefings. Instead, their silent escort brought them directly to a trailer in the middle of camp. Archibald's private quarters. The thought of being in such a tight space alarmed Taylor more than being among all those Peacekeepers. Outside, at least John could fly them away.

"You can blast us out of here if this is a trap, right?" Taylor asked John as the Peacekeeper leading the way banged on Archibald's door.

"I'm hoping not to do any blasting. We don't want to set things off," John said. Taylor gave him an exasperated look. "But yeah. We'll be okay."

They caught Archibald wearing a tank top and his uniform pants, dragging an electric razor across his cheeks. The old soldier had a good poker face, but Taylor noticed how his eyes widened a fraction to find John on his doorstep.

"Colonel Ray Archibald?" John began. "I'm—"

"I know who you are," Archibald replied. "Malcolm told us you were on campus. Come to explain the Mogadorian scout ship you crashed into my Academy yesterday?"

Taylor bristled at Archibald calling the place his, but kept her mouth shut.

"I am," John said politely.

Archibald turned to Taylor. "And you, Ms. Cook. Are you here to turn yourself in for processing? I believe you were paged around oh-nine-hundred."

"Hell no," Taylor replied.

"Good, then," Archibald said. "Come on in."

Archibald stepped aside and, in the same motion, dismissed the Peacekeeper escort. He wanted to be alone with them. Interesting.

The inside of Archibald's trailer was as Spartan and clean as the man himself. The only decorations were a pile of books on counterinsurgency tactics and a stack of washed TV dinner trays by the sink. Otherwise, it looked like Archibald barely lived here.

"You're lucky the Peacekeepers who brought you in are loyal to me," Archibald said as he shut the door. "Most of the others here would've taken you directly to Karlsson."

"What does that mean?" Taylor asked. "I thought you're supposed to be head of security."

"So did I," Archibald replied. He set aside his razor, found his shirt and started putting it on. "My position that we shouldn't be antagonizing the Academy's students and creating a dangerous environment hasn't made me very popular. The Peacekeepers coming in on Greger's orders are hard-line about enforcing Earth Garde's new policies."

"You know those policies are messed up, right?" Taylor asked, stepping in front of John. "People from the Foundation are manipulating Earth Garde."

Archibald sighed. "I'm a soldier. Ultimately, I can only follow orders. And right now, after Switzerland, the prevailing attitude towards you people is that you're dangerous weapons in need of regulation." His eyes flicked to John. "I'd hoped you were here to bring me some good news."

Taylor realized that in her eagerness to vent at Archibald, she'd pushed John into the background. She stepped aside and John gave her a grateful look.

"I'm here to inform you that tomorrow the *Osiris*, the Mogadorian warship at-large behind the moon, will descend at a safe distance up the coast from here."

"Jesus H. Christ," Archibald replied. "You know there's a standing order to nuke that son of a bitch as soon as it's in range?"

"Yeah, don't let them do that," John replied. "Thanks to the efforts of Taylor here and some other students at the Academy, the Mogadorians have agreed to surrender themselves and be relocated to Alaska. The war will finally, officially be over."

"Just as a new war gets started," Taylor murmured.

"Brief me," Archibald said. "Tell me everything."

Taylor sat back and listened as John unspooled the story just like he'd said. It was Taylor who had made contact with the warship while on assignment for the Foundation. It was Taylor who brought that information back to Nine, who contacted John. The Academy's students had helped prepare John to negotiate with the Mogs and had ultimately contributed to their peaceful surrender. When the background was finished, John gave Archibald the coordinates for the warship's landing.

John's earnest way of speaking made the lie sound pretty good. Archibald looked at Taylor with a newfound respect. So what if she hadn't exactly earned it? She deserved credit for trying to stop the Foundation, but no one at Earth Garde was going to give her a medal for that.

"I'll pass along your report to my superiors," Archibald said. "We'll get the area secured and prepare transport for the Mogadorians."

"And make sure they know we're here to help," Taylor added. "You know, if they're not forcing us to get brain surgery at the time."

"Okay, Ms. Cook," Archibald replied. "Point taken."

A walkie-talkie on Archibald's kitchen counter buzzed to life. "Heads up, sir." Taylor recognized the voice of LaRussa, the Peacekeeper who had gushed over John outside. "Static on the way."

Taylor tensed. That sounded like a warning to her.

"What does that mean?" John asked.

"It means we better step outside," Archibald replied. "Karlsson is on the way."

Sure enough, a large group of Peacekeepers had massed in a semicircle in front of Archibald's trailer. They carried a mix of weaponry—the electrified-collar cannons that Taylor had seen before, but also traditional shotguns and assault rifles. It was an ominous sight and Taylor immediately felt the urge to shrink back as she stepped outside behind the colonel. At least it was heartening that some of the soldiers' eyes widened nervously when John emerged behind her.

Greger stood in the midst of the Peacekeepers, a corny smile on his overly moisturized face. The liaison had donned a bulletproof vest beneath his tailored jacket. Taylor rolled her eyes. If they were going to hurt Greger, it sure wouldn't be with bullets.

"Colonel Archibald, I wasn't aware of a meeting with our most esteemed guest," Karlsson said, his eyes flicking at John.

"It's a security matter," Archibald replied coolly. "I was coming to brief you now."

"Mm-hmm," Karlsson replied. His smile widened as he looked at Taylor. "Hello there, Ms. Cook. I summoned you hours ago, but I suppose I shouldn't expect a teenager to be punctual. At least you showed up, unlike the rest of your classmates."

Faced with so many guns and soldiers, it took Taylor a moment to find her voice. She'd seen worse and deadlier in Mongolia. She wasn't going to be cowed by a bully and his thugs.

"I didn't come here for your bullshit processing," she said, her voice intentionally loud.

"Then you're in violation of the Garde Accord and—"

Taylor had been thinking about this moment since John first asked her to come with him. She'd been dwelling on everything that was wrong with Earth Garde and the Academy, everything that would need to be fixed. She hadn't actually put any of that into words, though; she hadn't rehearsed a speech or even consulted the other students. Taylor decided to wing it.

"Nope," Taylor cut in. "You guys at Earth Garde have proven that you don't have our best interests at heart, so we're done with that whole Garde Accord thing until we get some changes."

Greger chuckled. "You're in no position to make demands."

"First of all, we don't want anything installed in our brains or other parts of our bodies," Taylor continued, undeterred. "We want the guaranteed right to say no to any mission that Earth Garde sends us on—Earth Garde *or* any of its shady affiliate programs. Yeah, we know all about what you pulled with Ran and Kopano, Greg. That's not going to fly."

"*Greger*," the liaison corrected testily. "This is ridiculous."

Taylor didn't stop. She was on a roll now. "Plus, we don't want you guys deciding who's ready to graduate or what kind of jobs they should do. We want like a . . . a . . ."

"A council," John supplied.

"A council," Taylor said. "You can have some UN representatives on it, but there should be an equal amount of Garde, too. Human *and* Loric. Dudes like you have proven you can't be allowed to make decisions for people like me."

"This isn't debate club," Karlsson said with a snort. "You don't get to come out here and begin making demands. The world doesn't work like that."

Again, Taylor ignored him. Archibald was listening to

her. So were the Peacekeepers. Her message would get back to people above Greger. Maybe people who could be reasoned with.

"Until our demands are met and the Garde Accord revised, we aren't coming out of the Academy," Taylor said. "You don't scare us. And if you try to come on campus without permission, we're prepared to defend ourselves."

Greger's lips curled back. "Young lady, you are pouring gasoline on an already combustible situation. Earth Garde has determined what's necessary to protect humanity from your kind. Being firmly regulated will, in turn, make all Garde safer."

He made it all sound so sensible.

"Bullshit," Taylor responded.

"You're only making matters worse," Greger said. He turned to John, appealing to the Loric. "I'd hoped you were here to talk sense into Nine and the others. To lead by example. To receive your own Inhibitor . . ."

John's eyebrows went up at that. Maybe he'd thought the Loric would somehow be exempt from Earth Garde's new rule. After a moment, he pointed his thumb at Taylor. "No. Sorry," John said. "I'm with her."

"The Inhibitors are a compromise," Greger said, his voice more plaintive now. "I know it seems invasive, but it's for the best. Everyone will feel more comfortable—"

Taylor interrupted again. "I think I speak for every Garde when I say that we don't give a shit about your comfort."

"Uh, the thing is— You don't speak for all of us."

The Peacekeepers stepped aside to allow Melanie Jackson to step through their ranks. The blond-haired poster girl for Earth Garde looked a lot better than the last time Taylor saw her—covered in blood and mud, crying and shaking. She was back to her camera-ready glow, dressed in a snug blue-and-white Earth Garde uniform. Melanie pinned Taylor with a look of mean-girl condescension that took Taylor back to high school.

And she wasn't alone.

Walking up behind Melanie was the Chinese healer Jiao Lin who Taylor last saw working for the Foundation in Mongolia. She had traded in her Foundation-financed high fashion for a uniform identical to Melanie's. Jiao smiled when Taylor noticed her and wiggled her lacquered fingernails.

"Damn, it's so weird seeing you do this whole inspiring-leader shtick. When I was at the Academy, you were scared of your own shadow."

That came from Lofton St. Croix. The lean Canadian hadn't gotten rid of his matted, granola dreadlocks since joining Earth Garde, nor his smug sneer. His uniform didn't fit as well as Melanie's or Jiao's, probably on account of the quills protruding from his forearms and shoulders. He could project those little spikes at will. As he eyed Taylor, Lofton snapped one of his quills off his arm and began picking his teeth with it.

"How's Isabela?" he asked. "Still hot for me?"

"Okay, Lofton, we agreed you wouldn't talk," Melanie

snapped, and Lofton held up his hands in response. She turned her attention back to Taylor. "I'm glad you're here, Taylor. Honestly. Even if you're all mad and stuff. We're here to clear up some of the misconceptions about the Cêpan program and the Inhibitor chips. I'd like to come onto campus and talk to some of the students."

"No," Taylor said immediately. "No way, sellout."

"I think everyone on campus understands what's happening," John added evenly.

Melanie made a pouty face. "Come on, guys. You're being ridiculous. Don't you think the students deserve to hear both sides?"

Taylor ignored her, turning instead to face Greger. "You've got our demands. Let us know when you're ready to talk."

"Are you going already?" Jiao asked.

The Peacekeepers shifted and Taylor felt an imperceptible tightening of the circle around her.

"Easy now," Archibald said. Taylor got the sense that these soldiers listened to Greger instead of the colonel. He couldn't help them.

She felt the first tug then. Someone pushing her with telekinesis. Trying to force her down to her knees.

John must have felt it too because he quickly put his arm around Taylor's waist. There was a rush of air and then the Peacekeepers and Earth Garde receded away. She was flying. Well, John Smith was flying, holding Taylor against him with ease, like she weighed nothing.

"Sorry, I didn't mean to presume," John said. "But that

was getting ugly."

"No. We definitely needed to bail," Taylor said into the wind. She could see the full layout of the Academy below them—the dorms, the training center, the Peacekeepers massed at the border, their makeshift barricade that suddenly seemed flimsy. Her eyes watered from the crisp wind. "They aren't going to give up, are they?"

"No, I don't think so," John said. He started to float them downwards, towards the clear grass of the quad. "I know you want to make a safe place for our people. It's noble. I want that too. And I know you think that place should be here. But you need to consider the very real possibility that this place could fall."

Taylor's shoulders tightened. She pulled away from John as soon as their feet hit the ground. "So what are you suggesting? That we give up and let Earth Garde put their Inhibitors in us?"

"No. Of course not."

She laughed incredulously. "Then what? Should I convince the entire student body to leave the Academy and move to India with you?"

John Smith didn't blink.

"Yes."

CHAPTER FOURTEEN

ISABELA SILVA
LE ROYAL MANSOUR—CASABLANCA, MOROCCO

"OH MY GOD, THIS DUDE HAS SO MANY WATCHES!" Isabela cried out as she rummaged through Derek King's luggage. One by one, she slipped five expensive timepieces onto her arm, each one a different glittering metal. "Who travels with five different watches?"

"You are supposed to be looking for intel," Ran said from the other room, where she and Duanphen were tying up King's bloated bodyguard.

"Intel," Isabela muttered. "I don't know what that looks like." She held up her arm, clinking the watches together. "This would pay my family's rent for a year."

Isabela prepared herself for another reprimand. Sometimes it seemed like all these people did was chide her, even when she'd done a good job. All of them sitting around and watching while Isabela paraded about in her different forms, then endured hours of King Loser groping her and blowing his peanut-smelling breath all over her neck. She was entitled to go through his stuff and add the most expensive items to her growing hoard on that gross spaceship. It was only fair.

Surprisingly, Ran didn't say anything else. Instead, Isabela heard a grunt of pain and a thump as something hit the floor.

Isabela stood up from her crouch over King's luggage and called into the living room. "What was that? Did the fathead wake up?"

Duanphen appeared in the doorway to the bedroom, a weird little smile on her face.

"Hello there," she said.

"Uh, hey," Isabela replied. She started to slide King's watches off her arm. "I didn't find anything. You two finished?" She tossed a gold Rolex in Duanphen's direction. "Check that out. Guy's loaded."

Duanphen caught the watch in the air with her telekinesis, spun it around and then whipped it back at Isabela's head. Isabela was too surprised to even duck. She cried out as the watch struck her on the cheek, opening a cut there.

"*Vaca!*" Isabela shouted. "Why—?"

"Aw, come on now," Duanphen said with a laugh. "You had to know all that covetousness would end in consequences."

Isabela stared. It was Duanphen's voice, but she suddenly had one of those twangy American accents.

"Shit," Isabela said, realizing that while it might have been Duanphen's body stalking towards her, it wasn't Duanphen at the controls.

"You know, when I first read the file on you, I was like—hey, me and this girl are pretty similar. We both try on other people's skin. But the more I thought about it—and now, seeing you in action—I realized that we ain't the same at all. You're nothing but a petty liar. A little thief. Stealing people's forms. Tricking them. All for your own gain. It's downright devilish, what you do."

As Duanphen closed in on her, Isabela leaped onto the bed and then stumbled to the other side, putting the furniture between them. It might not have seemed like it to her companions, but Isabela had been paying attention when they talked about this Lucas bastard. She couldn't let him touch her or he'd be able to possess her. Or, if not that, he'd use Duanphen's electrified skin against her. Isabela wasn't eager to experience either outcome.

Duanphen circled around to cut off Isabela's path to the door. "Me, on the other hand? When I'm inside a person, I'm doing the Lord's work."

"My English isn't so good," Isabela said. "But that sounded nasty."

Isabela managed a glimpse through the doorway. She could see Ran slumped over in the other room, her body right next to the sleeping bodyguard. She was breathing, at least, but must have been shocked into unconsciousness by Duanphen.

She needed to stall. That was the right move. Either until Ran woke up or the guys came back down to check on her.

Although, if Lucas was allowed to touch Five or even Einar, the rest of them wouldn't stand a chance. Best to keep him talking, though, while she figured something out.

Luckily, Lucas seemed happy to flap his borrowed gums, rambling on through Duanphen.

"I see right into people's hearts and decide if they're worthy. It's my calling. There's no better judge on this plane of existence than me. This one, for example?" He shook out Duanphen's limbs. "Do you know how many people she's hurt? Hell of a lot. Beating people up for pocket change." He fired off a dramatic high kick. "What a sad, sorry life. What a waste of potential, slithering around in dark alleys, hiding from the Lord's light."

"You don't know her," Isabela snapped. "Shut up."

"I know she trusts you more than anyone else in this little group. She's got a crush on you." Duanphen made a face, like she'd tasted something sour. "Blech. Unnatural."

There was another option besides stalling. Isabela could go on the offensive. Knock this sicko out cold and send him back to his own body. That might mean hurting Duanphen, but she didn't think her friend would care. She used to do fight club. Girl was used to getting clocked in the head.

Isabela let a slow, confident smile spread across her face.

This trailer-trash zealot thought he could mess with her head? Please. She invented mind games.

Duanphen made another lunge towards her, then stopped abruptly when Isabela changed shape.

She'd seen pictures of the late Reverend Jimbo all over the bar where the Harvesters held a wake for their assassinated leader. She'd heard his voice on the recording Einar played them. Isabela's approximation of Lucas's father wasn't perfect, but it was close enough.

"Lucas!" Isabela boomed. "I'm up here with Jesus and we both think you're a piece of trash."

"Bitch!" Duanphen shouted. "You take that mask off!"

Duanphen sprung forward, her fingers crackling with electricity. It was a sloppy move and Isabela was quick, even as Jimbo. She ducked under Duanphen's grasping hand and swept her legs out from under her. Duanphen stumbled forward, crashing against the nightstand.

"Sonny boy, I can't believe you sprung from my saintly balls," Isabela crowed, bouncing back on her heels and into the living room where there was more room to maneuver. "You ain't right."

A wild look in her eyes, Duanphen shrieked and charged after her. Isabela stood still, let her come.

When he was almost on top of her, Isabela used her telekinesis to grab an unopened champagne bottle from where it sat chilling on the table. She let it fly, striking Duanphen right in the temple. The bottle exploded, foam and champagne spewing everywhere, shards of green glass tinkling onto the carpet. Duanphen fell down in a soaking heap right at Isabela's feet.

"Sorry," she said, changing back to her normal shape.

"Sneaky," Duanphen grunted, on her hands and knees. "Very sneaky."

Damn. Duanphen must have had an exceptionally hard head. Isabela had failed to displace Lucas. Not wanting to get too close, she danced backwards, looking around for something else to hit her with.

"You freak, get out of her!" Isabela shouted in frustration.

"Make me," Duanphen replied petulantly.

As Isabela looked on, Duanphen snatched up one of the larger pieces of glass from the carpet. Blood dripped down the side of her head, pinkish where it mixed with the champagne. Her eyes focused on Isabela. That crooked smile returned, giving Isabela a chill.

"Make me," she said again, calmer now, and then dug the glass into Duanphen's forearm.

"What're you doing?" Isabela shouted. "Stop!"

It was her instinct to race forward and try to stop Duanphen from hurting herself. Isabela realized that she'd made a mistake, but it was too late.

"Got you," Duanphen whispered, and brushed a bloody hand across Isabela's cheek.

The world fell away. A blackness closed in on her, like someone had pulled a hood over her head.

A glittering disco ball spun over Isabela's head, dangling from crisscrossed wooden rafters. Strobe lights flashed and a fog machine belched cool mist.

"Oh no," Isabela said.

She stood in the middle of an empty warehouse. Confetti and glitter and red plastic cups littered the floor. There should have been music—Isabela remembered music—but the only sound was the too-fast beating of her own heart, reverberating through the speakers mounted near the unoccupied DJ booth.

"No," Isabela repeated. "No, no, no."

This was the place. She'd been partying here just weeks before the invasion. Someone dropped a cigarette into a puddle of spilled paint thinner and the whole place went up in flames. She couldn't get out.

Isabela looked down at her hands. Wavy burn scars covered the backs. She tried to use her Legacy to transform herself, but it didn't work.

This wasn't real. It couldn't be. A second ago, she'd been fighting that freak in King's hotel room and now—

"This is in my head," Isabela said.

There was fire. She could smell the smoke but not see the flames. Sweat dripped down the back of her shirt.

Across the room, a neon exit sign flashed. Isabela ran for it, desperately needing to get out of this place. But even sprinting, it felt impossible to make any progress. The warehouse's makeshift dance floor kept getting wider and wider. And, somehow, the closer she got to the exit, the smaller the door became, shrinking into the wall like something out of *Alice in Wonderland*.

Isabela wiped a hand across her face. Her eyes were watering or maybe she was crying. The air was hot now. It burned her lungs. She was in hell.

"Don't be dumb," she said to herself. "This is all bullshit."

She forced herself forward. This room wasn't so big, the air not so hot. If this was happening inside her own mind—like a dream—then she should be able to exert some control.

Isabela willed herself to make it to the other side of the room and—just like that—she was there. The exit door was still shrunken, though. It was like the tiny portal of a dollhouse. Isabela needed to crouch down on the floor to push open the door with her index finger. Light spilled in from the other side. Isabela wedged herself in close to the wall, putting her eye up to the opening.

Through the door, she could see into the hotel room, where it seemed like only seconds had passed since she'd been fighting with possessed Duanphen. Isabela realized that she was peeking out through her own eyes, a fact which felt both disorienting and enraging.

"Let me go, you bastard!" she screamed into the tiny opening, but there was no response. No one could hear her. Or—if Lucas could—he was ignoring her.

Duanphen sat on the floor looking dazed, the girl getting paler and paler as blood seeped from the gash in her arm. She clutched at the wound in an effort to stop the bleeding.

"The good news for you is that the Foundation doesn't want ya back," Isabela heard her own voice say with a dreadful Southern accent. "Gosh, I suppose that's also the bad news."

And with that, Lucas kicked Duanphen in the face with Isabela's foot. Duanphen couldn't offer any defense at all—her head rocked back and she tipped over, unconscious.

"Stop it," Isabela whispered.

Lucas swung his gaze towards Ran—she was still out cold, slumped next to the bodyguard. He clapped Isabela's hands.

"Suppose them others should be along any second," he declared. He was narrating. He must have been able to sense that she was watching.

Lucas knelt down over Duanphen and cradled her head. Made it look like he was trying to help her.

He had Isabela posed just like that when Caleb burst in through the balcony doors.

"Holy shit!" Caleb exclaimed, seeing the wreck of the room, the carnage all around. "Isabela?"

Lucas made Isabela hold out one of her hands.

"Caleb," her voice said. "Help me!"

Trapped in that perpetually burning warehouse, eye pressed to the solitary opening, the real Isabela pounded her fists against the walls of her prison.

"Caleb!" she shouted. "Don't!"

But he couldn't hear her.

CHAPTER FIFTEEN

CALEB CRANE
ISABELA SILVA
LE ROYAL MANSOUR—CASABLANCA, MOROCCO

RAN WAS CRUMPLED IN A HEAP ON THE FLOOR NEXT to the hog-tied bodyguard. Duanphen was also unconscious and looked half-dead, clutched in Isabela's arms. A lot of blood. Too much blood. And Isabela wild-eyed, grasping for him.

Caleb took all these details in quickly, seconds after he kicked open the balcony door. He'd been dropped off there by Five, the Loric flying at top speed back to their cloaked skimmer. Einar had stayed behind in the penthouse garden to keep an eye on Derek King. If Lucas was still here, it was too dangerous to risk his possessing either of them. It was up to Caleb to sort this out.

"She attacked me," Isabela said. "I didn't know what to do."

If Lucas had been controlling King's bodyguard, then he

must have jumped to Duanphen when she used her electrified touch. Then, Caleb reasoned, he must have used
Duanphen to take out Ran, but encountered trouble when it
came to Isabela. Caleb knew that Isabela could handle herself in a scrap, could be vicious. She might have knocked out
Duanphen and sent Lucas flying back to his own body.

Or . . .

"I think I hurt her too bad," Isabela said shakily. "I didn't
mean to. Please, Caleb, help me stop the bleeding."

She didn't quite sound right, but then, that could've been
on account of Duanphen bleeding to death in her arms.

Still, there was only one way to know for sure.

"It's okay, baby," Caleb declared. "You're safe now."

Swift strides carried him across the room, where he knelt
down next to Isabela. She smiled at him and grasped his
hand.

"Calling me baby! What the hell is wrong with you, you stupid, stupid boy?" Isabela seethed, watching through the tiny
doorway as Caleb came too close. She saw her hand reach
out to pass along Lucas. Her fingers brushed against Caleb's
in what felt like slow motion.

The disco ball hovering overhead stopped moving, beams
of light frozen in midair. The warehouse began to come apart
in chunks. It was like Isabela's world was a puzzle and that
puzzle was sliding off a table, the pieces breaking free from
each other. Through the gaps, she could see the real world
through her own eyes—Caleb, Duanphen, the hotel room.

She felt herself being pulled into that space. Released.

Lucas was letting her go. Which meant he was taking over Caleb.

She readied herself. She would have only seconds to react. She'd need to hit Caleb hard and fast, put him down before Lucas could create any duplicates. The idiot had a good punch in the mouth coming for falling so easily into Lucas's trap.

"Come on," Isabela said, psyching herself up, clenching her fists in this bullshit dreamland and hoping that would make her hands ready when she regained control of her body. "Come on!"

But then, suddenly, the warehouse snapped back into place.

Lucas still had her.

The moment Isabela had taken his hand, her frightened mask slipped away and Caleb saw that same crooked smile he remembered from Italy. But now, a heartbeat later, that smile was gone, replaced by a brow furrowed in confusion.

"You . . ." Isabela sounded bewildered. She sounded Southern. "You ain't human."

"That's rude," Caleb's duplicate replied. "I have feelings, you know."

The duplicate grabbed Isabela in a bear hug, squeezing her tight and lifting her off her feet. She screamed in frustration and head-butted the duplicate, not at all mindful of the welt that immediately formed on Isabela's cheek.

"Go," the real Caleb said from his spot on the balcony. "Don't let him hurt her."

Four more duplicates charged into the room. Together with the original, they quickly wrestled Isabela's arms behind her back and secured her legs. One of them looped a forearm under her chin in a loose chokehold, the duplicate totally ignoring Isabela's teeth gnashing into its flesh.

"Devils!" Isabela screamed. "Get your hands off me!"

Objects swirled through the air—broken glass from a champagne bottle, a chair, a vase filled with orchids. One of Caleb's duplicates went down under this bombardment of telekinetic debris, but the others were able to maintain their grip.

"Cover her face," Caleb commanded. "Don't let her aim—"

A couch exploded through the balcony doors. Caleb dove aside at the last possible second. A pillow landed on his head, but otherwise the bulk of the furniture missed him. The couch broke the balcony's railing and sailed into the night.

As he picked himself up, Caleb hazarded a look below. There were red and blue flashing lights at the hotel's entrance. Police, at best. A highly trained mercenary kill squad, at worst. Either way, their cover here was blown. They needed to move. Where was Five with that ship?

The duplicates managed to cover Isabela's head with a pillowcase, making her telekinetic aim less accurate. Caleb sent two more duplicates into the room, one to try shaking Ran awake and the other to tie a tourniquet around Duanphen's

arm. That first-aid class everyone took at the Academy had
come in handy.

"Caleb?" Einar called down from the balcony above. "Are
you alive? Are you yourself?"

Caleb looked up. He could just see Einar's head poking
over the edge of the terrace.

"I'm fine," Caleb said. "Duanphen and Ran are down."

"Dead?"

"No. Hurt. And Lucas is possessing Isabela."

There was a whoosh of air as the skimmer descended at
speed, blowing Einar's meticulous hair out of place as it hov-
ered directly above him. A hatch opened up in the ship's
belly, a rope ladder dangling down in front of the Icelandic
boy.

"Knock her out and let's go," Einar said sharply. "We've
got what we came for."

Reluctantly, Caleb peered back into the hotel room, where
Isabela continued to squirm against his duplicates. She
twisted her body in such a way that he was worried that she
might dislocate something, but the duplicates did a good job
of restraining her.

"I don't want to hurt her," Caleb said.

"It's hurt her or leave her behind," Einar said, grasping
the bottom rung of the ladder. "Decide quickly."

Isabela clapped her hands as the Calebs overwhelmed her
physical body, the noise echoing in the empty warehouse.
"Yes! You're smarter than you look!" she cheered. Her lips

quirked to the side as one of the duplicates hugged her from behind. "Always looking for an excuse to grope me."

Suddenly, a curtain fell over the tiny aperture she'd been peering through. They'd covered her head with something so that Lucas couldn't see. That was a good move, she supposed, although it meant Isabela was stuck in here with nothing to do.

"I need you to bring him out."

Isabela jumped as a man's authoritative voice came from behind her. She spun around, but there was no one there.

"Are you kidding me?" A woman's voice answered the first. "Salma just checked in. She says they're close."

There was a crack in the wall opposite Isabela. It hadn't sealed back up after the mental prison briefly came apart when Lucas tried to jump into Caleb's duplicate. She glanced back at the tiny doorway that opened onto her own eyes— still nothing to see there—then walked towards the sound of the voices.

As soon as she moved, the room tilted. Upended. Like she was inside a cube that had been flipped on its side. She fell backwards, landing right next to the tiny doorway. The crack in the opposite wall was now high above her on the ceiling. And, to make matters worse, the fire that had died down when Isabela reached the doorway now started back up again, the room heating up, smoke billowing in from unseen crevices.

"Oh, so you don't want me to go that way?" Isabela said aloud, standing up on what had once been the warehouse's wall. She smirked. "Too bad I know your tricks now."

Isabela crouched down, her legs pulled in tight. This was her mind. Lucas might be able to keep her stuck in here and use her trauma to keep her scared, but, ultimately, he didn't make the rules. She did.

It was like pushing off the wall of a swimming pool. Isabela imagined herself gliding across water. She extended her legs and raised her arms and it was so. She floated towards the crack in the ceiling, spinning through smoke and the winking lights of the disco ball.

This was how she'd felt in those moments before the fire had claimed her. Dancing. Free.

She landed on the ceiling, right up against the crack where the light came through.

"That Karlsson fool is losing control of the situation at the Academy," said the man. "But an opportunity we can't pass up has presented itself. We need to get Lucas in position."

"And what if, at this very moment, he's eliminating Einar?" the woman asked in response. "You want to take responsibility for blowing that?"

Peeking through the crack, Isabela could see into a harshly lit white room. Above her, fluorescent lights were drilled into a concrete ceiling. She could hear the steady *beep-beep* of a heart monitor and glimpsed an IV bag nearby.

She was looking through Lucas's eyes.

Isabela got the sense that Lucas's real body—temporarily abandoned while he hijacked hers—was lying on a gurney. His wrists and ankles were bound to railings that ran up either side. The room was completely devoid of decorations—a cell, definitely—except for the nearest wall. A painting of Jesus cuddling a lamb hung there.

A woman stood over Lucas. She was in her forties but could have passed for younger; her lips and eyes had the tightened skin of someone who got regular work done. She seemed sharp and coldly beautiful, yet she was dressed in a frumpy woolen frock and a dowdy turtleneck. A prominent golden crucifix dangled from around her neck.

On the other side of the bed stood a man in his fifties, skin tanned to a leathery brown. He was well built and rigid in posture, which suggested a military background to Isabela. He wore a dark blue suit that bulged in the breast from the pistol strapped beneath. Isabela's attention was drawn to his right hand, which was covered by a mechanized glove with a digital interface on the back. Strange. She wondered what that did.

The man met Isabela's gaze and she reflexively shrank back from the crack in the wall, even though she knew he couldn't actually see her.

"You know his eyes are open," the man observed.

The woman looked down at Lucas's face, unhidden disgust in her eyes. "Yes. He does that sometimes." She snapped her fingers over Lucas's head. "I'm going to personally shoot you in the face when we're done with you," she told him, then glanced up at the man. "He's not aware while in this state."

"You better hope not," the man replied. He tapped a

sequence into the keypad on the back of his glove. "I'm going to bring him out."

The woman raised a hand in warning. "Again, I have to object. If he's in the middle of doling out his judgment and we yank him back, he'll be very upset. If he comes unglued and we're forced to sedate him, he'll be no good for whatever mission you want him on next."

The man gave her a level look. "That's why you're here. You're his Cêpan. You're meant to keep him calm."

"It's not so easy, Warden," the Cêpan replied.

"You sound afraid of him."

"I'm afraid of *all* of them," she hissed back.

Isabela took all this in. The woman was Lucas's Cêpan, part of that idiotic program they'd been talking about on the news. She was in charge of controlling him. And the man—Warden—was that his name or was it his job? Could this be the person in charge of the Foundation's holding facility?

"I see you," Isabela whispered through the crack in the ceiling. "I see you."

She memorized their faces.

One of Caleb's duplicates pulled Duanphen onto the balcony. She was still unconscious and looked deathly pale, but at least the duplicate had stopped the bleeding with a torn bed-sheet. With Einar on board, the skimmer dropped enough altitude so that the ladder dangled right next to Caleb. He wasn't exactly sure how he'd manage to drag Duanphen's limp body up there. Luckily, Five chose that moment to jump out of the skimmer's underbelly, floating down to the balcony.

"Damn," Five grimaced, after taking one look at Duanphen. "Here. Let me take her."

While Five flew back up to the ship, Caleb turned his attention to the hotel room. His duplicates were still restraining Isabela. A muffled stream of invective came from beneath the pillowcase covering her head—demons, sinners, judgment. Caleb couldn't understand most of it, but he got the gist.

With one of Caleb's duplicates gently shaking her shoulders, Ran finally came awake. Her first reaction was to backhand the duplicate away from her.

"Mean," the duplicate said, rubbing its cheek.

"Sorry," Ran replied. She did a full-body shudder, still feeling the effects of getting shocked by Duanphen. Her eyes quickly scanned the room—the damage, the blood, the team of duplicates wrangling a hooded and screaming Isabela. "What happened? What *is* happening?"

"Lucas," the duplicate reported, glancing sidelong at Isabela. "Most of my brothers are having fun wrestling, but I'm more of a gentle soul. I think we should try talking to this guy. Maybe some peer mediation. Explain that we don't *want* him to kill us."

"Hmm," Ran replied.

Caleb absorbed the duplicate that was apparently one of his softer sides and shouted to Ran from the balcony. "Come on, Ran! We need to go!"

She cocked her head at Caleb, nodded and then did the exact opposite. Instead of going for the exit, she walked to where Isabela was and yanked the pillowcase off her head. Immediately, objects began to whip around the room, tossed by Isabela's telekinesis. Caleb steeled himself, not sure how much damage his duplicates could take but ready to make more. He didn't have to bother. Ran swatted down each flying lamp and shard of broken glass with her own Legacy. When King's misplaced loafer came rocketing at her head, she snatched it right out of midair.

"Enough," she said. "Lucas Sanders. My name is Ran Takeda. Why—?"

Isabela's eyes lit up, that crooked smile spreading across her face. "The girl who blows things up. Oh, I know all about you."

"Why are you like this?" Ran asked pointedly. "Why would you use your Legacies to hurt us? Why work for the Foundation?"

"You're monsters," Isabela replied. "All of you. You deserve what you get."

"You're one of us," Ran said calmly. "Consider that your father told you nothing but lies."

"Consider that it's still a sin, even if you do it on accident," Isabela said with a sick laugh. "You know that's true, don't you, Ran? I don't even need to be in your mind to know what you are. What you've done. If only someone like me could've been there to stop you."

Caleb saw Ran's expression cloud over through the eyes

236

of his duplicates. He didn't understand exactly what Lucas was saying, but it had gotten to her.

"We should go," Caleb said. "Cover her head and bring her."

"Where is he being sent, anyway?" Lucas's Cêpan asked. The warden gave her a look, but she didn't flinch. "You need to tell me. If he comes out pissed off, I have to be able to spin this. Feed him some shit about a higher calling."

"California," the warden answered. "The Academy. Apparently, a high-priority target has appeared there."

"More high-priority than Einar?"

"Galactically."

Isabela recoiled. They were sending this monster Lucas towards her friends. She needed to get out of here, needed to warn them.

The warden hit a button on his glove and Isabela got her wish. She could feel the voltage passing through Lucas—the glove must have been keyed to his Inhibitor. Lightning crackled through the walls of the warehouse, breaking them apart. A scream of rage and frustration rang out at a volume that seemed impossible, like it could shear right through Isabela's brain. Instinctively, she clutched her ears and then—

One second, Isabela glowered at Ran while simultaneously jerking her head away from the duplicates trying to shove her head back into the pillowcase. Then, suddenly, she went completely slack in the Calebs' arms, like she had fainted. Caleb wondered what this new ploy from Lucas might be. It didn't matter; he wasn't going to fall for it. His duplicates gruffly shoved Isabela's head into the pillowcase and began dragging her towards the balcony.

Isabela's body jerked back to life, although she didn't thrash against the duplicates with the same reckless ferocity as before. A muffled stream of annoyed-sounding Portuguese came from under the fabric.

"Wait," Caleb ordered the duplicates. "Take that off her."

Caleb came off the balcony for the first time, potentially exposing himself to an attack. But, having listened to the boy rant and rave in his languid Southern accent, he sensed there'd been a change. Lucas's Legacy didn't seem to make him fluent in other languages.

Isabela tossed her head as the pillowcase came free. She blew a curl of hair out of her eye and fixed Caleb with a pointed look.

"I bet you're loving this," she said, puckering her lips at him.

Caleb stared into Isabela's eyes, looking for some kind of sign—he wasn't sure what. "Are you *you*?"

Isabela reclined in the arms of his duplicates, letting them carry her weight. She even made an attempt to kick her feet up. It suddenly looked more like they were practicing a dance number than restraining her.

"This isn't so bad, actually," Isabela declared. "I've been on my feet all night."

"It's her," Ran said flatly.

With a mental command, Caleb got the duplicates to relax. They fell back to a respectful distance from Isabela, causing her to pout as she nearly lost her balance. He didn't absorb them—there was still the matter of the local police, who were probably closing in on their location. His copies might still be needed.

"Are you okay?" Caleb asked. He stepped forward to touch Isabela's shoulder.

He expected the usual sharp reply, but instead Isabela put her hand on top of his. Her fingers trembled.

"That bastard . . . ," she said. "It was bad."

"What happened to Lucas?" Ran asked. "Where did he go?"

Isabela's eyes widened. "The Academy. They pulled him back to send him to the Academy."

Before Caleb could reply, his duplicates turned as one towards the door. Thanks to six sets of ears, Caleb heard heavy footfalls in the hallway, the familiar metallic clank of body armor, the rattle of guns pulled from their holsters. The authorities were here.

"We have to get out of here," he said. "Now."

Caleb left his duplicates in a wall facing the doorway. While the three of them retreated for the balcony, the door exploded inward, kicked off its hinges. Someone tossed a flash-bang grenade into the room, sparks and white smoke cluttering the air. In response, Ran lobbed King's charged loafer over the duplicates and towards the breaching cops.

Caleb couldn't see through the smoke, but he heard pained shouts in response to the detonation. They fired back into the room—bullets, actual bullets. One of his duplicates went down, shot in the forehead. The others marched forward, sponging up the gunfire until they could take no more, stalling.

Isabela went first up the ladder. Then Ran. Caleb was last. He'd barely gotten his foot on the bottom rung when the skimmer started gaining altitude. He clung on tight to the ladder, wind whipping across his face.

He glanced back at the hotel, at the penthouse garden. He could make out Derek King slumped over the table, a dark pool spreading across the tablecloth. There was a steak knife jammed into the side of his neck, King's own hand still clutched around the handle.

Einar had lied. Einar had killed.

And yet, after what these people had done to him—to Duanphen, to Isabela—how remorselessly they'd tried to hurt them . . .

Caleb couldn't bring himself to care.

CHAPTER SIXTEEN

THIS IS THE GREATEST DAY OF MY LIFE, KOPANO thought. He almost said it out loud, but he had a sudden vision of Taylor rolling her eyes at him, so he kept silent. Played it cool.

"Okay, do you see this here? Underneath the armory? That's the warship's core."

Even though he didn't geek out vocally, Kopano couldn't suppress the dopey grin. He thought back to that day during the invasion when he'd been swept up in a telepathic vision and declared to his family he was a Garde, only for them to tell him the whole thing was just a dream. He remembered how his powers had been late in coming, how he'd endured merciless teasing at school, how his classmates had tied him to a soccer goal and kicked balls at him, daring him to stop them with his nonexistent telekinesis. Where were those kids now? Back in Lagos, rushing through their math homework so they could go play pool. Oh, maybe they'd win a few bucks—*how awesome*. Really, really dope, you guys.

And where was Kopano? Former victim of their slander and abuse?

Oh, just planning a mission with John Smith. No big deal.

"Kopano," John said. "Are you listening?"

He wiped the grin off his face and nodded vigorously.

"Yes, John Smith."

"Just John is fine, man."

"Okay, John," Kopano said, then made a studious face and turned his attention back to the laptop John had borrowed from Lexa.

A 3-D blueprint of a Mogadorian warship was displayed on the screen. John tapped the spot he'd been talking about— the core—aptly named since it was positioned right at the ship's central point, arteries of connections fanning out from there to every corner of the spacecraft.

"You'll find the force field generator here," John continued. "Once the *Osiris* lands and powers down, it'll be safe to disconnect. We're not going to have that much time with the Peacekeepers looking over our shoulders, so we'll have to be quick."

Miki raised his hand. The three of them stood in an empty classroom, huddled around a teacher's desk. The diminutive Miki looked tired and twitchy—Kopano supposed a few weeks cooped up in a cell would do that to a person who was used to transforming into wind. Regardless, he seemed grateful to be released, albeit after a very stern and threatening lecture from Professor Nine.

"I have a question," Miki said. "No offense, but why do you even need us? I thought you had every Legacy."

John shook his head. "No, that's not what I do. It's true that I can copy any Legacy that I've seen, but I've never met any Garde with your powers before."

Kopano puffed up a bit. "So you can't do what we do?"

"Nope," John replied. "Not yet, at least. And anyway, just because I can copy a Legacy doesn't mean I can use it well. Not to mention, it's always better to work with a team." John rubbed the back of his neck. "That's something I need to be reminded about sometimes, but I really believe it."

Kopano clapped his hands. "Yes! So once our team is in the warship's core, what do you need us to do to get the force field generator free?"

"Well, I won't be going in with you," John said. "I've got to keep an eye on Earth Garde and the Mogadorians, make sure nothing happens during the surrender. You two will be sneaking in while that's happening."

Kopano and Miki exchanged a look. Neither of them had ever been on a Mogadorian warship before, much less taken one apart. The thought thrilled Kopano, but Miki looked uncertain.

"Don't worry," John said. "I'll show you the way."

John clicked around on the blueprint, zooming in on a refrigerator-size object amid all the Mogadorian tech.

"That's the generator there," John explained. "Obviously, the Mogs don't want these damaged, so it's surrounded by three layers of armor—carbon steel, titanium and a mineral native to Mogadore." He glanced at Kopano. "You might've seen it on Vontezza's weapon. The obsidian-looking stuff?"

Kopano nodded, touching his chest. "Yeah. It hurt when she whacked me."

"So you can imagine what a pain in the ass it is to strip that armor away, even with my Legacies," John replied. He looked at Kopano. "What I want you to do is phase through the armor, grab the generator and pull it free."

Kopano stifled a wince. Vontezza's weapon had caused him pain when it passed through him. He wasn't excited about coming in contact with that metal again.

John noticed his hesitation. "Will that not work? You can do objects, right?"

Kopano forced a smile. He couldn't let John down; couldn't squander this chance to do something heroic on behalf of the Academy. It was exactly the kind of opportunity he'd been waiting for.

"Yes," Kopano said. "I can do objects."

As a demonstration, Kopano picked up the laptop, then loosened his molecules. He waved his arm around, passing the computer harmlessly through the top of the desk. Then, he set the laptop back down where it'd been, restoring its density. The screen flickered, but otherwise everything was normal.

"That's good," John said. "But the generator is a lot bigger than that. Do you think you could try the desk?"

Kopano looked down at the desk, cracking his knuckles. It was bulky and metal with drawers filled with teaching supplies. Kopano considered the size. Yes, he was strong, and he could tip over this desk no problem, but it was awfully big for him to lift up. He put his hand on top of the desk and loosened its molecules. The laptop started to fall to the floor, but Miki caught it with his telekinesis.

"I don't see how I'll be able to lift something like this," Kopano said, frowning.

"Why not?" John replied. "If I'm understanding your Legacy correctly, you've just changed the density of the desk's molecules. You've altered them enough that the laptop fell through, but not so much that the desk is ghosting through the floor. That's your instinct kicking in. You're making sure that you don't completely trash the room by altering the physics. But, if you tried, couldn't you make it completely weightless?"

Kopano considered this. Mostly, he'd used his Legacy to pass through things, or harden his own molecules to become impervious to damage. He'd never considered messing with the weight of objects to move them around.

"I've never done anything like that," he mused.

"I'm sure Nine was working up to that," John said. "Want to give it a shot?"

"Hell yes, I do," Kopano replied.

He crouched down to grab hold of the desk—back straight, lift from the knees, proper form. As Kopano focused, he became aware of the desk's particles and how he was separating them, how they fought to keep their shape against the manipulation of his Legacy. His brain said that the desk should have weight, it should be too unwieldly for him to simply pick it up. But Kopano didn't listen to the logical part of his brain.

Kopano would show John Smith that he could help. That he was worthy of being a Garde.

He lifted the desk perpendicular to his body. It came easily, putting no more strain on Kopano's muscles than an empty cardboard box. Miki hopped backwards, but John stayed put, letting the desk pass harmlessly through him as Kopano maneuvered it.

"Very good," John said.

Kopano turned the desk the long way and hefted it all the way over his head, part of it disappearing into the ceiling. As it tilted, some of the drawers came open and papers fluttered free, these regaining their mass as they left the desk and wafted to the floor.

"This is fun." Kopano grinned, balancing the weightless and incorporeal desk on one hand now. "Do you think there's a car I could try on?"

Showing off now, Kopano tossed the desk from one hand to the other. He imagined himself juggling furniture later in the student union, not realizing his mistake until the desk crashed to the floor on its side between him and John. Drawers went flying, the floor tiles cracked and a good-size dent spread across the desktop. The second he'd lost contact with the desk, it had turned solid.

"Oops," Kopano said.

"Nice one," Miki said dryly.

John patted him on the back. "When it's the generator, maybe don't let it go until it's clear, okay?"

Kopano nodded. "Got it. Lesson learned."

Miki peered around the upended desk to look at John. "So what am I supposed to do?"

"Transport," John replied. "There's going to be a lot of attention on the warship and we'll need to get the generator moved before Earth Garde has a chance to secure the area. They won't let us just carry the thing away. So once Kopano's got the equipment loose, I want you to transform it into wind until we clear the area. Then, we'll teleport it back to New Lorien."

"We get to go to New Lorien?" Kopano asked, trying not to shout the question in his excitement.

"Yeah, we'll make a stop, drop it off," John said casually. He revealed a Loralite pendant on his neck, exactly the same as the one Nine had been wearing at the meeting in his office. "This will let us teleport there. The stone is keyed specifically to the Loralite in New Lorien."

"Sweet," Kopano said.

"And then we'll head back here as quickly as possible," John replied. His expression darkened. Kopano had heard about what happened when he and Taylor visited the Earth

Garde encampment. "I have a feeling things might take a turn for the worse soon."

"One problem," Miki said, patting the side of the desk. "I've never moved anything larger than a person in my wind form. I'm not sure I can do it."

"Well, we've got the rest of the day to work—"

The classroom door clattered open, interrupting John and causing Kopano to flinch. Vontezza stalked into the room, the Mogadorian girl still clad in her dented armor. Kopano took a step back, remembering their fight the day before, and Miki simply stared at her. She didn't pay attention to either of them, though, her imperious gaze instead boring right into John.

"I have been looking for you," she stated, annoyed.

"Vontezza, I thought we agreed you would stay out of sight," John said diplomatically. "Some of the students here might not be ready for someone like you."

"I cannot sit in that box and twiddle my thumbs while the fate of my crew hangs in the balance," she replied. For the first time, she noticed Kopano and Miki. "Hello, large one and small child I do not know."

Kopano could tell that Miki was trying not to stare or shy away from Vontezza. "Um, hey," Miki said. "I'm—"

Vontezza ignored him, instead focusing on the laptop John held, the blueprint of her warship still displayed there. "You are planning. Without me."

"Because you aren't going," John answered, pinching the

bridge of his nose. "We can't risk Earth Garde finding out you exist."

"I am the captain of the *Osiris*," Vontezza replied. "My crew may have agreed to surrender themselves, but I cannot let them do that alone. I must be there to ensure their safety."

"Vontezza—"

"You will need me," she said. "What is your plan? To send these two unbloodied Garde in while you pose for pictures? They will need a guide."

Kopano made a face. "I'm not—I've got plenty of blood. And I think we can find our way around a warship."

"Really?" Vontezza snatched the laptop away from John and thrust it towards Kopano. "There is the map. Show me what route you will take, thick one."

Kopano flippantly traced his finger from one side of the warship straight into its center. "I can pass through walls, remember? I don't need a route. I can just—"

Vontezza made a noise like an explosion, apparently the Mogadorian version of the wrong answer buzzer.

"What about the radiation?" Vontezza asked. "Can you pass through that, too? Or will it melt your molecules like it did so many of my people?"

Kopano's forehead scrunched up. He'd never considered what might happen to him if he phased through something toxic. His first instinct was that opening his atoms to some kind of poisonous cloud was probably a bad idea. However, John spoke up before he could voice that concern.

"What radiation?" John asked Vontezza. "You didn't mention that."

"Entire sections of the *Osiris* were damaged during the mutinies," Vontezza replied. "There are areas of the ship that are inhospitable even to the vatborn. Mere humans stumbling around the halls unguided will never make it to the core alive. You see? I am needed."

"You could just tell us how to get there," Miki muttered.

"No," Vontezza snapped. She stared at John. "I have already traded too much to come to this school that is falling apart. I will be there tomorrow to make sure that my crew are treated with dignity."

John's nostrils flared. Kopano could tell that he was struggling to keep his cool. Vontezza was arrogant, kind of mean and made Kopano uneasy. But he could see where she was coming from. It was, as usual, Kopano's tendency to try to smooth things over.

"I mean, I guess she is a good fighter," Kopano spoke up. "Couldn't hurt to have someone watching our backs in there."

Vontezza didn't say anything else, simply raising her sculpted black eyebrows at John.

"Fine," he said gruffly. "I don't want to spend any more time arguing about this. If you're going to come, though, you need to be a hell of a lot more incognito."

Vontezza glanced down at herself—the armor, the long black braid, the mace on her hip. "Incognito. Of course."

John breathed out through his nose and turned back to Miki. "All right. You want to show me how this wind stuff works? We can figure out how big of an object you can carry."

"Right now?" Miki asked.

"Right now," John replied, and extended a hand.

Miki grasped on to the Loric and the two of them transformed into a swirl of particles, breezing from one end of the classroom to another. When they reappeared, John put the back of his hand to his mouth and coughed.

"That's a weird sensation," he said.

"You get used to it," Miki replied.

John motioned to one of the smaller desks where the students once sat. "Okay, try carrying that with you. I'll do my best to help. We can figure this out together."

They transformed again—this time John didn't need to take Miki's hand—and the desk vanished with them. Kopano tried to track the swirl of their particles, but soon they'd blown open a window and were gone, moving their training session to a less confined area.

Kopano realized then that he was alone with Vontezza. And she was staring at him.

"Thank you," she said. "For acknowledging my rightness."

"No problem," Kopano said with a shrug. They stood there awkwardly for a moment. "Well, see you later."

As Kopano headed for the exit, Vontezza followed.

"What does this word mean?" she asked. *"Incognito?"*

"It means he wants you to look less like a Mogadorian and more like one of us," Kopano said. "A human."

Vontezza looked down at her gear. Kopano glanced at her as well—the ashen skin, inky-black hair, slightly sharpened teeth. She clicked her tongue against the roof of her mouth.

"Yes, I am willing to do that," she said, then paused. "But how?"

Kopano itched his earlobe in thought. "Maybe try getting a suntan or . . ."

He trailed off as they exited the classroom and ran into a handful of students. Kopano figured they had a class scheduled for the room and started to walk by them but found his path blocked by Nicolas Lambert.

"Son of a bitch, Maiken wasn't lying," Nic said. "There really is a Mog here."

It took Kopano a moment to recognize the tension in the air. Vontezza, behind him, identified it much more quickly. She paused in the classroom doorway, one hand straying down to the mace by her hip.

Kopano looked at the students assembled behind Nicolas. There was Anika Jindal, who could manipulate metals; that dude Ben from Brooklyn, who had sticky skin that let him cling to walls; and a couple of tweebs who Kopano had seen around but not really gotten to know. Kopano wouldn't have considered any of them his friends, exactly, but he knew them all and thought they were generally a good bunch. He'd never seen them look like they did now—angry and cold, all of them glaring past Kopano at Vontezza.

This was a mob.

"Guys," Kopano said tentatively. "What are you doing?"

"My older brother, Nathan, was a helicopter pilot for the Belgian Air Component," Nicolas said, ignoring Kopano and instead speaking directly to Vontezza. "He was evacuating people from Berlin when one of your skimmers shot him down. He died."

"You must be proud," Vontezza replied. "Your brother perished nobly in a victory for your planet. Such sacrifice is a great honor for your bloodline."

Kopano winced. "Okay. What I think she's trying to say is—"

"I should be *proud*?" Nic exclaimed. He looked incredulously at his cohorts, all of their expressions hardening further. "My brother is dead because of you animals and you think I should be proud?"

"Mogs killed my aunt just because she was out in the street," Ben said. "Should I be proud too, bitch?"

"You don't belong here," Anika added. "You should go back to your own planet."

"My planet is dead," Vontezza said flatly.

"Exactly," Anika replied. "That's where you belong."

Kopano held up his hands. He was still in between Vontezza and the others, nearly chest-to-chest with Nicolas in the tight hallway.

"Guys, this is stupid," he said. "I'm not saying you shouldn't be mad about what happened during the invasion, but Vontezza didn't do any of that. She came here to help us."

"Kopano, you're an idiot. Why would we ever need help from one of them?" Nicolas spat. "It's insane that she's even here, as if we didn't already have enough problems." He jutted his chin out, staring into Kopano's eyes. "Why don't you get out of here, man?"

"Yeah, whose side are you even on?" one of the tweebs said to Kopano.

"The war is over; there aren't sides anymore." Kopano didn't back down. "You all aren't thinking straight. Maybe we should talk this over with Professor Nine and John Smith. They can explain—"

"Enough talking," Vontezza interrupted.

As Kopano half turned to look at her, Vontezza unsnapped the mace from her hip and extended the weapon, the obsidian spikes shining in the light. The students all flinched backwards, except for Nicolas. The Mogadorian girl was an intimidating sight and none of them had actually seen combat outside the training center. Kopano hardened his molecules, ready to absorb attacks from either direction.

He was surprised when Vontezza tossed her weapon to Nicolas. The Belgian was taken aback as well, barely managing to catch the mace by its handle.

"You want to hurt me as retribution for your fallen," Vontezza said. "I understand and will not stop you."

"What?" Nic replied. "Are you nuts?"

"I should tell you that I cannot be killed," Vontezza continued blandly, like she was reading off a book report in front of class. "My Legacy is regeneration."

Anika looked to Nic. "You said Maiken was exaggerating about that part."

"It's bullshit," Nic replied, eyeing Vontezza. "There's no way some Mog would get a Legacy."

"It's the truth," Kopano inserted. "She heals automatically. I saw it."

"This is a good thing for you," Vontezza said to the students, her gaze sweeping over them. "You can beat me as much as you like and eventually my body will rebuild itself. Each of you can take a turn."

Everyone stared at her. Vontezza's dark eyes were hard and unblinking. She really meant it.

Ben and the tweebs no longer looked so strong in their convictions. They edged back down the hallway, swallowing and exchanging nervous glances. Anika stared at Vontezza like the Mogadorian had somehow become *more* alien.

"You'd seriously just let us like take turns bashing your head in?" Anika asked.

"Bash my head in, slash my throat, impale me," Vontezza rattled off these brutalities without inflection. She looked at Nicolas. "Will you be first, then?"

Nicolas hadn't moved. He kept adjusting his fingers on the hilt of the mace. Kopano could tell that his hands were sweaty. The others were all watching him—they didn't want to push this any further, but they were also taking their cues from the Belgian. They wouldn't back down until he did.

Kopano kept silent. He was worried that anything he might say would only egg Nicolas on. He stood by, waiting for the tension to break. Or, waiting for Nicolas to take a swing. He would stop him, if it came to that. He wasn't going to let the superstrong Belgian hurt anyone, even if Vontezza was literally asking for it.

Finally, Nicolas snorted.

"You're a freak," he said, glaring at Vontezza. "An animal. And you shouldn't be here. We should've exterminated all your kind the second you lost the war."

Nicolas tossed the mace on the floor, where it clattered around and dented the tiles. He scowled at Kopano and then began to slowly back away. His friends followed.

With her telekinesis, Vontezza picked up her weapon and secured it. She nodded to Nicolas.

"If you change your mind, I will be here," she said. "Waiting."

When they were gone, Kopano breathed out a long sigh of relief. Vontezza, meanwhile, seemed unaffected by the entire incident.

"Would you really have let them do that to you?" Kopano asked.

She looked at him, a tiny vein pulsing in her tattooed neck.

"You should not have stood against your friends," she said, dodging the question. "They will remember that."

"We need to look out for each other until this mess with Earth Garde is sorted out. We're all on the same side here,"

Kopano replied. "They'll realize that, eventually."

"You are honorable," Vontezza said. "But unfit to lead."

"Um, thanks?"

"Now," Vontezza said, her piercing gaze locked on Kopano. "Show me how I might become more human."

CHAPTER SEVENTEEN

NIGEL BARNABY
THE HUMAN GARDE ACADEMY—POINT REYES, CALIFORNIA

"I HEARD THEM PAGE YOU BEFORE, DEAR," BEA Barnaby said, once again seated on the edge of her cot with her legs primly crossed. "I do hope that you aren't in any trouble."

Nigel sat across from his mother, the metal chair dented from his outburst following their previous encounter. He smiled thinly. Bea didn't know it yet, but this would be the last time they spoke down here. It'd taken a day spent making sure none of his freaked-out classmates decided to flee campus, but Nigel had at last come to a decision about what to do with his mother.

"You know I've never been much for authority," Nigel said. "Kinda my thing."

"Yes, I suppose this is when I should blame your rebellious

behavior on that contemptible punk rock," Bea said. She lowered her voice, as if letting Nigel in on a secret. "But, truth be told, your father and I were never ones to play by the rules either. You get that from us."

Nigel bristled. The woman knew exactly how to press his buttons. Knowing that she was doing it didn't seem to help.

"I'm not like you," he replied with more passion than he would've liked.

"No, of course not," Bea replied with an indulgent smile. "It's happening like I predicted, isn't it? This mad little Academy is being brought under control." When Nigel didn't immediately respond, she continued, her voice more sincere than taunting. "You must know it will be easier if you don't fight it. Safer. For both of you," she added, glancing away from Nigel.

Taylor stood at the back of the cell with her arms crossed.

"You don't get to have this place, Bea," Taylor said. "Or maybe you do. But it'll just be a lot of empty buildings. You don't get to have us."

"I like you, Ms. Cook," Bea said. She turned her attention back to Nigel. "I like her. She touched this whole conflict off in a way, didn't she? Our reports had her down as meek and pliable, afraid of her own Legacies. We didn't expect her to be so volatile when we recruited her."

"Kidnapped me," Taylor corrected.

"Yes, well, I admire a young woman with convictions, even if we fundamentally disagree." Bea lowered her voice again, speaking to Nigel. "Perhaps you two should date."

Nigel snorted. "Mum, I'm gay."

Bea raised an eyebrow and sighed. "Will these little rebellions never cease, Nigel?"

Nigel wanted to lunge forward and strangle her. Bea, of course, chose that moment to double over in a fit of coughing, the back of her hand pressed to her mouth. When she straightened back up, her eyes were red-rimmed and flecks of black ooze writhed in her pale cheeks.

"Last chance to be of use, then," Nigel said quietly. "Do something good for a change."

"Last chance before what?" Bea asked, her voice raspy. "Is this the last time you'll offer to heal me in exchange for information? Is that why Taylor's here?" Bea scoffed. "Please."

"Tell us who the Foundation has inside Earth Garde," Nigel said. "Tell us everyone that's been compromised."

Bea made a face, like the question was silly. "We have sources, I'm sure. Like that frumpy headshrinker you keep locked up down the hall. Sad little thing cries herself to sleep most nights." She tapped her lips in thought and Nigel noted the dead black spot beneath her fingernail. "Perhaps there are a few high-ranking collaborators within the organization. If they exist, I honestly don't know who they are. If you're looking for some mythical enemy that you can put under citizen's arrest and end all your problems, you're wasting your time. The Foundation is a hydra and you will never have enough swords."

"Tell us about Greger Karlsson," Taylor said.

"Who?" Bea replied.

Nigel studied his mother's expression. She honestly looked baffled. The name hadn't rung any bells.

"He works for Earth Garde," Nigel said. "They've put him in charge of drilling holes into our brains."

"Oh, that Swedish striver?" Bea chuckled. "What do you want to know? If I remember our reports correctly, Karlsson was the type of man to never pass up a promotion. Ultimately, though, bureaucrats like him are a dime a dozen. They've got no real power and are easily replaced. Not worth the investment."

"What do you have on him?" Taylor pressed. "We know how the Foundation leverages people. What are you doing to make him act like this?"

Bea cocked her head. "Sometimes we apply pressure, that's true. But I wasn't aware of any operation concerning Karlsson. If he's involved in regulating your kind, consider that he honestly believes it's the right thing to do. Is that such a far-out viewpoint, dear? Do you think the Foundation is blackmailing every person who believes Garde are a danger to humanity? We're rich, but not *that* rich."

Nigel's lips compressed. He turned his back on Bea so that he could make eye contact with Taylor.

"Anything else you want to ask her?" Nigel said. "Or can we stop wasting our time?"

Taylor considered that for a moment. "Do you feel any remorse?" she asked Bea. "For the people you've hurt? The people you've killed? For the messed-up world that you greedy assholes have helped create?"

"Oi, there's an interesting line of questioning," Nigel said, turning back to face Bea. "Basically, my lovely friend here is wondering if you've still got a soul, Mum."

Bea looked unamused. "Do you feel remorse for saving the life of a killer, Ms. Cook?" she countered. "Does it bother you that in sparing Einar, you've no doubt endangered the lives of countless others?"

"Yes," Taylor said without missing a beat. "That does bother me."

Bea nodded as if she suspected as much. "When you've grown up, you'll learn how to set those feelings aside."

"Maybe," Taylor said. "But until that day, I guess I'm going to feel guilty for a lot of things. Like what I'm about to do to you."

"Right," Nigel said, standing up and getting out of the way. "Have at it."

Taylor pushed off the wall and came towards Bea. Nigel was at least pleased to see his mother flinch. Even as a prisoner, Bea thought she was in control. But, when Taylor roughly grabbed the older woman's face in her hands, he saw a brief flash of fear in Bea's eyes.

"Relax, Bea," Nigel said. "You've won."

Bea let out a low moan as Taylor healed her. Nigel could see the veins of the Mogadorian ooze crackle beneath his mother's skin, the stuff somehow struggling against Taylor's Legacy. It took a couple of minutes—Nigel had seen Taylor heal bullet wounds quicker—but eventually Taylor let Bea go, wiping some sweat off her forehead. Bea sank back on her cot, breathing heavily.

"Feel better now?" Nigel asked. He looked to Taylor. "Did you cure the bitchiness while you were at it?"

"Doubt it," Taylor said.

Bea looked up at him with a mixture of surprise and disappointment. "Why—why would you do that? My health was your only leverage . . ."

Nigel rolled his eyes. It was always about the angles with his mother. She was displeased that Nigel had forfeited his one advantage, like she'd been taking some demented pride in her son's hardball negotiation stance.

"Because we're done talking," Nigel told her. "I'd been thinking that if I kept you down here long enough, I might be able to pry some information out of you. Maybe even catch sight of a spark of decency in that black heart of yours. But, not only are you full-blown evil, you're bloody useless. I don't think you know anything that can help us. I think you're scared. Maybe of Einar, maybe of some of your old friends at the Foundation who think you've lost the thread. You've been happy down here, letting us keep you safe. Well, that's over now, love."

Nigel took Bea by the arm and stood her up, brushing creases out of her sweat suit.

"What do you plan to do?" Bea asked, and for once Nigel thought he detected a shakiness in her tone.

"We're turning you over to Earth Garde," Nigel said. "You, Linda and that tit whose name I always forget."

Bea guffawed. "I'll be free before the sun sets."

"Maybe," Nigel said with a careless shrug. "We're also sending along all the evidence we've got. Taylor and I recorded statements about what you've done. Killing those soldiers in London, the warship in Siberia, that mess in Iceland. How you orchestrated Sydal's death. I think we covered everything. Plus, you know, all the recordings of our little chats in here. Those don't look so great for you."

"My lawyers—"

Nigel shut his mother up by hugging her close and giving her a peck on the cheek.

"Bea, I don't care," he said in her ear. "If Earth Garde's as corrupt as you say it is, then at least we'll know for sure when they set you free. And, if maybe you're overestimating your own clout and they drag you off to The Hague in chains, well, that'll be a sunny day, won't it? Either way, you won't be my problem anymore. I'm emancipating myself."

His mother, for once, fell silent. That was good—Nigel didn't think he had another speech in him.

Nigel and Taylor escorted Bea into the hallway where the others were waiting. Professor Nine, Malcolm and Agent Walker had already brought Dr. Linda and Alejandro Regerio out from their cells, the two of them shackled together at the feet and waist. Regerio was doubled over, wheezing, and Nigel quickly got the picture that he'd tried to escape and received a punch in the stomach from Nine as a reward.

"Lady Barnaby!" Nine exclaimed. "Welcome to the party!"

"This is futility defined," Bea said, keeping her chin high

and that upper lip plenty stiff.

Nine tossed Nigel a length of chain. "You want to do the honors?"

"Happily," Nigel replied, and set about securing his mother to the other two.

When it was done, Nigel dropped back behind the prisoners, letting Nine and Walker take the lead on escorting the shuffling group out of the subbasement. There was some humor, at least, to be found in the sight of his mother duck-walking behind Dr. Linda.

"You okay?" Taylor asked as she sidled up beside him.

"Oh, I'm right as rain," Nigel said, trying to keep his tone light under Taylor's probing gaze. "I'm officially an orphan. Most free I've ever felt."

"I'm not very close with my mom either," Taylor said. "I mean, she's not part of a global conspiracy, she's just kind of spacey and crappy with keeping promises. But, you know, I get it. I always thought one day she'd come around and realize what a cool person I am and want to hang out with me."

"If Bea ever thinks I'm a cool person, I'll jump off a bridge," Nigel said. "But thanks. And thanks for healing the evil wench."

"No problem. Sparing her from a slow death, wow, we *really* showed her," Taylor said.

Nigel snorted. "Yeah. Hope she learned her lesson."

Their dour procession made it out from beneath the Academy and continued across the quad. They passed by a small group of tweebs working on their telekinetic control. None of them said anything, but Nigel could sense them staring. His shoulders knotted together, a feeling of shame welling up in him. That was his mom, there. Evil queen of the Foundation. Everyone have a look at the rotten tree he'd descended from.

The sun was already getting low as they crossed the lawn and headed beyond the barricade. Omar and Lisbette stood guard there and Nigel knew there were a couple others hiding in the trees, waiting to signal if the Peacekeepers tried something. They'd almost made it through one day of being an unsanctioned Academy. Nigel allowed himself a small smile. At least his mother would be wrong about her prediction that she'd be free by sunset.

No one spoke. The only noise was the wind whipping across campus and the clinking of chains. Finally, as the ruined track came into view, Dr. Linda cleared her throat.

"I want to apologize for what I did," she said, her voice small and scratchy. "I realize it's no excuse, but I was coerced . . ."

"We included that in our report, Linda," Malcolm said, not unkindly. He fingered the USB drive with all their Foundation-related evidence loaded onto it.

"Yeah," Nigel added. "Hopefully the fascists go easy on you, Doc. And just so you know, I didn't think our sessions were a complete waste of time."

"Thank you, Nigel," Linda replied. "That's nice of you to say."

The wreckage of the Mogadorian skimmer came into view. It was guarded by a handful of Peacekeepers in radiation suits. They started at the Academy group, all of them hoisting those Inhibitor cannons that Nigel got all too familiar with during that game of capture the flag.

"Hold!" a voice shouted from near the trees. Colonel Archibald appeared with another group of armed Peacekeepers, although this bunch didn't raise their weapons. Archibald must have seen their approach on the security cameras and come out to meet them.

Nine held up their group, keeping them at a safe range from the Peacekeepers. "How's it going, Archie? We brought you a present."

"What now, Nine?" Archibald asked, narrowing his eyes at the three prisoners. "You know I'm under orders to bring you in." He glanced at Taylor. "*All* of you."

Nigel snorted, but for once kept his mouth shut. No reason to fan the flames further.

Nine turned to look at Walker. "Over to you, Karen. If you end up in prison, it's been nice knowing you."

"Yeah, good luck to you, too," Walker replied, accepting the USB drive from Malcolm. Then, she gave a yank on Regerio's chain and pulled the trio of prisoners forward. With her other hand, she held up her badge. "Colonel Archibald! My name is Special Agent Karen Walker and I'm working under the remit of the intelligence agency known as Watchtower. These three people stand accused of a number of capital crimes. I'm formally requesting your assistance and protection until they can be transferred to an appropriate location."

Archibald listened to all that with his usual stoicism,

then grunted something to his men. A couple of the Peace-keepers came forward to help Walker with her charges.

"Think it'll stick?" Taylor murmured to Nigel.

"Do you?" Nigel replied.

"I think we can trust Archibald," Taylor said. "He'll at least try."

Nigel watched the Peacekeepers take charge of his mother. He waited for her to look over her shoulder or make some snide comment in parting. But Bea never so much as glanced back at him. It was over between them. Done. Nigel hoped to bask in the satisfaction of seeing his mother corralled, but all he felt now was that same sense of loneliness that pervaded in his earliest days at Pepperpont when he would stay up nights hoping his parents would come pick him up.

He was well and truly on his own now.

With a brief glance at his soldiers, Archibald crossed the field to approach the Garde. He kept his hands raised the entire time. Nigel noted dark patches of sweat on the man's armpits. Seemed everyone was equally nervous.

"I'm getting transferred out tomorrow," Archibald said without preamble. "They want me to oversee this Mogadorian surrender. After that, I'll be reassigned somewhere else. Most of the Peacekeepers who were loyal to me have been rotated out as well."

"Well, wish I could say it's been fun," Nine said gruffly. "Peace out."

Archibald suppressed a glower at Nine's comment. "They would've stormed campus today if I hadn't stalled them.

Well, John Smith's arrival also spooked Karlsson. For now, he wants to make things as uncomfortable for you as possible, hoping you'll surrender. But tomorrow, when I'm gone and John's gone . . ."

"They're coming in," Taylor said.

"This is mad," Nigel said, waving a hand in the direction the Peacekeepers took his mother and the other conspirators. "You realize you Earth Garde lot are being played by the Foundation, right? We just handed you a pile of evidence!"

"And I'll do my damnedest to make sure that counts for something," Archibald replied. "But this is a heads-up, because I appreciated the work we were doing here, whether you believe that or not. The Earth Garde coalition is falling apart. These Foundation people you're after, they're just taking advantage of the situation—fear, distrust, corruption—it's everywhere. And it's not going away overnight, no matter how many bad guys you bring in."

"Heartening," Nigel said.

"So what you're saying is that we're going to have to fight," Nine said.

"Or run," added Taylor.

Whatever else was said, Nigel didn't hear it. He drifted back towards the student union. His mother was in custody, taken down as much as someone like her could ever be. His father was dead. His best friend was halfway around the world with his dad's killer. And here, the Academy, which had finally started to feel like home to him, was on the verge of being swallowed up.

Fear, distrust, corruption.

And nothing would change. That was basically what Archibald had said.

Nigel thought back to the invasion. How he'd rallied the first few Human Garde to race off to fight the Mogadorians. He'd thought that he was going to be a hero.

What had Nigel ever done that had made a bit of difference?

He found himself standing in the student union. The place was noisy and active, students bustling around, chatting with each other as they prepared dinner. Omar Azoulay waved to him from the kitchen. They'd gotten to work without Nigel's prompting this time. They were taking care of each other.

The TV was tuned to the news, where, of course, the anchors were talking about the situation with Earth Garde. "At this hour, we're hearing that there's skepticism from many European countries about the so-called Cêpan program, with many advocacy groups claiming that the forced installation of Inhibitors is a bridge too far and perhaps borders on child abuse. While nothing's been confirmed, we're hearing additional rumors that some countries, such as Germany and Canada, are considering pulling out of the UN-backed Earth Garde coalition . . ."

Nigel took a deep breath and looked around. He smelled baking bread and curry. Someone was laughing in the kitchen.

His mother was wrong. She'd always been wrong. He

couldn't let her thinking infect him; he refused to inherit her cynicism. There was still good to be done in the world. It started here, with protecting these people, with making sure that they had a safe place to learn and grow and become the heroes this messed-up world needed.

Nigel clapped his hands. "Oi, ready to teach me how to boil water?" he yelled over to Omar. "Got a spare apron for me?"

As Nigel started across the student union, the TV suddenly turned off. So did the overhead lights. Nigel glanced over his shoulder and saw that the lamps that lit the Academy's pathways were off as well.

Earth Garde had cut off their power.

CHAPTER EIGHTEEN

"HOW ARE YOU FEELING?" RAN ASKED.

"I am breathing," Duanphen replied. "That is enough."

Duanphen sat against one of the bulkheads, her injured arm cradled in her lap. She still looked deathly pale from all the blood lost in Morocco. Dark purple bruises spread from her temple to where her right eye was nearly swollen shut. While Ran crouched in front of her, Duanphen's eyelids began to flutter and her head lolled to the side. Gently, Ran touched her cheek.

"You need to stay awake now," Ran told her. "You might have a concussion."

"Isabela hit me with a champagne bottle," Duanphen declared.

"Yes, I know."

"I *said* I was sorry," Isabela said from across the cockpit's seating area, where she huddled with her knees pulled tightly to her chest. Caleb was next to her, staring off into the distance while one of his duplicates paced back and forth in front of him. No one had bothered to mention that Caleb had popped a clone. They were all too tired and rattled to bother.

"It's fine," Duanphen replied dreamily to Isabela. Then, something clicked on in her mind and she leaned forward to peer around Ran. "I don't have a crush on you. That was a lie."

Isabela tossed her hair. "I wouldn't blame you if you did."

"Okay," Duanphen said, leaning back. "Good."

"We would make a hot couple," Isabela said thoughtfully.

The duplicate stopped pacing to look from Isabela to Duanphen and back, seeming to consider this statement. Caleb looked up, realized there was a second him walking around and immediately absorbed it.

"How's her arm?" Caleb asked.

Ran took Duanphen's hand and carefully turned her arm over so that she could examine the gash in her forearm. The stitches weren't the neatest Ran had seen in her life—no one would mistake them for the work of an actual doctor—but they were straight and clean and they'd successfully stopped the bleeding.

"It looks okay, actually," Ran said.

"One of the only things my idiot Cêpan taught me was first aid," Five said as he climbed out of the pilot's seat, the skimmer set on a course to Mexico. The Loric had been the one to stitch Duanphen's cut closed, his thick hands surprisingly gentle. Now, he stood over Ran's shoulder and looked down at his handiwork. "You want me to take a turn keeping her awake?"

Ran stood up, arching her back. "Yes. Thank you."

Five took her place on the floor in front of Duanphen, his one eye watching her closely. They'd loaded Duanphen up on some painkillers that Einar had stashed and she was loopy enough to put her legs in Five's lap. He didn't move them. Instead, he awkwardly patted Duanphen on the shin—he'd broken that bone during their first meeting, or so the story went, then carried her back to Einar's ship and made a splint for her.

Lucas had called them monsters. Ran didn't believe that, though. None of them were beyond saving.

"Any word from our friends at the Academy?" Einar asked. He sat on the arm of the copilot's seat, his body angled to face the rest of them. He didn't glance up from his tablet when he spoke.

Isabela uncurled enough to check her cell. Now that they knew the Foundation was using a precognitive Garde to track them, one little flip phone didn't seem like such a big deal. They had tried calling the Academy as they fled Moroccan airspace, but the call went straight to voice mail. Isabela had left a message—*"Professor Dumdum, it is Isabela. There is a body-snatching Garde that's super into Jesus headed your way. Call back, please!"*—but they hadn't gotten a response. That didn't bode well.

"No service," Isabela said. "Maybe once we're across this ocean . . ."

"It's possible that Earth Garde cut off their communication," Einar said contemplatively. "It's what I would do."

"Shouldn't we be going there?" Caleb asked. "If they're in danger . . ."

"We can do more to help them by not flying directly into Earth Garde's clutches," Einar said curtly.

"No, instead we're flying straight to a Garde prison," Caleb responded. He looked at Ran, probably expecting her to back him up. She thought of Nigel and the others back at the Academy, already surrounded by Peacekeepers who planned to enslave them, and now Lucas was headed there for some nefarious purpose. It wasn't an easy call to make.

Ran reluctantly shook her head. "They can take care of themselves," she told Caleb gently. "And, right now, I think we can do more to help them from the outside."

Caleb didn't respond. He looked down at his feet, hands balled up in front of him. Clearly, something was still eating at him, and Ran didn't think it was entirely the fate of their friends at the Academy.

"Do we even have a plan yet?" Isabela asked.

Ran wondered the same thing. She went to stand next to Einar, glancing at the information displayed on his tablet. She saw a floor plan for a large cube-shaped building that was then divided into many smaller boxes. A very efficiently constructed prison. Einar gave Ran a sour look—he liked to be the one in control and wasn't yet ready to do his whole briefing thing—but relented when Ran placidly gazed back at him.

"This is the prison where King said Lucas would be housed. The locals used to call the place *La Caldera* . . ."

"The boiler," Isabela said.

"They'd sweat confessions out of criminals there," Einar said with a nod. "Or the cartels would rent cells to torture their enemies. The Mexican government shut it down for corruption a few years back and that's how the Foundation snapped it up. Since then, they've installed a number of high-tech upgrades."

"You learned all this from King?" Ran asked.

Einar nodded again. "He was nice enough to grant me access to his company's internal server. Blackstone still had details of the prison from when they staffed it in the early days, before the Foundation cleaned it up so they could rent it to Earth Garde."

It occurred to Ran that they hadn't carried out the rest of their plan back in Morocco. They'd wanted to set King up for arrest on the casino floor, but had gotten sidetracked running for their lives. That meant King was still in play.

"King will cut off your access soon, won't he?" Ran asked. "He could warn the Foundation."

Einar hesitated. "Yes. You're right. I'll make sure to download what we need. As for warning them, we'll just have to take our chances."

Caleb made a noise, like a solitary laugh that got caught in his throat. He was staring at Einar in the usual way he did right before an argument broke out. But, for once, he didn't say anything. He just sat there grinding his teeth. That silence concerned Ran.

"What is it, Caleb?" she asked.

"Yes," Einar added, meeting Caleb's eyes. "Do you have something to add?"

The question hung in the air for a couple of seconds and something passed between the two boys; Ran wasn't sure what. The skimmer bobbed back and forth on a rough wind and Duanphen let out a low moan.

Finally, Caleb spoke. "Who were those guys back there? The ones who came in shooting?"

"If I had to guess, it was a security detail assigned to King, kept off-site so that they would've give the trap away," Einar said with a shrug. "Or, they could have been local cops. Interpol. Peacekeepers. Overzealous hotel security. At present, there are no shortage of people who'd like to take shots at our kind. Why does that matter now?"

"I just never thought it would get like this," Caleb replied, looking down at the floor again. "For you, maybe. I could see why they'd want to shoot at *you*. You've earned that. But they didn't care who they hit when they came into the room." Caleb tapped his forehead. "One of my duplicates took a bullet right here. That could've been me."

Ran hadn't even considered this. She'd been in enough dangerous situations since developing her Legacies that a few bullets no longer fazed her.

"And unleashing that Lucas guy on us . . . ," Caleb

continued, his eyes drifting over to Duanphen. "She could've died. He cut her open like she's not even a person."

"He's sick," Isabela added. "Crazier than any of you."

"That's why we're going to get him, aren't we?" Five asked gruffly. "Can we get back to talking about *el crackpot*?"

"*La Caldera*," Einar corrected, but he was still looking at Caleb. "What do you say, Caleb? Should we move on?"

It surprised Ran to hear a bit of patience in Einar's typically clipped words. Caleb crossed his arms and rubbed his shoulders—Ran could tell there was something nagging at him, he looked too haunted for this to just be about a duplicate getting shot—but he eventually nodded in agreement. "Go ahead. Tell us how we get to Lucas."

"It won't be easy," Einar said, paging through floor plans on his tablet. "The prison is fifty miles west of the nearest city, in the middle of the desert. Only one road leads in and the surrounding area is nothing but scrubland."

"Was our plan to drive up and knock on the door?" Isabela asked.

"I'm just painting a picture," Einar said. "There's a wall . . ."

Ran eased the tablet out of Einar's hands and flipped it over so the rest of them could see the prison's layout. He paused for a moment, then cleared his throat and continued.

"As you can see, there's a wall five hundred yards out with an initial checkpoint. Then, past that, another stretch of open ground covered by snipers in the guard towers. Beyond that is the fortified main entrance."

"So, we don't go that way," Five said. "We've got a ship that can turn invisible. We land on the roof and blast our way in."

"That seems to be the better option, but there are still issues," Einar said. "For one, I stole this skimmer from the Foundation. They know its capabilities. I don't know for certain that they can beat our skimmer's stealth mode. But I do know that they've installed antiaircraft weaponry on their roof. There's a chance we could come under fire."

"Does this ship have any weapons?" Caleb asked. "Could we shoot back?"

Five grunted. "No. The weapons are down. Honestly, this piece of shit is barely holding together."

Isabela stared at him. "We're over the ocean and you're just now telling us that?"

"I thought everyone knew," Five said. He knocked on the metal floor beneath him and the skimmer seemed to groan in response. "We'll be fine."

"Easy for you to say," Isabela countered. "You can fly."

"Okay, say we land on the roof," Caleb said. "What then?"

"Well, even if we take them by surprise, there will still be some sentries to get by. But then, as we move inside . . ." Einar highlighted the top story of the prison. "This floor is the guards' barracks. The staff works in five-day shifts, sleeping on the premises."

"We'd be breaching at their strongest point," Caleb said with a frown.

"Yes," Einar said. "Not ideal."

"How many guys they got?" Five asked.

"Based on the rooms in this blueprint and assuming they're fully staffed? I'd estimate three hundred."

"I can take three hundred," Five said with a shrug.

Isabela snorted. "You sound like Professor Nine."

Five glared at her. "Take that back."

"These Peacekeepers won't be like the ones guarding the Academy," Einar said. "I don't think even you can do this alone, Five."

Five wilted a bit when Einar spoke. "I wouldn't be doing it *alone*," he muttered. "Ran's good. Caleb is a small army by himself. *We* can take them."

Ran tapped her finger on Einar's tablet. "Does it get easier? Assuming we can make it through the barracks?"

"The second floor houses the medical center, the control room, the warden's office and the armory," Einar replied. "Assuming we can push through the barracks, it's likely we'll find a second wave of Peacekeepers waiting at the armory."

"What can we do from the control room?" Caleb asked.

"Their surveillance cameras feed there. The prison's internal defenses are operated from there as well."

"What kind of defenses?" Five asked.

"Titanium doors for a lockdown, gas dispersal mechanisms in the vents and electrified tiles. They don't mean for Garde to escape this place, much less break in."

"Oh, there are traps," Isabela said. "Of course."

"Sounds like Nine's obstacle course," Caleb said.

Einar went on. "The ground floor is a central processing

area, a cafeteria for prisoners and a small yard for exercise. The two basement levels are nothing but isolation cells. That's where we'll find our target."

"Once we make it to the control room, we'll have the advantage," Ran mused.

"Yes and no," Einar replied. "There's also something here they call the *Skeleton Key*. It's a remote mechanism keyed to the warden's biometrics that gives him control of the prison's systems. We'll need to track him down."

Isabela leaned forward, her voice more serious now. "I saw this warden. I know what he looks like. The Skeleton Key is a silly glove thingy he wears."

Caleb raised an eyebrow. "How do you know that?"

"Something got screwy when Lucas tried to jump into your duplicate," Isabela replied. "I could see out through his eyes. He was in a cell with the warden and one of those Cêpan people. The warden activated his Inhibitor to bring Lucas back to his own body."

"Could you shape-shift into the warden?" Ran asked.

"Of course," Isabela replied. "I made sure to memorize the bastard's face."

"Perhaps that might be an easier way in than fighting down from the roof," Ran suggested. "At least for Isabela."

"They've got retinal scanners at the front gate," Einar said, looking to Isabela. "Can your shape-shifting beat those?"

She thought for a moment. "Maybe."

"Maybe," Caleb repeated. "You'd be taking a big chance."

Isabela turned to look at Caleb, and Ran noted a look of

resolve on the Brazilian's face that she'd never seen before.

"I want to get this guy," she said icily. "What he did to me—it can't happen to anyone else."

Einar cleared his throat. "Well, our options appear to be either brute force or subterfuge, neither of which seem to have a high likelihood of success."

"Why not both?" Five asked, looking at Einar. "No offense, but if it comes to a brawl, you and Isabela won't be much help. Better off trying every angle."

"We'll be outnumbered and spread thin, either way," Einar said. He glared down at the tablet, like it had betrayed him by not presenting an easier way in.

"Sounds like a suicide mission," Duanphen said, her head lolling to the side. "Fun."

"We cannot think like that," Ran replied. "Taylor told us that they could be holding other Garde in this place. Sam Goode, Number Six, maybe others that Earth Garde and the Foundation have taken prisoner. If we can make it to the cells and set them free, the battle could turn in our favor."

Caleb began ticking off his fingers. "We fight our way in. We take over the control room. We track down the Warden and his Skeleton Key. We make it to the cells and start letting Garde loose. We find Lucas . . ."

A silence settled over the cockpit. They weren't only contemplating the enormity of the task before them, Ran knew. They were also grappling with a bigger question, one that they'd avoided discussing even though all of them had probably thought about it.

It was Ran who finally said it out loud. "When we get to Lucas, what do we do with him?"

"He needs to be stopped," Isabela said.

"And how do we accomplish that?" Ran asked. "Specifically?"

Five grunted. "Fine. I'll be the one that say it. We kill him."

Ran peered down at Five, keeping her expression neutral. "He is confused. Damaged. Does that make him a monster? Should we be the ones who decide that there's no saving him?"

Five met her gaze for a moment, then looked away. Ran honestly wasn't sure about the answers to her own questions. She hadn't made up her own mind about what to do with the deranged son of the Harvesters.

Isabela didn't waffle. "Piss on that. I've seen his mind, Ran. There's no saving this one."

"I agree with Isabela," Duanphen said weakly.

"He's got an Inhibitor inside him and he can't jump into my duplicates," Caleb said. "We could contain him. Take him prisoner."

Isabela leaned away from Caleb. "And what if he escapes? Then whoever he hurts next will be on us."

Einar pinched the bridge of his nose. "I made a pledge not to hurt any of our kind. But Lucas . . . I don't know."

"Where does it stop?" Ran asked. "When do we become no better than those we're fighting against?"

Another strong gust of wind caused the skimmer to sway

back and forth. Five stood up and went to the controls, not looking in Ran's direction. Isabela came to sit next to Duanphen to make sure she didn't fall asleep. Einar took his tablet back from Ran and left the cockpit. Caleb leaned back against the wall and closed his eyes, his legs bouncing restlessly. Ran stood there, waiting.

No one had an answer for her.

CHAPTER NINETEEN

ON THE EVE OF BATTLE
THE HUMAN GARDE ACADEMY—POINT REYES, CALIFORNIA

"I'M SORRY," TAYLOR SAID. "MY OLD ROOMMATE would've been much better at this."

Taylor held up a mirror so that Vontezza could examine her handiwork. It had taken no small amount of concealer and blush to put some color into Vontezza's face, the makeup not easy to apply by candlelight and with Vontezza constantly flinching away from her brush. Now, the Mogadorian sneered at her own reflection and swatted the mirror away.

"Disgusting," Vontezza said. "I look like a clown."

From the couch on the opposite side of the pod, Kopano laughed. Taylor turned away from Vontezza to glare at him. This whole ordeal was his fault, volunteering Taylor to teach a Mogadorian to put on makeup. Like she didn't have enough problems.

Catching Taylor's glare, Kopano raised his hands. "I'm sorry. I should've known you wouldn't be good at makeup, being such a natural beauty yourself."

Taylor groaned at his clumsy attempt at a save. So did Rabiya, who'd been observing the whole makeup demonstration from the doorway of her room.

Vontezza rubbed both her hands across her face, which only made matters worse. Taylor cringed and Rabiya stifled a laugh. Sensing them watching her, Vontezza stood up abruptly and marched to the bathroom.

"This is idiotic," she growled. She grabbed the front of the flannel shirt she'd donned instead of her armor and twisted it. "These clothes are useless, too. I hate this planet."

Maybe she was exhausted from the last few days. Maybe it was being in her dorm room where she'd shared so many memories with Ran and Isabela. But the more agitated Vontezza got, the funnier the situation became. Taylor found herself loosening up for the first time in a while.

"I hate this planet," Taylor repeated, hiding a laugh as she flopped down on the couch next to Kopano.

"Be careful," Kopano said in a stage whisper. "If you make her really angry, she'll make you hit her with a mace."

Vontezza didn't hear them. She was too busy savagely scrubbing at her face with soap and water.

At first, Taylor had been annoyed that Kopano volunteered her untrained makeover services to Vontezza. But now, she felt grateful for the distraction. She leaned against

Kopano and he put his arm around her.

"You've got a big heart," she said, feeling suddenly sincere in her loopy state. "You're like pathologically determined to help everyone you come in contact with. Even Mogadorians."

"Isn't that why we're here?" Kopano asked. "But yes, you're right. I am great."

Taylor laughed softly and leaned up to kiss his cheek. She sensed Rabiya disappear back into her room at that point and felt kind of bad for the PDA. But oh well. This might be their last night on campus and this was her room. She'd grab any moment of happiness she could.

Vontezza emerged from the bathroom with her hair down, the massive braid unraveled into a wavy curtain of black that fell to her hips. She pushed it to one side so that it covered her tattoos.

"My people lived among Earth's population for years," she said. "It should not be so difficult to blend in."

"That was when no one knew that Mogadorians existed," Kopano replied.

"There was a teacher at my school with dark hair and a pale complexion," Taylor said, remembering. "Someone keyed his car after the invasion."

"Because he was Mogadorian?" Vontezza asked.

"No, obviously not," Taylor replied. "Just because he looked like one of you."

Vontezza stared at her blankly. "I don't understand the point of your story, blond one. I am a trueborn, not some weak teacher. And I don't own a car."

Taylor sighed, leaning against Kopano. "You're fun to have around."

"No," Vontezza replied. "I am not."

Rabiya emerged from her room and tossed a bundle of clothes to Vontezza. The Mogadorian snapped them out of the air like a knife had been thrown at her.

"Try that on," Rabiya said.

Vontezza untangled the clothes and held them out in front of her. A dark blue hijab and matching scarf.

"Not that wearing a hijab is inconspicuous in this country," Rabiya said. "But at least they won't be able to tell you're Mogadorian."

"Yes," Vontezza replied as she pulled her head into the garment and then carefully began stuffing her hair inside. "This is acceptable."

"Good idea," Taylor said to Rabiya.

"Yeah," Rabiya replied, looking away from her and Kopano. "Thanks."

The door to the pod cracked open and Nigel poked his head inside. He did a double take when he first spotted Rabiya standing in the doorway to Ran's old room, then scowled and looked at Taylor.

"Right," Nigel said by way of greeting. "Everyone's meeting at the student union. You ready?"

Taylor eased herself out from under Kopano's arm. It was nice while it lasted.

"I'm ready."

When they ran out of candles and battery-powered flashlights, the Academy students made torches. They cut green branches from the trees, wrapped cotton gym shirts around their ends, dipped them in kerosene and let Omar breathe on them. The pathway from the dorms to the student union was lit by a row of these and Kopano couldn't help but smile at his classmates' ingenuity. He pulled one of the torches out of the ground and carried it, waving the flame back and forth in front of him.

"Careful with that," Nigel said.

"This is very cool, don't you think?" Kopano asked. "Like a movie."

"We're under siege, mate. But I'm glad you're having fun."

Kopano squinted towards the student union. He could see shadows milling around in there, all the remaining students and instructors left on campus—except for the handful that had drawn guard duty at the barricade. He smelled hamburgers and hot dogs.

"Yeah, maybe we're in trouble," Kopano replied to Nigel, patting his smaller friend's bony shoulder. "But don't you feel it? We are together. We're going to win."

Taylor glanced over her shoulder at them. "Is he being irrationally positive again?"

"You know it," Nigel replied. "Kopano, when they drilled that Inhibitor into your head were you like '*Oi, this is great, it don't hurt near as much as I thought it would!*'"

Kopano grinned. "That does sound like me!"

They were making fun of him, but Kopano could sense that his positivity was working. He saw how Nigel's posture straightened and how Taylor walked a little taller. They knew he was right.

As they neared the student union, they bumped into John and Nine heading in the same direction.

"You ready to inspire everyone?" Nine asked Taylor.

"You sure you don't want to do the talking?" she replied.

"Better coming from you, I think," Nine answered. "I'd probably just curse a bunch."

"I could say something, if you want," John put in.

Taylor hesitated. "Honestly, it's probably better if you just stand there and look, uh—"

"Silently handsome," Nigel supplied.

"Sure," Taylor continued. "That. People are comfortable knowing you're here. It makes them feel safe. But when it comes to talking about our situation, I think that should come from one of us. Maybe once I get them used to the idea, you can jump in."

"Makes sense," John replied, holding the student union door open for them. As Taylor entered, Kopano noticed how John looked at her. He wasn't leering or checking her out—it was worse than that. John looked at Taylor the same way that Kopano often felt himself looking at Taylor. With a mixture of admiration and longing. Kopano's smile faltered just a bit.

As he was last through the door, Kopano put a hand on John's shoulder. "Do you have a girlfriend back in India, John Smith?"

"No. Not exactly," John said, giving Kopano a weird look. "I had a—well, I had something for a while, but it didn't work out. It's, uh . . . it's complicated."

"Compli—*oof*—"

Before Kopano could get out his follow-up question, Nicolas Lambert bumped shoulders with him. The student union was packed, so Nic had an excuse, but Kopano could tell he'd done it on purpose. John didn't notice and was actually probably relieved to get away from Kopano anyway. Nic shot Kopano a look, then went to stand with Anika and Maiken.

Nigel sidled up next to Kopano, staring down Nic. "Prick's got it out for you because you stood up for the Mog girl," he said. Kopano had told Nigel about the incident earlier and seen the anger flare in his roommate's eyes. No one hated bullies more than his British friend.

Kopano shook his head, grateful at the moment that Vontezza had volunteered to prowl the woods on the Academy's perimeter rather than attend the torchlit assembly.

"He'll get over it," Kopano said. "What's he going to do? Bump my shoulder and mean-mug me? I can handle that."

"That's just how shitheads like that get started," Nigel responded grimly. "Might need to nip it in the bud if we want a proper unified front."

"It's okay," Kopano said with a wave of his hand. "Let it go."

Nigel's eyes narrowed and continued to track Nicolas. Kopano took a deep breath and turned his attention elsewhere. Miki stood with his old friends in the tweebs, nodding encouragingly as one of them demonstrated a tiny spark jumping from his fingernail—a newly discovered Legacy. The remaining faculty, including Malcolm and Dr. Chen, were gathered on the second level, watching the students from above. Kopano did a quick head count. There were about a dozen teachers up there, less than a quarter of their original number. Still, not bad. He respected them for sticking it out.

Everyone was together. Unified. Kopano thought that was awesome. He spread his arms out, put one around Nigel and the other around Simon who happened to be standing next to him, and squeezed.

"This is what we've been training for," Kopano declared. "It might feel like we're in trouble, like this is an end—but it's not. This is the *start*."

"Okay, mate," Nigel replied, patting his back. "Calm down."

The room fell respectfully quiet when Taylor climbed onto a table in the center. The torches cast dramatic shadows across her face as she looked around at the assembled students, trying to make eye contact with as many of them as possible. Kopano had told her to do that. Eye contact and good posture, he'd told her. She'd rolled her eyes, of course, but he was used to that.

"Today, I told representatives from the UN what we expect from them," Taylor said. She spoke normally, but her voice carried well. That was Nigel's doing. "I told them that we refuse to let them put Inhibitors in us. I told them that we want a bigger say in what kind of missions we're assigned to once we graduate from the Academy." She glanced up at the balcony and nodded at Professor Nine. "I told them that we want to be represented by people we trust, who have our best interests at heart."

"And then they turned our power off," Maiken said. Some students grumbled in response.

"Yeah, they told me this isn't a negotiation," Taylor replied. "They don't care about what we want. We pissed them off by ignoring them today. I've got it on pretty good authority that tomorrow, they're going to try to remove us by force."

An anxious murmur went through the crowd. Kopano noted a lot of nervous glances between students. However, just as many of his classmates appeared to steel themselves at the news.

"I know it feels like us against the world right now," Taylor continued. "But that's not true. Not everyone at the UN is bad. Look up at the gallery—" She gestured to where Dr. Chen and the remaining instructors stood. "There are people within these walls that agree with us and believe in the Garde. Before they turned off our power, I saw people on the news arguing on our behalf."

"There were just as many saying we should be locked up," Simon murmured. Kopano frowned at him.

"I want to believe that people are good," Taylor said. "I want to believe that the UN will come to their senses. But until that happens . . . we fight."

Another ripple went through the room. Kopano felt his classmates squeeze in a little closer.

"We don't want to hurt any of the Peacekeepers. But we're going to defend ourselves," Taylor's voice got a little louder, a little harder. "We're going to show them that we won't be pushed around."

"Hell yeah!" someone yelled, Kopano wasn't sure who. He was more focused on a couple of tweebs at the back of the room, neither of them older than thirteen, the two of them huddled together and looking near tears.

"I know this is asking a lot," Taylor went on, softening her tone now. "Some of you are a million miles from home. You already miss your families and your old lives. And now I'm up here asking you to basically become outlaws." She shook her head. "It's crazy, I know. If you told me when I first came to this Academy that one day I'd be giving a speech like this, I probably would've peed my pants a little."

Some light laughter from the crowd. Taylor let that subside before going on.

"Maybe, you're thinking, the deal the UN is offering doesn't sound so bad. They say they'll only use the Inhibitors as a last resort. You're a good person. They won't ever need to shock you or control you." She pointed towards the doors of the student union and the dark night beyond. "We aren't going to stop anyone from leaving and joining them. I wouldn't hold it against anyone that wants to play it safe, that doesn't want to take the risk."

Taylor paused, as if she was waiting for someone to make

a break for the door. Everyone looked around, eyeing each other, waiting for the same thing. No one walked out.

"But if you *are* considering that, let me tell you about a healer that I met when the Foundation first kidnapped me," Taylor said. "His name was Bunji, although he couldn't tell me that himself because Bunji couldn't speak. He'd been shocked so many times by an early version of the Inhibitor that he was basically a vegetable. His Legacies still worked, though. There was a woman with him—a nurse, maybe, or one of these people they're trying to pass off as a Cêpan— and she could get Bunji to use his healing Legacy. They had him trained for that. He wasn't a person anymore. He was a means to an end."

Kopano had heard that story before and still his stomach turned at the thought. Looking around, he could tell the story had a similar effect on many of his classmates.

"They did that to a healer," Taylor continued, her voice low. The flickering torchlight made Kopano think of telling ghost stories. "Not someone with a dangerous Legacy. Just someone that didn't listen. Someone that wouldn't do what they asked. Can we really trust that won't happen to us? Shouldn't we have a say in how we live our lives and use our Legacies?"

The murmurs of agreement were stronger now. Kopano smiled fiercely. No one was looking at the door anymore.

"Maybe you've noticed I keep saying the UN instead of Earth Garde," Taylor said, her voice rising again. She was good at this. "They make Earth Garde sound so great, right?

Try really hard at the Academy and one day you'll get to wear a cool uniform and hang out with Melanie Jackson." Taylor snorted. "There's three Garde out there with the Peacekeepers that claim to represent Earth Garde. One of them is Melanie. One of them is a girl who used to work for the Foundation. The other's a total dunce. Just three. How many of us are there?" Taylor looked pointedly around the room. Then, she pointed up to Nine and John. "How many of the Loric are out there? None. And how many are in here?"

Taylor paused, her lips compressed, her eyes narrowed. Her angry face. Her determined face.

"Earth Garde isn't out there," Taylor said. "They don't get to call themselves that. Earth Garde is right here. It's *us*. We *are* Earth Garde."

"Damn right," Nigel yelled. "We are Earth Garde!"

Kopano joined in. "We are Earth Garde!"

Maiken. Simon. Miki. "We are Earth Garde!"

Nicolas. Omar. Rabiya. "We are Earth Garde!"

Everyone. "WE ARE EARTH GARDE!"

"Good," Taylor said, once the shouting subsided. "Then if you're with me, here's what we're going to do . . ."

"Our goal is to hold the Academy and prevent any of our people from falling into Earth Garde's clutches," Taylor told the room. She looked up at the balcony, where John and Nine stood together. "But if we feel like that's a losing fight, we've got a backup plan. John?"

Maybe it was a little showy that John chose to float down from the second level so that he could stand next to Taylor on the table, but she didn't mind. It was a relief, actually, to have the attention on someone else for a while. All those shining eyes looking up at her were starting to freak her out.

They trusted her. They really thought she knew what she was doing.

John explained what he'd been building in India. Taylor, a little dazed from giving her own speech, didn't really listen. Her eyes found Kopano in the crowd. He flashed her a thumbs-up.

"With one more force field generator, I'll be able to secure the area," John was saying. "But we don't want to give away New Lorien's existence before it's safe, which means you guys will have to hold out here until I have everything installed." He glanced at Taylor, then up at Nine. "Hopefully, it won't come to running. We want to keep this Academy open. We want to work with Earth Garde—"

"But we also want to live free," Taylor added. She looked around. "Any questions?"

Of course there were questions.

At some point, Taylor and John climbed down from the table. Nine and Malcolm descended from the second level to explain how things would work. They elected team leaders. Some people trickled out for guard duty, others to rest and still more to work on defenses for tomorrow. Taylor let the activity swirl around her and carry her forward. She talked to as many of the students as she could. Of course, many of them seemed nervous, but they were also resolute and upbeat.

They felt ready.

The pep rally was all well and good. Taylor did a bang-up job. But Nigel knew that for a movement like theirs to be successful, someone had to be willing to get their hands dirty. He was happy to take that on himself.

He was his mother's son, after all.

Nigel remembered how guys like Nicolas operated back at Pepperpont. The little aggressions like a shoulder bump or a snide remark that didn't seem so bad at first—nothing you couldn't tolerate—that gradually escalated into grander humiliations and finally brutal cruelties. Those prep school pricks had hurt Nigel badly enough without Legacies. What were people like Nicolas and his cronies capable of if left to their own devices?

So after the meeting let out, Nigel kept an eye on Nicolas.

He watched from the shadows as Nicolas had a quiet conversation with Anika and a couple of tweebs on the lawn in front of the dorms. He watched as that guy Ben joined them, all of them huddled together, plotting something.

It was the same group Kopano told him about; the wannabe lynch mob that had gotten in Vontezza's face. Nigel wasn't exactly crazy about having a Mog on campus either, but if John Smith vouched for her, then he figured she must be decent enough. Nigel was more concerned with the kind of damage that Nicolas and his friends could do to the Academy. Were they so pissed off about Vontezza's presence that they'd sell out to Earth Garde?

When the six of them left the torch-lit expanse of the lawn for the empty Academics Building, Nigel became even more suspicious. He'd been around the Foundation enough to know what a conspiracy looked like.

Nigel muted his footfalls so that the others wouldn't hear him padding across the tile floor behind them. Thanks to all the lights being out, it was easy to trail them. He watched the group file into an empty first-floor classroom. Figuring that no one was around, Nicolas and his crew didn't even bother to shut the door.

Nigel edged along the hallway, not exactly sure what he should do. It would be just one of him against six others. He knew that he should get help. That would be the smart move. But it had been a long day and something inside Nigel had frayed along the way. He was tired of shadowy cabals and secret meetings. He was tired of losing.

"What did he say to you before he left?" That was Anika's voice. Nigel stood just outside the door, his back against the wall, listening in.

"He said he would protect us," Nicolas answered. "Said those bastards wouldn't even see him coming."

That was it, then. Another betrayal. Nicolas had made contact with someone from the other side and arranged to keep his little clique safe. They'd probably blown the secret of New Lorien, too.

Before he even knew what he was doing, Nigel lunged into the room. He was so, so sick of this. Visions flashed through his mind—the sneering faces of the Pepperpont boys as they loomed over him, the dark tunnels beneath Patience Creek, Einar whispering in his ear, his mother's back as she walked away from him. He wanted to make someone hurt.

Nigel whistled. It was a little trick he'd been working on in the training center. He used his Legacy to ratchet up the volume into a piercing, teeth-grinding siren. Then, he shaped the vibrations into an arrow, focused and aimed the whistle right for Nic's eardrum. Take down the biggest one first, that was the rule of the schoolyard.

Nic howled and fell off the desk he'd been sitting on, clutching the sides of his head. The group had been arranged in a circle and now all of them stood up in alarm. A bag of tortilla chips one of the tweebs was holding spilled everywhere. As Nic writhed on the ground, five sets of wide, panicked eyes focused on Nigel.

"What are you doing?" Anika shouted, flinching as Nigel redirected his whistle in her direction. "Stop it!"

Something didn't feel right.

For one, Anika held a box of tissues in front of her to ward Nigel off. There were also way too many snacks for a conspiracy. And wasn't that the Sharing Bear—an old plaything of Dr. Linda's that she once tried to get Nigel to hold a one-sided therapeutic conversation with—on the floor next to Nicolas?

Nigel stopped whistling, glaring at the others. But no one tried to attack him. Nic, groaning, managed to sit up. He gingerly touched his ear and winced.

"Right, then, what the hell is this?" Nigel demanded. "If you lot think you're going to sell the rest of us out to Earth Garde—"

"What are you talking about?" Nic yelled. At that moment, he was both angry and a little deaf. "We aren't selling out, you asshole!"

"We're on your side," Ben said nervously. "I mean, I thought we were."

Nigel pointed down at Nic. "I heard about what went down with you and the Mogadorian. Saw you trying to intimidate Kopano. I know your bloody type—"

"Yeah, we tried to scare off that psycho Mog," Nic replied sharply. "But we didn't—ugh, you really hurt my ear, man."

Anika came forward with her hands raised, her voice gentle. "We realized that all of us lost people during the invasion," she said. "We thought, instead of taking out our feelings on other people—or hideous aliens—that we should talk about what happened to us."

Nigel wiped a hand across his eyes. "Bollocks. I just assaulted a support group."

"Don't make it sound so lame," Nicolas snarled.

"When you came in, Nic was telling us about the last

conversation he had with his brother," Anika said. "Before he was killed in the invasion."

Nigel took a step back. At that moment, he wished that he had Kopano's Legacy so he could just go transparent and sink through the floor. The others were all staring at him, afraid of what he might do next. Paranoia, cynicism, rage—that was his mother's legacy to him. Nigel felt like he might be sick.

"I'm—I'm sorry," he stammered. "I'll go."

His cheeks were hot and his eyes were wet as Nigel left the room. He wanted to run. To get as far away as possible.

As he stumbled through the dark hallway, Nigel was vaguely aware of movement behind him. A strong hand clasped his upper arm and turned him around. Nicolas, back on his feet, a small trickle of blood visible in the cup of his ear. Nigel braced himself. He'd been punched before. He deserved to be punched again.

"Hey—hey, man, stop—" Nic said awkwardly.

The fit Belgian loomed over Nigel, but he didn't look angry. It took Nigel a moment to register the unfamiliar expression on Nic's face. Sympathy.

"I've heard, uh, about what happened to you," Nic continued. "Maybe you should stay. Talk with us. Or just listen. You know, if you want."

Somehow, Nigel found himself pressed against the larger boy's chest. He shuddered. Nic patted his shoulders, squeezed the back of his neck.

"Okay," Nigel said. "But don't tell anyone about this."

Nic snorted. "Yeah. You neither."

Hours after her speech, Taylor peeked through a tangle of metal desk legs, watching the woods. It was late and everything was quiet. There weren't any Peacekeepers lurking out there. Her four hours of guard duty—she'd volunteered for a late shift—were almost up. She'd spent the entire time rehashing her speech and the discussions afterwards. Did she say the right things? Did she forget any details? Could they tell how nervous she was? Standing up in front of her classmates and pretending that she wasn't just some farm girl from South Dakota but a leader, someone who knew what she was talking about.

"Sure fooled them," she softly said to herself.

Footfalls behind her broke Taylor from her thoughts. She spun around to see Maiken approaching. Taylor's shift was over.

"Go get some sleep," Maiken said. "You look beat."

"Thanks," Taylor said dryly.

Taylor padded towards the dorms along the torch-lit path. She glanced up, saw a shadow perched on the wall near the roof and waved at Nine. He waved back from his vantage point. Knowing Nine, he probably wouldn't sleep tonight. And, despite what Maiken said, Taylor didn't feel like she could either.

It occurred to her that, for the first time in hours, she was free. There was nothing left for her to do. She could breathe. She wouldn't waste that time sleeping.

Taylor knocked gently on the door to Kopano's pod. She figured that she looked a mess; hair wavy and matted, eyes tired. She didn't care. Anyway, it was dark.

Kopano came to the door quickly. He wore just his pajama pants, which were a little too short for him—he'd grown a couple of inches in the months since their arrival. He held a candle, the tiny light flickering in his dark eyes. He lit up when he saw her, a look that Taylor never got tired of.

"Good," Taylor said. "You're still awake."

"I *should* be sleeping," Kopano replied, leaning in his doorway. "I need to be up very early for my mission with, ah, what's-his-name."

Taylor tilted her head. "John Smith. Your idol."

Kopano snapped his fingers. "Yes. Him."

Taylor brushed off this weirdness. "Is Nigel here?"

Kopano looked a little crestfallen that she was at his door asking about his roommate. "Um, no, actually. I don't know where he's gotten off to."

"Good," Taylor replied and put both her hands on Kopano's chest, pushing him back into his room. "I'm spending the night."

"You're—"

Before Kopano could fully respond, Taylor went up on her toes to kiss him. She needed this. Change was coming. Danger was on the horizon. All that. Taylor didn't know what tomorrow might bring for either of them. This could be their last chance to act irresponsibly. She was going to take it.

Kopano scooped her up with one arm and her legs found their way around his waist. He set the candle down. She slammed the front door with her telekinesis.

Nobody got much sleep that night.

CHAPTER TWENTY

KOPANO OKEKE
THE *OSIRIS*—PFEIFFER BEACH, CALIFORNIA

"IT IS WAY TOO EARLY FOR YOU TO BE SMILING like that," Miki said, knuckling some sleep out of his eyes.

"Yes, I agree," Vontezza said, her sharp tone only slightly muffled by the hijab and scarf wrapped around her head. "What is wrong with you, large one? Has your mind broken?"

Kopano sucked in a deep breath of the cold morning air. The sun wasn't even up yet and the three of them were standing outside the administration building, waiting for John Smith to finish a last-minute meeting with Professor Nine. Kopano tried to turn down the wattage of his dumb smile, but it wasn't easy.

"Sorry," he said. "But isn't this exciting? We're about to

do something that will help ensure the safety of our people. It's cool!"

"My people," Vontezza replied grimly, "are about to surrender themselves to life in a detention center."

"Which is where the rest of us will be headed if the UN has their way," Miki added, equally jaded.

Kopano blew out a sigh and waved his hands. "You two. Everything will be *fine*. I know this. The world is good."

"Idiot," Vontezza grumbled.

Of course, Kopano couldn't tell them the real reason that he kept smiling, despite the life-and-death circumstances they and their classmates faced that day. It wouldn't be gentlemanly.

"*Sock on the door wouldn't have killed ya*," Nigel had grumbled that morning as Kopano left their room.

That too had made Kopano smile. He couldn't help himself. It was a glorious day.

Just then, John emerged from the administration building. Unlike the others, he appeared relatively well rested. At some point since the night before, he'd trimmed the patchy blond beard. Kopano supposed he wanted to look fresh and authoritative for his interactions with the military.

"Good to go?" John asked.

Vontezza pointed her thumb at Kopano. "This one won't stop showing his teeth."

John considered this for a moment, ultimately deciding that it wasn't worth commenting on. He turned to Miki. "So

I'll handle the flight to the landing site to keep you fresh for moving the generator."

Miki coughed into his fist. "That's good. I'm still a little worn from yesterday."

"Spot me, though, okay?" John said. "Make sure I'm doing it right."

"Sure," Miki replied, then looked at Kopano and Vontezza. "Just so you know, the wind transformation can be a little weird at first. Remember that you're air and the air doesn't need to breathe."

Vontezza's brow furrowed. "What?"

Kopano nodded sagely. "Cool mantra."

"It's not—" Miki sighed and held out his hands. "Let's do this."

They all linked hands. One second, Kopano could feel Vontezza's cold fingers and Miki's sweaty palms and then the next—whoa, his body came apart, he was rising, spinning into the sky, moving fast. He wanted to scream—not in fear, but the way one did at the top of a roller coaster—but he didn't have the mouth to do it.

Kopano could see in 360 degrees. The dark sky above him, the flicker of an orange sunrise to the east, the ocean to the west and the Academy drifting away below him.

They flew southward. Kopano was vaguely aware of the others, their particles intermingling. It felt the same as when you could sense someone standing right behind you. He couldn't speak with them, though. He couldn't tell Miki how freaking amazing his Legacy was. He couldn't do anything, really. He wasn't piloting the course, he was just a passenger. So, Kopano relaxed and enjoyed the view.

Eventually, his mind wandered back to the dorms and that morning. Taylor in his bed, sleeping on her stomach, a strand of blond hair in her mouth. She snored a little bit and Kopano had wondered when the last time she actually slept was. He didn't want to wake her up, so he leaned over to kiss her cheek and left without a word. She deserved all the rest she could get.

I'm going to link the four of us telepathically now that we're getting closer, John's voice said in his head, jarring Kopano back to alertness.

It was strange enough to be disembodied without the added weirdness of John's telepathy. For the first time that morning, Kopano's giddiness gave way to discomfort. He hoped the Loric hadn't been reading his mind a second ago.

I wasn't, John said in answer.

Oh, you heard me? Kopano thought back, concentrating for once on not being too open-minded.

I hate this! I demand my flesh be restored! Vontezza's inner voice came through as a screech that made Kopano's mind throb.

Kopano felt a sudden sinking sensation and his stomach dropped. That shouldn't have been possible, considering he was wind and didn't have a body. The falling sensation only lasted a second, though, and then he was back to swirling weightlessly through the air.

Sorry, lost my grip for a second there, John thought.

Don't worry, Miki replied, his mind a whisper. *I got us.*

Vontezza's freaking out a bit so I took her out of the tele-pathic link-up, John added.

Kopano chose not to worry about the fact that he'd almost fallen out of the sky. Instead, he turned his attention to what was below. They were coming in from the north, over the ocean, but already Kopano could see—

They brought an army, he thought to the others. *Wow.*

A Mogadorian warship really brings 'em out, John replied.

They flew over a massive aircraft carrier. A dozen jets waited on its deck, their pilots and crew milling about, ready for action. Flanking the aircraft carrier were a half-dozen ominous gunboats, their funnels belching smoke, cannons along their sides glinting in the dawn.

They sailing up to the Academy after this? Miki asked.

Let's hope not, John replied.

So much weaponry, Kopano added. *Didn't you tell them the Mogs were surrendering?*

I did. But they're all about overkill. There's probably a nuke down there somewhere.

Seriously? Kopano replied. *That's intense.*

I'm going to take us around. Get a view of everything.

They gusted over land. Pfeiffer Beach was secluded, its sand glittering purple in places, rock formations jutting dramatically out of the surf. It was surrounded by cliffs with only one viable pathway in. John had chosen a good place for the *Osiris* to set down; if anything went wrong, the Mogs could be easily contained.

The military would make sure of that. There were thousands of soldiers down there. Kopano recognized the white helmets of Peacekeepers but also the green fatigues of the US Army and Marines. There were tanks stationed in the parking lot. Kopano could only see so far, but the roads appeared to be blocked off for miles.

An open stretch of beach was marked off and flagged for the landing zone. There were barricades and trenches set up around that, heavily armed soldiers manning them. There was only one clear path leading away from the landing zone—that was where they'd walk the Mogadorians—and it led to dozens of armored vans that would be used for prisoner transport.

They set all this up in less than a day, Kopano thought. *What chance would the Academy have against an attack of this magnitude?*

I don't know. But even this much manpower won't break through the force field I want to build, John replied. *I'm going to take us in closer, look for the command tent. Miki, make sure I don't screw up. Wouldn't be great if we just randomly popped out of thin air.*

They flew in lower, down towards the parking lot where tents were set up at a safe distance from the beach. They circulated through soldiers smoking cigarettes and drinking coffee out of thermoses. Next, they swept over a cordoned-off area where reporters and their crews were setting up to get coverage of the warship's arrival.

The military encampment was organized like a nervous

system, so they found the command tent at the heart. A group of very serious men hung out there, going over satellite images of the surrounding beach. Ray Archibald was among them. None of them noticed when a stray gust of wind ruffled their papers.

Okay, I'm going to break off from you guys here, John said. *I'll keep the telepathic link going as long as I'm able. Miki, there were some rocks overlooking the landing site that I think you guys could wait at unnoticed.*

I saw the spot, Miki replied.

You aren't worried they'll try to capture you or something? Kopano asked.

No. At least, not until the warship is down, John replied.

He separated from them and Miki took full control of their wind formation. Surprisingly, they moved quicker and Kopano felt more secure—Miki was better at this. As John appeared above the command tent, making himself known by gently floating down to the ground with his hands raised, the rest of them flew up to the cliffs that overlooked the beach.

Miki put them down on a narrow ledge high above the landing site. An outcropping of rocks blocked them from sight by the soldiers below, but it was possible for them to peek over and take in the army's sprawling show of force. The ledge fed into a shallow cave and, as his body regained its shape, Kopano became aware of the taste of salt and the fluttering of bat wings.

Kopano's legs wobbled beneath him. Vontezza straight

collapsed onto her hands and knees, letting loose a full-body shudder.

"Gah! I hated that!" she cried.

"It was dope," Kopano said. "After spending the last year cooped up on a warship, I'd think you'd love the open skies."

"You thought wrong," Vontezza replied.

Miki sat down on the rocks with a weighty exhale. He looked pale and drained. The journey south had taken something out of him.

"You good?" Kopano asked.

Miki nodded. "Even with John doing most of the work, that was a long way for me. I haven't practiced much."

"You'll be okay to take us back?"

Miki bit the inside of his cheek. "Yeah. Yeah, don't worry."

Vontezza stood up and pressed herself against the edge, glaring down at the warship's welcoming committee. "This pathetic army would be no match for the *Osiris* if it was at full strength."

Kopano chose not to respond to that. "So. What do we do now?"

"We wait," Vontezza replied. "The sky is lightening. It won't be long."

She was right.

Guys, John's telepathic voice made Kopano jump. *It's here.*

Kopano looked up. At first, the *Osiris* was nothing more than a dark disc against the pale sky—it could've been a drone up there, Kopano thought, or a really high-flying Frisbee. That didn't last. From down below, Kopano heard soldiers yelling and the metallic creak of missile systems aiming. Fighter jets screamed by overhead, flying in formation towards the warship. They looked like insects buzzing in front of a moon.

"It's enormous," Miki whispered.

Kopano could only nod. For once, he was at a loss for words. The beach darkened as the *Osiris* blotted out the sun. Seeing the warships on his tiny TV in Lagos had not done the massive vessels justice. The scarab-shaped war machine made Kopano's knees shake. As it got lower and lower, descending obediently towards the landing zone, Kopano was amazed that he'd once thought the army below was impressive.

A scary thought occurred to him. "You're sure—you're sure your people won't snap and open fire," Kopano said to Vontezza. "Right?"

The Mogadorian girl stared at the *Osiris* with pride. "I disabled most of the offensive systems before I left," she said. She stroked her fingers across the mace on her hip. "I left my weaponsmith Koramu in charge. He would not betray my wishes. He is madly in love with me."

Kopano blinked. "In love . . . you have a boyfriend?"

"No," she said sharply. "Can you shut up now? I wish to enjoy my people's last moments of freedom."

For as threatening as the *Osiris* appeared, Kopano still picked up details that hinted at its tumultuous last year. One side looked as if it had a bite taken out of it; jagged barbs of metal pointing outward indicated that a massive explosion had emanated from inside the ship. Black curls of smoke drifted up from gaps in the warship's armor. The cannon along the *Osiris*'s belly drooped uselessly, thick icicles melting along its sides.

The ship touched down with a groan that shook the valley. Helicopters circled overhead and Kopano edged back into the shelter of the cave, touching Miki's shoulder so that he would do the same. Vontezza, however, kept up her vigil from the rocks.

The surrender went down faster than Kopano would've thought. A booming voice on a megaphone bellowed instructions at the warship. A ramp unfurled from its side. The soldiers below readied their weapons.

The Mogadorians exited the warship in a regimented two-by-two column, unarmed and without armor, their hands on their heads. Kopano edged closer so that he could watch with Vontezza. He expected all the Mogs to be upright and hard-edged like her. Instead, they looked mostly bedraggled and sad, skinny and underfed. Many of them limped or stumbled as they made the walk down the gangway and along the cordoned beach path. These weak ones were shouted at by soldiers brandishing assault rifles. There was a moment when Kopano worried a soldier might shoot up the entire crew just because one starving Mogadorian fainted. When the line of Mogs reached the soldiers, they were handled roughly—thrust down to their knees, patted down and zip-tied and then hustled towards the armored transports.

Vontezza sucked in a shaky breath. When Kopano turned

to look at her, she had hidden her face behind Rabiya's scarf.

"You okay?" he asked.

"Shut up," she replied. "Yes."

Kopano looked down at the shuffling horde of Mogs. "Kinda sad, really."

"Reminder that they would have enslaved our entire planet," Miki said.

"Still," Kopano replied.

"You're weak," Vontezza said quietly.

Hey. John Smith's telepathic intrusion made them all jump. *The crew is clear of the ship, but the soldiers won't be doing a sweep until all the Mogs are locked down in the transports. This is your chance to get in. Be quick.*

Miki stepped forward, hands extended. "You heard the boss. Ready?"

Kopano took Miki's hand, but Vontezza hesitated.

"You remember the map of my ship, yes?" she asked. Miki nodded. "There is an antechamber near the entrance. Take us to it. It will be safest to approach the generator from there."

Vontezza snatched at Miki's hand and then they were aloft again, floating down from the cliffs, a gentle breeze with a purpose. Kopano got an up-close look at the Mogs— pale, skinny, dead-eyed—as the soldiers wrestled them into custody. "Freaks aren't so tough now," a soldier said. He was glad when they'd passed over them and breezed through the open entrance of the *Osiris*.

The interior of the warship was as forbidding as Kopano

expected. He tried to take in as many details as possible as Miki swooped them through the cavernous hallways. The Mogadorians didn't design for comfort but for functionality. They also seemed extraordinarily partial to chrome panels and muted crimson lighting. There were signs everywhere of the mutinies Vontezza had described—collapsed ceiling panels, scorch marks, deep laser-caused scars in the walls. Discarded equipment littered the floor—armor and blasters and other gear—as if the Mogs had just dropped all that weaponry on their way out the door.

Kopano lost track of the twisting and turning hallways. Luckily, Miki had been paying attention to the map. He set them down in the middle of a branching chamber. As he got his legs under him again, the smell nearly knocked Kopano over. The warship stunk—refuse, fuel spillage and over-cooked meat all mingling together. His eyes watered.

"Nice place," Miki said warily.

Kopano's eyes darted around, scanning for danger. Surprisingly, this section seemed to have been kept much cleaner and battle-free than the other spaces they passed through.

Vontezza grabbed a stray backpack from the floor and approached the far wall, which was covered floor-to-ceiling in small drawers labeled with Mogadorian script. She selected one of these drawers, tugged it open and withdrew three small pouches, which she deposited into her backpack. When she moved onto another, Kopano stepped forward.

"Uh, what are you doing?"

She pointed down the hallway. "The generator is that way. My people should have left the way unlocked."

"What about all the radiation leaks?" Kopano asked.

Vontezza sighed. "I lied about that. Go. Do your errand. I will catch up."

"But—"

She spun to face him, shaking a pouch in his direction. It sounded like it was filled with dirt.

"These are our honored dead," Vontezza said. "I will not allow their remains to fall into the hands of the humans. Let me do what I must and then I will join you."

Kopano exchanged a look with Miki, the smaller boy shrugging in response. Without another word, they jogged off in the direction of the core.

They didn't encounter any traps or stray Mogadorians on their way, just more battle-scarred walls, discarded ration bags and broken bits of armor. Within minutes, Kopano bounded down corrugated steel steps into the engine room. Just like in the blueprints, the armored generator waited in a central location. The room was hot—the engines still cooling from the warship's descent—and eerily silent.

Kopano cracked his knuckles and looked at Miki. "Ready?"

Miki motioned to the generator. "All you, large one."

"I really don't want that nickname to catch on," Kopano replied.

Kopano went transparent and stepped through the generator's armored shell. He slipped by the first two layers without an issue, then paused as he reached the innermost carapace, the one made of the same obsidian material as Vontezza's mace. He took a deep breath of air and reminded himself that he was doing something heroic for his friends. Then he pushed forward.

Kopano gasped as an icy sensation coursed through his every molecule. It was as if millions of needles were stabbing into his cells. The urge to harden his form in self-defense came over him, but it would be deadly to do that now, and would leave Kopano bonded to the Mogadorian alloy permanently. He focused on enduring the pain and urged his body forward.

The generator came into view. The confines of the innermost shell were tight; no room for Kopano to go fully solid. He wrapped his arms around the generator, got in as tight as he could, hugging the thing close. Even then, his back was still partially inside the obsidian, his spine howling in pain.

Kopano concentrated. It was like surgery, in a way. He pictured the schematic of the generator, reminding himself which pieces he needed to take with him and which he could sever and leave behind, just as John had instructed. Then, he tuned himself to the machinery, aligning its molecules with his own, while struggling not to expose himself to the dangerous material behind him. He was pretty sure he had a grip on it.

"You can do this," he whispered to himself.

Holding the generator, Kopano threw himself backwards. A shower of sparks cascaded downwards as the generator disconnected from its coils. Miki had to jump aside as Kopano and the refrigerator-size piece of equipment tumbled back into the relative safety of the engine room. He stood up carefully, still holding the generator—it was weightless as long as he maintained his grip. Now that he could see it in full, it looked like a giant battery. He set the piece down in a clear area and, with a happy exhale, turned himself solid.

"Easy," Kopano declared to Miki. "No problem."

Miki pointed at his chest. "You're bleeding."

Kopano looked down. Indeed, splotches of blood were soaking through the front of his shirt. He peeled it away from his skin and saw that his chest and arms were covered in tiny pinpricks, so small that Kopano didn't even feel any pain. For a moment, he felt faint. What would have happened if he'd stayed pressed into that alloy longer?

"Okay," Kopano breathed. "Maybe not so easy."

Miki went to the generator and laid a hand against it, ready to transform again. "Where's Vontezza and John? We should bail."

"John Smith," Kopano said aloud, at the same time as he forcefully thought the words. "We're ready to go."

There was no response. Kopano hadn't noticed it happen, but it seemed as if the telepathic link was severed.

Miki sniffed the air. "Do you smell—?"

Smoke. It hit Kopano's nostrils before Miki could finish his sentence.

An anguished scream echoed from above. Kopano and Miki both spun around as Vontezza staggered into the engine room, crashing hard against the landing above.

She was on fire. The Mogadorian girl's entire back was enveloped in flames, her clothing and flesh crackling, peeling away. Her dark eyes sought them out.

"Go!" she screamed hoarsely. "Run!"

CHAPTER TWENTY-ONE

THEY REACHED MEXICO WITH THE SUNRISE. RAN had spent the entire flight looking after Duanphen, which meant that neither of them had slept. Duanphen lay on one of the cold metal benches in the narrow auxiliary room attached to the cockpit, and Ran sat on the opposing bench with her legs curled beneath her. Sunlight filtered through the grates in the wall and Duanphen sat up a bit, shielding her eyes.

"How are you feeling?" Ran asked. She touched the other girl's forehead, relieved that she didn't have a fever. That was good. It meant her wound hadn't gotten infected.

"Light-headed. Exhausted," Duanphen responded. "You?"

Ran shrugged one shoulder. "Complicated."

Duanphen squinted. "Is that . . . is that a feeling?"

Before Ran could answer, Number Five called back from the cockpit.

"We're almost there!" he shouted. "Everybody, get your shit together."

Ran stood. Duanphen sat up gingerly, still favoring her wounded arm—Five's improvised stitches looking red and raw.

"Are you sure you're up for this?" Ran asked, speaking quietly so the ones in the cockpit wouldn't overhear. Their plan for attacking the Foundation's prison was haphazard at best. It was desperate and Ran had the feeling that everyone onboard this skimmer was careening towards a certain death.

Duanphen nodded once. "I'll be fine. Besides, what other choice is there?"

"We could drop you on the way," Ran replied. "If you aren't up for fighting . . ."

"The fighting will find me, eventually," Duanphen said. "It always has."

Ran frowned at that but put up no further argument. They all knew what they were getting into when they joined Einar. Ran herself had been looking for a way out from Earth Garde's control, a way to avoid using the Legacies that she often hated. But today she would almost certainly use them again. To hurt people. It would be for a good cause, she told herself, to liberate other Garde from the control of the Foundation. To stop Lucas from harming anyone else. That was reason enough.

Ever since the invasion, it felt to Ran like she had been propelled along a dangerous river. From Patience Creek to the Academy to Iceland to Switzerland to here. And every time she tried to break free of the current, the waters caught up to her. Maybe this was her fate—all their fates—to always be fighting.

The skimmer felt very small, suddenly. She wished that she could go outside and run until she stopped thinking.

"I'm going to get the others," she told Duanphen.

Ran padded into the rear compartment. She headed towards the storage closet that Isabela had turned into her private bedroom, pausing in the hall outside when she heard voices. Caleb was in there with her.

"You talk in your sleep," Isabela said, the complaint softer than usual.

"Sorry," Caleb replied quietly. "I . . . I dreamed about the hotel."

Ran peeked around the corner. Caleb and Isabela lay on the floor, propped on some pillows, Caleb's head resting on her chest. Isabela idly played with his hair, staring up at the ceiling. They didn't notice her, so Ran popped her head back out and leaned against the outside wall. She suddenly missed Nigel very, very much. Someone to talk to, someone to rely on and trust. When this was over, she told herself, she would have to make amends with him.

"The knife was just sticking right out of his neck," Caleb said, his voice near a whisper. "I keep seeing it."

"Don't think about it," Isabela said firmly. "That man

would have killed us all. He doesn't deserve an ounce of your sympathy."

"That's the thing," Caleb replied. "I'm not—I don't feel bad about it. I'm . . . I'm glad he's dead. That's what scares me. What if I turn into someone like . . . ?"

"Hush," Isabela said. "You'll never be anything like Einar."

The pieces clicked for Ran. During the fight with Lucas back in Morocco, Einar had been left alone with Derek King and taken the opportunity to murder him. Caleb must have seen. It made sense now why Einar wasn't at all concerned that King would report their actions or cut off their access to Blackstone's server. He was out of the picture.

Ran felt cold. They were all complicit in what Einar had done. They had listened to him, allowed him to go free, journeyed across the globe with him. Like Caleb, Ran didn't know how to feel. Maybe the world was a better place without Derek King in it. Maybe it was now safer for their people. But what gave any of them the right to decide that? And weren't they only driving the world closer to the war that Five cynically predicted?

She cleared her throat and stepped into the doorway. Isabela and Caleb stopped talking immediately and looked up at her.

"It's time," she said simply. "We're meeting in the cockpit."

"Oh, good," Isabela replied. "Get the almost-dying out of the way early today."

Ran allowed herself a tense smile, then turned to go.

Behind her, she heard Isabela speak quietly to Caleb.

"You know, it's not too late to run away," she said.

"You don't really mean that, do you?" Caleb responded.

Isabela sighed. "No. I guess not."

Ran returned to the cockpit. As usual, Five hunched in the pilot's seat and Einar sat beside him, glued to one of his tablets. Duanphen stood behind them, going through some stretches, albeit sluggishly.

"I don't like this plan," Five was saying to Einar when Ran entered. "You'll be too exposed. We can take a couple of days to scope out the situation and find a better way to get you in."

"I'll be fine," Einar replied dismissively. Five sat back sullenly, barely glancing up from his controls when Einar held up the tablet for him. "Look, your old friend is going to speak."

"He always loved speeches," Five muttered.

As Ran came nearer, she could see that Einar was watching an often-buffering live stream from a news network. A Mogadorian warship descended onto what looked like the California coast. She leaned over Einar's shoulder to get a closer look.

"What is happening?" Ran asked.

"Madness, isn't it?" Einar replied, looking up at her. "The last Mogadorian warship is surrendering itself. Apparently, John Smith organized this with some help from your friends at the Academy. John's supposed to be giving a statement to the press soon about his thoughts on the changes to the

Garde Accord. Smells like a PR stunt to me."

"Hopefully he's better at talking than you," Isabela said as she entered the cockpit, Caleb crowding in behind her.

Ran could tell by the curdled look on Einar's face that the remark stung. He'd never gotten over how much negative attention his grand speech in Switzerland had gotten.

"Maybe that's why Taylor and those guys haven't been answering our calls," Caleb mused. "Too busy with this."

The news feed cut away from the warship and the line of Mogs exiting its confines, switching to a crowded press area where John Smith was surrounded by soldiers and reporters. Considering they were on the run and had recently been shot at, it was odd to see how the soldiers reacted to John, practically knocking each other out of the way in their efforts to shake his hand and salute him.

"I helped bring down the Mogadorians, too," Five said quietly. "No one's ever saluted me."

"One day, they'll respect us like that," Einar said, his voice almost wistful.

"No," Ran replied. "They will not."

She put a hand on Einar's shoulder and squeezed until she could feel his bones beneath her fingers. Einar winced and looked at her sharply, his eyebrows raised. Five also noticed the tension and turn to appraise Ran. She kept her expression cold and neutral.

"The humans know what John sacrificed during the invasion. They know that he fought alongside them," Ran said, looking at Einar. "What have you done that is close to that?"

"I've sacrificed," Einar said. "I—"

"You have done nothing but hurt people," Ran continued over him. "Perhaps you had a troubled upbringing. Perhaps the Foundation brainwashed you. Perhaps now you think you are defending the Garde. All of these are excuses that you use to justify the destruction you cause."

Einar glared at her. "Where is this coming from, all of a sudden?"

"When we are done in Mexico, I will be leaving this group. You are sick," she said, glancing over at Caleb and Isabela. "And you are making us sick with you."

Einar at last pulled away from Ran's grip and stood up so that he was in her face. He let the tablet go and Five caught it. The Loric seemed more interested in the broadcast than coming between Ran and Einar. Caleb, Isabela and Duanphen all stood by in silence, too. Perhaps this wasn't the most appropriate time for this confrontation, what with all of them about to stage a raid on a top secret prison, but Ran needed to get this off her chest.

"I don't need you," Einar said to Ran. "All you Academy brats have been nothing but trouble since the day you begged to join us. I'll be glad not to have to babysit you. None of you have the stomach to do what really needs to be done."

"Neither do you," Ran said.

Einar scoffed. "Please, I—"

"If you truly wanted to unite the Garde and keep them safe from humanity, then you would turn yourself in and pay for what you've done," Ran said. "But you are a coward.

So, instead, you want to turn us all into monsters like you."

The tiny hairs on Ran's arms stood up. Einar's teeth were clenched, like he was making a concerted effort not to attack her, and still she felt his telekinesis radiating off him. She sensed that he wanted to tear her apart. Caleb and Duanphen both edged forward. Isabela watched with narrowed eyes. And Five . . .

"Oh," Five said. "Oh, fuck."

That gave Ran pause. She'd heard Five curse plenty of times, but she'd never heard his voice sound so small, like a little boy.

He held up the tablet where John Smith's speech to the press had begun, turning up the volume. Immediately, Ran could tell there was something off with the way he spoke.

"I know there's been some people out there saying how they don't like the changes to the Garde Accord and they don't think Inhibitors are the way to go," John said, speaking into a dozen microphones. "But I think it's a great idea."

Ran's eyes narrowed. On-screen, John smiled crookedly.

"God willing," he said, "I'll have an Inhibitor in my head by the end of today."

That wasn't right. Ran didn't know John that well, but she knew he would never—

The Foundation pulled Lucas out of Morocco because of a high-priority target.

All those soldiers shaking John's hand.

"Now, if you'll excuse me," John said, all good manners. "There's a whole rebellious Academy that I've got to get under control. Including some folks who are right here under our noses."

John leaped into the air and took flight. It was a rocky maneuver, not a smooth takeoff, and he nearly knocked over a cameraman on his way up.

"That was him," Isabela said, her voice shaky. "Lucas. He . . . he . . ."

"He has John," Five said. "He's unstoppable."

Ran remembered Patience Creek. It was a Mogadorian that time, some woman with a weapon that let her siphon off part of John's power. She'd barely survived that.

Lucas was going to the Academy. He claimed, as John, that he was going to get them under control. But Ran had seen Lucas's brutality, his apathy towards human life. He wouldn't stop at chipping her former classmates. He would kill.

She made eye contact with Einar, the two of them still standing uncomfortably close together. Ran took a step back. Einar nodded. For now, the two of them agreed to put their differences aside.

"Five," Einar said, trying to find some of his usual pompous confidence and struggling. "Speed up. We've got a prison to attack."

CHAPTER TWENTY-TWO

TAYLOR COOK
NEW LORIEN—THE HIMALAYAS, INDIA

IT WAS EARLY THAT MORNING, WHEN THEY WERE all still in relatively good spirits. When they thought they could win. Before everything went to hell.

"Everybody got a hold on me?" Nine asked.

Four hands squeezed Nine affirmatively. His bicep, his shoulders, his back. He gave a little shimmy in response.

"I like this," he said. "It's relaxing."

Taylor sighed and pinched Nine's arm. He seemed to be in a better mood this morning than he'd been in recent days. Maybe he was feeling that same weird giddiness that came over Taylor sometimes when she faced impossible odds. Even so, he needed to stop screwing around.

"Hurry up," she told him. "We've got a lot to do."

"Yeah, yeah," Nine replied. "Okay, I've never actually

tried this thing out before, so if we teleport directly into a volcano—my bad."

"Oi," Nigel groused. "You're scaring Simon with that talk."

"Actually not," Simon countered. "It's highly unlikely there would be a Loralite stone inside an acti— *Ulp!*"

Nine reached up and squeezed the Loralite pendant that hung around his neck. There was a flash of azure light and that head-over-heels sensation that was disorienting enough to cut off Simon. One moment, the five of them were huddled together in Professor Nine's office and the next they were halfway across the world.

The first thing that Taylor noticed was the cold. It was different than the damp chill of Northern California; brisker and biting. She dropped her hand off Nine's arm so that she could hug herself, rubbing her upper arms.

"I did not dress warmly enough," Rabiya said with a commiserating glance at Taylor.

Nine spread out his arms. "Well, here it is. The nicest cave we'll ever live in."

They stood in the back of a domed cavern where a large outcropping of Loralite jutted out from the floor. The stone walls were a polished blue-gray that reflected the shimmering Loralite; Taylor got the sense that the walls had been recently scrubbed or scraped. At the center of the cavern was a round wooden table, big enough to comfortably seat at least twenty people, a Loric symbol that matched Nine's pendant burned into its center. Sunlight poured in through the cave's entrance along with a small flurry of snow.

A girl sat on the edge of the table, facing away from them, a sketchpad in her lap. When Nine made his declaration, she turned to face them, her eyes alight. She had auburn hair streaked with white that hung loose to her shoulders. She wore a full-length winter coat with fur trim, unzipped, a T-shirt depicting a cartoon Vishnu beneath. It became clear when she hopped off the table that, although she wasn't more than fourteen or fifteen, the girl was tall and gangly, all elbows and knees like she'd just endured a growth spurt.

"Oh, wow, hi, Nine," the girl said, trying to mask her obvious excitement with a bit of blasé chill.

"Ella?" Nine exclaimed, practically screaming, no chill at all. "Holy shit! Is that you?"

And then they were hugging, the girl's—Ella's—arms around Nine's neck, him picking her up so that her long legs kicked at the air, both of them laughing.

"One of the OGs," Nigel explained to the blank expressions of the Academy students. "Number Ten, I think? Maybe? Telepathic and clairvoyant. I think she died once."

"Interesting," Simon said. He pushed his glasses up the bridge of his nose as he looked around, taking care to memorize every detail of the cavern.

"It's so good to see you," Nine said, holding Ella at arm's length. "Damn. What are they feeding you up here? You're so *tall.*"

"Stop," Ella said, pulling her coat around her and shying away. "I hate this height. Every day I think about using my

Aeternus to change back."

"Nah," Nine said with a dismissive wave. "It looks good on you."

Nine tossed the compliment out there casually; he was already walking by Ella to get a better look at the cave. Taylor could tell the girl was practically swooning, though, like Nine had just made her life. Nine was, of course, as oblivious as always, and he hadn't even introduced them. Taylor took it upon herself to stick out her hand in Ella's direction.

"Hey there," she said. "I'm Taylor. We're from the Academy."

Ella shook her hand and Taylor quickly introduced her to the others. The Loric girl gazed at each of them in turn, studying them, a flicker of bright blue in her eyes that wasn't the reflection of the Loralite.

"It's good to meet you all in person," Ella said. "John said we might have some guests soon. I hope you like the place."

"Bit nippy for my taste," Nigel said.

"You get used to it," Ella replied.

"Himalayas," Nigel said wonderingly. "They got rock clubs up here?"

Ella chuckled. "No. Not really."

Nine had made his way over to the table, where he picked up Ella's sketchbook. The drawing was of them—well, not them exactly—but five shapes silhouetted in the glow of the Loralite stone. She was a pretty good artist.

"You knew we were coming," Nine said.

Ella shrugged shyly. "I had an inkling."

"You doing that a lot?" Nine asked. "Looking into the future?"

Ella pulled a strand of hair across her eyes. "Not really. Knowing the future changes the future. It's too messy. I try not to peek."

"So you don't have any idea how we do today," Taylor said. "If we win."

Ella shook her head. "If I told you that you were going to be victorious, then you might get cocky and not do the things that made you win in the first place. And if I told you that you were going to lose—"

"We might all go jump off the mountain," Nigel interrupted. "Got it."

"I do know your plan, though," Ella said, smiling at her in a way Taylor found a little creepy. "Seems pretty solid to me. Not that you asked. But since you're worried."

"You know what we're planning," Taylor repeated, not quite believing.

"You're planning to use Loralite to teleport squads of students around campus. Play cat-and-mouse with the Peacekeepers until you wear them out." She pointed at Rabiya. "That means relying on her a lot. You don't entirely trust her because she used to be with the Foundation."

Taylor glanced at Rabiya. She was about to say something to the contrary but knew that would be patronizing. Rabiya regarded her coolly and said nothing.

"You *can* trust her, though," Ella continued. "At least as far as this battle goes." Speaking quickly, Ella turned to

Simon. "You're here because you can transfer knowledge. Cool Legacy, by the way."

Simon half bowed. "Thank you. It doesn't get enough respect."

"You're going to transfer your knowledge of this place into some stones so that Garde can teleport here from any of the Loralite you've placed around campus. Just in case you need to retreat. It's smart. Might save some lives." Finally, Ella turned to Nigel. "And you're just here because you don't have anything better to do until the fighting kicks off."

Nigel smirked. "Actually, I was supposed to be cleaning the toilets, but seems like a waste of time when we might be high-tailing it later today."

Nine clapped his hands. "Oh man, Ella, I missed this! It's like a magic show."

Taylor pretended not to be disturbed by the ease with which Ella laid out her thoughts. Apparently, the telepathic weren't much for boundaries. "I don't know if it's even worth saying this next part," Taylor began.

"Go for it," Ella said. "Talking is fun."

"We were hoping to get a look around, since there's a fifty-fifty chance we might be living here," Taylor said.

"It's more than just this cave, right?" Nigel asked. "We've got a lot of people . . ."

"Let me give you the tour," Ella replied, looping her arm through Taylor's and pulling her towards the exit. "John's been a little weird about this place since his vision. Been insisting that we get the force field set up before allowing anyone to come here. But, well, I'm pretty proud of what we've built and I think we should show it off."

"Wait a second," Nine said, catching up with them. "He didn't mention any vision to us."

"I tell him to keep his head in the present, but he doesn't listen," Ella said. "I guess he saw some kind of explosion here. Like we were being bombed or something. And that's why he's so bent on the force field."

Taylor and Nine exchanged a look. This was supposed to be their safe place to retreat to; at least, that's what John had promised them. Now, suddenly, there was talk about explosions and bombings.

"Oi, so we're going from an Academy under siege to the next Hiroshima?" Nigel asked, putting Taylor's anxiety into words. "That what I'm hearing?"

Ella sighed. "John could've seen one of like a million possible futures. It doesn't mean anything. Besides, who would want to bomb us? We're not hurting anybody."

Taylor frowned at that. Despite being a little weird and invasive, Ella seemed like a sweet girl. She'd also spent the last couple of years living in John Smith's mountain utopia. She didn't know what the real world was like anymore.

"What does Marina think of all this?" Nine asked. "Is she around?"

Ella's lips pursed and her eyes darted to the side. Taylor didn't need to be telepathic to pick up that signal; the girl had some bad news.

"Marina, um, well, her and John had a bit of a falling out,"

Ella said, trying to sound diplomatic and adult. "She left a few weeks back. We haven't heard from her."

"What did they fight about?" Nine asked.

"When Marina saw that Five was back, she . . ." Ella gave Nine a look and shrugged, like he could fill in the blanks. "Anyway, John didn't seem to care. So I guess Marina took off to go look for Five by herself."

The drama between the Garde didn't much interest Taylor, so she walked on a little ahead. She burrowed her hands into the pockets of her sweatshirt as she reached the cave's mouth. As she was the first one out, she was also the first one to jump back, screaming in surprise as she came face-to-face with a monster. The head of an eagle on the body of a lion, with huge wings that kept shifting to shake loose snow.

Simon skidded to a stop beside her. "*Mon dieu!* It's a griffin."

It *was* a griffin. And then it *wasn't* a griffin. Before Taylor's eyes, the huge beast shrank down into a totally adorable beagle. A Chimæra. Taylor had heard talk of the creatures, but never actually encountered any of the Loric animals. In the days after the invasion, Earth Garde had taken them all into custody. The dog panted happily at her, then bounded past so it could paw at Nine's legs.

"Bernie Kosar!" Nine shouted. "My dude!"

"Sorry about that," Ella said to Taylor and her startled classmates. "BK nests up here. Keeps watch. Makes sure that we don't get any unexpected guests teleporting in."

Taylor nodded mutely. She was already beyond the

presence of a Chimæra, too busy being awed by the view.

"Beautiful," Rabiya said. Taylor nodded agreement.

They were high up the mountainside, surrounded on all sides by white-capped peaks. From the rocky landing they stood on, a switchback path led down to a small village. Dozens of quaint little cottages were spaced evenly along the path. At first, it looked to Taylor like the houses would surely crumble off the mountainside. Then, she noticed the stone foundations that attached them to the rocks beneath. Not attached—*connected*. It was as if the bases of the homes had risen fully formed from the rocks. That was no ordinary construction. Legacies built those.

There were more of the newer-looking houses down in the village, interspersed among the villagers' original construction, blending in. Enough space for a few hundred new occupants, at least.

"I know they don't look it," Ella said, "but the houses are warm. We've got running water. Electricity most of the time." She glanced at Nine. "John wants to put in a training center, but was waiting for you to help build it."

Nine smiled at that but said nothing. Like Taylor, he was looking down at the tableau and imagining the possibilities.

"The force field will be big enough to protect all of this?" Taylor asked.

"Well, technically, it'll be three force fields cobbled together," Ella replied. "But yeah."

A truck rumbled into view on the road leading into the village. Taylor stepped forward to take a closer look, her stomach clenching as she spotted armed soldiers hopping down from the truck's bed.

"Don't worry, they're cool," Ella said, sensing her agitation. "They're the Vishnu Nationalist Eight. A little militia that's dedicated to protecting us."

Nigel scratched his cheek. "Huh. That hasn't been our experience with army boys."

"Yeah, well, the villagers are nice here, too," Ella continued. "We try not take to take advantage of their hospitality. We help out down there however we can and they protect us from outsiders."

Taylor stared down at the picturesque village. It was cold and remote. It was secluded and safe. It was farther from home than she'd ever been. She glanced over at Nigel and found that he was watching her. He raised his eyebrows in question. She blew out a sigh, her breath misting before her.

"So," Ella said, since the Academy guests had all gone quiet. "What do you think? Could you live here?"

"It's nice," Taylor said. "I think it could be good. For a backup."

The serenity of the view was broken by Nine's pocket buzzing incessantly. He pulled out his cell phone, his brow scrunching up.

"Damn, I've got better service in the Himalayas than at the Academy," he grumbled. Nine held up the phone so Taylor could see. "We've got like twenty messages from Isabela."

Back at the Academy, Rabiya created a Loralite stone in the center of the student union, the cobalt mass breaking right through the floor tiles.

"We'll fix that later," Nine said.

She made another one inside the entrance to the dorms. Another outcropping sprang up from the training center. She placed one on the Academy side of their makeshift barricade, jutting out of the central road that led into campus.

Finally, Rabiya grew a chunk of Loralite on the beach, hidden among some rocks. At that point, she and Taylor were alone. Everyone at the Academy was on a strict buddy system, so Taylor had to stand idly by as Rabiya did her work. Nine and Nigel had gone off to organize the students into squads, while Simon was busy imbuing bracelets with knowledge of New Lorien. Those bracelets would be distributed around to students they could rely on to evacuate others if the need arose—Maiken, Nemo, Omar and, at Nigel's insistence, Nicolas.

Walking along the beach as she waited, Taylor thought about Isabela's message to them. A crazed Harvester who happened to be a Garde, working on behalf of the Foundation, who could steal bodies. And he was headed to the Academy. Of course they could add that to their problems. Isabela didn't answer her phone when they tried to call her back, so there was nothing more they could do about it.

"I guess the best plan," Nine had said, "is to not let any strangers touch you."

Taylor stubbed her toe on something hard in the sand. An empty bottle of champagne. She crouched down, brushing sand off the green glass. She and her friends must have left that bottle out here on New Year's Eve after sneaking it out of the faculty party. She smiled softly. That was a good memory. A good night. Well, right up until Nine had come to tell Nigel about his father's passing.

"I'm done," Rabiya said, coming up behind her. She glanced at the bottle in Taylor's hand. "I see that in addition to organizing a defense of the Academy you are also picking up litter."

Taylor hadn't realized how far away she'd roamed from Rabiya and the Loralite. "Sorry," she said. "Got into my head a bit."

Rabiya shrugged nonchalantly and they started back along the shore. "You really like it here," Rabiya said after a moment, when she caught Taylor gazing out at the water. "You don't want to go."

"It's funny, because I never wanted to come here," Taylor replied. "But now I feel attached. It's like the place where I really grew up."

Rabiya nodded and fell silent again. Taylor was surprised by her own candor. She guessed that she was feeling extra sentimental in what might be one of the day's last quiet moments. What had Ella said about Rabiya? That Taylor could trust her—with today's battle, at least. That meant there was *something* Taylor couldn't trust her about.

"Do you think he's okay?" Rabiya asked. "Kopano, I mean. Aren't you worried?"

Ah. Or *someone*.

Taylor didn't feel any ill will or possessiveness. Maybe she was a bigger person than that, or maybe she just had too much else to worry about that Rabiya's little crush on Kopano didn't rate. As they reached the Loralite, Taylor smiled at the other girl in a way that she hoped was reassuring.

"Kopano will be fine," Taylor said. "Nothing can hurt that guy."

CHAPTER TWENTY-THREE

KOPANO OKEKE
THE *OSIRIS*
PFEIFFER BEACH, CALIFORNIA

NO SOONER HAD VONTEZZA SCREAMED OUT HER warning than a shape burst into the engine room behind her, moving at a speed that wasn't human. In the crimson light of the Mogadorian ship and with the addition of the flames leaping off Vontezza's back, Kopano at first mistook their attacker for some kind of devil—right out of the boring biblical comics his mother used to bring home for him instead of the good superhero stuff. That was the thought in Kopano's brain when the demon punched Vontezza in the side of the head with enough force to snap her neck. The Mogadorian's body collapsed and tumbled down the corrugated steps, landing in a burning heap at Kopano's feet.

In the back of his mind, Kopano knew that Vontezza regenerated. She would be fine. Most likely. Even so, his instincts were to lurch forward and try to help put out the fire on her back.

He came up short, though, when he saw who stood on the landing above.

John Smith. John Smith was the devil.

"Always wanted to kill one of them things," John said, his voice weird and twangy. "All that vermin scurrying around on our beautiful planet. Can't be tolerated."

Kopano stared. He didn't know what to say. These words didn't make any sense coming from John. The Loric had likely killed tons of Mogadorians during the invasion. He'd also organized this peaceful surrender and never once called the Mogs anything like "vermin." What the hell was going on?

"I'm here to accept your surrender," John continued. "You and then those other rebels over at that Academy. They said I'm supposed to show you mercy." John looked at his hands, flexing his fingers. They glowed white-hot. "But mercy might be hard on account of how much power's in this one."

"John, what—?" Kopano started to say but stopped himself. He wasn't stupid. The way John spoke, the way he smiled, the way he'd so callously dispatched Vontezza. That wasn't John. Kopano didn't know how, but Earth Garde had found a way to take control of the Loric. This was worse than an Inhibitor, though. Someone else—someone clearly deranged—was in possession of John's body.

"It ain't so bad where they'll put you," John said, starting down the steps into the engine room proper. "A little warm.

Food isn't great. But sometimes they let you loose to do God's work."

Kopano glanced over his shoulder. Miki stood there, frozen, one hand still on the force field generator.

"Miki!" Kopano yelled, snapping him to attention. "Get that back to the Academy! Warn them!"

Miki opened his mouth as if to object, but he must have done the same mental math as Kopano. If they flew out of there together, John would be right behind them. He might even overtake them and get to the Academy first.

Someone needed to stay behind to stall him.

And that person was Kopano.

"Now, now," John said. He aimed his open hand at Miki, a blossom of flame spilling forth.

Miki was wind before the fire touched him. The force field generator disappeared with him, a swirl of particles, Miki indistinguishable from the machine. Kopano saw how the flames curled and billowed at the sudden draft that rose up and out of the engine room.

"Slippery little critter," John said, and aimed another fireball at Kopano.

Kopano lunged forward. He turned transparent, darting through the fire, and grabbed the staircase that John stood on. The steps lost their density and John, off-balance, fell through them. Kopano grabbed him as he fell, snagging the front of his shirt, and hardened the molecules of his fist. He punched John square in the face, breaking his nose and bouncing him off one of the room's many control panels.

"If you are in there, John Smith . . . ," Kopano said, trying to keep his voice from shaking. "Fight! Fight against this thing that has control of you!"

John stood up, laughing and snuffling blood back up his nose.

"I got him in a real cozy place. A little spaceship he likes to imagine sometimes, watching some girl bleed out. Maybe he can hear you, but there ain't nothing he can do," John said. "I was put on this Earth to stop things like him. Things like you."

Kopano stood firm, ready to dodge aside at any moment. This one liked to talk. That was good. That could buy Miki precious seconds to get back and let the others know what they were up against.

"What are you?" Kopano asked. "You must be . . . you must be some kind of Garde."

"I'm a blessing," John replied, nasally, agitated. "These Legacies are corruption. An affront to the Almighty. I was made to root them out."

"You sound like my mom," Kopano replied. "She prays for me all the time."

A huge smile spread on John's face. "That must be why I found you first. Your mother's prayers were answered!"

John sprang towards him. He was fast and superstrong, but Kopano had noticed something about the way he wielded the fire. It was imprecise. Whoever was controlling John Smith wasn't as skilled at using his Legacies. Maybe he didn't even entirely know what John could do. A small advantage was better than nothing.

Kopano let John pass right through him, his fist smashing into the armored core where the force field generator used to reside. Then, Kopano grabbed him from behind and turned them both transparent. He muscled John forward, into the armor, until his face and chest overlapped with that Mogadorian alloy. John hissed in pain. Maybe, Kopano thought, if he could hurt him enough, this possessor would flee John's body.

"Release him!" Kopano yelled. "Go back where you came from!"

Metal shrieked as John let loose a powerful wave of telekinesis. The layers of the core peeled back like the petals of a flower, then flattened against the floor, away from the two of them. John shucked free of Kopano's grip, spun and flung out his hands, hurling Kopano across the room with another burst of telekinesis. Kopano turned himself transparent so that he didn't ram into any of the equipment.

"There's so much power in this body," John said, laughing. "Gosh, it's so easy. All I have to do is think of something and . . ."

John held out his fist and, in the blink of an eye, it was encased in ice. Cracking and hissing as it grew, the ice enlarged into a pointed lance, which he plunged right for Kopano's chest.

Kopano let the ice pass right through him, stepped clear and smashed it with one punch from his hardened fist. John hardly seemed to notice. He'd already moved on to shooting silver beams out of his eyes, turning parts of the Mogadorian warship into stone.

He was playing, Kopano realized. Screwing around.

"So much power," John said, looking down at his hands again. "This is what it feels like to be a god."

On Kopano's left, a tank of coolant that had been damaged in their fight suddenly burst, spraying chilly mist into the humid confines of the engine room. Kopano leaped back to get out of the way.

When he looked back up, John was gone.

Maybe he'd lost interest. Maybe he'd accidentally triggered John's teleportation Legacy and sent himself halfway across the planet. Maybe he was on his way to the Academy.

From up above, Kopano heard voices and boots. The soldiers were breaching the warship. Maybe they were drawn to the sounds of battle or maybe John Smith led them here. Either way, he needed to go.

Kopano crouched down over Vontezza's still-smoldering body. By any definition, the girl was dead. But she could come back from that, couldn't she? He couldn't leave her behind. Kopano patted out some last flames on Vontezza's back and started to gather her up.

The metal floor creaked as something moved behind him. Kopano spun around just in time to see John reappear— invisibility, of course, he'd never even left the room. He held a broken section of pipe that he'd picked up somewhere, swinging this for Kopano's chest.

Once again, Kopano went transparent. John stood there,

holding the pipe in the ghostly space of Kopano's shoulder. Kopano wondered how long this fool would go on like this. John had many tricks capable of doing damage, but Kopano only needed one move to avoid them all.

"I can do this all day," Kopano said with a smile.

"I can see the strings that connect you to the power," John said almost dreamily, his gaze becoming unfocused. He waved at the air, pointing from Kopano's heart to the floor. "It's hideous. Blue light coming up from the ground, sent from the underworld. I wonder what happens if I . . ."

John made a cutting motion.

Kopano howled as his shoulder exploded in pain. He had become solid around the pipe that John held inside him. Bone and muscle were pulped as Kopano's body reasserted its mass. It was agony; like getting shot from inside his body.

His Legacies were gone. John had ripped them away.

"Aha, there you are," John said. He touched Kopano's cheek with his free hand. "Human again. That feels nice, don't it?"

With his other hand, John jiggled the pipe that was now plunged into Kopano's shoulder and sticking out his back.

The pain was unbearable. Even so, Kopano grabbed for John's neck with his working hand. Clawed at him. Ripped at him.

The metal made a wet ripping sound when John used his superstrength to pull it out of Kopano. And that was it.

Kopano's eyes rolled back in his head and he collapsed.

Kopano's eyes fluttered open once as John dragged him by the ankle out of the Mogadorian warship. His head bumped across the metal floor and he felt chilled all over. There was a hole in him—not just the one in his shoulder—some bigger part of him was missing. He tried to use his telekinesis to shove John away from him and couldn't. He was still cut off.

A flash of heat from Kopano's shoulder made him moan. John glanced over his shoulder.

"There, there, fella," John said. "We'll get ya patched up."

Kopano squeezed his fist tight. He clenched something there, cool and sharp against his skin. He needed to hold on to that. Even if he passed out again, he needed to . . . needed . . .

Kopano came to once again, this time with the sun shining in his face. He felt the grit of sand on his cheeks. Steady hands held him down. They were doing something to his wounded shoulder. The pain was still there, but further away now, a distant ache, like it was someone else's shoulder that had gotten torn apart. He felt drugged and sleepy; it was a struggle to stay awake, to focus.

Two grim-faced Peacekeeper medics knelt over him. One of them realized he was alert and met his eyes.

"You've been badly hurt," he said simply. "Don't try to move."

There was a weight around his neck. A collar. Kopano looked past the medics and saw a third Peacekeeper holding one of those Inhibitor cannons. Kopano was hooked up to its electrified steel cord. The Peacekeeper watched him close, finger on the trigger, ready to shock him at the slightest provocation.

"What's he got there?" the Peacekeeper standing over him asked. "In his hand?"

One of the medics pried Kopano's fingers open and lifted John's medallion. Kopano had ripped it off him during their fight. He couldn't let him teleport to New Lorien. It was a small victory, but maybe it would protect the others.

"Some weird alien thing," the medic said, tossing the medallion into the sand. "Bag it up."

Kopano sensed that he could slip free if he wanted to. His Legacy was back. But he was weak. So, so weak. He didn't think that he could muster the energy. He'd lost a lot of blood. Too much, maybe.

But wait. If he could use his Legacy, that meant—

John Smith. Where was John Smith?

"Do you have any idea what you've unleashed down here?" a familiar voice shouted.

Kopano turned his head just enough so that he could see Colonel Archibald pacing back and forth across the sand, a satellite phone pressed to his ear. The man's cheeks were rosy with anger.

"All due respect, sir, I don't care how badly you want the Academy situation sewn up," Archibald barked into the phone. "The asset you've selected is completely unstable."

Archibald paused to listen for a response. Kopano could tell by his white-knuckle grip on the phone that Archibald wasn't happy with whatever was said.

"I don't have eyes on him, sir. He's on the loose and he's taken possession of some heavy ordnance. Nuclear grade. If you don't pull him out now, you're endangering the lives of every student at the Academy," Archibald snarled into the phone.

Kopano felt a pinch at his shoulder. Darkness began to creep in at the edges of his already blurry vision. He was fading. He clenched his teeth, tried to stay awake.

The last thing he heard before slipping back into unconsciousness was Archibald's final, grim pronouncement.

"He's liable to kill them all."

CHAPTER TWENTY-FOUR

ISABELA SILVA
LA CALDERA—DURANGO, MEXICO

THE TOWN OF DEL NORTE WAS, BY ISABELA'S estimation, barely a town at all. It was one of those in-between places, used by people on their way to something better. No more than a dozen buildings poked up from the dust, all of them built conveniently along the highway—a gas station, a ramshackle inn, a sad little cantina. Beyond the buildings were parked trailers, some of their vinyl sides sun-bleached and filthy, others gleaming new and silver, standing out in the desert sun. There were, at a quick count, more mobile homes than buildings.

Del Norte was the first livable place on the road out from La Caldera. It's where they figured some of the prison guards would have eyes. A good place to get their attention.

Isabela walked slumped forward with her hands bound

in front of her. She stumbled theatrically, dragging one foot behind her. Einar gave her arm a hard yank and shoved her onwards. It was just the two of them now, walking right down the middle of the road where everyone could see. No more hiding.

A man filling up his pickup truck at the gas station stared at them as they entered the town. Einar stood straight and proud, his pale skin already getting pink from the desert sun. Isabela, at his side, looked very much like his prisoner. She flashed the man at the gas station an imploring look.

"I think it will be funny when they shock you," Isabela said to Einar under her breath. "They will definitely shock you, right? And you'll be flopping all around. But then I will be on my own and—"

"What?" Einar asked. "What are you saying?"

Isabela glanced at his face. Einar's mind was clearly somewhere else, when it should definitely be on this very dangerous and stupid plan that Isabela already regretted agreeing to.

She hissed at him. "I was asking what will happen if they zap you with an Inhibitor."

"Oh," Einar said. "The Foundation sent me on some of the beta tests for Sydal Corp. Typically, if I could maintain consciousness, one shock would only put me down for three minutes or so."

"Three minutes that I will be on my own," Isabela replied. "Assuming they don't shock you too bad."

"Three minutes that my life will be in your hands," Einar

said absently. "I trust you, Isabela. This will work."

The words were confident, but the tone was all wrong. Einar sounded wounded and shaky.

"What is *wrong* with you?" Isabela snapped. "Are you having a heat stroke?"

Einar blinked, hesitating. "Do you think Takeda was right? About me?"

"Oh my God," Isabela moaned. "You choose *now* to develop a conscience?"

Einar shoved her up the wooden steps of the cantina and through the swinging doors. The inside of the restaurant was dim and muggy. A large bug—Isabela thought it was some kind of mutant cockroach/scorpion hybrid—skittered across the floorboards. A middle-aged man and woman, probably husband and wife, stood at the counter. They openly stared at the two new arrivals. There was only one other customer, a bent old man who barely glanced up from his plate of eggs and beans.

"Breakfast," Einar demanded. *"Por favor."*

Without a word, the couple scurried into the kitchen. Isabela saw the recognition in their eyes, though. Even here, in this remote Mexican village, they knew Einar. He was the most wanted person in the world.

Dragging her by her tied hands, Einar led Isabela to the counter. He shoved her onto a stool and sat down next to her.

"I've always had a conscience," Einar said after a few moments of heavy silence. "I'm not . . . I'm not a monster."

Isabela snorted. "Okay."

"We all haven't had the luxury of being part-time paci- fists like Ran," Einar continued. "Some of us didn't have a choice but to fight."

"Good, good," Isabela replied. "Maybe you can debate this with Ran after we're done."

"For our people to survive, someone has to be willing to get their hands dirty," Einar continued like he hadn't heard her. "Someone has to fight the Foundation on their level, in the dirt, with violence and blood, so that you Academy brats can go on being honorable."

Isabela was about to respond when the husband returned from the kitchen with two plates of rubbery eggs and gelat- inous beans. No sooner had he set these down in front of them than he darted back into the kitchen, probably to slip out the same back door as his wife had. Isabela glanced over her shoulder and noticed the old man was gone too. They were alone.

Einar dragged a fork through the beans, breaking apart the skin atop them.

"But maybe Ran is right," Einar said. "Maybe I need to decide when it's time . . . when it's time to stop. When I've done enough."

Isabela studied the cloudy, conflicted expression on Ein- ar's face. She thought about Lucas, how the boy had trapped her inside her own trauma, how he'd nearly killed Duanphen and probably would've slaughtered them all. She leaned in close to Einar.

"Today is not the day you go soft, okay?" she said into

his ear. "Maybe you are a monster. But you're right. We need a monster to fight a monster. I don't care about right and wrong. I don't care about winners and losers. I want to survive. I want my friends to survive. And for that, you have to keep being bad."

Outside, four sets of tires screeched to a stop. Truck doors opened and slammed shut. In the quiet of the restaurant, they could hear the metallic jangle of weaponry. Isabela pushed her wrists against the bonds holding them together.

Einar took a deep breath and pushed aside his untouched food.

"Do it," he said calmly. "Make it look good."

Isabela smirked. "You know I will, baby."

She lunged forward, grabbed the back of Einar's head and slammed his face into the bar. He cried out in pain, a cut opened up on the bridge of his nose. Even though the blow hadn't knocked him out, Einar let his body go slack against Isabela. She looped her bound hands around his neck and yanked him off his stool. He was light. The guy needed to eat more.

Breathing heavily, Isabela dragged Einar out the front door. The harsh desert sunlight greeted her. So did thirty armed guards. They all wore body armor printed with desert camouflage, presumably the uniform for La Caldera. The guards wielded a mixture of anti-Garde Inhibitor cannons and traditional assault rifles.

"Hold your fire!" the point man shouted as Isabela burst into the light.

"About goddamn time!" Isabela shouted back as she dumped Einar in the dirt. "They snatched me four hours ago and you're just getting here *now*? Unacceptable!"

Since walking into town, Isabela hadn't been herself. She had taken the form of a middle-aged man with silver hair and a leathery tan. She added some bruises around the eyes and some scuff marks on his hands, to make it look like La Caldera's warden had put up a fight. She didn't even know the warden's name and she'd only heard him speak a few sentences. That would have to be enough.

Isabela strode forward with the confidence that her own men wouldn't shoot her, worried that at any moment they might see through her disguise and do just that.

"This idiot child got sloppy and let me get the drop on him," Isabela said brusquely, nodding her head at Einar's crumpled form. She held her wrists out to the nearest guard. "Stop staring and cut me loose."

The guard hesitated, staring at her. From his place sprawled in the dirt, looking bloodied and unconscious, Isabela knew that Einar was using his Legacy. Amplifying the confusion and bewilderment in the guards. But thirty was a lot of minds to control.

The guard swung his weapon aside, pulled a knife from his belt and cut Isabela's hands free. He turned to look at the team leader and so did Isabela, talking quickly, giving the guards no time to find their balance, to recall their training.

"We gotta move," Isabela ordered. "They got a shape-shifter on the inside." She held up her bare hand, where the warden wore his mechanical glove. "It's got my Skeleton Key." She motioned to Einar. "His people are on their way. They got a breakout planned."

One of the guards had crouched down to get a closer look at Einar. She whistled through her teeth. "Holy shit, sir, that's Magnusson."

"You think I don't know that?" Isabela snapped. "Get an Inhibitor on him quick before he comes to and makes us all act like chickens."

Another guard snapped to attention, pointed his Inhibitor and fired a collar around Einar's neck. He depressed the trigger and Einar cried out in genuine pain, his body arching as electricity jumped through his synapses.

That was the plan. Make them think Einar wasn't a threat. Make them believe Isabela was the real deal. Let them get in close and create more confusion.

Without Einar using his Legacy to further confuse the guards, the thirty men and women arrayed around Isabela now looked at her warily, on edge. Some of them tightened their grips on their weapons. Others, though, watched her respectfully, awaiting orders. She hadn't sold them all, but she was getting there.

"I've got to radio this in," the team leader said, reaching for a walkie-talkie strapped to his shoulder.

Isabela stopped him. "No. You'll alert the shape-shifter that we know. Give up our advantage." The team leader's eyes narrowed, but Isabela pressed on. She pointed at one of the guards with an Inhibitor cannon. "Zap me with that thing if you don't believe me. I can take it."

She *hoped* she could take it. Isabela had plenty of practice maintaining a form through pain and discomfort. Back when Einar's gang had jumped her in California, she'd held on to her shape through a car wreck and a beating. As long as she could stay conscious, she could beat the Inhibitor.

"That won't be necessary," the team leader said. He pulled a mechanical scope from his hip. "I've got the portable retinal scanner."

Isabela swallowed. She would've rather taken her chances being shocked. She wasn't confident that she'd mastered the warden's shape down to that tiniest of details. She snuck a look at Einar. He was out. No help there.

She stood firm before the team leader. "What are we wasting time for?" She widened her eye. At the same time, she subtly increased the swelling on the warden's cheek and added a popped blood vessel by her pupil. If she failed the test, maybe she could blame it on her black eye. "Do it."

He scanned her. Isabela forced herself not to blink as the laser bounced across her pupil.

The device beeped. Isabela couldn't tell if that was a good sound or a bad sound. The team leader stared at her for a moment. She waited. A guard on her left hefted his rifle a bit, getting ready to train it on her. Isabela stared him down.

The team leader reached for his walkie-talkie.

And held it out to her.

"Sir, if we're breached, we should at least reach out to Lyon," he said. "Give him a heads-up."

Isabela stifled a sigh of relief; it wouldn't do to show them that. Instead, she nodded impatiently. She didn't know who Lyon was or what she was supposed to say, but now that these men had bought their ruse, it would work to her advantage to cause trouble back at the prison. Maybe the men there would go ahead and arrest the real warden, make things easy.

"Make it so," she told the team leader, then turned around to inspect Einar. "Can't believe we got him. Everyone here's going to get a medal."

The team leader spoke into his walkie-talkie. "This is Roberts, requesting a line to Security Chief Lyon."

"Lyon, here," a gruff voice responded. "What's the situation there, Roberts?"

"Are you with Warden Pembleton?" the team leader—Roberts—asked.

"Not at the moment," came the response. "You need him, too?"

"No," Roberts said firmly. "Because *I'm* with the warden. You've got an imposter in there, Lyon. Get every squad on alert."

Isabela stifled a smile. Perfect. The infighting at the prison would hopefully spread out the guards and cover the approach of the others. This plan might actually work. But first, Isabela had to keep these soldiers on her side.

She grabbed the nearest guard's shoulder and shoved him towards a truck.

"Move out!" she bellowed. "We are under attack!"

Within seconds, they'd piled into their armored SUVs

and were tearing down the desert road towards the prison. It was only five miles away. A short ride with these jacked-up soldiers doing close to one hundred, all of them ready to kick some ass against an enemy they were at that moment letting inside. Isabela rode shotgun with Roberts and two other guards. They'd taken Einar in a separate truck, juicing him once more with the Inhibitor to be safe.

"Sir, if you don't mind my asking, how did these freaks get to you?" That was Roberts, not taking his eyes off the road as they careened across the burnt terrain. "I didn't think you'd left La Caldera in weeks."

Isabela didn't have an answer prepared for that, so she sucked her teeth and narrowed her eyes. "Are you my superior officer, Roberts? Do I report to you?"

"Sorry, sir," Roberts responded quickly.

The prison appeared, rising up from through the heat haze that blurred the horizon. A sandstone fortress surrounded by tall fences, just as ominous as Einar had described. The place was completely unshaded from the scorching heat. Nothing could live out here. Isabela got the sense of movement on the rooftop, snipers watching their haphazard approach.

Roberts worked up the courage to speak again. "How do you think they'll come at us, sir?"

Isabela opened her mouth to give him the brush-off again. As she did, a flare went up from the prison's roof. A rocket. It cut through the blue sky and exploded some hundred feet above the building.

At first, Isabela wasn't sure what had happened. Some

kind of misfire or warning shot? It looked as if the rocket had simply blown up in midair.

But then Einar's familiar skimmer flickered into view, its cloaking system failing as black smoke poured from a hole in its side. Isabela leaned forward, straining against her seat belt. The small ship banked onto its side, avoiding a second missile, but then corkscrewed out of control. The skimmer crashed onto the prison's rooftop, sending up a glut of flames and dust. Even at this distance, the impact rattled the SUV.

"Go!" Isabela screamed, doing nothing to hide the panic in her voice. "Get us there now!"

CHAPTER TWENTY-FIVE

TAYLOR COOK
THE HUMAN GARDE ACADEMY—POINT REYES, CALIFORNIA

TAYLOR RAISED HER HANDS ALONG WITH HER VOICE. "Faculty and students who aren't fit to fight! We're going to teleport you somewhere safe. Please grab as much luggage as you can carry for the students that're staying behind. We might need to follow in a hurry and can't be looking for our stuff!"

The student union bustled with activity, most of it around the new growth of Loralite in the room's center. A line was formed there, mostly made up of teachers who shouldn't be put in harm's way and the younger Garde who wouldn't be helpful in a fight. There was a stack of backpacks piled there. Nine had ordered everyone to pack what he called "bug-out bags"—warm clothes, food and water, whatever small items from home they couldn't bear to leave behind.

In a flash of blue light, Rabiya appeared, returning from another trip to the Himalayas. She was only back for a couple of seconds before moving close to Dr. Chen. The dean of academics teetered a bit, multiple backpacks slung across her shoulders, carrying as much as she possibly could for the students. A couple of young tweebs steadied her, these two also huddling close to Rabiya, all of them linking hands.

"It's a bit disorienting, so you might want to shut your eyes," Rabiya told the group in what was quickly becoming her customary warning.

"My dear, I've always wanted to bend space and time," Dr. Chen replied. "Let's do this."

And with that, Rabiya teleported them out.

Lexa stepped up before Taylor and Nine, a laptop bag slung over her shoulder.

"With all our systems down, I'm no good here," she said. "I'm going to New Lorien. I'll watch out for the little ones."

"Ella will be stoked to see you," Nine said. The two of them hugged and then Lexa made her way over to the Loralite stone.

Dr. Goode came up to them next. He didn't carry any luggage. Instead, he held an Inhibitor cannon, which he must have been studying in his lab.

"I'm staying," he said firmly. "I've been in plenty of fights before."

Nine shook his head. "Nah, Malcolm. I don't think so. If something goes wrong here, we need you safe. You've got a lot of wisdom and shit." He lowered his voice to a whisper, but Taylor could still hear. "Unlike me, you actually know how to run an Academy. Wherever it might end up."

Malcolm frowned, considering this. "I can be of use. Might I remind you that these people imprisoned my son?"

"And we've got people out there looking for him," Nine said. He lowered his voice. "If things go bad today, I'll tell Sam you say hi when I see him in prison, then wait for you to rescue us."

Taylor touched Malcolm's arm. "Thank you for everything, Dr. Goode. But we don't want anyone to stay who can't teleport out on their own."

Malcolm sighed. Resigned to leaving, he thrust the Inhibitor cannon in Taylor's direction.

"Here," he said. "Give the scabs from Earth Garde a taste of their own medicine."

Taylor smiled. "We will."

The crowd in the student union gradually thinned as more and more people were teleported to safety. Taylor looked around at the remaining Garde. They weren't so many now.

"Do you think this is enough?" she asked Nine quietly. "To hold them off?"

Nine grinned at her. She could tell he was enjoying this. "Even if it's not, we're going to give them one hell of a fight."

The doors to the student union burst open and Maiken sped inside. Maiken had been assigned to keep watch at the barricade with a couple of others. Taylor knew what her

presence here meant. Before Maiken could even start breathlessly speaking, Taylor was headed to the door.

"It's happening!" Maiken said. "They're coming!"

There was only one direct way into the Academy. One way
out. A winding road that only straightened as it emerged
from the woods. That had given Taylor pause all those
months ago. Made it seem to her like the Garde were trapped
inside.

Taylor couldn't count the Peacekeepers who marched
through the woods in a regimented line. One hundred.
Maybe two. There were more back at the encampment, she
knew. This was only a first wave. Greger Karlsson testing
their resolve. Even so, the Garde were outnumbered something like four to one. The barricade that they'd assembled
yesterday and now hid behind felt suddenly flimsy. The
tangle of desks and tables wouldn't hold back an army. Not
for long.

But the Garde behind it might.

The soldiers stopped about fifty yards away, dressed in
body armor and carrying Inhibitor cannons. Some of them
held grappling hooks attached to ropes, probably meant to
tear down the students' haphazard wall. The Garde peeked
through openings in the barricade or peered over its top. The
Peacekeepers surely knew they were there; they could definitely see them through the gaps. But Taylor had taken care
to make sure the glowing Loralite stone behind the students
was hidden behind a thick lunch table. She didn't want the

Peacekeepers to know about that. Not yet.

Taylor thought back to capture the flag, how team after team had been beaten by an organized squad of Peacekeepers, at least until Isabela broke the game.

Back then, everyone had been showing off, trying to catch Greger's eye and look good for Earth Garde. They'd been working in teams, yes, but they'd also been working for themselves.

Now, they were together. They were an Academy united.

"YOU ARE IN VIOLATION OF THE GARDE ACCORD!" Greger's voice rang out through the trees, booming out of a megaphone. Taylor couldn't actually see him. He was no doubt a safe distance behind the Peacekeepers. "SURRENDER IMMEDIATELY OR WE WILL BE FORCED TO USE . . . TO USE FORCE!"

Taylor had her own megaphone. It was Nigel, standing right next to her. As Taylor yelled back, he amplified her voice.

"WE DON'T WANT TO FIGHT YOU!" Taylor responded. "BUT IF YOU ATTACK US, WE ARE WITHIN OUR RIGHTS UNDER YOUR PRECIOUS GARDE ACCORD TO DEFEND OURSELVES!"

Her message delivered, Nigel squeezed Taylor's shoulder.

"Good luck," he said.

"You too," Taylor replied.

Nigel jogged away from the barricade, touched the Loralite stone and teleported away. He had another role to play.

"Remember, don't hurt any of them too badly," Taylor

said, her voice carrying down the line of Garde positioned on their side of the wall. "Focus on disarming them. The Inhibitors are connected to their armor by tensile cords. We want to—"

"We *know*, Taylor," Nicolas said from on her left. "We're good. We're ready."

At some unspoken command, the Peacekeepers started forward. Their faces were stoic and hard. Taylor didn't recognize any of them. The familiar ones, those who had worked with Archibald, they were gone.

"Push!" Taylor yelled.

As one, the Garde shoved forward with their telekinesis. To the Peacekeepers, it must have felt like a wave of force rolled over them. Some toppled onto their backs, scrambling for balance in the dirt. Others hunkered down and weathered the telekinetic burst like a strong wind, trying to raise their weapons all the while.

"Give me chaff!" one of the Peacekeepers yelled.

Taylor heard the *putt-putt* of two grenade launchers and then the air between the Garde and the Peacekeepers filled with swarming bits of metal and flashing lights. They had used this trick during capture the flag. All the detritus wreaked havoc on a Garde's precision telekinetic control. It hurt Taylor's eyes just looking into the cloud.

But they were ready for it.

"Maiken!" Taylor yelled. "Anika!"

In a blur, Maiken swept around the barricade, sprinting at top speed while pulling with her telekinesis. She dragged some of the chaff clear in her wake. The rest Anika pushed to the ground with her magnetic control. A couple chunks of metal flipped loose from the barricade, caught in Anika's pull, but nothing that they couldn't live without. Just like that, the air was clear.

The Peacekeepers had made up some ground, though. They were closer.

"Grappling hooks!" one of the Peacekeepers shouted. "I want to be able to see our targets!"

A handful of soldiers scrambled forward to try flinging their hooks at the barricade. It was a waste of effort. Taylor didn't even need to give the command; the Garde along the wall batted aside the hooks with ease, leaving the limp ropes lying in the grass.

"Push!" Taylor yelled again.

Once again, the Garde rammed them with telekinesis. More Peacekeepers buckled under the pressure and fell back. Others kept coming, pressing forward and aiming their weapons. The shock collars would never make it through the gaps in the barricade, so the Peacekeepers didn't bother firing those. Tranquilizer darts, on the other hand—the projectiles sounded like rain as they bounced off the Garde's twisted metal cover.

Something whistled by Taylor's ear. To her left, Ben from Brooklyn gasped as a dart stuck him in the neck. He fell into the grass, nearly knocking down the Garde next to him. He was unconscious in seconds, the sedative working fast. One of the tweebs grabbed him, pulled him to the Loralite stone and teleported to safety. It was the only dart that wasn't intercepted by their blockade or telekinesis.

"Okay, we warned them," Taylor said through her teeth. "Disarm!"

As one, the Garde stopped *pushing* with their telekinesis and started *pulling*.

They yanked tranquilizer guns and Inhibitor cannons out of the Peacekeepers' hands. The weapons were attached to their body armor, but that was okay. In fact, it was perfect. Taylor focused on two Peacekeepers, ripped their weapons away and then tangled their cords together. She then yanked on that doubled cord and used it to clothesline a third soldier. Next to her, Nicolas pulled two Peacekeepers that he'd connected in a similar way into Taylor's bunch, getting their wires gnarled up further. Omar used the ropes from the grappling hooks to entangle a few more Peacekeepers. All the Garde used the same technique—they ripped weapons away and used them to bind the Peacekeepers into one large group.

By now, the soldiers were more focused on screaming at each other than they were on fighting the Garde. They bumped heads and knocked into each other, fell to the ground in kicking heaps, tried to shove one another away. Some of them smartened up and started to clip free of their body armor. It was too late for that.

The sight made Taylor smile. They'd managed to snare virtually all that first wave together. All of them connected.

"Pull!" Taylor shouted. "Now! Pull!"

With the combined power of their telekinesis, the Garde pulled the struggling Peacekeepers towards them. They rolled through the dirt or tried to ineffectually grab tree roots. Some of them tried to get their weapons free from the mess of bodies and cords, but to no avail.

"Open it up!" Taylor shouted.

With his superstrength, Nic pushed aside a trio of stacked cafeteria tables, creating a wide gap in the barricade. They dragged the soldiers through the opening. Shouting and grasping, some of the Peacekeepers managed to grab hold of chunks of the barricade, straining to stop their momentum. The Garde were stronger.

Taylor backed up as the jumble of soldiers clamored behind their wall. She backed up until she was right next to the Loralite stone.

Soon, the entire squad was dumped right at her feet.

She reached down and gripped the ankle of the nearest Peacekeeper. Then, she reached back and touched the Loralite stone.

A flash of blue light and, suddenly, the sound of thundering water.

Taylor stood on a hillside overlooking Niagara Falls. She'd been there once with her father when she was a kid. It worked just like Nigel said. Picture a place with a stone and the Loralite would carry her there.

Her, and the hundred or so Peacekeepers she was connected to.

The soldiers lay on the hillside, blinking and disoriented.

One of them turned onto his side and puked. Another nearly rolled into the water but was stopped by a couple of his buddies. Taylor stood over them all.

"One-way trip, guys," she said. "Enjoy your vacation."

She pictured the Academy, touched the Loralite and teleported home.

When she reappeared, only seconds later, a shout went up from the other Garde. Ahead of them, the trees were nearly clear of Peacekeepers. The handful that Taylor hadn't teleported away were retreating.

"Holy shit!" Nic bellowed happily. "I can't believe that worked!"

"We should do that again," Anika said.

"We could try," Taylor said. "But I don't think they'll fall for it twice. Get the wall sealed back up."

Taylor looked over her classmates. Some of them, like Nic and Anika, seemed pumped up and ready for more action. But there were others whose eyes looked a little sunken or were sheened with sweat. One of the tweebs, she thought his name was Danny, bent over at the waist to catch his breath. Telekinesis was a muscle and not all of them were up for a protracted fight.

"Second wave coming at ya," said Nigel's voice in her ear. The Garde closest to Taylor all jumped as they heard Nigel too. "Mostly on foot, but they've got a couple trucks. Might try ramming through."

Taylor turned towards the administration building. Nigel's shape was visible on the rooftop, the highest spot at the Academy. From there he'd be able to keep an eye on things and then call out orders. With all their technology compromised, he was the closest thing they had to walkie-talkies. Taylor waved to indicate that she'd heard him.

"Okay," Taylor said. "There's another group coming in with vehicles. Get ready."

Taylor peeked through a gap in the barricade. The Peace-keepers weren't visible yet. They were approaching more slowly. Cautiously.

Something buzzed by overhead. Drones. Four of them zipped out of the woods and began circling in a formation around the Garde.

"Knock 'em down!" Nic shouted.

Taylor squinted, catching a glint of something in the trees. She spotted one of the Peacekeepers, hunkered down behind an oak, waiting. He wore goggles and a gas mask.

"Wait!" Taylor shouted, but it was too late.

Her classmates reached out with their telekinesis, easily grabbed hold of the drones and smashed them to the ground. As soon as the robots hit, their payloads exploded. Mustard-colored tear gas spread in a cloud around the Garde, choking them.

The next group of Peacekeepers marched forward. Goggles, gas masks, tranquilizer guns and handheld shock sticks that were basically cattle prods.

Tears streamed out of Taylor's eyes. The air burned her throat. She heard an engine rev and tires squeal, but couldn't see the truck through the smoke. She leaped away from the barricade seconds before the crash—desks and tables flying through the air, breaking glass, screams.

Taylor shouted through haggard coughs.

"Fall back! Fall back to the dorms!"

CHAPTER TWENTY-SIX

CALEB CRANE
LA CALDERA—DURANGO, MEXICO

IN THE CLOAKED SKIMMER, THEY WATCHED FROM above as Isabela and Einar turned themselves over to La Caldera's guards. As soon as they were reasonably certain that the two of them wouldn't be executed, Five swung the ship towards the prison. They picked up speed. A lightning bolt aimed at their enemies.

"Strap in, we're landing hard," Five warned. "I'm putting us down right on the roof. Right down their throats."

In the copilot seat, Caleb pulled the belts across his chest and tightened them. Behind him, on the benches, Ran and Duanphen secured themselves as well. Caleb's leg bounced up and down. He was anxious. He always got this way before a fight. The battles he'd been in before—Patience Creek, the Harvesters' headquarters, Switzerland—those had kind of snuck up on him. He'd never willingly charged towards certain death. His dad probably would've been proud, even if it was currently taking all of Caleb's self-control not to pop a nail-biting duplicate.

The smoldering desert shot by beneath them. The prison came into view. Closer.

Sweat beaded on Caleb's neck.

Closer. Almost there.

Red lights lit up across the skimmer's console. An alarm sounded.

"Shit!" Five barked. "They're painting us!"

"What does that mean?" Caleb asked.

"It means—"

Caleb didn't see the rocket fired from the prison's roof, but he heard it. A high-velocity shriek and then an explosion that yanked him taut against his restraints. Burnt air rushed into the cockpit, stinging Caleb's eyes.

At the controls, Five let out a feral growl. His skin was metal now as he activated his Legacy, tapping into the steel ball bearing he kept hidden behind his eye patch. He wrestled with the controls and rolled them to the left. Caleb hung from his seat, only the belts keeping him from falling forward into the skimmer's cracked windshield. A second rocket whistled by, grazing them, but doing no more damage.

A warning siren keened incessantly from the console. Mogadorian script flooded the display. Caleb didn't need to understand the language to know what that meant. They wouldn't be flying this skimmer out. If Five couldn't get the ship under control, that wouldn't be a problem anyway. They'd all be dead.

Straining against his seat belt, Caleb looked into the compartment behind them. A huge hole had been ripped in the side of their ship, just feet from where Ran and Duanphen were strapped in. As the ship rolled, their bench began to come loose from its moorings, pulled towards the sucking air beyond. Ran looked dazed, bleeding from a cut on her temple. Duanphen held on to her with one arm, the other struggling to detach her tangled seat belt. A couple stitches on her forearm popped from the strain. Duanphen gritted her teeth.

"Hold on!" Caleb yelled. He loosed a trio of duplicates and they tossed themselves into the rear compartment, lunging for the girls and their bench, heedless of their own safety. A piece of shrapnel detached from the opening and ripped through the head of one duplicate, but the other two made it. They threw their weight into the bench, held Ran and Duanphen down, kept them from flying out.

"Brace yourse—!" Five screamed.

They hit the roof with a jarring, deafening impact, and rolled. Concrete churned beneath them. The skimmer's console flashed and beeped, all manner of catastrophic damage being reported, none of it mattering.

Caleb's head banged against the cockpit ceiling and for a moment everything went black.

Five slapped him hard across the cheek. Caleb blinked

back to awareness. He was upside down. Everything was upside down.

"If you're alive, you need to move!" Five shouted. "We're exposed!"

Gunfire. Bullets pattered against the skimmer's compromised armor. Tiny holes opened up inches from Caleb, beams of sunlight shining through the smoke and dust.

Five put his shoulder into the skimmer's windscreen and knocked it free. With a roar, he flew from the spaceship and charged their attackers.

Caleb unbuckled and fell onto the skimmer's roof, which was now its floor. Crouching low to avoid stray bullets, he hustled into the rear compartment and found Duanphen and Ran also unbuckling. They were singed and cut up, but none of their injuries were too bad. The three of them exchanged looks. There was no time for words. They knew what needed to be done.

Get out there, Caleb said to himself. *Protect us.*

He made as many duplicates as he could. Found himself peering out through fifteen sets of eyes.

The Calebs led the charge onto the rooftop, surging through the hole in the skimmer's side. Many of them were cut down immediately as the prison's guards took aim on them with their rifles. No Inhibitors. No tranquilizer darts. These men weren't here to take prisoners, only keep them.

Ran, Duanphen and Caleb followed behind the wall of Calebs, hunkered low. Caleb counted at least twenty guards on the rooftop, with others streaming up from the stairwell at the far end. Every duplicate that fell, Caleb tried to replace. His muscles felt taut and dehydrated, he was cramping up, but not from the heat. He was spreading himself thin.

Caleb clenched his fists and made more. More bodies to throw at these bastards.

Ahead of them, Five smashed into a group of guards. He ripped their weapons away with his telekinesis, punched through their visors with his hardened fists. When one tried to get away, Five turned his skin to rubber and snagged him around the feet, lifted him and bashed him face-first into the rooftop.

As they edged forward, Ran picked up bits of debris, charged them and hurled them into a pocket of guards. The ensuing explosion knocked many of them down, scattered others.

A pair of guards had circled around the crashed skimmer and tried to get in behind the Garde. Caleb didn't see them coming. He was too focused on what was ahead of them.

Duanphen saw what was happening. She shoved the guards' guns aside with her telekinesis, grabbed each of them by the throat and shocked them until they collapsed.

From the other side of the roof, a sniper drew a bead on Five. The first shot pinged harmlessly off his metallic chest, but the second one hit Five in one of the dark, ooze-tinged spaces that his Legacy didn't cover, right below the collar. Through the ears of his many duplicates, Caleb heard the wet, sucking sound the bullet made as it entered Five's body.

The Loric grunted and fell down to his knees. He'd been

hurt. Caleb had almost convinced himself that wasn't possible.

Caleb sent a surge of duplicates rushing forward to cover Five. They huddled around him as Five gasped for breath.

"Are you okay?" Caleb asked through five different mouths.

As Caleb's duplicates watched, the bullet reappeared, pushed out of Five's body by the congealed ooze. His lips were wet with blood, but he nodded once at Caleb, then flew forward in a blur. Five grabbed the sniper, spun him and chucked him off the roof.

Another explosion generated by Ran and the guards started to fall back. Caleb's duplicates tackled some of them as they tried to escape, pinned them down and pummeled them until they were unconscious.

A guard in the stairwell doorway fired wildly at them with his sidearm. With his other hand, he screamed into a walkie-talkie. "This is Lyon! We're being overwhelmed up here! We need reinforcements!"

"How do I know this is really Lyon?" came the response over the walkie-talkie.

"What?" Lyon screamed. "Are you out of your fu—?"

Five was on him. He grabbed the walkie-talkie and smashed it into the guard's face, then shoved him out of the way.

Caleb liked what he heard. Their ruse with Isabela and Einar had actually worked. The guards were disorganized and distrustful.

Suddenly, the rooftop was quiet. The gunfire had tapered to a stop. All around them, guards moaned in pain or were unconscious. At least, Caleb hoped they were unconscious. Actually, he realized grimly, he didn't care either way.

They took cover in the stairwell. Caleb remembered the map. Their next floor down would be the guards' barracks. They'd encounter more resistance there.

"Everyone okay?" Caleb asked. He realized he was shouting. All the gunfire had deafened him a bit.

"Yes," Duanphen said, nodding. She looked pale and a little woozy, leaning against the wall to catch her breath. Caleb wasn't sure how much longer she would last.

"Fine," Five replied, but then he coughed, more blood bubbling up from his lungs. He spit it onto the steps. *"Fine,"* he said firmly, before Caleb could ask him again.

Ran said nothing. She met Caleb's eyes and looked away, her mouth a hard line. This attack was against everything she stood for, yet she'd come along anyway.

They moved down the stairs towards the barracks. One of Caleb's duplicates led the way, ready to absorb more gunfire if any guards leaped out at them.

Before they could make the next landing, the door to the barracks burst open and a squadron of guards filled the stairwell. Five growled and started to lunge forward, but Ran put a hand on his shoulder to stop him. She had noticed the same thing that Caleb had through the eyes of his duplicate.

These guards weren't heading *up.* They were heading *down.*

"Get the armory secured!" one of them said. "Then figure out what's happened to the warden!"

They waited for the guards to hustle down the stairwell, then Caleb and the others slipped into the barracks. They were looking for the path of least resistance.

"It's too quiet on the roof!" a guard shouted. "I want eyes up— *Oof!*"

A second group of guards were exiting the barracks as soon as Caleb and the others entered. Duanphen shocked two of them before they even got their weapons up. Five slammed the head of another through the plaster wall. Caleb's duplicates and some precise telekinesis from Ran took care of the rest. It was over in seconds without a single shot fired.

"Missiles and rifles and snipers," Five growled raggedly. "These assholes aren't so tough up close."

The rest of the barracks appeared deserted. They moved through them quickly, passing by bunk beds, piles of magazines and round tables with multiple games of poker abandoned in progress. Seconds later, they reached the showers—communal stalls, tile floors, the strong aroma of mildew.

"This is the place," Caleb said.

Ran nodded and stepped forward. "Stand back."

She knelt down and placed her hands on the tiles. Soon, a whole section of them glowed with the crimson energy of Ran's Legacy. The floor vibrated slightly beneath them and Caleb took another step back. He knew that she was reaching down, charging more than just the top layer of the floor.

Einar had noticed this spot on the blueprint. Told them it might be a shortcut.

The charge set, Ran jumped backwards and took cover in the hallway with the rest of them. It was a three count until the floor exploded, sending a shower of tile and stone spraying into the hallway.

When the dust cleared, Caleb sent a couple of duplicates to peer into the hole. Water poured from pipes that looked as if they'd been sheared clear in half by Ran's precision detonation. Down below, an empty hallway waited. They would be right outside the warden's office and the control room.

"Let's go," Five said.

He floated down, then helped the others as they jumped from the floor above. Ran was the last one to make the leap. Caleb thought that she hesitated, maybe wavered a little bit on the edge. Charging the floor must have taken something out of her.

Five caught Ran when she jumped. She started to pull away from him, but Five held her by the upper arm.

"Hey," Five said. "What the hell?"

He held up his hand. Where he'd touched Ran's side was covered with blood.

"Scratched," Ran said. "It's nothing."

Her voice sounded weak. Caleb took a step towards her. "Ran? Are you . . . ?"

Gruffly, Five yanked up Ran's shirt, exposing her abdomen. Two dark, puckered holes marred her stomach. Gunshot wounds. Caleb's eyes widened; she must've gotten hit during that first battle on the roof.

"I'm okay," Ran said, looking down at the wounds. "They don't even hurt."

No sooner had she said that than Ran's legs buckled. Five caught her around the waist and held her up.

"No, no, no," Five growled. "I actually like you, Ran. You aren't dying on me."

Ran smiled wanly. "That's nice, Five."

Five pointed to the control room. "Get in there and check the monitors," he told Caleb. "They've got to have a healer locked up here. They *have* to."

"We need to find the warden and that Skeleton Key thing," Caleb said. "Get the place unlocked."

"Einar's on it," Five said. "He'll get it done."

"We should check his office. Maybe he left something behind," Duanphen said.

They split up. Caleb went into the control room and the others into the warden's office.

As soon as he stepped into the control room, a guard lunged out from behind the door and pointed a pistol at Caleb's chest. He popped a duplicate just in time to absorb the first shot, then ripped the man's gun away before a second shot could be fired. Caleb floated the gun over to himself and aimed it at the guard.

He raised his hands. "Okay, kid, okay. I'm sorry. I'm just doing my job."

"You would've killed me," Caleb said flatly. He thought of Ran, gut-shot in the other room, maybe dying if they didn't get lucky and find a healer locked up here. "You'd kill all my friends."

"We're just defending ourselves," the guard said. "From *you*."

Caleb's finger twitched on the trigger. He didn't fire. Instead, he ejected the weapon's clip, then used his telekinesis to fling the empty gun into the guard's face. The weapon struck him right between the eyes, knocking him out.

Duanphen appeared in the doorway. "I heard a shot."

"It's over," Caleb said. "Help me look."

The two of them were confronted with an overwhelming network of screens and control panels. Caleb's first thought was to try something on one of the computers—open the cells, for instance—but everything was password protected. Caleb turned to the screens.

"Where's the damn warden?"

"There," Duanphen said, pointing to one of the dozens of monitors that streamed every inch of the prison.

On the screen, the warden led a large group of guards through the first floor's intake area. The warden in question also carried an Inhibitor cannon with Einar attached to its leash. That was Isabela, a fact Duanphen quickly realized as well.

"No, wait, *there*," Duanphen said, pointing at a different monitor.

The warden—the *real* warden—led a second cadre of guards, all of them heavily armored. They were headed down a stairwell, on a collision course for Isabela and Einar.

Caleb squinted at the monitor, trying to catch a glimpse of the mechanical glove that controlled the prison's systems. He spotted it.

"Tell Five there's nothing to find in the warden's office," Caleb said. "We need to go help the others."

As Duanphen left, Caleb took a moment to take stock of the monitors that broadcast views of the cells, praying that he'd see a healer there.

On one screen, Daniela Morales stood with her ear pressed against the door of her tiny compartment. She must've been able to tell there was some kind of disturbance in the prison. Caleb grimaced, realizing that her presence here meant that Earth Garde had turned on Daniela. That was maybe a little his fault.

On another screen, a young woman knocked out a set of push-ups. It was only when she sprang to her feet and furiously banged her fists against the reinforced door that Caleb realized who she was. Number Six.

In a different cell, Caleb spotted Sam Goode. He was lying down on his cot with an IV hooked up to his arm.

And there, on another screen, Caleb saw the enemy. A scrawny boy with wild curls, also unconscious in his bed, while a woman dressed like a Sunday school teacher kept watch over him. Lucas.

Finally, Caleb spotted a boy with dark, curly hair, huddled on his bed and shivering. It took Caleb a moment to remember his name. Or, anyway, his nickname.

"Meatballs," Caleb said. "Hell yeah, Vinnie Meatballs."

Caleb rushed out of the control room and over to the warden's office. He was just in time to see Five finish bandaging up Ran's side using a first aid kit he'd found. The warden's office was decorated in a way that suggested its owner would be totally cool imprisoning and torturing teenagers—the taxidermy heads of animals ranging from buffalo to mountain lions, a bearskin rug, a blown-up picture of the warden shaking hands with Dick Cheney. Caleb was glad to see the place had been trashed as Duanphen and Five looked for the Skeleton Key.

"There's major reinforcements and a healer if we can get them free of the cells," Caleb reported. "The real warden and a lot of the guards are heading for the first floor. Einar and Isabela . . ."

Five nodded, then looked to Ran. "You ready?"

She didn't look good to Caleb. Ran was pale and appeared unable to fully straighten. Five had to support most of her weight.

"Let's finish this," Ran said.

"You stick close to me," Five replied. "Blow stuff up. I'll take care of you."

"I can do that," Ran replied.

"Here, let me help," Caleb said.

He made a duplicate to ease in on Ran's other side. They might need Five to fight, after all. He created a second duplicate to take point as they exited the warden's office and

started towards another battle—all of them hurting, bloodied, maybe even dying. But still pressing on. They could
only go forward.

"Wait," Duanphen said, stopping in the office. "What are
those?"

Caleb had missed them in his quick perusal of the office.
Hanging from a nail beside the mounted head of a buck were
two strange pendants. These looked like the latest additions
to the warden's gross trophy collection. The two medallions
gave off a faint blue glow that was unmistakable to Caleb—
Loralite. Each of them were etched with a Loric symbol that
he didn't understand.

"What the hell?" Five said. With his free hand, he yanked
one of the pendants off the wall. "My people make these,
they—"

Five's fingers brushed the Loralite. There was a flash of
blue light.

For the briefest of moments, through the eyes of his duplicate that was supporting Ran, Caleb caught a glimpse of a
strange cave. A cave on the other side of the world. A cave
crowded with familiar faces. The faces Caleb saw were panicked and frightened. They were running from something.

And then, being too far away from Caleb, the duplicate
evaporated. His window into New Lorien closed.

Caleb and Duanphen stared at each other. The other pendant remained on the wall, swinging gently.

Five and Ran were gone.

CHAPTER TWENTY-SEVEN

NIGEL BARNABY
THE HUMAN GARDE ACADEMY—POINT REYES, CALIFORNIA

FROM THE ROOFTOP OF THE ADMINISTRATION building, Nigel watched as everything his mother had promised about the Academy came true. It was falling. Just like she said it would.

They had started out so well. Nigel had cheered when Taylor managed to teleport that entire first squad of Peacekeepers away, her crazy-ass plan working to perfection. Plus, there'd been the Peacekeepers who attempted to sneak in via the beach. They slammed their speedboats right into a series of icebergs that Lisbette had hidden in the shallows. With most of the other Garde tied up with Taylor, Nine personally teleported down there to handle the bedraggled Peacekeepers that waded ashore.

Now, Nigel watched as his classmates sprinted away from

an expanding cloud of tear gas. Their barricade was down, the road into campus unblocked except for some scattered debris. The Garde took shelter in the dorms. A team of Peace-keepers with gas masks gave chase. Nigel knew that Taylor had another trick up her sleeve, but he didn't think it would be enough. There were too many soldiers.

In a flash of light, Nine teleported in from the beach using the rooftop Loralite stone. He was scuffed up—knuckles bloody, a burn mark on his neck, but otherwise unharmed.

"Did you have fun?" Nigel asked.

"Felt good, haven't gotten a solid workout in a while," Nine replied, cracking his neck. "How we looking?"

"She's trying the dorm maneuver," Nigel said. "The other side's got too many bodies, Nine. They'll just keep coming."

"And here I was hoping they'd pull back once we showed them our mean faces," Nine said.

"You having a laugh?" Nigel replied. He shook his head. "We might as well be playing capture the flag down there, mate. They'll keep sending more men. No reason for 'em not to. All we're doing is inconveniencing them. Would be just as effective to chain ourselves to the trees or burn our bras, yeah?"

Nine gave him a look. Nigel knew what it sounded like he was suggesting. That unless they hurt the Peacekeep-ers—*really* hurt them—there was no way they'd stop their attack on the Academy. But Nigel wasn't like that. He wasn't like Einar, willing to sacrifice everything for the cause.

He wouldn't kill Peacekeepers, no matter how screwed up things got.

"I'm just saying, we can't win," Nigel continued. "The rest of us should evacuate the hell out of here. Let 'em have this dump."

Nine made a face when he referred to the Academy as a dump, but let it go. "If they know we're going on the run, they'll start looking for us," Nine said. "If they start looking for us and find New Lorien before John's got his whole force field network hooked up—"

"Yeah, yeah, I know," Nigel cut in. "We hold out until we get the signal. I know the score. Don't mean I don't feel like a right idiot up here . . ." Nigel peeked over the edge of the roof. He'd seen enough Peacekeepers plow into the dorms. He cleared his throat. "Hold that thought, trap to spring."

Nigel smirked as he pictured the fifty or so Peacekeepers that had charged after the Garde. Right that very second, they were probably kicking over couches or peering under beds, searching for the Garde they thought were hiding in there. Except the Garde weren't hiding. As soon as Taylor's crew hit the dorms, they'd used the Loralite stone to teleport to the training center.

"NOW!" Nigel shouted, funneling the sound so that it rattled the training center's windows.

Taylor and the other Garde spilled out of the training center with a war cry and charged towards the dorms. The few Peacekeepers standing watch outside the building looked completely spooked. Soon, they collapsed under telekinetic shoves, or were knocked out with redirected darts from their own tranquilizer guns. A group of Garde, including Nic, split off to tip over the trucks the Peacekeepers had driven through the barricade.

Meanwhile, Nigel jogged to the other side of the roof, the side closer to the dorms. Nine joined him and they focused their telekinesis. Together, they started pulling down the blast shields.

When Nigel first learned about the little jail beneath the Academy, he'd wondered what other "safety" features their school came equipped with to potentially keep the students in line. It turned out there were titanium panels installed over every window in the dorms, just in case a Garde ever lost control and needed to be locked in. If the power wasn't out, they could've brought those shields down with the press of a button. Instead, they had to use telekinesis.

Nine and Nigel sealed the windows that they could see while Taylor and her Garde ran around to the sides and yanked down the metal plates there. Soon, every window in the building was battened down. Then, Lisbette erected a thick barrier of ice across the front doors. Within minutes, they'd successfully trapped fifty Peacekeepers inside the building.

"Right, then," Nigel said. "Job well done."

Another small victory over the Peacekeepers, which they were able to celebrate for exactly the amount of time it took Nigel to make that comment. Then, twice the number of soldiers they'd just locked into the dorms came charging out of the trees and smoke.

"Shit," Nine said. "I gotta get down there."

"Take me with you," Nigel said. "I'm done playing human megaphone. All our traps are sprung. We bare-knuckle it from here on out."

"What's that saying you British guys have?" Nine asked as he grabbed hold of Nigel. "Once more into the bitches?"

"Yeah," Nigel said dryly. "That's it."

They didn't bother with the Loralite. Instead Nine ran them straight down the side of the building and they hit the ground at a sprint. Well, Nine did. Nigel quickly lost pace with the Loric. He was a dervish of flying black hair and shining mechanical arm—trucking a Peacekeeper here, ripping a tranquilizer gun free from one there.

The latest wave of Peacekeepers made it chaos on the ground. Nigel heard Taylor shouting above the fray.

"Use the tranquilizers against them! Stay tight!"

She couldn't keep the Garde together, though. There were too many enemies. The Garde scattered and started fighting individual battles or else booked it for one of the buildings where there was a teleportation stone. The Peacekeepers swarmed them.

A few yards ahead of Nigel, Anika sent a cloud of tranquilizer darts flying back towards their shooters. As she did that, another Peacekeeper rushed her from behind, jabbed a shock stick into her back and electrocuted her. Anika fell to the ground and the Peacekeeper pulled a shock collar off his belt, but Nigel whistled sharply into his ear and the Peace-keeper fell back.

Maiken zoomed by and snatched the collar out of the reel-ing Peacekeeper's hand. While Nigel knelt next to Anika and tried to get her back on her feet, Maiken zipped through the lines of Peacekeepers, ripping away their equipment as she passed. That worked well until one of the soldiers fired an Inhibitor cannon at the ground—he missed Maiken entirely with the collar, but the tensile wire snagged her legs and she fell onto her face at speed. The Peacekeepers were on her before she could get back up.

"Come on, come on," Nigel said to Anika, trying to help her stand. "We need to get you out."

A heartbeat after Nigel got Anika to her feet, there were three Peacekeepers bearing down on them. With a shout, Nicolas intercepted them. He clotheslined two of the sol-diers, then kicked another one in the chest—the force sent the man flying across the field. Nicolas waded into the heart of another pocket of Peacekeepers. As he did, Nigel noticed three tranquilizer darts sticking out of his back. He wouldn't last long.

"Can you shoot?" That was Nemo, who was suddenly right next to Nigel. She held a tranquilizer gun in each hand and floated a third one nearby with her telekinesis. There was a cut on her scalp, causing her aquamarine hair to turn dark purple.

Nigel snatched the gun out of the air. "Thanks—"

A Peacekeeper was on them, trying to yank barely

conscious Anika away from Nigel. He aimed the gun Nemo had given him and fired a dart into the man's neck. When he looked up, Nemo was gone. Another group of Peacekeepers were incoming.

Dragging Anika, Nigel fled to the nearest building. The training center. He'd get Anika there, then go back for someone else. He wouldn't let any Garde get taken. That was the best he could do.

Nigel thrust open the doors of the training center. The Loralite stone grew just a few yards away, Nine's sadistic obstacle course looming behind it. He was almost there when the Loralite lit up and—

"Do you jerks think you're the only ones who know how to use these stupid rocks?"

Woof! A fist struck Nigel right in the belly, the punch packing enough power to lift him completely off his feet. He collapsed to his hands and knees, retching and gasping. Anika fell beside him.

Melanie Jackson whipped off her gas mask and tossed it aside. Lofton St. Croix had teleported in with her, spikes protruding from his shoulders and arms, ready for battle. Their Earth Garde uniforms weren't even a little dirty.

"I knew they'd put a stone in here," Lofton said proudly.

Melanie snapped her fingers at him. "Get collars on them," she ordered.

She frowned at Nigel. "Why are you guys even fighting us? You know Earth Garde's doing the right thing here."

Nigel was too winded to respond. Not that he would've

known where to begin with this airheaded sellout. Instead, as Lofton approached brandishing a shock collar, Nigel pushed them with his telekinesis. Melanie and Lofton used their own telekinesis to stabilize themselves, only allowing Nigel to shove them back a few feet. But that was all Nigel needed.

He just needed to get them onto the course.

"Stop being a dick," Lofton said, starting forward again.

Nigel knew every one of Nine's traps. He knew there was a redwood log attached to chains that swung down from the ceiling right at the start. He'd been knocked on his ass enough times that he'd never forget that stupid battering ram. He reached out with his telekinesis and slid open the compartment in the ceiling, let the log fall free—

Melanie saw what he was doing. At the last moment, she simply reached up and caught the log, holding it above her head like it weighed nothing.

"I don't know who built your bootleg training center," Melanie said. "But the one in Washington is way— *Hhkk!*"

The Inhibitor collar snapped around Melanie's neck and sent a jolt through her before she could finish speaking. As her muscles spasmed, Melanie lost her grip on the log and dropped it on top of herself, pinning her to the floor.

"Put that on your poster, bitch," Taylor said.

Taylor stood in the training center doorway, holding the Inhibitor cannon. She gave Melanie an extra shock to make sure she was out, then tossed the weapon aside. Taylor's eyes were red-rimmed; there were traces of blood in her hair and smudges of dirt on her cheeks. She had two tranquilizer guns shoved into her pants and a glare on her face that was savage enough to freeze Lofton in his tracks.

"You," Taylor said.

Lofton paused for a moment, then dropped the Inhibitor and raised his hands to clutch at the sides of his head. He looked down at Nigel in terror.

"What are you doing?" Lofton screamed. "Your sonic attack is destroying my equilibrium!"

Lofton fell over, flopped around and then lay still.

Nigel managed to suck in the first solid breath since Melanie punched him, and staggered back to his feet. He stared at Lofton. He hadn't done anything to the guy. "What the actual fuck?"

Lofton opened one eye. "Dude, they said it was either come here and fight or go to Garde prison. Just pretend you messed me up and I'll stay down. My Cêpan will never know the difference now that Melanie's out."

"Christ," Nigel said, slapping his forehead. "You're a moron."

Nicolas barreled into the training center with Maiken's unconscious body slung across his shoulder. He set her down next to Anika, then fell to his knees in front of Taylor. She immediately set to work pulling darts out of his back and healing him.

"We're losing," Nicolas said breathlessly. "For every one

we take down, another two show up. Plus, I think they've got a healer of their own. I swear I knocked out the same dude twice."

"That's Jiao," Taylor said coolly. "We need to find her. Take her out of the fight."

Nigel peeked out through the doors. There were still battles happening all across the grounds. As he watched, Omar drove a group of Peacekeepers back with his fire breath. Nearby, a group of tweebs guided tranquilizer darts into the backs of some soldiers. A new cloud of tear gas bloomed near the student union, and Nigel watched Nine emerge from within it, a stolen gas mask pulled over his face.

"We can't win," Nigel told Taylor bluntly. "We need to start pulling people out—"

A huge piece of metal appeared out of thin air in front of the training center and crashed to the ground, tearing up chunks of grass as it skidded to a stop just in front of Nigel. His first reaction was that the Peacekeepers were now dropping invisible refrigerators on them. Luckily, before Nigel could voice that stupid thought, Miki appeared, stumbling towards him. The kid looked a proper mess—gaunt, dark circles under his eyes, near exhaustion. He collapsed and Nigel bounded forward to catch him.

"John Smith," Miki said weakly. "He's coming to kill us."

CHAPTER TWENTY-EIGHT

ISABELA SILVA
CALEB CRANE
LA CALDERA—DURANGO, MEXICO

THE FIGHT AT THE PRISON WAS ALREADY GOING when Isabela's truck pulled up to the front entrance. The other SUVs skidded to a stop nearby, her escort piling out, weapons at the ready. The body of a guard came flying off the roof—thrown, obviously—and landed directly on the windshield of one of the trucks. Isabela stifled a smirk. That had to be a good sign, right? Her friends had not only survived the skimmer crash, they were winning.

"Go! Go!" Isabela bellowed as the warden. "Get in there and kick some ass!"

As the guards sprinted in formation through the entrance, Isabela caught up with the one that was handling Einar. He was still stuck on the end of an Inhibitor, feet moving robotically beneath him as the guard dragged him along. A very un-Einar-like line of drool dribbled from the corner of his mouth. How many times had they shocked him on the way here? Were those three minutes he needed to get his shit together cumulative?

Isabela put her shoulder into Einar's guard and snatched the Inhibitor from him. "I'll take it from here, officer," Isabela said. "Bastard is my prisoner."

The guard didn't object. After all, Isabela was his boss. He joined the rest of his comrades as they kicked open the doors of the prison. They trampled into the central intake—a large room bisected by a series of chain-link fences and checkpoints. Isabela remembered from Einar's discussion of the prison that the floor here could be electrified at any moment in order to bring down an escaping Garde. She shuffled her feet uncomfortably.

"I want that imposter warden brought down here ASAP!" she yelled. "Be careful. He's got my Skeleton Key."

Some of the guards set up a perimeter in the main room while the others split off to check ancillary hallways. Isabela's eyes tracked to the gated staircase that led to cells below. They needed to get down there.

Something exploded on a higher floor and water began to trickle down from the ceiling.

With the guards distracted, she shook the Inhibitor around Einar's neck.

"Einar?" she said quietly, out of the corner of her mouth. "You with me?"

Einar's head lolled to the side and he swayed on his feet;

his eyes had trouble focusing on her. Isabela resisted the urge to snap her fingers in his face.

"Give him another shock, sir," one of the men suggested. "If you think he's coming to."

Shouting. A second group of guards poured into the room from the level above, their weapons raised and ready. They outnumbered the squad that Isabela had wormed her way into by at least two to one. Even so, Roberts and the rest of his people took up defensive positions around her. She had the guards aiming their guns at each other, so at least that was going according to plan.

"Stand down, men!" the real Warden Pembleton commanded as he entered the scene. His voice was more booming and pompous than Isabela had given him credit for. "You're being tricked!"

"Imposter! Take him into custody!" Roberts shouted back.

"He passed the retinal, Roberts!" said one of the guards on Pembleton's side.

"So did ours," Roberts countered. "He—"

"Roberts!" Pembleton called off the name, crisp and clear. "Whitehall! Stewart! Big Stewart! Jeffries!"

It took Isabela a moment to realize what Pembleton was up to. He was rattling off the last name of every man on her side of the standoff. When he was finished, he waved a hand in her direction.

"Now you, freak," he said darkly. "Name even five of my men and maybe we won't blow your head off right away."

Dozens of blank, glaring faces confronted Isabela. Their

rifles aimed in her direction. Even the men she'd come in with looked doubtful now, skeptical. She sensed some of them edging around to put her in the crosshairs.

She'd heard one name over the walkie-talkie. What was it . . . ?

"Lyon!" she called off, trying to match the warden's style.

"Lyon's down," Pembleton said coldly. "But good effort."

One of the guards beside her chambered a round.

A dark, quaking terror came over Isabela then. The feeling of anxiety was so powerful that it made her want to curl up into a ball. She couldn't even run; there was nowhere to go. No escape. No other forms to change into. Never had she been this scared before, even when the Harvesters had her pinned down in a meat locker, even when Lucas had her trapped inside her own mind. That was how she knew that she was about to die.

Three of the guards screamed, threw down their weapons and ran out the front door. Others fled into adjoining hallways or up the stairs, gibbering and shrieking, their minds broken. Some of them fired off shots into the air, spraying their guns randomly at unseen menaces—a couple were wounded that way, went down, crying and moaning.

The warden himself did what Isabela would have if she wasn't frozen in place. He crouched down into a ball, covered his head and rocked back and forth, whispering nonsense.

Soon, the room was nearly empty, except for a few remaining guards that were hiding under desks.

Einar smiled.

"To know me," he said, "is to fear me."

The terror slowly seeped out of Isabela. Her hands were still shaking when she transformed back into her true form and then handed Einar the Inhibitor cannon. With a sneer at the mechanism, he detached himself from the collar.

"Why didn't you . . . ?" Isabela swallowed an acidic lump. "Why'd you do that to me?"

"Sorry," Einar said quickly. "Too many people in the room. Impossible to be precise. The fear won't last long once they're away from me." He hesitated. "I could've opted for a more . . . permanent solution. Except I didn't want to risk you or our new friend here getting caught in the crossfire."

Einar said all that as he stalked across the room to stand over Pembleton. Isabela wondered if he was telling the truth about why he didn't simply make the guards murder each other. Perhaps Einar really was going soft. Whatever. Isabela didn't care; that he saved her life was all that mattered.

The warden looked up at them with dewy eyes and a pouty lip, then lunged forward to cling to Einar's leg. "Thank God you're here!"

Isabela's lips curled back in a mixture of delight and disgust. To see a man who only moments ago was oozing confidence and ready to kill her turned into a pathetic child by Einar's emotion manipulation was strange to say the least.

"Yes, thank God for me," Einar said coldly. He pulled the warden to his feet by his tie. "Now, shall we go somewhere safe? Down to the cells, perhaps?"

Caleb and Duanphen edged cautiously down the hall. Without Five and Ran, they would be severely outnumbered if they came across too many guards. From looking at the monitors, Caleb knew there was a bunch of them in the armory, geared up and waiting for orders. Unfortunately, the stairwell was on that end of the floor, which meant they had to improvise.

Grunting, three Calebs forced open the doors to the elevator. Caleb peeked into the empty shaft and saw that the car was stuck on the ground level. An alarm buzzed—something down there was keeping the doors from closing. He exchanged a look with Duanphen.

"We don't want to be pinned down," she said.

"You have a better idea?" Caleb asked.

She shook her head.

All the same, Caleb sent a duplicate down first. When his double landed on the roof of the elevator, someone on the inside screamed. That was strange.

Caleb's duplicate punched open the maintenance grate and dropped into the elevator. An unconscious guard was sprawled in the entrance, the elevator doors repeatedly bumping into the side of his head. A second guard—awake, but curled into a ball—shivered against the elevator's back wall.

"Is he gone?" the guard asked. "Is he gone?"

Caleb's duplicate blinked. "Huh?"

"Einar got to them," Caleb reported back to Duanphen.

"Come on. The coast is clear."

They dropped down into the elevator, the guard shying away from them. Duanphen reached out and, as gently as she could, electrocuted the terrified man until he passed out.

"Was that really necessary?" Caleb asked.

"Yes," Duanphen replied. "Einar's tricks do not work forever."

They made their way through the prison's ground level, coming across a few guns discarded on the floor where the guards dropped them in their fear. The way down to the basement cells was completely clear, every gate and door already unlocked.

"They've been this way," Caleb said. "Must have found the warden."

"Yes," Duanphen agreed. "They—"

They got lucky that the first gunshot struck a chain-link divider and ricocheted away, otherwise Duanphen and Caleb wouldn't have had a chance to duck low and run as the guards opened fire. Duanphen was right—Einar's emotional manipulation didn't last long. A dozen La Caldera grunts had already regrouped. Or maybe these were the ones from the armory. It didn't matter. They were shooting.

The two of them flung themselves downstairs, towards the cellblocks. Caleb made a couple of duplicates to try to slow down their pursuers, but they were gunned down before they could do anything. Luckily, there were tight corners down in the cells, providing cover, letting them get ahead. Although, if Caleb correctly remembered the blue-prints, they were quickly going to run out of hallways to hide in.

"Prison," said a voice. "Do me a favor and electrocute anyone carrying a gun."

Caleb skidded to a stop in front of the speaker. A groggy-looking guy wearing a pair of taped-together glasses. His voice sounded tinny. Almost mechanical.

Sam Goode.

Shouts of pain went up from behind Caleb and Duanphen as the prison's electrified floor activated beneath the guards giving chase. "Fall back!" Caleb heard one of them shout. "They're in the system! Someone get to the control room and override these floors!"

"That's the thing about high-tech prisons," Sam said staggering forward and rubbing his arm where an IV tube had just been removed. "They're really easy to talk to."

"Nice job, baby," Six said. She emerged from one of the cells, flexing her fingers, clearly itching for a fight. "You bought us some time."

"There will be more coming," Sam said with a sigh. "There are *always* more guards in places like these." Finally, his eyes flicked to Caleb and Duanphen. "Ah. Here's some more of our rescuers."

"Caleb, right?" Six said.

"Uh, yes, ma'am," Caleb replied, never missing an opportunity to be intensely awkward in front of a girl he didn't know.

"Ma'am, shit, did you get hit in the head or something?" Six looked at Duanphen. "And you are?"

"Duanphen," she replied, then leaned her shoulder against the wall, holding her arm where some of her stitches had popped loose. Caleb had forgotten how hurt she was. Hell, until that moment, when he nearly collapsed in front of Sam and Six, he hadn't realized how exhausted he was himself. His muscles were sore, his cells vibrating, his ears ringing. It had been a day.

"You're hurt," Six said, looking at Duanphen. She glanced over her shoulder. "There's a healer, I think. Daniela! Bring the healer!" Six turned again to peer down the corridor. "We might want her to put a wall up until we can figure out an escape route," she said thoughtfully.

"You've got a ship, right?" Sam asked Caleb.

"Crashed it," Caleb responded. "Your dad was hoping we'd find you. We figure Earth Garde turned on you because of what you could do to their Inhibitors."

Sam touched his temple. "Yeah. They chipped all of us. Kept me unconscious most of the time so I couldn't mess with them. But I took care of them as soon as I was woken up and got free."

"Where are the others?" Six asked. "Einar said you were here with Five and Ran."

Caleb eyed her. She'd said that so casually. Six must have picked up on the weird look Caleb gave her, because her eyebrows furrowed.

"Huh. I am weirdly okay being rescued by Five and that

terrorist kid who actually seemed nice," she said.

"You talked to him? Einar?" Caleb asked.

"Yeah," Sam answered for the both of them, then looked at Six. "You called me *baby* a second ago."

"Ugh. I did? I *did*." Six shook her head. "What is wrong with me? I feel super upbeat, even though this is a total cluster."

"Einar must have used his Legacy on you. It'll wear off soon," Caleb said. "Where did he go?"

Six shrugged breezily. "I'm not even mad about it." She pointed over her shoulder. "He went that way. Looking for someone. Told us to get the prisoners sorted out."

Caleb started in that direction, then remembered Six had asked him a question. "Oh. Five and Ran teleported out accidentally." He held up the remaining Loric pendant. "This yours?"

Six took the amulet from him. "Nice. Thank you. That's our ticket out of here."

Daniela led a huddled group of Garde around the corner. With the exception of Vincent, most of them were complete strangers to Caleb. They all wore the same tan jumpsuit and all looked like they were close to starving to death.

"Oh, damn, you *are* here!" Daniela shouted, greeting Caleb by throwing her arms around his neck. "Einar said you were. Thanks for busting us loose, my dude."

Caleb was happy to see Daniela, of course, but he couldn't shake the way that she spoke about Einar. It was the same tone that Six used. Like Einar was their old buddy.

He'd *made* them like him. That way, none of the other Garde would ask questions or get in his way while Einar dealt with Lucas.

They had never actually come to a decision about Lucas. If the bit of news they'd seen was any indication, the body snatcher was in possession of John Smith. He could be doing untold damage at that very moment. Caleb knew they had to get Lucas back into his own body. What to do with him after that? Caleb wasn't sure.

But he knew he didn't want Einar making that decision on his own.

"I'm going to go check on the others," Caleb said. He glanced at Duanphen. "You good?"

She nodded. Vincent stood nervously before her and started to heal her wounds.

"Hurry back so I can teleport everyone out of here," Six told him, holding up her pendant. "And tell Einar I said hi."

Caleb jogged down the corridor in the direction Einar had gone. After rounding a couple bends, he found Lucas's cell. Caleb could tell because the warden's unconscious body was crumpled outside the door alongside the body of an out-of-place woman oddly dressed like a suburban mom. That must have been Lucas's Cêpan. Caleb supposed it was a good sign that those two were still alive. Maybe Einar had learned restraint.

Did he want him restrained, though? What should be

done about a Garde like Lucas? Exhausted, Caleb knuckled his forehead and kept a duplicate from popping loose. He wasn't in the mood to debate ethics with one of his clones.

Before Caleb could get any closer, Isabela exited the cell. Alone. She shut the door behind her and used the warden's glove—she wore that now, the real thing—to lock it. She jumped when she realized Caleb was there, then smiled faintly and walked towards him.

"Please," she said, "can we get the hell out of this place?"

Caleb craned his neck to look past her. "What's happening? Where's Einar?"

Isabela put her hands on Caleb's chest and gently pushed him back a step, away from the cell.

"Leave it alone," she said.

Caleb squinted at her, trying to discern if she was under some emotional manipulation. Her eyes were as sharp as ever, though.

"It's over, Caleb," Isabela said. "No one is coming out of that cell."

CHAPTER TWENTY-NINE

HUMAN GARDE ACADEMY
NEW LORIEN
LA CALDERA
THE END

EVERYONE STOPPED FIGHTING WHEN JOHN SMITH descended on the center of campus. Peacekeepers and Garde alike, none of them knew what to do when the most powerful being on the planet landed in their midst. He gave off a vivid white glow—John's Lumen Legacy—emanating from his head and shoulders, creating a sort of halo effect. The troubled boy in control of John's body thought this looked cool.

The silver object that John cradled in his arms gave everyone pause. The thing looked like a giant bullet and, in a way, it was. Down the coast, at Pfeiffer Beach, the military had the missiles on hand just in case the Mogadorian warship went on the attack. Even though the warhead bore the yellow-and-black nuclear warning, it wouldn't be powerful enough to cause a large-scale fallout event. It would only destroy, say, two city blocks.

Not that Lucas knew any of that when he dumped the weapon in the grass with a *thump*, causing the nearest Peace-keepers to scuttle backwards. All Lucas knew was that he could make the thing explode. Which was perfect for what he had planned.

While the others focused on John's glow or his bomb, Taylor zeroed in on the bloodstains splattered across his shirt. Her hands shook.

"Kopano," Taylor whispered, hiding behind the door of the training center. "What—what did he do to Kopano?"

Nigel squeezed her shoulder. "He's a survivor. I'm sure—I'm sure he's fine."

But Nigel didn't sound sure. Taylor clutched the necklace Kopano had given her and tried to focus on the battle ahead.

It hadn't taken long for them to put things together once Miki described what happened at the *Osiris*. John's sudden turn towards the dark side. Isabela's warning about the body snatcher. It all made horrifying sense.

"Why did you stop?" John's words carried across campus as he addressed the staring Peacekeepers. "Get these animals in line!" When none of the soldiers immediately responded, John dramatically rolled his eyes. "Sheesh. I gotta do every-thing, huh?"

John's eyes flicked to the nearest Garde—Lisbette—and he waved his arm in her direction. A wall of fire exploded from John and rolled towards her, quickly evaporating the wall of ice Lisbette summoned to protect herself. The raw power of the fire, all unfocused fury, enveloped a couple of Peacekeepers, too. Other Peacekeepers rushed forward and tackled Lisbette, not to take her into custody, but to pat out the flames burning her clothes.

"STOP THIS!" a voice boomed over a megaphone. "STOP THIS AT ONCE!"

Later, when Taylor had a chance to think, she almost admired Greger Karlsson for his courage. At some point, once the Peacekeepers started winning, he'd made his way closer to the battlefield, dressed in a set of ill-fitting armor borrowed from one of his soldiers. Now, he stood twenty yards from John Smith and stomped his foot, trying his best to look authoritative.

"You aren't authorized to bring that body into combat!" Greger shouted. "The situation here is under control. You're to return to base at once so that we can install an Inhibitor in Number Four." He glanced at the dormant warhead and swallowed hard. "*Those* are your orders! Not this *madness*!"

John paused to consider this. A crooked smile spread across his lips.

"There's an exodus happening right under your nose, little man," John said. "Don't you see that? Don't you know what's at stake?"

"I gave you an order!" Greger screamed back. "You are—!"

"No," John said simply. His eyes flashed silver.

Taylor gasped as the silver beam struck Greger in the

forehead and turned his head to stone. His body swayed for a moment, his face forever frozen in a mask of fear, and then toppled over. Before cutting off the stone-gaze, John swept the beam across a number of other Peacekeepers.

"Oops," he said.

The stillness after John's arrival finally broke. People on the quad ran in every direction—the Peacekeepers fleeing for their encampment, the Garde sprinting towards the buildings that contained Loralite stones. A few of the braver Peacekeepers attempted to hit John with tranquilizer darts, but those were deflected by telekinesis and their shooters quickly flattened by the same force.

"RETREAT!" Nigel bellowed from the training center's doorway, his voice carrying across campus. "GET OUT!"

A lightning bolt scorched the earth at Nigel's feet and sent him flying backwards, where Nicolas just managed to catch him. The sky had clouded over suddenly with dark, ominous clouds. More lightning snapped down from the heavens, shearing through buildings and setting the grass on fire, shattering windows.

"This place is a monument to corruption!" John shouted, his arms spread wide, commanding the storm. "It cannot be allowed to stand!"

He stomped his foot.

The ground began to shake mightily. An earthquake rumbled through the Academy. Behind Taylor and the others, the elaborate obstacle course began to creak dangerously.

Across the way, the dormitory wiggled impossibly, an entire building swaying on its foundation.

"John Smith holds back, you know?" John said—or the boy controlling John said—as he flattened a fleeing tweeb with a blast of telekinesis. "He doesn't want to scare y'all with what he can do. He doesn't know how beautiful it could all b—"

A metal fist clocked John in the jaw and knocked him off balance. For a moment, the tremors stopped and the sky began to clear.

"All right, you motherfucker," Nine said, squaring up with John. "Get off my campus."

In the training center, Taylor ran to Nigel. He twitched and coughed as Nic set him on the ground, smoke rising off his singed denim vest.

"I'm good, I'm good," Nigel said, swatting their hands away and trying to stand up. "We have to help Nine."

"No," Taylor replied swiftly. "No. You have to make sure everyone gets out. Teleport to New Lorien. Wait for as many of our people as you can. But don't wait too long. You have to destroy the Loralite there, Nigel. You can't let him follow us."

"He can just fly there," Miki said. "He can fly *fast*."

Taylor pointed out the door, to where the force field generator was getting pelted by hailstones. "He can't fly through *that*," she said, hoping it was true. "Get it to New Lorien. Lexa and Malcolm will figure out how to hook it up. We just have to buy time and stay ahead of him. Isabela and the others are searching for this body snatcher. They'll come through."

Miki grabbed Nicolas. "You're strong, right? Help me get the generator."

At a nod from Taylor, Nicolas barreled into the gathering storm to grab the machinery. Meanwhile, Taylor sensed movement behind her. She turned in time to see Lofton, with Melanie in his arms, reach for the Loralite stone.

"Uh, sorry, but I don't want to die," Lofton said, right before he teleported somewhere else. Washington, probably.

"Wanker," Nigel muttered.

With Nine distracting John, the earthquake had subsided somewhat, but the damage was done. A beam came loose from the ceiling and crashed through the obstacle course. The building wouldn't be standing much longer.

"You need to go," Taylor said to Nigel. *"Go."*

"What about you?" Nigel asked. "What are you doing?"

With her telekinesis, Taylor grabbed a weapon. A black marker from the dry-erase board where their training assignments were posted. She began to hurriedly scribble something on the inside of her forearm.

"I know what we're up against," she said. "I've got an idea."

"He made an earthquake! The entire Academy is collapsing!"

"Oh God! My arm! My arm is broken!"

"Professor Nine can't fight him alone—we have to go back!"

"He's got a bomb!"

"It hurts! It hurts so bad!"

Screams greeted Five and Ran and, briefly, a Caleb, when they teleported into New Lorien. Five braced himself for danger and hugged Ran close to protect her, but no one was paying any attention to them. They weren't in the middle of a battle, they were in the middle of a retreat. There were other people teleporting into the cave via the same Loralite stone, new shapes appearing every few seconds.

"Students," Ran said weakly, just as bewildered at the sudden change as Five. "The Academy?"

Ran's eyes bounced over the faces. She saw Miki collapsed against one wall. She spotted a small group tending to Lisbette who'd somehow been badly burned. She caught a glimpse of Nicolas dragging a large piece of machinery out of the cave, into a blustery snowstorm, Lexa jogging along at his side.

"John Smith is killing everyone!" a tweeb named Danny shouted as he appeared next to them. "He's—" Danny shut his mouth when he spotted Five, his splotchy skin covered in blood, his single eye glowering. "Oh."

Malcolm Goode immediately shouldered through the crowd when he noticed Five and Ran. His mouth hung open in shock.

"Five? Ran? How—?"

Five grabbed Malcolm by the front of his shirt and shoved him backwards until his back hit the grand table in the middle of the room.

"What is this?" Five shouted. "Why am I here?"

Gasping a bit under Five's grip, Malcolm noticed the pendant still clutched in his fist. He tapped Five's hand.

"You—you must have teleported in. This is New Lorien, it's John's—"

"Don't care," Five said.

He released Malcolm and set Ran gently onto the table. She was bleeding through the bandages that Five hastily applied in the warden's office. She felt light-headed, could sense herself ebbing away. Still, she smiled gently at Malcolm. She was glad to see his face. She was glad to see all of them.

"She needs a healer," Five said gruffly. *"Now."*

Malcolm's eyes cast about. "I don't see . . ." He shook his head. "Taylor, our healer, is still at the Academy. We've come under attack and—"

A wild look in his eyes, Five turned towards the Loralite stone they'd teleported in from.

"I need to go back," he snarled. "My friends—my *only* friends—are in the middle of their own fight. Trying to save your asses."

"Is there . . . is there Loralite there, Five?" Malcolm asked cautiously. "Because if there's not, then there's no way . . ."

Five's skin turned metallic and his fist clenched. He seemed close to losing it. Even though it hurt her, Ran leaned forward and placed a hand on his shoulder.

"Stop," she said. "They need our help here, Five. Or at the Academy."

Five took a shuddering breath. His lips were red with his

own blood from some injury deep inside him that he was still ignoring. He looked at Ran with wet, fearful eyes. He was afraid for her, she realized.

"You need a healer," Five said. "You need—"

"There's a doctor in the village, I'm told," Malcolm said. He shouted across the room to a girl with a badly bruised face that Ran barely recognized as Maiken. "Maiken! I need you to make a run—"

In a flash of light, someone new teleported into the cave. A slow smile spread across Ran's face.

"Head count!" Nigel shouted breathlessly. "Where we at?"

Rabiya yelled back to him from the mouth of the cave. "Almost everyone! Still missing Taylor and Nine . . ."

A gangly blond girl—Ella, Ran realized—stood up from where she'd been meditating in one of the few clear spots in the cavern.

"I sense him," Ella said, looking at Nigel. "He's coming."

Ran recognized the look on Nigel's face. He was conflicted. Hesitating about something. She didn't know what—this entire situation was basically chaos to her—but she knew the decision was eating at him.

"You have to do it," Miki said, his voice small and weak. "We can't chance it. Destroy the stone."

"Wait," Five snapped. *"What?"*

Ran squeezed Five's arm. Destroying the stone would cut them off from the Academy. From a healer. But if that's what the Garde needed to do, then Ran would take her chances with the town doctor.

Nigel sucked in a deep breath. Ran knew that motion too and she smiled again, even as she continued to bleed out. That was how Nigel prepared for one of those shrieking punk rock notes that he loved so much. The kind that could shatter glass. Or stone.

But then he saw her. His eyes widened. The breath whistled out of him as he hesitated.

"Ran?" he said.

Behind him, the Loralite stone lit up anew.

John Smith waved a hand over his face where Nine had broken his jaw, healing the damage. Then, he laughed, practically grinning at Nine.

"A true demon in the flesh," John said. "This day keeps getting better."

"Dude," Nine said. "You're nuts."

Lightning struck the ground around him, but Nine threw himself forward, charging towards the possessed body of his best friend.

The ground shook, but that was of little consequence to someone with Nine's antigravity Legacy, balance and speed. He flung himself through a burst of fire, dodged around a stabbing icicle and aimed a punch for John's temple. Just one good shot; that's all he needed. That would be enough to make it all stop.

He felt his strength go out of him. His Legacies sapped. Cut off. Stupidly, Nine had hoped that this imposter wouldn't know how to do that.

John caught his fist in midair, crunched his fingers through Nine's metallic knuckles and yanked. In a moment that Nine found humiliatingly familiar, John ripped his cybernetic arm free from the moorings on his shoulder. In the same motion, he kneed Nine in the stomach, putting him down on the ground.

"Oh well," John said, looking down at him. "Nice try, partner."

With his telekinesis, John wrapped Nine's own metallic arm around his neck and began to choke him. Nine clawed at the metal, gasping and coughing, trying to work his fingers underneath it to get himself some air. Without his enhanced strength, though, there was little he could do. Nine started to see spots. The world got darker.

"Praise be!" Taylor shouted. "I prayed and thank God you've come!"

John's grip on Nine's neck loosened as he turned to look at Taylor walking towards him with her arms raised high above her head. She stumbled a bit—the ground was still shaking—and flinched with each hailstone that pelted her on the cheek. But on she came, hair wet, eyes wide and teary, like some kind of apocalyptic vision.

And on her forearm she'd drawn the symbol for the Harvesters. The snake and scythe she'd seen tattooed on her father's farmhand all those months ago, before she even knew that she was Garde.

"I've been waiting so long for the harvest to come!" she shouted into the rain, trying to remember all the stupid platitudes she'd heard in the past. "The culling of the snakes that crawl up from our corrupted Earth! You can help me, right? You can take these awful Legacies away!"

John grinned at her and let Nine drop, the Loric completely forgotten. She saw something in his face then—he was like a boy, eyes shining with eagerness, delighted to find a kindred spirit.

"I knew it," John said. "I always knew there'd be others like me out there. Ones who understood their own sickness."

John left Nine in the mud and glided towards Taylor. As he came, he used his telekinesis to pick up the warhead, the gleaming bomb floating nearby.

"This body had a vision," John said, referring to himself. "It showed me what I have to do. It showed me the way."

Taylor remembered what Ella said—John's vision of an explosion in New Lorien. How that'd driven him to seek out the force field generators. How meddling with the future only screwed things up. By looking forward, John had only assured this moment would come. It was difficult for Taylor to keep her faithful smile in place with the knowledge of what this monster was planning to do.

"Can I help you?" Taylor asked.

"You can be my witness," John said grandly. He landed in front of her and took her hand. "Come on, now. Let's go see where the evil has scuttled away to."

"First," Taylor said, stalling. "Will you pray with me?"

John hesitated, so Taylor amped up the wattage of her smile. The Academy seemed deserted now, but she wanted to buy Nigel a bit more time to get everyone clear and destroy the Loralite in New Lorien.

"Of course," he said. He closed his eyes and tilted his head back. "Our Father—"

Taylor lunged forward and stabbed a tranquilizer dart into John's neck.

His rage was immediate and terrible. The ground shook violently and the front of the student union collapsed, the stone façade crumbling. Jagged bolts of lightning slashed into the ground beside Taylor, knocking her down.

John pulled the dart out of his neck. He blinked his eyes. Glared at her.

"You shouldn't have done that," he whined. "Snake!"

Then he was on her. Hand around her throat. And up they went, flying, his fingers generating heat that charred Taylor's skin. She struggled, but John was too strong, and the tranquilizer wasn't working fast enough.

He drove her down, through the open roof of the student union, and smashed her back-first onto the Loralite stone. Taylor felt her ribs crack, at the very least. The breath went out of her. John held her down there, then reached back with his telekinesis and called the warhead to him. Taylor tried to push it away with her own telekinesis, but she could barely slow it down.

The bomb touched John's palm.

Nigel, Taylor thought. *Please. Don't let him in.*

Pinning her beneath him, John pressed his free hand to the Loralite.

A flash of blue.

No, Taylor thought. She would've screamed it if she could. *NO!*

And then, they were in the cave. Nigel stood just feet away. Beyond him, the terrified faces of all the other Garde. Taylor saw Ran—somehow, Ran was there—bloody and pale, staggering towards her.

"Too late," John said. Somehow, Taylor knew he wasn't talking to them. He was talking to someone else somewhere else. "You're too late."

John—the thing controlling John—he didn't hesitate. He poured all his power into the warhead. Fire and lightning and pressurized telekinesis. Pure rage, channeled into the bomb.

He laughed as it exploded.

The room filled with white light.

In a subbasement prison hundreds of miles away, Einar and Isabela stood over the prone body of a boy. For such a monster, Isabela thought, he wasn't that scary in person. In fact, he was sort of sad. His dark curls fanned out on the pillow beneath him, his ribs poking up through his jumpsuit, dark circles under his half-open eyes. He looked so small and so, so young.

"What should we do?" Isabela asked, looking to Einar.

"*We* should do nothing," Einar said.

Einar held the warden's pistol loosely in his hand. He tapped it against the side of his thigh.

"I thought I could be a leader. Thought I was so gifted, so smart. But I'm like . . . I'm like him," he said, staring at Lucas. "I'm bad."

Isabela didn't say anything. She edged back from Einar. Something in her made her feel calm. Something inside her told her to walk away.

"Leave us. Get the others out of this hell," Einar said. "Let me do this. So the rest of you can be good."

In Mexico, a gunshot.

In the Himalayas, John Smith regained control over his own body with a frustrated scream. He fought against the sedative coursing through his system, fought to reel back in the insane force of his Legacies that had been discharged so carelessly.

He was too late. Too late to pull all that power back.

His cave lit up in white. New Lorien. Gone in an instant.

Ran Takeda sucked in a deep breath. She sucked in—

She pulled in.

She opened her every molecule.

She made space.

It was one of the first tricks she learned. Sitting on the beach outside the Academy, pushing the raging energy inside her into an egg, then yanking it back out. The result? A hard-boiled egg.

She'd done it to Nigel in Iceland. Charged him up, pulled the energy back. The result? Her best friend's heart started.

Ran did that now. She pulled energy in. Swallowed heat and force and destruction. She let it all collect inside of her.

More.

And more.

Then, silence.

The cave stood. Quiet and cold. The Garde and their allies blinked their eyes, dropped their hands that had been shielding their faces, stood up from the ground. They all stared at her.

Ran vibrated. She was white-hot. She felt like the sun.

She stood over the warhead. The bomb was cold and empty.

It was inside Ran now. Fighting to get loose. Tearing her apart.

Nigel's was the first face she saw. It was his expression that made Ran know it was bad. She couldn't tell that all her hair had burned off. She was barely aware that she was glowing. That there were fissures on her skin cracking open, burning energy glowing through, aching for release.

"Ran?" Nigel said, tears on his cheeks. "What . . . what did you do?"

"*Nakama*," she said, her words crackling with power. "I love you. I'm sorry."

Without thinking, she reached out to touch Nigel's cheek, to brush his tears away. He let her, even though her touch left fingerprints scalded on his cheek. He tried not to flinch. He tried to be strong like her.

"No, Ran," Nigel said. *"No."*

"I can't . . ." Ran's voice was barely a whisper now. She couldn't find air that wasn't boiling. Her insides were melting away. "I can't hold it."

She saw John Smith stumble towards her, looking like he might pass out. But someone shoved him aside.

"Not you," Five said to John. "You make this worth it."

And then, Five's arms were around her. His metal skin melted as soon as he touched her, molten steel dripping down to pool on the cave's floor. That didn't stop him. He carried her and they flew out of the cave.

Once, there was a prophecy about Five drawn on one of those walls.

Now, he chose his own fate.

Up, up, up.

The Himalayas disappeared beneath them. The sky got darker.

Higher.

Ran heard Five shudder. His grip loosened. She could see bone in his arms, where his skin had burned away. She looked up at him, wanted to apologize, tell him to go, but Ran couldn't speak. The force was too much. It was eating its way out of her.

It was time.

She sought out Five's eye. He looked back at her. At peace.

"You were right," he whispered. "We do have these Lega-cies for a reason."

High above the Himalayas, the girl who made things explode detonated for the last time.

AFTER

A TOP SECRET LABORATORY—LOCATION UNKNOWN

"I THOUGHT THESE THINGS TURNED TO ASH WHEN you killed them," a man said, sounding bored.

"Only the ones they grew in vats do that," responded a woman. "Didn't you read the briefing?"

"Skimmed it," the man replied. "That's pretty fascinating. Cloning division is on that, right?"

"Yeah. Wish I was assigned there instead of down here trying to figure out why this one isn't decomposing like the others."

Vontezza Aoh-Atet's eyes snapped open. She gasped, filling lungs that had been dormant for—days? weeks?—she couldn't be sure. She sat bolt upright on the cold metal slab and made a quick assessment of her situation. She was nude in a brightly lit room that smelled like formaldehyde. There was a line in marker drawn down her sternum, presumably where the two scientists—at that moment, stumbling away from her in shock—planned to cut her open with the array of scalpels that gleamed on a nearby table.

"Unacceptable," she said, then lunged off the table and punched the male scientist in the throat.

The woman screamed and dove for a button on the wall. That would call for help, probably. Vontezza couldn't allow that. At least, not until she found her armor.

Vontezza swept the woman's legs with her telekinesis, then leaped on top of her. She floated a scalpel to her, snatched it out of the air and pressed it to the woman's neck.

"Where am I?" Vontezza asked. She noted the strange emblem on the woman's lab coat. A logo for something called Sydal Corp. "How long have I been dead?"

"You're—you're in Vancouver," the woman stammered. "And weeks, I think. I don't know. I just got transferred here."

"Vancouver," Vontezza said, tasting the unfamiliar word. "How far is that from Alaska?"

The complete destruction of Sydal Corp's Vancouver research station went unreported on the news.

THE HAGUE—SOUTH HOLLAND, THE NETHERLANDS
"State your name and role for the record."

"Karen Walker. Formerly of the United States Federal Bureau of Investigation. Formerly an agent for the clandestine organization known as MogPro. Most recently, assigned to a top secret operation known as Watchtower within Earth Garde."

"Please begin, Ms. Walker."

"Ladies and gentlemen of the court, what I hold in my hand is a vial of corrupted Loralite, better known as Mogadorian ooze, a substance created by Setrákus Ra. This sample was recovered by an agent of Earth Garde, Caleb Crane, after he served on a protection detail for the late Wade Sydal. It is my sworn testimony that Mr. Sydal operated outside the Garde Accord to further his own self-interest, his efforts to reproduce dangerous alien technology. He was funded in these efforts by a group of people calling themselves the Foundation . . ."

SOMEONE'S EXPENSIVE VILLA—SANTIAGO, CHILE

Caleb did one last lap through the heated water, then climbed out of the infinity pool and toweled off. The afternoon sun beat down on his shoulders, a nice reprieve from the cold of New Lorien. The towel was puffy and soft—rich-people soft, Caleb thought. Of course, the villa was decadent, just like all the places Isabela chose to stay at. Caleb sighed. He liked it here, but it also made him nervous. These spaces reminded him too much of the abandoned haunts of the Foundation that they'd traveled through all those months ago. He still felt the urge to look over his shoulder. Maybe that would never go away.

"I forgot to ask who you're posing as this time," Caleb said as he padded across the deck to where Isabela reclined on a lounger.

She tipped her sunglasses down her nose and eyed him. "Do you really want to know that, Boy Scout?"

Caleb thought about it. "No. I guess not."

This was the third time that Caleb had come to see Isabela and the third different mansion she'd been squatting in. He didn't ask her how she found these places or where she got her money. They had an unspoken agreement that certain topics were off-limits. Like Mexico. The one time Caleb brought that up, a dark cloud had settled over Isabela for the rest of their visit. She didn't want to think about that—about responsibility or the fight or any of the things they'd done. She wanted to live the good life.

So, Caleb let her.

He sat down on the lounger next to Isabela. Duanphen got up from the one on Isabela's opposite side and dove into the pool. After everything, Duanphen had decided to stick with Isabela rather than come to New Lorien. That made Caleb happy. He felt good knowing someone was watching out for Isabela.

There was another change that Caleb never remarked upon. Whenever Isabela checked in and invited him to one of her mansions, it inevitably had some kind of pool. And at those pools, with only Caleb and Duanphen around, she wore her true form. Scars and all.

"You're ogling me," Isabela said.

Caleb swallowed. "Sorry."

She smirked, never happier than when she could make him uncomfortable. "I don't mind."

"Have you been watching the hearings at all?" Caleb asked, eager for a change of subject.

Isabela snorted. "Of course not. What am I? Boring?"

"They're going pretty well, I think," Caleb continued lamely. "We might be able to come out of hiding soon."

"I like hiding," Isabela said. "I think you like it, too."

Caleb reached for his shirt, pulling it on. Then, he picked up his medallion and slipped it on over his head. The Loralite stone keyed to the cave in New Lorien glimmered in the afternoon sunlight.

"You know, we're building something there," Caleb said. "I think it'll be good. We could use your help, if you wanted . . ."

Isabela swatted him away. "Every time with this. No, Caleb. I don't want to build anything in some cold-ass monk cave under a force field. I'm good."

"You still have your pendant, though, right?"

She sighed. "Yes, yes. The ugly thing is wrapped in a sock in my bag."

"Because you're welcome whenever. I miss . . ." He looked away. "Everybody misses you."

Isabela stood up abruptly. Caleb had pressed too hard, broken one of their unspoken agreements.

"I'm going in," she said. "You?"

"No," Caleb replied. "I've gotta get back."

"Okay," she said, and pecked him on the cheek. "See you next time, Caleb."

"See you," Caleb replied.

Caleb watched Isabela saunter over to the pool. He was about to touch the Loralite stone and teleport home when she turned back to him.

"Caleb?"

"Yeah?"

"Don't stop asking me, okay?" Isabela said.

Caleb smiled. He could do that.

THE HAGUE—SOUTH HOLLAND, THE NETHERLANDS

"State your name and role for the record."

"Colonel Ray Archibald. Former head of security at the Human Garde Academy."

"Your statement, Colonel?"

"In my time at the Academy, I had the pleasure of witnessing a number of gifted young Garde realize their potential. It is my belief that the mission of the Academy and Earth Garde was pure, at least at first. However, these institutions were gradually corrupted by insidious outside forces that—"

"Excuse me, Colonel, but we have heard sworn testimony from your men that your judgment may be clouded. May I ask why you were relieved of duty?"

"I allowed a Garde who was in my custody go free."

NEW LORIEN—THE HIMALAYAS, INDIA

"We teleported! We teleported! It was dope! Can we do it again?"

Obi and Dubem, Kopano's two little brothers, launched themselves at him. Laughing, Kopano wrapped them both up in a hug, squeezing them tight. It'd been more than a year since he last saw them, when he'd snuck away from Lagos in the dead of night. Now they were here, high up in these strange mountains, staring at him with wide, glistening eyes.

It was family day at New Lorien.

"We read all your emails," Dubem told Kopano in a rush.

"Over and over," Obi added.

"I can't believe you fought the great John Smith," Obi said. "And nearly beat him!"

Dubem jabbed Kopano's sternum. "Until he ripped your heart out of your chest!"

"Has he ever apologized?" Obi asked. "He should!"

"Hush about that," Kopano said, looking around, making sure John wasn't in earshot. "John doesn't like to talk about that day. And, anyway, it wasn't really him."

Kopano rubbed his shoulder at the memory. Any lingering pain was all in his mind. John had apologized, right after he personally healed Kopano's shoulder. It was John that had come to get Kopano after all the chaos of that day. Colonel Archibald hadn't argued. He'd let Kopano go without so much as a question.

The two of them didn't talk much. It was strange to be around John. Even though it wasn't really him that had nearly killed Kopano—and so many others—seeing him brought back strange memories. The Garde were all here, in a place that John built, but John himself tended to keep his distance. Kopano hoped that it would get less weird in time. After all, John used to be his idol. But being a hero, Kopano had learned, was not always glorious.

"What do you want to see first?" Kopano asked his brothers. He gestured down the path to the longhouse that had recently been built at the edge of the village. The one with *PROFESSOR NINE'S FUNHOUSE* spray-painted in ominous script on the side. "Do you want to try the obstacle course? You can train like a genuine Garde!"

"First, I need a bathroom. Does this place even have toilets?"

That came from Udo. Kopano's father ambled down the pathway from the cave, rubbing the sides of his prodigious beer belly. He patted Kopano gruffly on the shoulder.

"You look taller. That's good," Udo said. He rubbed his arms. "It's too cold here. Where is the alien that warms things up?"

Kopano rolled his eyes—so often the subject of eye rolls himself, it felt good to do it to someone else—and looked beyond his father. The pathway behind him was empty. There was no one else.

"Where's Mom?" Kopano asked.

His brothers looked down at their shoes. Udo cleared his throat.

"She did not want to come," Udo said frankly. "She thought the Academy would cure you. This—?" He waved his arms. "This, she does not understand at all. I told her it was a free vacation, but no, the woman would not listen. She told me that she'll pray for you."

Kopano forced his smile not to falter. "Yeah. I'll pray for her, too."

Udo dug his elbow into Kopano's ribs. "The pretty girl who teleported us here, she spoke very highly of you. Is she your lady friend?"

"No, Dad," groaned Dubem, speaking on Kopano's behalf. "That was Rabiya. She's just his *friend*. Taylor's the *girlfriend*."

Kopano grinned at his brother. He truly was a student of Kopano's many rambling emails. He turned away from his family for a moment, looking around, and spotted Taylor standing on an overlook up above with her own father.

"She's up there," Kopano said. "We're all having dinner later. I beg you, Dad, please don't talk."

Up above, Taylor saw Kopano pointing at her and waved back. All week, he'd been filling her head with warnings about his father. Udo didn't look so bad from where she stood, strutting around, pretending like he wasn't impressed by anything. She saw the way that Udo kept stopping himself from patting Kopano on the back. He was proud, she would tell Kopano later, he just didn't want to show it.

Brian Cook whistled through his teeth. Her own father had arrived earlier that day and never even tried to hide his awe.

"Pretty far cry from South Dakota," he said. "From California, even."

Taylor nodded. They stood on a favorite perch of hers, just a short hike up from the mouth of the cave. She came up here often to stare out at the mountains and the village below. There were new buildings being constructed every day—more cottages along the switchback path, a new wing on the school that they shared with the villagers, a bigger hospital so that they could bring in patients from outside. It was growing. They were rebuilding what they'd lost.

They also lived under the perpetual glow of a force field, the dim blue light always visible in the sky above. Taylor hoped they wouldn't need that forever. The territory they'd been granted by the Indian government was a bit of a gray area. The UN didn't acknowledge their existence, but the neighboring countries did. No one had made a move on them yet, especially not with the hearings ongoing.

"Do you like it better?" her dad asked, breaking a silence that Taylor didn't realize had dragged on. "Than California, I mean."

"I think I do," Taylor said. "It's a change. But I think it's good."

She didn't mention what they'd lost to save this place. Who they'd lost.

"Well, it's a long truck from the states, assuming your teleporting friend doesn't sneak me off every time I want to see you," Brian said, sighing. "How much is a plane ticket to Nepal, anyway?"

"We're building something here, Dad," Taylor said, turning to him. "But we don't want to do it alone. The Loric had these people called Cêpan. They didn't have Legacies themselves, but they helped train the Garde. Helped them make sure they were doing the right thing. We're looking for people like that, who might want to live here and help us."

Brian nodded. "Yep. Sure. Seems like a good idea." Then, it dawned on him what Taylor was really saying. "Hold up. You mean . . ."

"I destroyed the farm," Taylor said. She pointed down the hill at one of the new cottages. "Least I can do is get you a mountain estate."

THE HAGUE—SOUTH HOLLAND, THE NETHERLANDS

"State your name and job for the record."

"Beatrice Barnaby. I'm a philanthropist."

"Mrs. Barnaby, your name has come up quite a bit in our investigation."

"Truly, I have no idea why."

"The Foundation, perhaps?"

"The Foundation was an organization I was very

tangentially involved with. Its purpose was to locate Garde from non–Earth Garde nations and provide them with the means of escaping what were often terrible conditions in their home countries. From our earliest days, we had the full support of Earth Garde. Our purposes were strictly humanitarian. All of this conspiracy talk is pure lunacy."

NEW LORIEN—THE HIMALAYAS, INDIA

Family day. After months in the Himalayas, it was the first time the Garde would be letting in outsiders. It took planning. They needed to contact the families, first of all. Then, the ones who wanted to visit, they needed to design plans to sneak away. Many of their parents were under constant surveillance. Nigel helped out in every way he could—from logistics to teleporting. It was good for him to always be working.

But then the day came and there were happy people all around him and Nigel wanted to puke.

Obviously, no one would be coming to see him.

So he hiked down the mountain, through the village and out onto one of the craggier paths that led farther down. He'd done all these hikes over the last few months. Turning into a real nature lover. Not punk rock at all.

He knew Ran would have loved it up here. It was days like today that he missed her the most.

Nigel touched the scars on his cheek where her fingerprints were still burned. Taylor hadn't even asked him if he wanted those healed. She knew better.

Eventually, Nigel came to a crystal-blue stream fed from

the ice at the top of the mountain. The water bubbled and bent as it coursed downwards over the rocky terrain. He followed along the curving bank until he reached the force field, as far as he could go. The water smashed up against the energy barrier and diverted to the left and right, creating an icy puddle.

Something caught his eye. Movement beyond the force field. He squinted.

"What the shit is that?" Nigel asked the air.

Nigel waded into the water, not caring about the cold soaking through his sneakers. There was something familiar out there, butting its head up against the barrier again and again. He needed to get a closer look to be sure.

"No way," Nigel whispered.

Nigel raced back to the village, up the mountainside and into the cave. The visitors had all been teleported in by then, so the space was empty except for whoever was standing guard over the stone. At that moment, it was Marina. The Loric girl had returned to New Lorien shortly after the exodus from the Academy. Her relationship status with John Smith was a popular topic around the mountain, although they never talked about that when she came to the weekly group-therapy sessions Nigel and Nic had organized.

Marina sprang to her feet when Nigel burst in. "Hey! Is everything okay?"

"I need . . ." He took a breath. "I need to go outside."

"Should I call down to the Vishnu Nationalist Eight?" Marina asked. "Do you need an escort?"

"No, no," Nigel panted. "I'll be quick."

Nigel touched the Loralite stone and pictured one of the smaller chunks that they'd hidden outside the force field's boundary. In a flash of light, he stood in a snowy thicket outside New Lorien.

"Please still be there, please still be there . . . ," Nigel said as he jogged back up the mountain, towards the blue glow of their shield, along the dried riverbed.

It was a giant tortoise that Nigel spotted outside the force field, although by the time he reached it, the Chimæra had transformed into a ram, butting its horns ineffectually against the energy barrier. Nigel chuckled and wiped a hand across his eyes. The creature was stubborn. Just like its old owner.

Nigel whistled. "Oi, remember me, mate?"

The Chimæra turned its head, spotted Nigel and transformed back into its turtle shape. That was its preferred form. The one that Nigel had last seen it take when it fled into the ocean, ahead of the Earth Garde soldiers who wanted to imprison it.

The tortoise trundled over and laid his chin down right across Nigel's sopping feet. It remembered him. Of course it did. Nigel bent down and stroked its smooth head.

"Hello, Gamora," Nigel said, smiling for the first time in months, remembering what Ran had named her old pet. "Where ya been, mate?"

THE HAGUE—SOUTH HOLLAND, THE NETHERLANDS
"State your name."

"I . . ."

"State your name, please."

"Einar. Mag— Magnusson."

"I'd like the court to note that my client is equipped with an Inhibitor that sends a low-grade shock through his system every six seconds. That makes it extremely difficult for him to focus for any sustained period. Additionally, the conditions he's being kept in are far from ideal and—"

"Thank you, counsel. Begin, please, Mr. Magnusson."

"I have . . . I have hu— hurt people. Many people. Kidnapped. Killed. The Found— The Foundation. Took me. Molded me. I am— I am here now to take— to take respons— *responsibility*. I know their names. The one—the ones who profited. Who helped me. Will you—will you finally *listen*?"

NEW LORIEN—THE HIMALAYAS, INDIA

"I'd like to say, I'm still very much against this idea," Malcolm said, peeling off his rubber gloves. "Even now that I've helped you do it. I don't like it."

John Smith sat up from where he'd been lying on his side. It was a simple procedure really. Just a small cut at his temple, the insertion of the chip and then done. Taylor brushed her fingers across his head, healing him. John could've done that himself, but he'd asked her to be here so she might as well pitch in.

"Twice now an enemy has been able to use my powers against our people. I can't let that ever happen again," John said.

Malcolm shook his head. "Well, like you requested, I've

given bio-keyed remotes to Nine, Six, Sam, Marina and . . ." He turned to look at Taylor.

She touched her front pocket where she'd stuck the thin remote. The device that would shock John Smith into submission was no bigger than a lipstick.

"I still don't understand why," Taylor said to John. "Why me? The other Loric and Malcolm I get, but . . . why trust me with this?"

"Because I trust you to do what's necessary," John replied. "I trust all the others, too, obviously. But we have history. They might hesitate, in the moment. I don't think you will."

Taylor chuckled. "I don't think Nine would hesitate."

"No," John admitted. "I'm honestly surprised he hasn't shocked me already. For fun." He hopped off the table. "We should get going. They're waiting for us."

The three of them left John's cottage—just one of the many along the path leading up to the cave, no bigger or smaller than any of the others. There were other Garde walking in the same direction. Lisbette and Nicolas were coming up. They smiled and waved at Taylor, but slowed down when they noticed she was with John. Picking up on the vibe, John bent down and pretended to tie his shoe so that they could walk by.

"They'll get over it," Taylor said to John, his hurt expression obvious. "I mean, you broke my back and *I'm* over it."

"I know," John said quietly. "For a year, though, I dreamed of filling this place with our people. Of doing great things.

And now, you're here, it's happening and—I don't feel like one of you."

"John Smith! Stop using your gloomy charms on my woman!" Kopano shouted. He charged up from behind and grabbed Taylor around the waist, squeezing and kissing her neck until they almost fell off the path. In spite of himself, John laughed.

"Stop, stop, gross, stop," Taylor said, slapping at Kopano.

He let Taylor go, only so he could bounce up and down and rub his hands together. "I am so pumped, you guys! We're going to go live! Whose world do you think we'll save first?"

Kopano slapped John on the back, then ran on ahead. Taylor turned to John.

"See? You'll be one of us again in no time."

"Ow," John said, rubbing his shoulder. "Now I'm not sure I want to be."

They entered the cave and found it filled with Garde, all of them gathered around the massive wooden table that John had carved. Their conversations didn't stop when John and Taylor entered.

"Your parents sound totally badass," Six was saying to Miki.

"Yeah, they're pretty cool," Miki replied. "You should come say hi to them tonight."

Six stroked her chin. "I feel like I could get really into ecoterrorism."

Sam groaned. "Please don't say stuff like that, Six."

"I really wish you'd stop turning my traps to stone," Nine said to Daniela, rubbing his bicep. "I gotta keep chiseling the gears. It's a pain in the ass."

"Sorry, bro." Daniela shrugged. "But stone-vision fixes everything."

"Also," Nine continued, turning to Rabiya, "teleporting from one side of the course to the other doesn't qualify you for best time."

"Says you," Rabiya replied.

"You ever heard of this band Journey?" Caleb asked Nigel.

"Yeah, mate, they suck," Nigel said.

"I know. My dad *loves* them." Caleb said. "Maybe we should ruin some of their songs with badly played covers."

Nigel grinned. "Yes. Nigel and the Clones reunion revenge tour, coming soon to a very unprepared village!"

Taylor draped her arms around Nigel and Caleb, smiling at them, taking it all in. There were almost forty of them in here and more still squeezing their way inside. It was like a party.

"Okay, everyone!" Lexa shouted, getting their attention. She leaned over a laptop attached to a holographic projector that displayed a rotating globe over their big table. That had been Daniela's idea. "We're coming online!"

The website was simple. Type "GARDE" into any search engine and the top result brought you to a plain black screen with a single question and a box to enter text.

The question: "HOW CAN WE HELP?"

At first, once Lexa made the website live, nothing happened. But then their in-box began to ping, messages scrolling down faster than Taylor could keep track of. Lexa brought them up one by one on the projector and they read through them together. Some of them were gross and weird, some of them obviously fake, some of them simply asking if this whole thing was for real. But there were others . . .

A sick mother in Ghana who was being swindled for her medicine.

A boy trying to break away from a gang in Colombia.

A conservationist in Sri Lanka who was worried about elephant poachers.

Anything that seemed real and necessary, Lexa dragged to the globe and populated a dot there with the request's details. Soon, their entire map was glowing. These weren't people like the ones that the Foundation "helped." This wasn't for pay or for status. This was all about doing good. About serving humanity.

The room fell silent as they slowly realized just how much work there was to do. Then, without even realizing they were doing it, everyone there turned towards John. They were looking for direction. It was all a little overwhelming.

John was smiling. He hadn't even noticed their eyes on him. "It's perfect," he said quietly. "Just like I imagined."

Taylor stepped forward and clapped her hands.

"So," Taylor said. "Where do we start?"

DON'T MISS A SINGLE PAGE OF THE ACTION-PACKED, #1 *NEW YORK TIMES* BESTSELLING I AM NUMBER FOUR SERIES

HARPER
An Imprint of HarperCollinsPublishers

THE WAR MAY BE OVER—BUT FOR THE NEXT GENERATION, THE BATTLE HAS JUST BEGUN!

THE ADVENTURE CONTINUES IN THE LORIEN LEGACIES REBORN SERIES!

JOIN FAN FAVORITES SIX AND SAM ON A NEW JOURNEY!

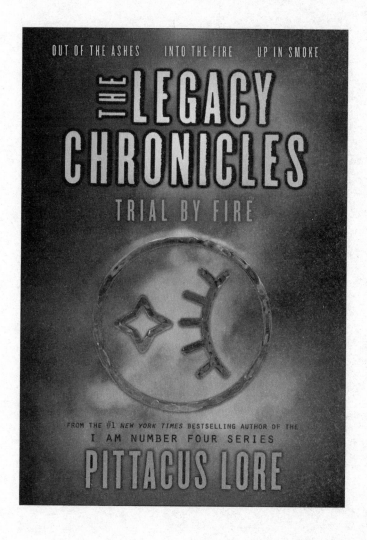

DELVE DEEPER IN THE LORIEN LEGACIES WITH THESE COMPANION NOVELLAS!

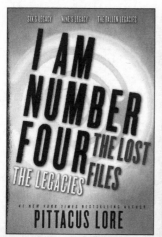

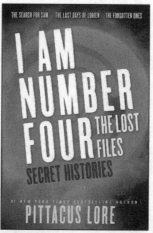

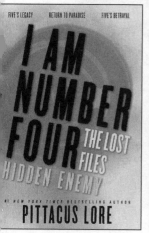

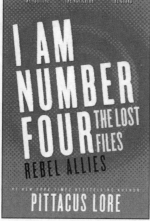

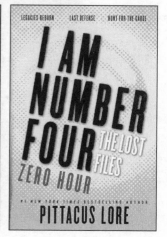